THE PAPER CHASE

THE PAPER CHASE

RON WELLING

The Book Guild Ltd

First published in Great Britain in 2018 by
The Book Guild Ltd
9 Priory Business Park
Wistow Road, Kibworth
Leicestershire, LE8 0RX
Freephone: 0800 999 2982
www.bookguild.co.uk
Email: info@bookguild.co.uk
Twitter: @bookguild

Typeset in Adobe Garamond Pro

Printed and bound in Great Britain by CPI Group (UK) Ltd, Croydon, CR0 4YY

ISBN 978 1912575 602

British Library Cataloguing in Publication Data.
A catalogue record for this book is available from the British Library.

FSC www.fsc.org
MIX
Paper from
responsible sources
FSC® C013604

To Margaret,
My wife of 56 years

To Margaret,
My wife of 56 years

1

Clearing border control and then customs at Gatwick Airport on a Friday afternoon was chaotic and Claire was beginning to feel weary. She met Rick in the arrivals hall. It was dusty from the building work being carried out, the space to linger and meet was tight, just squeezed between escalators and hoardings. Through a melee of people Claire saw Rick and she welcomed a tight hug and kiss from him.

'Let's get out of here, you look tired,' Rick said as he took her travelling bag and Claire held his other hand.

'Just a Friday afternoon, that's all,' Claire said.

'We'll soon shake that off, but I hope you liked Barcelona.'

'It's a great city. The sun, the sea, and with a lot to see around the centre, I liked the place.'

'So welcome home to the cold of London. Tell me how you got our man out there to pay up what he owed so easily.'

'Leave it until we get in the car, Rick, it's just too noisy here and you're walking too fast.'

'I'm sorry, it's me, you should know by now I always walk at a trot.'

They reached Rick's car and within a few minutes were leaving the dark of the concrete building and heading along the motorway to London. Claire closed her eyes as her head rested on the top of the seat and she could feel Rick's closeness in the car with their mutual silence. With light traffic they arrived in Mayfair and Rick's underground garage within an hour.

On a summer's evening his penthouse apartment, which had a wide-sweep view of the Thames, was a place that Claire found easy to relax in. She gratefully sank into an armchair and sipped a glass of cool Chablis. The past two days she had spent tidying up a business problem in Barcelona where Rick was owed money. She now slowly unwound from the travelling and the tension of trying to follow a Spanish businessman as he spoke quickly in his halting English. For Claire, it had been an interesting time but she could now forget all about chasing after money in Spain, she would take time to change and be comfortable to welcome the coming evening when she could really enjoy Rick's closeness.

'Okay, tell me about Señor de Freitas. Was he friendly or did he try to run away when you asked him for cash?'

'He smokes too much and to get him to part with his cash was not easy. I thought it was never going to happen. Even when we met in the lawyer's musty and dark office he started by saying he didn't think he should pay up all the outstanding rent. Thirty thousand euros he owed, but should he pay half, should he pay two thirds, he kept on hinting, until I looked away as if I was going to walk out. In the end I persuaded him to clear the lot and he authorised a bank transfer,' Claire said.

'Thanks for what you've done, Claire. The cash is all in the bank but I shall sell that property as soon as the market picks up. And anyway, employing people in Spain is a nightmare, so never again.'

'Perhaps that's what makes Barcelona so enticing, it's laid back, friendly and runs very slowly on its gourmet offerings.'

'I've not been for the last ten years. Sometime we'll visit again, together,' Rick said.

'It was a perfect hotel you found for me. I could have stayed longer than three nights it was so good. Right on the waterfront, high-rise and Michelin-starred restaurant, what's better than that? So, please take me again sometime soon,' Claire said.

'I've called the lawyers off the case. Who needs lawyers when there's Claire Watts, who's even better at sorting knotty problems? Some day you must tell me what you really did before our paths crossed a couple of years ago. I'm still very curious to know what makes you so efficient and effective,' Rick said as he sat with a sigh next to Claire.

'My past is very simple. I've told you many times that I worked for my uncle until he died and he left me a lump of cash. So let's leave it there shall we?'

'You're clever, Claire, and you're good at sorting out the risky bits on the edge of my business that sometimes go wrong. So thanks for what you do.'

'No, I'm not clever. Trade, commerce, boiled down to its nuts and bolts, is like life, that is, simple if you let it be. But what I don't understand is why on earth did you buy such a property, right in the middle of Barcelona?' Claire asked. 'It was quite rundown and not surprising it gave you so many problems.'

Claire wanted to change the subject away from her past. What she had done two years ago that led her to be with Rick was a fragile area of her life. Of course she had never worked for her uncle and she had certainly not been left money. But Claire's story was easy, it hid the real reason why she had come to be with Rick and it stopped more probing by him.

'When I look back, like a lot of other things, Barcelona looked a good bet at the time and the advice was right too. But now I've been looking at some more London properties as there's quite a lot going around the capital at the moment,' Rick said.

'Do I get a success fee for clearing Barcelona up for you? And my expenses for this one, please? My bill is in my bag, unless I tear it up now,' Claire said and laughed at her tease.

'You're so good at sorting these little problems I'll pay you whatever you want, Miss Watts. So let's have your account,' Rick said and squeezed Claire's hand.

‘So what have you been doing while I’ve been cornering one of your deals to pay up?’

‘You’ll like this. I’m going to France tomorrow to have a look at a chateau and vineyard near Bordeaux. It’s on the market and I might buy it. And if it’s good we’ll spend some time out there and drink some of their wine. They produce a fine Merlot and a Cabernet Sauvignon, but, Claire, in the last couple of days I’ve been thinking,’ Rick said.

‘That sounds ominous.’

‘You said you were going to have your flat redecorated. But do you feel safe on your own in London? I mean, a lady like you walking at night to your apartment is likely to attract attention from some rough sleepers looking for easy prey. Why don’t you give up your flat and move in here where you now spend a lot of your time anyway?’ Rick asked.

‘I don’t want to upset your schedule, especially when you have to be away on business or if you’re working late,’ Claire replied.

‘Don’t worry about that, just move in here as if it’s your home and you’ll avoid the hassle of having two wardrobes full of clothes.’

‘Okay but one condition then. You won’t ask me to do the cooking. I’m no good at that,’ Claire said, and looked closely at Rick with a grin.

‘No, we’ll eat out or use the concierge service, they have a good menu and it’s fast and efficient.’

This was Rick as his easy, organised self and for an unsettling moment Claire saw the contrast with Harry Stone. He was a man from her past and a man that Rick knew nothing about. And Rick must never find out about Harry Stone and how she had worked for him. But Claire was not sure how long she could hide it and she shuddered at the thought as she looked away.

‘I’ve got a surprise for you,’ Rick said.

‘I’m listening.’

‘Take your time to change and then I’ve got a limousine coming to take us to The Ritz. We’ll arrive in style and I’ve booked a table for dinner as I thought you've earned some glamour after the last few days plodding around in the heat of Barcelona,' Rick said.

'What can I say? Rick that's great, I like your surprise. The Ritz, that's a new place for me and I shall dress up for it,' Claire said, suddenly excited at the thought of this smart dinner in an elegant place.

Claire had a reviving bath and dressed carefully. It gave her more time to think about moving in with Rick. She was enjoying the London scene with him, Rick was becoming an important part of her life but it could quickly come crashing down if her past, working with Harry Stone, was opened up. And that could easily happen.

It was exactly two years ago that Rick had been severely beaten in a quiet Cotswold village. He was kicked in his face and all over, an attack that left his right arm shattered in four places and a permanent scar over his right eye. Claire had been there with him when it happened and she had been very frightened on that night when they should have been enjoying dinner together. But the gangland thugs had got the wrong man; they thought they were doing Harry Stone over. And Rick never knew the truth and she could never tell him. Living with Rick now, Claire sometimes felt she was living a lie which, with every day, was becoming more difficult to hide from.

But the attack was now in the past and Rick always brushed it aside as if it could happen to anybody. Rick's recovery had been slow, Claire had nursed him and the thought of Harry Stone had gradually been pushed aside. But Claire still felt a tinge of nervousness when she looked at Rick's face and saw the scar over his eye, a scar that would always remind her of what really happened.

As they sat down at the calm but busy bar in The Ritz, Claire looked at Rick and felt almost as if she needed to tell him about the past and explain it was not her fault the dreadful mugging had happened. Could she clear the air once and for all and put Harry Stone right away to be forgotten in the distant long-ago? That thought had been tempting on many occasions because telling the truth had always been Claire's way. Tonight, though, she knew that it was just not possible.

'You're very quiet, Claire. Anything wrong?' Rick asked.

'I'm trying to adjust quickly from Barcelona to The Ritz. It's such a very interesting place, but, otherwise, I'm fine and ready to go for dinner.'

The menus were long. Some offerings Claire did not understand so she ordered sea bass, an easy dish that she knew she could enjoy.

'You do seem to find all the elegant places. I mean this is so grand, exclusive without being glitzy,' Claire said as they listened to the music of a harpist who was playing in the lounge.

'You need a few connections and a tip or two here and there to keep the wheels oiled, and then you can get in most places just when you want,' Rick said.

'Okay, let's test that. There's one place you haven't taken me to yet and that's the Chelsea Flower Show. Take me there next year if you can, Rick, and then I'll teach you all about gardening,' Claire said.

'Have you ever had your own garden? You've never told me about it,' Rick said.

'It was nothing exotic or tidy like what you see at Chelsea. But living in London I miss the wild garden I had.'

'Okay, so we'll go next year. That's a date. Is there anywhere else you'd like to go?'

'No, just for now let's leave it as The Ritz, what else could a girl want?'

'Do you still enjoy sorting these little problems like Barcelona for me? They do smooth out the business quirks that have to be cleared up,' Rick said.

'Of course, going to all the different places is what I really find interesting, and sitting behind a desk at a computer all day is no longer for me. So you just keep finding the problems and I'll keep sorting them out for you,' Claire replied.

Claire had only worked in Rick's office for a couple of months and that was two years ago. It was while Rick was recovering from the mugging. She had gone as a temp through an agency, and now even with Rick's easy, calm manner, she knew she could not return to work there. It would revive all her unwanted memories of how Harry Stone had manipulated the path so that she could spy on Rick's business empire for him, the Trifoni Group. Housed in a glass tower near Hyde Park, it was a slick place to work and had its own tempo and Claire, at that time, had felt the buzz of the business and a growing closeness to Rick.

But this evening dinner at The Ritz was special and the evening drifted by. Claire always felt easy in Rick's company, where conversation was about everything that was going on in the world and then about nothing in particular. Rick was wealthy, he owned most of the Trifoni Group where he bought and sold businesses, just like Harry Stone wanted to but could never balance reality with his own enlarged ego. And Rick had been attracted to Claire the day she first worked in his office. She was very stylish, she was confident under pressure, she was efficient and organised, and a leisure life away from work had quickly grown between them since that time.

'Can we fix a date for you to make the move into my apartment?' Rick said as dinner was ending. 'It'll be good for both of us and you could still be busy doing all the things you want to do.'

'Yes, when we get back after dinner I'll look at my diary and we'll make it soon, is that okay?'

'Leave it all to me, I'll arrange the removal people for you, Claire. You won't have to do a thing.' Rick watched as the waiter poured the last of the champagne into their glasses and he leant closer to Claire across the table. 'When you're ready to take on something new I've got another project I'd like you to have a look at for me.'

'That's not why you brought me here for dinner is it? To oil the wheels like your normal business deals?'

Rick laughed and held Claire's hand across the table. 'I would never do that. And tonight is a thank you for Barcelona until the next time.'

'So, go on, what is it that needs sorting?' Claire asked with a relaxed, teasing smile.

'Close to home this one. Nice part of the West Country.'

'Would that be some place I can catch up on some shopping?' Claire asked.

'Listen to this. Just a few months ago I bought a slice of a supermarket business based down in the West Country. Not a big set-up, just a dozen oversize shops. They call themselves Blake Markets, and Martyn Blake, the man who started it all, is still there. They seem to know what they're doing but they're up to something and they're starting to run dry of cash. It might be quite okay, it might be sinister, but cash is draining away. So can you fit in making a visit to ferret around for a couple of days, just to see what goes?'

'Blake Markets? You don't mean "black markets" do you?' Claire joked as she leaned closer to him.

'I hadn't thought of that but I like it. Yes, black markets, you obviously know how these things work.'

That halted Claire for a moment. Of course she knew all about black markets, the black economy, because that was the way Harry Stone always worked. Nothing above board, always on the edge with him. She pushed the thought away and looked more closely at Rick.

'What do you mean by something sinister going on? The word "sinister" always sounds deadly threatening to me.'

'I don't know. Maybe somebody with their fingers in the till or loads of stuff from the shelves going missing. But see what you think of Martyn Blake, I've got him coming into the office next week and I'd like you to come along and meet him. There's money draining away down there and I need to know why,' Rick said.

'Sounds very interesting.'

'There's a smart lady called Gina who works alongside Martyn Blake, she runs it all behind the scenes, and is in charge of what happens day to day there. She's very quick and alert and I'm told is very helpful. So a simple job this time, Claire.'

'Yes, of course I'll go but give me a couple of days to get my breath back from dealing with the Spaniards.'

Claire picked up her small clutch bag which was resting on the table. Of course she would probe into the supermarket business for Rick, she liked the diversity of work she did for him and, with their growing closeness, Claire wanted it to continue. She had seen a new world in the past two years. Visits to Glyndebourne, the Centre Court at Wimbledon where they had front row seats and even to a party in a marquee at Henley, where it had rained too heavily to even look at the river, were memories that lingered. As they left the table Claire knew their closeness had grown beyond just sorting a few awkward money problems.

'While you're away in France I'm taking a few days off, I need to do some shopping and to meet with my close friend, Jennie. Just to catch up on a few things. You must meet her one day,' Claire said.

'You've talked about her often so I'd like that. But I'm off to France tomorrow to probe around this very interesting chateau and vineyard. I need to learn a bit first about how to make wine so it may be a few days that I'm out of London,' Rick replied.

Half an hour later the limousine took them back to Rick's apartment and as always Claire would sleep well in the quietness that night. And it suited Claire that Rick was going to be away tomorrow as she was going to drive out from London with Jennie to make a visit for much more than just a catch-up on a few things. Claire was going to tidy up a problem that had been nagging at her for two years and it was a difficulty she could never tell Rick about.

2

After Barcelona and with a 'thank you' dinner at The Ritz with Rick, Claire had planned to take time out visiting her favourite shops in the West End. New clothes, summer outfits for holiday-time with Rick, shoes, and even a new watch were on her list. But Claire had a curious excitement at her promise to Rick to call on Blake Markets, the supermarkets in the West Country. Martyn Blake sounded an interesting person but Claire sensed maybe this would not be a quick and easy visit. Rick had told her something was going on down there, something sinister even, and next week Claire would meet Martyn Blake in Rick's office. Rick would quiz him but Claire was sure that it would leave many unanswered questions and she would easily go to find the answers.

But, for Claire, today was more important as she had her own problem to resolve. Claire was going to return to Arrow Hall and, after meeting a few days ago in Harrods for afternoon tea, Claire had persuaded Jennie to come with her. Arrow Hall was once an eye-catching Elizabethan manor house, a place which had stood in the Essex countryside as the finest notable historic building for many miles around. But it was now just a pile of rubble as two years ago a fire had blazed rapidly through the dry timbers of the old house razing it to the ground. It had been an arson attack from a drug ring, a vicious group of thugs who had followed Harry Stone from the Caribbean, and who had demanded protection money which he had not paid.

Claire had lived in her own flat in the West Wing of Arrow Hall while she had worked for Harry Stone and she had been anchored there by its 500-year history. She had traced the records back, starting with Sir William Wholinge who built the Hall and even with a visit from James I who had stayed there in 1610. But that meant nothing to Stone, he had ignored the history and he had let the historic building become run-down. Even the garden, which had a dried-out moat, had never been tended or cared for as Stone had been too mean to employ a gardener, someone he would always have seen as lazy unless his back was bent over a spade.

The fire had changed everything. Before that dreadful day Stone had promised Claire the money to renovate the house and she had carefully drawn up plans with an architect that would have breathed new, refined life into the Hall showing up its historic past. Claire had been very excited about this project but Stone's promise of money was hollow. It had been no more than a bribe to entice her to take on spying on a competitor, Rick Austen. Renovating Arrow Hall had been overtaken by Stone's greed and the plans died with the fire that had consumed the old house.

After the fire Claire had left quickly. She had stayed with Jennie and Roger in Newbury for some time. She had nowhere else to go. Jennie had always been there as a friend and Roger sometimes advised Harry Stone, when he would listen, and when he wanted to raise some cash for a deal he was working on. Although Jennie disliked Harry Stone intensely, at least Roger's contact with him would let Claire know what he was doing.

Claire was now living in London in an elegant part of Knightsbridge where she had her own apartment. But there the roads were bare of greenery and it was always too busy and noisy with ever-moving traffic. She was beginning to feel the contrast with the space in the three acres of wild garden that surrounded Arrow Hall. The old timber-faced façade of the house and the gentle Essex countryside, where she had known the freedom of the overgrown garden and farmland which surrounded the house, was the picture Claire had clung on to. And a visit to Chelsea Flower Show next year with Rick would be a day which would inevitably leave her with feelings on what Arrow Hall could have been. If only Harry Stone had kept his promise to renovate the Hall and had the gardens laid out.

Forebodings that Harry Stone would sometime come back to upset her life with Rick still lingered with Claire. Her time living in Arrow Hall was not yet settled and today it gave Claire a compelling reason to visit the ruins, a place she had not visited since the fire. This morning Rick had left early for Bordeaux searching for a vineyard estate to buy and it gave Claire time on her own. At midday she arrived at Jennie's Newbury house where Jennie was waiting for her with an eagerness as if she were a long-lost friend. It was a good start to a difficult day for Claire.

'You look smart for a drive to a desolate house in the country, Claire.'

Claire laughed, but she liked Jennie's compliment.

'I need to see what's left of where I lived for seven years, just for one final time so I can close it off from thinking about it every morning. One day I hope it might be rebuilt to just as it was, but I doubt if that is ever going to happen. Even with the insurance money, Harry Stone would be too mean to do it.'

'When we get there, take your time and don't let your memories upset you,' Jennie said.

A quarter of an hour later they left Newbury but with tangles of traffic it was some time before they came to the familiar Essex countryside, with its greenness from trees and many hedgerows. It had a comforting pull for Claire. They drove slowly down the lane that led to Arrow Hall, with trees that almost met in an arch over the road, then rounded a bend and reached the large iron gates to the grounds that were still open. The gates had rusted and a green coating of mould from years of dampness rested on them. They had stayed open for as long as Claire could remember but they were part of the history of this place and today they were a welcoming sight.

Claire could not hide the memory of driving down this lane two years ago on her way to Arrow Hall. It was a time when she was going to confront Harry Stone, let him know her spying on Rick was finished. But on that day Claire had met Stone standing at the large oak front door to Arrow Hall, flames behind him crackling to the sky. Then she had watched the fury and anger on Harry Stone's face, and the scene now tumbled back in front of her as if it was happening today all over again. Claire was very pensive, as even though this visit was not for nostalgic reasons she knew that it would open up her past in all its bare detail. But today, Claire had come for another purpose and she was feeling very tense and unsettled.

As Jennie stopped the car just past the gates, the sight that confronted them gave Claire a shock. Hoardings painted in a dark grey hid the remnants left from the arson attack and long random grass mixed with thistle weeds was growing in what was once the dried-out moat. The empty space looked miserable and abandoned. A few metres beyond the ground piled with rubble stood the old stable block which had not been caught in the flames. Claire let out a sigh of relief, as it was in that stable block that she would search for something important, something that would keep Harry Stone at a distance from her.

The memories for Claire of living at Arrow Hall became instant. She had lost all her clothes, family photographs, some jewellery inherited from her mother, two telephones and a laptop. At the time of the fire Claire thought a line had been indelibly drawn under her life at Arrow Hall but Harry Stone had thought differently and Claire now sat with Jennie in the car with the engine running. She was just staring at the derelict site that was once a historic and magnificent building. Its 500 years of history were no longer there and Claire gasped and put her hand over her mouth.

'This is just too dreadful. I shouldn't have come,' she said, and a tear crept from her eye.

Jennie put her hand on Claire's arm and watched as she stared at the blank hoardings in front of her. It was very quiet for a few seconds and even Jennie, who had never visited Arrow Hall before, felt the pain that Claire showed in the deep frown over her eyes.

'Do you want to walk around?' Jennie asked.

'Yes, but I can't believe how Harry Stone could ever have let this happen.'

'Come on, let's just go and walk in the garden for a few minutes,' Jennie coaxed.

They found a gap in the fence and walked in the long grass along the middle of the old moat to the house. They came to the place where Claire thought her apartment in Arrow Hall had been and she looked away as if she might see some of her possessions still lying on the ground. But the place had hardly been disturbed since the fire and weeds and long grass had grown, hiding any semblance of the house that had once stood there. The stable block, separate from the house, still stood as if in defiance of the fire and Claire silently recalled Anton, Stone's handyman as he called him, who had lived in a room up the top of the stairs.

'I did think sometimes in my wildest dreams maybe I could come back and live here again, if it's rebuilt,' Claire said. 'But I can now see that's never going to happen.'

'Have you ever thought of buying this place just as it is?' Jennie asked.

'I could never do that, and I don't have that sort of money. And Arrow Hall was a Grade I listed Historic England building, so anyone buying it will have all sorts of planners poring over the place. The cost will be high but if only someone would take hold of it and rebuild it as it was, as I remember it… well how good that would be.' Claire looked away and wiped a tear from her eye.

They had only been there a few minutes but Claire had seen enough. This site was now an ugly place filled with weeds, long grass and who knew what was lurking under the rubble, maybe even a snake or two. Claire took from her purse a small key and without saying anything she left Jennie behind and walked slowly to the stable block. There were tall weeds around the small building, undisturbed this summer, and Claire trod carefully to push open the broken front door. She tentatively walked up the worn wooden stairs to the first floor, wary that maybe the place had been vandalised since the fire.

It was dank inside but it was how she remembered it, all part of her haunting memory of Arrow Hall. Inevitably the room had been vandalised and she pushed her way through a pile of broken furniture that Stone had left in the building to rot. Claire found a small safe in the corner enveloped in cobwebs and if it had not been for its cast-iron build and weight she was sure it would have been removed by somebody trying their luck. But it was empty of money and it just held papers that to Claire were far more valuable. Harry Stone knew of this hiding place but he never came to it and he had no idea what was stored there.

With no fear or phobia to inhibit her, Claire wiped the cobwebs away with her hand. Her key fitted into the small opening on the safe's front, as she knew it would, and she twisted her fingers with childish excitement.

Claire took a thin file from under a couple of roughly bundled US dollars and quickly opened it. She found some notes in her own handwriting and she counted the pages, one to six, that were all just as she had left them. She breathed out heavily as she closed the safe and left to walk down the stairs, the file under her arm. She had deliberately left the key in the safe; it was now completely empty and maybe it would stop any would-be vandal from hurling bricks at the safe to try to break it. Jennie caught up with Claire as she looked back at the open door of the decrepit building.

'What have you found?' Jennie asked.

A positive smile spread over Claire's face as she held out the dusty file she had taken from the safe. She opened it and showed the first page to Jennie.

'What on earth have you got there?' Jennie asked.

'These are the codes Harry Stone needs to access his two Panama companies that have bank accounts which I set up for him. He's got at least $50,000 in each account, cash he secreted from the sale of five diamonds and two Rolex collectors' watches that had been given to him on a property deal in South Africa. He sold all these through a currency exchange contact he had in Soho who cleared the money into his Panama accounts, all underhand and without anything in writing.'

'Claire, I can't believe you were involved in all that, and does Roger know what Stone's been up to?'

'I doubt it. He hid everything from the Revenue men, Harry Stone trusts no one, he wanted his business and banking deals to be right out of sight and hidden as far away as possible. The Panama bank accounts now hold dead money until he gets hold of these codes,' Claire said.

'Be careful, you never know what Harry Stone will do to get his hands on them particularly if he needs the money that much,' Jennie said.

'That man is always short of cash but only I know where the passcodes were hidden. And I can't even imagine his anger had he known today that I'd opened the safe in the old stable block to Arrow Hall. I had the Panama account passcodes written down in these papers, even firmly fixed in my head, and Harry Stone might even think they were lost in the fire, that's as much as he knows where they were.'

'I hope his money is still there in the Panama accounts if it hasn't been touched for two years,' Jennie said.

'Yes, it'll all still be there. These accounts are secret and private but because he couldn't face working at a computer he doesn't know how they operate or where the codes are. But Jennie, don't you see these sheets of paper hold my insurance. After the fire, when I went to work for Rick, Harry Stone thought I'd walked out with all his business secrets and I'm afraid he'll go to Rick sometime soon to sprinkle lies about me and how he thinks I cheated him. But these codes are his cash and if he wants to get hold of it he'll have to stop his nasty, intimidating threats,' Claire said.

'But why come now to get them? I mean the fire was a long time ago.'

'I'm moving into Rick's apartment in a couple of days; Rick knows nothing about Harry Stone and these are my only security to make sure that's the way it's going to stay.'

'Why don't you just give Stone these access codes and tell him to go away?' Jennie asked.

'I will need to have his promise first about leaving me alone but even then I'm not sure I could ever trust him.'

Claire held the thin file tightly under her arm but Jennie sensed that this was more than just a visit here to recover access to Harry Stone's hidden money.

'I can see this visit means a lot to you,' Jennie said.

'Yes, of course it does. I had heard that the stable block had not been burned down but I needed to pluck up courage to come here and see for myself,' Claire said.

But Claire paused. The place was already bringing back haunting memories of how Stone did his business and as she looked around the derelict site she could recall him again shouting down the phone in an argument, his way of talking to people.

'Harry Stone and hot money go together, he will never change. He was always dealing on the edge, bending the law as he saw it. And he did not understand that Arrow Hall was an important historic building and this place will now just be left to rot away,' Claire said.

'You know Harry Stone too well. You worked very close to him, Arrow Hall meant so much to you but please stand back and move on, Claire. Look at your life here from a distance and try to blot Harry Stone out.'

'That man has a big ego, I've seen his rages and I know one day soon he'll try to get to me. And I find that frightening.'

'Stone runs to Roger when he needs cash to prop up a deal he's into. But Roger will never tell him where you are,' Jennie said.

Claire thought for a moment, unsure.

'Please, Jennie, give Roger a message for Harry Stone. Tell that man I'm never going back to help him tidy up everything he left in a mess. Like the insurance claim on Arrow Hall, he had wanted me to deal with it for him but that's not going to happen. He had odd bundles of cash secreted around the old house and the insurance company said they were not covered because he had not told them how much he had hidden. So if he goes to drop lies about me to Rick he needs to know I will then shred these precious Panama bank account papers of his.'

Claire walked towards Jennie's car and stared at the ground. And yes, she had spied on Rick, a betrayal that had led him into a very nasty beating at the hands of the same senseless hoodlums who had been chasing Stone. But spying was never Claire's way, Stone had lured her into it and, whenever she looked back to that time, she shuddered.

'Does Rick ever ask why he was beaten up?' Jennie asked.

'No, never, I've never told him, and he never wants to talk about the attack. I don't think he remembers what went on. It was a vicious assault, the police asked lots of questions and I had to be careful what I said because I knew the truth. But then they left it as just another mugging. I shall never forget the horror of it all, with Rick unable to speak in his hospital bed with bandages all over him,' Claire said.

'Does Rick know you've come here today?'

'No, that's a dark secret. I've never told him about how I lived at Arrow Hall, I couldn't. What would he say if he knew about this place? I just can't think of it, but I often ask myself if I'm deceiving him still.'

They drove through the heavy open iron gates and as they left down the tree-arched lane, Claire did not look back. They found the nearest country pub, The Sportsman, which Claire had often visited when she lived at Arrow Hall. It now had a new landlord, and Claire was not recognised, but as they entered the small low-ceilinged bar it still brought more memories flooding back.

'Rick took me to The Ritz for dinner as a thank you for clearing up some money problem he had in Barcelona. I often did that sort of work for Harry Stone but I never remember him taking me to dinner at The Ritz to say thank you. Jennie, I just don't want my life with Rick ever to stop and Stone talking to Rick… well let's not go there,' Claire said.

'You underestimate how much Rick likes your company and there's no reason it should stop. But next week let's forget all this and we'll have another run around the shops together,' Jennie said.

'Yes, that'll be good. I'll fit it around another problem job Rick has asked me to deal with. A supermarket business in the West Country. He thinks something's going on and I've promised to go down to probe into what's happening.'

'Sounds interesting but don't stay too long because it's time to have one of our lunches. And that'll wipe Stone and his dodgy deals right away,' Jennie said.

'Today's my sign-off from Harry Stone, I promise,' Claire said with a gentle laugh, the first today, which relaxed the tightening muscles of her face.

Claire held the folder tightly that she had found they sipped glasses of cheap wine, the best that this country inn offered. But in this centuries-old pub, Claire's memory of Harry Stone was like a misty cloud that never cleared. It left Claire feeling very unsettled.

On the drive back to London they spoke very little and, with firm dates for shopping and lunch, Jennie said goodbye to Claire as she dropped her off at her small flat in Knightsbridge. Once inside, and now alone with Rick away, Claire remembered the desolate site that she had seen that day. It was not Arrow Hall as he knew it. She put her head in her hands and gently sobbed.

3

Harry Stone left Marine House, the Regency mansion he was renting on Brighton seafront. It was the early afternoon. He had a call to make on his building site in Sudbury. Converting a derelict Victorian hospital into high-end apartments was not going well and even before he got to the site Stone's temper was rising. Leaving the major road he drove slowly and with winding bends in the lane and following a tractor until it reached its farm entrance, Stone's frustration and irritability doubled. It was now beyond his normal short fuse with anything that got in his way and it did not help that today he was driving a bright red Ferrari, a car that was more suited to a Formula 1 circuit than squeezing into the country byways he had been following.

The building site in Sudbury was only guarded by loose iron gates and as he swung his Ferrari into the muddy entrance, he saw this place too was very still and silent. He slammed the door of his newly valeted car and, as he walked quickly away from it, water from a muddy puddle splashed over his foot. It took his cold mood beyond what he could control and Dave, his man on the site, moved away warily. But then the stillness of this place was suddenly broken with menacing taunts shouted across the mud. It made Stone stop for a moment and he stared at the ghostly building in front of him.

‘This place stays empty, mate! You bring us some proper cash, what you owe us, that’s fivers, tenners, notes paid into our hands right here. You do understand don’t you, mate? You do know what grubby money is?’

Dave held his arm out to bar the way of two hefty men wielding builders’ trowels as if they were weapons they would use given half a chance. They had shouted to Stone over Dave’s shoulder almost as one voice and Stone saw the two men move closer to his red Ferrari. They peered through its window for a few seconds before the taller brickie, trowel still in hand, opened the driver’s door. He looked at his mate for a moment and laughed as if he wanted to show who was really in control in this place. Ignoring his very soiled sweatshirt and stained oily jeans he was about to sit inside on the cream leather of the seat when Dave’s voice boomed across the mud. It commanded instant attention and for a moment stopped the men’s sneering jibes towards Stone.

‘Boozy! You get out!’ Dave shouted. ‘Don’t spoil mister’s car, just leave all this to me.’

Boozy obeyed, and still waving his trowel ambled away towards a Portakabin with a defiant look back. He joined a gang who were talking and smoking and all staring at Stone as if he were a large orangutan in the zoo that might soon show some daring trick high up in a tree. Suddenly there was raucous laughter from the idle group as they watched this bloke with his very expensive motor and clean shoes, both incongruous in this place. He did not come here to work and get his hands dirty, he only came when he needed to measure how the building was growing. But that just gave them even more reason to taunt him and laze around the site.

Stone bawled at Dave as he walked towards the half-finished building, still feeling the stares and shouts of derision directed at him.

‘Get these layabouts off my back, won’t you? I hired you to make this place run and where is it now?’

Dave, in his knee-length boots, splashed through a puddle to face Stone.

'I've told you many times, boss, what to expect, so it's no use you walking away from it now. You owe these boys three weeks' wages, three weeks of grubby notes that they can roll up and put in their pockets away from the missus. You won't do that, so they get more angry each week and just tramp around. And don't expect any more work done here until you let 'em have what they ask and pay up. In fivers and tenners. And some friendly and final advice, sir, it's not going to work like the way you want it and you need to know that bricks don't get laid and concrete don't get poured without readies stuffed in brown envelopes. Or at least not where I come from. You want this nice building finished and your cash back then that's…'

'No, *you* listen. I can't get bunches of notes for them just like that. My bank asks too many questions. So forget it. And is this final? This lot of skivers and idlers are not going to work anymore to get this place finished?' Stone asked as he moved back towards his ostentatious red car.

Dave was adamant. 'No, nothing'll happen here, boss, until you pay up. And just so as you really know, the boys don't like you turning up in that flash motor of yours. It makes 'em think you're really rolling in the readies and they want some of that too. So next time, why don't you call me and I'll come and get you in my diesel rust-bucket.'

Stone, stopped in his tracks, turned. 'How much do I owe? How much to get this site moving again?' He spat the words out with growing irritation.

'A hundred and fifty grand. That's what it'll take. And all in crisp notes. Some for the boys and some for the suppliers who bring the stuff onto the site. You don't pay up in some cool money, like, quick, you'll find someone'll come and dig the whole lot up and then bury you right in the middle of it. These boys are happy to lay around for a short time but they won't hang around too long, so take it from me – you should go and find some cash to pay 'em like quick.'

'This is the last time I tell you, Dave – that's not going to happen, and the demand from that lot for a hundred and fifty grand in notes is absolute moonshine. Anyway, haven't we just paid eight grand for windows, so are you having me on?'

'Have you really never dealt in cash?' Dave shouted.

'Shut it, Dave. I've already said I don't do bundles of cash on demand so they'd better understand that.'

Dave let out a hollow laugh and turned away. Not for the first time had he seen a stark contrast between a wealthy man, tiptoeing and squirming in the mud, against the realities of working on a building site, drenched in puddles of dirty water that splashed everywhere. But Dave, a big man from London's East End with builders' thick, rough hands, for a moment checked himself. He knew that his boss was walking into something much deeper than just getting the boys working again.

'This place isn't your scene is it, Mr Stone?' he said.

'I know how to deal with this mob and I didn't come here today to get a blast from you,' Stone replied.

'Okay, then, but when you leave this idle site and drive off in your very shiny motor, remember this. There is a big noise. Part of a network that runs what happens on sites like this. Boozy and his mob look to 'em when they want a bit of help. Wide boy, drug dealer, heister, the network man, call him what you want, and he'll be around soon. So please watch out, Mr Stone. He'll come and get you.'

'I'm not listening to all this nonsense, so shut it,' Stone said.

'My advice, then, sir, is to get off from here, like a hundred miles away, and like, quick. While you still owe 'em you're going to be watched closely by their real boss man who'll bring some dirty underworld racketeering that'll soon swill around this place.'

'If they're trying an extortion racket on me they'll soon know how I deal with those tricks. This is my site, I own it. So tell 'em

I'm the boss here, and don't let any of these layabouts forget that. End of story.'

For a moment Stone looked at Dave with a scornful stare, unused to having a lecture from people he employed. He hesitated by his car, unsure whether he should just get in and drive away or wait to hear more from Dave. But then he still had more to say.

'Tell all these layabouts and their big mate, whoever he is, that if they don't like it they'd better get off my site. So they've got two days before I come back to clear 'em out,' Stone said.

'Don't do that, boss. They're already angry and you'll get in a right big fight if you try.'

'Forget it. Shut up, Dave. You give me a call tomorrow to tell me it's all working. Okay? Got it?' Stone snapped.

Dave quickly moved away, treading easily in the mud, and he then stared at Stone. That man owed a hundred and fifty grand. Dave knew this place and if Stone didn't pay up he would be drawn quickly into a ring of gangland dealing, and once in, he would be crushed if he ever tried to get out. But his boss was not listening, he never did.

Stone opened his car door and sank into the leather seat, giving no thought to the sleek lines of the shining red Ferrari as being out of place. Building sites were nothing new to Stone. In his teens, some fifty years ago, he had been at the dirty end, scraping around for cash like Boozy and his mates. But now he owned this place and nobody was going to take that from him. With a hefty slam of the door he noisily inched forward, splattering mud over the windscreen and at Dave. For a short moment Stone wondered why he had ever bothered to come here.

Stone could now see he had lost control of his building site. Even Dave, a man he paid to give the orders, had let Boozy and his mates make their demands just as they wanted. Turning a long-abandoned Victorian hospital into upmarket flats would make money, Stone was sure of that, it always did. But today, Boozy and the other layabouts were idle, mooching around the site with a can or two of Heineken and a rolled cigarette. They had a television, radio and kettle for tea in their own Portakabin. They could slip a bet or two on the horses from their smartphones or even at the bookie, just a short way down the road. They really had time they could kill and that was how they would let the hours drift by. And Stone's new building would not grow.

Leaving the site, Stone glanced up to stare at the façade of the old building. It still had the outline of a red brick arch that in its day had led to the courtyard garden, giving the lot a genteel outward appearance of Victorian quality, even grandness. Stone had always admired Victorian architecture, it was an age in which he could have lived comfortably, top of the pile and relaxed in the servile surroundings.

But the architect had just last week told Stone there were other problems with the building which had lurked hidden away until now. The foundations of the old red brick frontage had caused wide cracks to appear in the walls that had been built above them and the architect's advice, which Stone had ignored, was anyway beyond what cash he could find to rectify the problem.

Stone put his foot towards the floor of his Ferrari, felt the power, and decided at that moment that he would just leave Sudbury alone, he would not return until the crowd of skivers were back at work. He did not have a hundred and fifty grand in used notes and that was the end of it.

As evening closed in, with red clouds silhouetting a sinking sun, Stone left the silent Sudbury site with his anger rising. He drove quickly for a few miles to shake the place off, but it did little to calm his mood. There was a gloomy stillness in the air with threatened rain and Stone drove above the limit along a country lane towards the motorway, his mind whirring about five-pound notes, even a fistful of tenners. Boozy, with his trowel, standing like a school kid bully behind his mates was a picture he could not let go.

He braked hard and pulled over for an approaching car on the narrow road. He did not want any more scratches to an expensive motor from a low hedge in a country lane. They cost big cash to repair, cash that he did not have. The driver of the approaching car was in a bright yellow hi-vis jacket with sunglasses that hid most of his face and Stone stopped to let the car pass. But it swung in front of him and nudged against his front bumper. Out of the gloom there was a blast on a horn and a green van noisily loomed almost from nowhere against his rear bumper. Stone was closed in.

Stone's heart beat quicker from this annoyance and he felt a throb in his temples. His powerful car was stationary, going nowhere, and he was suddenly helpless in the quietness of the country lane. Before Stone could move, the driver in the hi-vis jacket was knocking on his windscreen. He was a big, broad man with a bald head that shone even in the gloom of the evening, dense black eyebrows and a rippling thick neck, with ears that projected wide of his head. It gave an appearance that was intimidating and demanding. Stone only half lowered his window and slipped lower into his seat.

'Harry Stone?' the bald man shouted.

'Yeah, what the hell are you at?'

'Out!' the man demanded, his accent broad cockney.

'Who're you?'

'Call me Xavier. Simple, easy to remember even for people pretending to be the boss, eh, Harry?'

There was another blast from the horn of the green van behind, as if the sleepy lane needed wakening, and Stone turned to see the driver and his mate staring at him through the windscreen. Without thinking he grabbed his car phone to call for help but the bald man saw Stone's move and laughed croakily with menace as he wagged his finger in Stone's face. He had stubbed his cigarette on the road only thirty seconds before.

'Those boys are with me so you ain't got no way out from here, mister. Keys before I come and get 'em. Come easily and you won't get hurt. At least not this time.' Xavier held out his hand.

'You're crazy! Go and do your heist somewhere else.' Stone struggled with the words, feeling hot and prickly.

'Last time, Harry. Out, and keys,' Xavier barked.

Stone felt the large body looming over him and touched the smell of violence closing in. He eased himself from the driver's seat and moved away, conscious that he was being watched closely by the two men in the van that was nudged up tight behind. It was the threatening charge of Boozy and his mates all over again, but this time, here in this deserted lane, he was cornered and he was alone.

Xavier stood back and looked over Stone's Ferrari with a mocking grin that said he was in charge. 'How much these wheels worth, Harry?'

'What the hell's that got to do with you?'

'My mates who deal in motors reckon two hundred and fifty grand. At least. Not many like this around I'm told. The number plate at the front looks good, it's a bit special, with your initials all over it and if the plate at the back has the same number too they're worth a bit on their own.' Xavier laughed with a taunting sneer and, after pushing Stone away, ignoring his soiled jeans, he slid into the driver's seat of this expensive and flashy red car. He held the steering wheel as if he were driving and pressed the horn which made a blast even noisier than the green van nudged up close behind.

'I don't know what you're playing at but you're not taking it,' Stone said with his usual defiance of anything he did not like.

'For a start this'll do nicely. The boys on the site want a bit of collateral against the hundred and fifty grand you owe. Hasn't Dave told you all about it? The notes and how the boys with their families and little kids are all starving waiting for you to pay up. Now come on, Harry, that's not fair is it?'

'Get out of here. I said you're not taking it!' Stone shouted.

'You watch me. Maybe one day you'll get it back, maybe not. Depends how we do business from here, Harry.'

'I don't *do business* with people like you,' Stone said. 'I don't do crumpled notes in dirty brown envelopes that've come from some violent smash and run, or dirty tablets and powders that you peddle. So the site'll get paid *my* way, and that doesn't mean you take my wheels when you want.'

'You watch and see, mate. You got a mobile?'

'What are you after?'

'Let's have it. You can walk home from here.'

Stone felt cold. He shivered, stepped back, and without a word took his phone from his jacket and threw it onto the passenger seat of his car. He was outnumbered by these big thugs, and this was not the time or place to fight. But there would be another time, of his choosing, when he would deal with these chancers.

'Thanks, Harry,' Xavier said. His tone was almost conciliatory and his large face creased into a teasing smile.

'I'll smash you, I've got people who know how to deal with scum like you so you just watch out,' Stone said.

'Shut it, Harry. We'll tell you when we're good and ready to do business, so you just listen. It may be we got a deal for you. You play it our way and we could look again at the hundred and fifty you owe. And if you do as we ask you might even get these nice wheels back sometime. If you don't do as we ask… well, Harry, my friend, let's just wait and see, but you'll work it out with us, because smart people with money like you always do.'

'You won't get away with this, you thug,' Stone shouted as the bald man noisily shifted the Ferrari into gear.

There was a throaty laugh from Xavier as he looked straight at Stone and lines creased Stone's forehead. For a moment he felt desperate, frightened even.

'I said we'll call. We know exactly where you live in that smart house on that flashy Brighton seafront. So you just wait, my friend, and be patient, while we enjoy these nice Ferrari wheels for a few days.'

'I'll call the cops. They'll soon see my motor, a bright red car like that shows up anywhere, so watch it 'cos I'm coming for you and your mobsters,' Stone said.

'Wouldn't go to the cops if I was you, matey. Just remember

those brickies and roofers on the site. You know, that lot who want to be paid in notes? I saw them come up to you with their tools, they looked a bit like weapons didn't they? Only Dave kept them away. Stopped something nasty happening to you, and you need to know I'm the only person who can keep it that way. So, Harry, wherever you are you can't run and hide.'

Stone thought he heard a police siren blaring into the evening air, perhaps even approaching down the narrow lane, and he walked away from his car, hoping to call for help. But the sound died away – it was only a noise from the motorway a mile or two distant, no doubt the police chasing another car.

In a fit of anger Stone wanted to thump the large face that was grinning at him from the wheel of his Ferrari but he was caught, totally helpless. He just stared and then waved his fist at Xavier in his car. But Xavier ignored this desperate gesture and again gave a mocking laugh, staring back intently at Stone. And in that moment, alone and cornered, Stone could smell the trouble that would come in dealing with these hoodlums.

Stone was now shivering, feeling cold in the early evening air. He watched his Ferrari, with it's headlights ablaze, as it was noisily driven away at speed, going far too fast to be safe down this narrow country lane. Too intent on watching his car disappear, Stone did not see or hear the driver from the green van with his mate as they walked up behind him. The wide metal bar hit Stone on his right shoulder with a force that sent him stumbling forward. He fell in a heap, face down on the wet road.

'That's just in case you might forget we're around, Harry,' the attacker said. He walked away quickly to the van, and his mate, laughing, ran to drive the car away. It was just a few seconds later that one after the other raced past Stone to the ends of the lane and with loud blasts from their horns made a deafening sound.

Stone was fit and lithe but this had stunned him and he lay in the road for almost a minute before he propped himself up. His hand automatically went to his shoulder to feel the damage. He sat dazed in the empty lane for another thirty seconds then rolled over, and seeing a tear in his trouser leg over his knee, struggled slowly to his feet. In an automatic gesture he ran his hand through his hair just to smooth it, and again felt his shoulder. As he moved his arm the pain was too great and he let it hang limply by his side.

The attack had happened quickly and noisily, but it was now very quiet. Xavier and his mates were gone and suddenly Stone was alone. It was getting dark and starting to rain. He had no phone, no car, and holding his jacket lapel tightly to his neck, Harry Stone started to trek slowly along the lane. His shoulder was sore and throbbing, and the injury to his leg slowed his progress. The rain intensified and water dripped freely from his hair. Getting wetter and wetter, he trudged on for over thirty minutes, with no traffic passing him, before he came to a small thatched cottage with a gleaming light shining from a front window. He breathed a sigh of relief as he sheltered under a narrow canopy and rapped hard with the brass dog's head that was the knocker on the front door.

It was opened half a minute later by a heavy-set elderly lady leaning on a stick. Stone smiled and stepped back, trying not to look intimidating in the growing darkness, although his dripping, dishevelled appearance was much less than inviting.

'Very sorry to trouble you,' he said, 'but my car's broken down. A mile up the lane. Do you please have a phone I may use?' Stone spoke slowly and met the lady's gaze.

She stared at Stone and peered over his shoulder as if looking to see if there was anyone with him, and then, with natural caution, she leaned fully on her stick and half closed the door.

'Wait a minute and I'll get the phone. I don't let strangers in,' she said bluntly and clumsily turned away.

From his wallet Stone found Dave's number, and as he waited he moved closer to the doorstep to shelter, and swore to himself. He shuddered, for a moment unbelieving at what had happened just a mile down this deserted lane. Should he call the police from this lady's doorstep and tell them about his car? More than two hundred thousand pounds' worth of precious machinery that had been carjacked by a man called Xavier?

His thoughts were interrupted as the elderly lady returned and gave the phone to him and then held the door almost shut. Had she already phoned the police as a precaution, Stone wondered, as he waited for Dave to answer.

The call was quick. Stone handed the phone back to her with a five-pound note for her trouble but she did not take the note, letting it fall in the rain on the step. Without saying goodbye she firmly shut her front door and Stone heard a bolt being drawn to secure it. Dave arrived ten minutes later. Stone was now feeling colder and very annoyed. But he would get his own back, he would get the word out about his expensive car and he would clear away this blatant chancer who called himself Xavier. And the thugs who were behind him.

'Are you all right, Mr Stone?' Dave asked as Stone got into the old and mud-splattered 4x4.

'You should have warned me about that lot. Taken my car and my phone. And that fat-faced fool hit me hard on the shoulder. I could have been dead lying in that road. So let's get out of here,' Stone replied and put his hand up to smooth his hair.

'I did try to tell you, Mr Stone. There's a man on top of the pile who looks after all the boys on the site. So, some advice, sir. Don't get drawn into his ring of drugs and extortion like a sucker.'

'Shut it, Dave!' Stone shouted, his usual answer when he didn't want to listen.

'Where do you want to go?'

'The pub at the end of the lane so I can clean up and get a drink.'

Dave said no more, and put his foot hard on the pedal as Stone slumped back into the seat and momentarily closed his eyes. But as Dave drove at pace Stone became alert.

'What do you know of a gangster who calls himself Xavier? What game's he trying to play on my site?'

'You owe wages in cash to all the boys and Xavier's there just to remind you. It's what he does,' Dave replied.

'What? Using a crowbar on my shoulder to steal the Ferrari?'

'Listen, boss, turning a derelict Victorian hospital into upmarket flats without paying cash off on the side don't work. No bank accounts, just simple clean cash in their hands at the end of each week. That's how they work.'

'Whoever this madman is you let him know, like quick, that I don't splash cash around like that, okay?' Stone said.

Dave gripped the steering wheel and a tight look of exasperation spread over his wide face.

'Please boss, treat Xavier as serious. He's got a network that's all over London. Your car's gone, the site at Sudbury's a mess of mud with nobody working and he ain't going nowhere. So you gotta deal with him.'

Stone, feeling the throbbing ache in his shoulder, stared through the windscreen, and it was as if the road in front was now opening up like a crater, a large hole into which he was falling. Shivering with cold, and uncomfortable, with his hair still dripping with rain from his lonely walk, Stone snapped.

'Get me to the pub and then go and get that lot of crooks sorted. That's what I pay you for!' Stone shouted.

Dave stopped, his seat belt not fixed Stone's head hit the windscreen and stars danced in the growing dusk of the day. This was another heist in a country lane and momentarily mesmerised he tried to open the door. It was locked and Dave, red-faced, turned to his boss.

'Sorry, boss, my fault, just avoiding a dog running across the lane. Are you okay, sure you don't want me to run you to Brighton?' A smirk spread across Dave's face.

'Call me in Brighton when you got some better news, got it?'

Dave dropped Stone off and quickly sped away. Stone was volatile and Dave had seen enough for one day.

Stone walked into The Weavers, a half-welcoming pub and

fiddled in his back pocket for some cash. Within two minutes he was sitting in a cosy but empty bar with a double Glenfiddich in his hand. He shouted across to the barmaid to call him a cab to take him to Brighton. She looked at her only customer, disbelieving. Nobody shouted like that and from someone so wet and dishevelled, with a trouser leg torn and jacket with a large oil-stained blot on the shoulder, this was an unlikely request. In any case she did not see it as her job to call for cabs.

'Phone's by the door, taxi numbers are on the wall. Top one's best. But they'll want cash up front.' She waltzed away to sit on a stool and stare at her newly polished nails

Cash up front for a cab ride? What's new? he thought in his mounting confusion. Stone paid the cabbie three fifty-pound notes before they left. The cab smelt of stale cigarette smoke and the woman was loquacious, wanting to tell her life story, divorce included. But Stone had been there himself and he told her to be quiet. He closed his eyes and for a few minutes slept.

Cold and irritable, Stone arrived in Brighton after ten that evening. He left the cab outside Marine House, the impressive Regency building that looked straight across to the pebble beach and the width of the sea. This house was four storeys high, with two elegant columns flanking the front door. He lived here on his own with just a housekeeper, Jo, who came each day to keep the place tidy and Vlad, a man who chauffeured him when he felt lazy. It had now been home for two years, ever since Arrow Hall had been torched and burnt to the ground. But Xavier now knew of Marine House, and it would not be long before he was snooping around. It made Stone wary.

At the end of this wet summer's day Stone was tired and he wearily climbed the steps to his front door. Jo had left a small, neat pile of post on the hall table. Stone scanned it quickly and without thinking placed the unopened envelopes on a growing pile of unpaid bills on the kitchen table.

He took off his jacket and shirt to examine the hurting shoulder more closely. There was no blood, just a dark black bruise spreading down his chest. He swore and poured a whisky from a decanter on a side table in the large sitting room. He walked to the small balcony where he stared across to the empty beach and a row of hanging lights that flickered gently in the night-time breeze. Harry Stone was now very angry and promised himself there would be a time and place for revenge. He paced the room for a minute and then again slumped onto the deep sofa. The clock over the fireplace showed nearly midnight. For the next five hours Stone slept uneasily, stretched out on the sofa of his elegant Regency living room.

***

Roger Garon often took his work home where it was always quiet in his Newbury house. That evening a nephew had taken an hour of his time asking him to find some cash for a scuba diving enterprise he had hoped to open in the Caribbean. The sheer fantasy of the hoped-for fun his nephew was seeking made Roger become short of patience. It was late in the day, and he needed to finish some other papers, but when he walked into his study to make some notes on his nephew's visit his phone rang.

'Who's that?' a rough voice asked sharply.

Roger held the phone away from his face for a moment and looked at it surprised.

'I might well ask the same,' his cultured voice replied slowly.

'Just holding this phone for a mate and you're one of the numbers I've got here and I'm finding out who they are.'

'Are you now?' Roger responded.

'Look, mate, do you know Harry Stone?'

'Why do you want to know?' Roger's intuition told him to be careful at the mention of Harry Stone, and he flicked on the 'record message' button.

'Well, it's like this, Harry has lent me his phone and I'm finding out if one of his mates can help him.'

'Does he need help?'

'Mister, do you know Harry?' the caller persisted.

'I might, but you'd better tell me what's going on here.'

'You his lawyer?'

'That really is no business of yours,' Roger said crisply. 'But for the record I'm not.'

'Okay, mate, but you sound a bit throaty whoever you are. Harry's jumped right deep into a pile of mess, he's up to his neck, he don't know how to handle it and one day soon I'll make sure he drowns in it. But Harry looks like a man who can find a bucket full of cash when he needs it, so tell him I called.'

'Why should I do that?' Roger said, trying to sound casually disinterested.

'Don't you want to know, mister? Or is Harry somebody you don't care about? What if one day soon he's found floating in a bag in the water off Brighton beach?'

'Are you threatening me?' Roger shouted. He heard an intake of breath in the phone.

'Put it like this. Harry owes me and my set of boys a large bunch of cash all in notes, so I'm just checking around to see what sort of mates he has.'

'What's your name?' Roger asked.

'Just call me Xavier. Most of me mates do. And I run the boys at building sites all over the place and that includes Harry's site of half-built flats at Sudbury.'

'I know nothing about Sudbury so leave it, Xavier, or whatever you call yourself. I don't like the sound of your threats so run away before I have this call traced.'

'Okay, mister, just so you know everything, Harry has not only lent me his phone but I've got his nice Ferrari wheels for a time. Goes fast and makes a deep, loud thumping noise when I put my foot on the pedal, and that's without the radio turned up, and it keeps our mate Harry close. He's never going to walk away from what he owes.'

'If you're making demands on Harry Stone, don't make threats too. Or else I'll advise Harry Stone to call the police.'

'We're following where he goes and from what I see that man's too sensible to go to the cops. And if he does, we'll take him out from his big house down by the seaside and get physical, eh mate?'

Roger had heard enough and he snapped the phone off. The call had lasted exactly two minutes. The caller had a coarse, mocking tone and Roger took what he had said seriously. Anything to do with Harry Stone always raised alarm bells, and this call confirmed once again what he had always known about the murky world that man moved in. What was going on this time, he wondered?

There was a deep frown on Roger's face as he thumbed some notes in a bulging file now lying on the floor in his study, that he had been getting ready to send to the security shredders. Roger only kept this wad of papers to remind himself how often he had tried to advise Stone, and his warnings had all fallen as quickly into Harry Stone's waste bin as a crumpled ball of white paper. Run a deal alone and then call for help when it was collapsing and when money was needed to support it, was Harry Stone's way. But today this call had been sharper, more menacing, than usual.

At that moment Roger called Fender & Co. He wanted to know more about this man Xavier, was he a chancer, someone just testing his luck, or someone who could get physical to show the reality of his menace? Fender & Co could dig the dirt on anyone, Roger had found many times, and with their agents they could work anonymously to find out who this man really was. Delving into the layers of the underworld, scammers, fraudsters or just violent heavy thugs trying extortion, was what they got paid for.

An anonymous male voice quickly answered Roger's call.

'Search something for me, please,' Roger said softly as if he did not want the call to be overheard.

'Is this urgent?'

'Yes, very.'

'What is your code, please?'

'Code orange, eleven twenty-four,' Roger answered crisply.

There was a short pause. The voice replied, 'Your file's coming up.'

'Right, please be accurate and in your usual way, very discreet,' Roger demanded.

'As ever. That's what we do, sir. Details please,' the man's voice from Fender & Co said, sounding alert for this instruction.

'Research from your files and wherever it takes on the ground about a man calling himself Xavier. Don't know if that's his real name but he might be part of some organised syndicate and at this time I'm told on a building site in Sudbury, a site owned by a man called Harry Stone. Runs the boys there, whatever that means,' Roger said, remembering the note he had made of the call. 'He maybe works on other sites around London too, but I want everything he's up to, criminal convictions, bank accounts, and his money flows, who his connections are – total info so I can see what he's about. And you won't miss him because he's driving a bright red Ferrari around town. I've got a mobile number he might be using and you can trace if it helps. Forty-eight hours, please, for a prelim.'

Roger reeled off Stone's mobile number and the personal number plate of Stone's Ferrari. It was a number he easily remembered as Stone had taken him for a ride in the loud car just to show off soon after he had acquired the thing. And at that time with Stone's foot never too sure on the pedals it had left Roger wanting to get out. The voice from Fender & Co broke in and gave a short confirmation that the response Roger had requested would be dealt with very urgently. A minute later Roger joined his wife, Jennie, who was finishing her nightcap gin and tonic and ready to retire to sleep.

'What's been keeping you so late in the study?' Jennie asked.

'I've had a call about Harry Stone. Something funny's going on.'

Jennie shivered. She disliked Harry Stone, she knew how Claire felt about him, and just the sound of his name made her wary.

‘What’s he up to now?’ Jennie said.

‘It was a very rough voice on the phone and he says he’s taken Stone’s big red Ferrari.’

‘That man deserves all he gets,’ Jennie said.

‘I know he’s got two property projects running and it sounds he’s doing another of his underhand deals in the black economy. Something he’s not told me about and something that’s not working out.’

‘When I went with Claire yesterday to the pile of rubble that is the ruin of Arrow Hall, Claire picked up a dusty file of papers. She said they hold the codes Stone needs to access his Panama bank accounts and Claire thinks he’s got a few thousand dollars stashed away there.’

‘Yeh, and he’ll call on Claire when he needs that cash. His Panama accounts are like gold to Harry,’ Roger said.

‘The next time you see Harry Stone, Claire says to tell him that she’s got his Panama codes. And more than that she’ll shred the lot if he ever calls on Rick,’ Jennie said.

‘Claire needs to be careful. Harry’s a vindictive man.’

‘I don’t understand why he can’t leave Claire alone and get on with his low-end business without her?’

‘When Arrow Hall was burning he was sure Claire had gone behind his back. He saw it that she had run away and never came back to help him clear up the mess,’ Roger said.

‘For goodness sake, Roger, tell the man that Claire’s moved on. Stone digging up the dirt of his own dodgy past helps nobody.’

Jennie finished her drink, she had heard enough and she went to her bedroom. But Roger sat still for a few minutes. He often helped Harry Stone in his schemes but he usually walked away when it was right on the edge. And now something was going on with a man called Xavier which Roger smelled from the call had the ring of menace. But half an hour later as he too climbed the stairs for a night’s sleep, Roger could have no way of knowing how Claire would be dragged into the vicious circle of nastiness that was now surrounding Stone.

4

Dave drove at speed but was slowed as he entered the maze of streets that was London E12. He knew where he was going, he knew this part of London well and even liked the smell of the place but he had an unsure feeling after the phone call from Xavier at seven that morning. It was the urgency in Xavier's voice and where he was now being directed to that just did not sound right. The traffic quickly thickened and his satnav led him to Dundee Road. There were rows of long narrow side streets, places he remembered from his childhood, and he found a space to park between the wheelie bins that were stationed outside each Victorian terraced house.

Leaving his car he walked the hundred yards that took him to an address of a charity shop, one of many in Dundee Road. Several people milled in its open aspect. It was selling second-hand clothes, books, bits of furniture and almost anything else it could put into its window. Dave had no time to look further, he turned away and walked up the uncovered concrete stairway at the side of the shop. This surely was not the right place to find Xavier. With his fist Dave banged on the door of the flat that stood one storey up. A dog barked with a piercing growl and Dave stood back, startled.

Holding by the collar a jet-black pit bull terrier with glaring eyes and showing its long white teeth with slobbering jaws, Xavier came to the door. He had a sweat-stained T-shirt and dirty jeans held with cord below a large belly, and he had a stubble growth of several days. The animal barked again, Dave felt the menace from its snarl and although he had always thought Xavier had money when he wanted it, this place was barely showing it.

'Hello mate. You found me okay?' Xavier shouted above the noise of the dog.

'Keep that thing away from me,' Dave said as the pit bull started barking close to his feet.

'Not too friendly today, is he? Perhaps he wants his dinner,' Xavier replied with a laugh.

'You called me. But I ain't got much time,' Dave said, trying to ignore the animal.

'Come in,' Xavier said, and backed away into the dark, narrow hallway.

He held the dog tightly and opened a side door to push the animal in. It jumped back at the door, still snarling and scratching at the wood, and Xavier smiled. He led Dave into a small untidy room that overlooked the road. It had a sofa with no cushions, two upright chairs and a single curtain that half obscured a very dirty window. The whole place was sparse, dingy and malodorous with a mixture of mustiness and cigarette smoke.

'Want a cup of tea? Or something stronger?' Xavier asked as Dave sat on the edge of the sofa.

'No thanks, I can't stay long. But you want to talk about Harry Stone?' Dave blurted.

'Yeh.' There was a grin on Xavier's stubbly face as if he had forgotten why he had asked Dave to call.

'Do you live here all the time? Is this your pad?' Dave asked, looking at the dirty carpet and the peeling paper on a side wall. The dog was still barking but more muffled as if it was settling at Xavier's command.

'I come and go. Depends what I've got on. You know what I mean?'

Dave did know what Xavier meant, and after Harry Stone's

carjacking he was not surprised to find him dossing in a tip that he could move from quickly. With a man like Xavier there would always be people he would rather not see come knocking on his door.

'I run the site at Sudbury and you do know Harry Stone don't like dealing with the sharp end of the building game. He only ever visits the place when he thinks something's going wrong,' Dave said.

'I'm going after him. The man's not going to walk away from paying the boys right up and all in ready notes. I got his motor and I keep his motor until he comes round, but looking at him he'll play hard and try to twist out of it, won't he?' Xavier asked.

'All I know is Harry Stone'll do his own thing, his way, whatever that is.'

'Listen. I've got some cash come my way, like a quarter of a million in used notes. The Revenue man don't know about it and I got to get it looking like clean money so he don't ask questions when I do use it. And I gotta do it like quick. Got it, Dave?'

'Yeh, but why're you picking on Harry for clearing this cash?'

'I want to try him out. He looks like a man who's got money and knows people who'll help him deal with it. Anyway I'm searching around for new contacts because I've got a lot of cash flowing in from St Vincent where I've got a mate. And don't forget, Dave, our man Harry owes the boys at Sudbury a lot of readies.'

'Why do you keep that dog? I can hear him scratching at the door.'

Xavier ignored Dave, lit a cigarette and stared through the grimy window.

'I'm sending one of my boys down to Harry Stone's place. I want to watch him 'cos he's now got to do this washing job for me. I'll try the soft stuff first, because looking at him, he won't take much roughing up. But then I might get a bit tough, just like what he had to feel when I took his motor,' Xavier said.

'Where'd you get a quarter million in notes?' Dave asked and immediately wished he'd left it.

'It's like this, mate. My friend in the Caribbean needs some bundles of notes he's sent me cleared up very quickly from a bit of trading he's been doing. And I've got a lump on the side too. Had a nice job couple of months ago. South of the river. A bit of breaking and entering took out trays of diamonds and some classy watches from a couple of dozy shops. Add a bit of protection cash from a few pubs round that way and that means a bag of notes to be made clean, away from people who want to put their finger in my pie. But I don't want to spill too much, do I?' Xavier said and laughed, which led to a deep smoker's cough.

'I don't want to know your deals 'cos what I don't know I can't talk about, okay?' Dave said.

'You stay around, Dave. You got work to do for me.'

'Yeh, but that man will never do that dangerous work of money laundering, he's volatile, he'll blow it all wide open.'

'You go and talk to Harry. Tell him he's got to find one of his mates who has a business that has lots of cash takings through the till. You know, a set-up like a supermarket, football club, garage, car dealer, bookies, pubs with all those betting machines, you know 'em, they're all out there, all with takings in hard cash. But the clever bit is where his mate then pays my bundles of notes into their bank all nicely mixed with their own cash just as if my money's theirs and no one notices. And then in a few weeks' time, when I give him a special invoice for work my building business never did but wants payment for, his mate'll send it back down the wire. Nobody knows the invoice is phony that I've given him but that's what washing cash is. Cash goes in as grubby notes one end and comes out clean as a cheque or down the wire, for payment of a pretend job well done at the other end. It's like magic. And Dave, you tell Harry, when my cash is back, washed clean, he's maybe got a bit more time to clear his debt to the boys,' Xavier said and again laughed.

'Look mate, I just want to be left out of any cash running deal. There's already some odd-smelling stuff being dealt around the site at the moment. Those boys not only don't want to work, they want to get high, and that place is grinding to a halt. Nobody's worked for a week now and if everyone's going, so am I,' Dave said.

'You stay there, mate. It looks like a good place that could become valuable without Harry messing it. Just wait and see what happens. Okay?'

Dave ignored the comment as Xavier stood, lit another cigarette, walked to the window and peered into the busy street.

'Sure you don't want a cup of tea, mate?'

'No thanks, I'm too busy to drink tea,' Dave replied and then kept silent for a few moments, only punctuated by the aggressive growl of the dog locked away next door.

But Xavier was in full flow, his eyes were glazed and he was not going to stop.

'Listen, mate. I told Harry I'd be in touch when I nicked his nice motor. I can see it in the lines of his face, he's hungry. But is he legit himself? Could I trust him with a large amount of used notes to be washed clean? Would he run away with it? I don't know but I'm gonna find out, you see?'

'You're talking of money laundering. That's risky stuff. I've said leave me right out of it,' Dave said.

'Stone owes the boys money, mate, so he's got my attention until I want to let him go. You know what I mean?'

'Yeh, I know what you mean but you got his motor to cover that, so lay off him is what I say, mate. You don't know how hot-headed that man is,' Dave said.

'And my boys tell me Harry's got a big house by the sea. That must be worth a million or two, eh Dave?'

'Nothing to do with me, Stone's big lot down in Brighton, so leave it can't you?'

Dave got up from the sofa and moved towards the door. It set the dog barking with an increased ferocity noise and Dave backed away. 'That thing can't get out can it?'

'Not until I say so, mate. So you're safe and don't look so scared,' Xavier said.

But Dave was now becoming unsettled. He could not get out quickly enough, he had heard things he did not want to know, and besides, how could he talk to Harry Stone about laundering cash for Xavier? Stone was a man who was unpredictable at the best of times.

'You do this run for me, look after the site, do what I ask, and I'll make sure you're okay, mate. Got it?'

Dave had never thought that Sudbury would become valuable but that was not his part of the deal to worry about and, as all he wanted to do was make sure concrete was poured in the right place and bricks laid in the right sequence, he pushed it aside.

Xavier stood close to Dave as they entered the hallway and his breath was odorous from drink. The dog barked fiercely again and Xavier bellowed at it to stop, together making a din that would penetrate down the stairs, right into the street.

'Like I say, mate,' rumbled Xavier, 'Harry knows he's got a problem, washing my money is his way out. If he walks away we rough him up and he really won't like that.'

'Yeh, I'll go talk to him, but you leave the heavy stuff off until I'm gone,' Dave said.

Xavier ignored him and thumped on the closed door where the dog was scratching the thin wood that kept him in.

'You can hear my pet shouting can't you, mate? He wants out and I might just let him loose on Brighton seafront sometime, you know, when Harry is taking a mooch in the dark. This doggy's pretty good around the building work too, and he'd have a good sniff at Sudbury.'

'Not when I'm around. I don't like dogs,' Dave said, and he quickly ran down the outside stairway.

There was another loud laugh from Xavier and he again kicked the door where he had enclosed the fierce animal as it set off on a barking frenzy.

Dave left this unlovely place hurriedly as he wanted to get away from barking dogs. Xavier, working from an unlikely place and with alcohol odour at this time of day staining his breath, frightened

Dave. It was a far distant picture from what he thought he would find. But where was the flash Ferrari that Xavier had nicked from Stone? Dave looked along the road but there was no sign of a roaring piece of metal that was Stone's very valuable car.

Just round the corner from Xavier's dosshouse there was a large old-fashioned pub. It had high windows with etching in the glass of the beers sold there and bars for those who came from work with dirty clothes separated from those who were at leisure and wanted a softer seat and beer at a higher price. Dave walked quickly to put distance between himself and Xavier's unlovely squat. He was very unsure that Stone, even with all his cunning, could ever compete in the ruthless world that he was being dragged into. Washing bundles of illegal cash to make them look clean was a dirty business.

Dave slipped into the pub and eagerly sipped his beer in the bar for those who came from work with dirty clothes.

5

The carjack in the country lane left Stone very angry. His shoulder was aching with a dull throb, Stone had not seen this heist coming and even Dave had not warned him of trouble from the deserted site at Sudbury. Stone swore to himself. He was distracted as he wandered aimlessly into the large sitting room of this elegant house and the pain in his arm did not help his mood. His Ferrari was an investment worth money, not just a motor car, and even though by now it would be well hidden he would send Vlad to find it.

And, today, he would have to get his second car back from the local garage. It was a Porsche and it was having deep scratch marks down the passenger door repaired after being driven by Vlad too close to a bollard. It was Stone's harrying that had made Vlad try to park the wide car in too narrow a space and now it was a costly repair.

His call to the garage took two minutes. The car workshop promised to deliver the Porsche back straight away and Stone walked down to his garage in the dark shade behind his house. Stone had never wanted these two valuable cars in the first place. They were too showy for his low profile, he had already been taunted at Sudbury from Boozy and his mates for driving a Ferrari onto the site and he would soon cash them in for big money.

It was a deal in the black economy for a bundle of notes that had led Stone to own them. As an investment, just a year ago he had piled batches of loose cash into a used car lot on the eastern edge of London. But he soon found it was not the best place for dealing big upmarket flashy cars that he thought would make him a quick return. Ferraris and Porches were really out of place, too pricey for a rapid turnover and the car lot folded. Stone did not argue, he stepped in and he took back what he thought he was owed. A bright red Ferrari and a valuable Porsche with a soft top became his. They satisfied the debt. And at the finish the car lot in the East End left only an office full of paper strewn over the floor, paper that recorded only some of the dealings of the place that was now bust.

Ten minutes after his call a wide-eyed girl with long blonde hair drove the Porsche easily into the tight bay in Stone's garage, her touch deft and controlled. Harry Stone knew all about a car with ego-touching power, how dangerous it was in the wrong hands, and even the road rage he had caused several times himself behind the wheel of this vintage motor car. The girl smiled easily as she eased from the low driving seat.

'Mr Stone, all dents repaired and you're ready to go again.' She stood and looked at the car as Stone gave an approving nod.

'Yeh, looks good.' Stone held his hand out for the key which the girl was twisting in her fingers.

'How would you like to pay, Mr Stone?'

'I'll bring the credit card in tomorrow. Okay?'

'Sorry, sir. Can't do that. Can't hand you the keys until we have payment. Instructions from the boss.' She stared at Harry and smiled.

'Come on sunshine,' Stone said, 'you know I'm not going to run away.'

'The boss says the bill is building up and he needs the money.' Her smile widened, showing obvious enjoyment at keeping the keys twiddling in her fingers.

For a moment Stone looked at her wide smile; he felt no embarrassment, yet he was becoming irritated and unsure how to handle her demand.

'How much?' he snapped walking aimlessly around the car as if to inspect the work that had been done.

'With petrol and other accounts that are already outstanding, it's five thousand, six hundred and seventy-eight pounds. We'll leave the fifty-two pence off.'

'I haven't got time to come to the garage just now. I've got some urgent business that means I've got to get on. So I'll call with my card details, okay?'

Stone immediately knew that was not going to be okay as he watched the girl walk with purpose and stand right in front of the car and then lean against its bonnet. Whatever Stone said, the girl from the garage was going to block its movement.

'To save you time, I've brought the card machine with me. Works almost anywhere, but I guess we may need to go outside into the fresh air to get it to connect. How's that?'

Stone had not seen this coming. He paid bills when he wanted to, not when they were demanded, but the reality that now faced him was a blonde young woman from the accounts department of the local garage. He fumbled in his wallet and produced a gold American Express card.

'Let's go,' he said, walking quickly as he led her to the daylight of the garage exit.

In the bright light of a summer's day Stone paid the account. The card had a high credit limit, not even his accountant knew it existed, and it would get him off the hook of being held hostage by his own garage. At least until the next time. Stone felt the heat of the sun on his forehead as he tapped in his PIN code.

The girl from the garage had a smug look on her bright, fresh face as she gave Stone the key to the Porsche and then walked slowly away. This was satisfying. She had been sent to do a job and had finished it well, happy to see this outwardly affluent man comply with her demands without blinking. She gave Stone an almost mocking grin. He turned away.

'Thank you, Mr Stone,' she said. 'My boss will be pleased.'

Stone did not look back as he walked to take a closer look at the car. He was angry over the large bill but this hold-up for cash was not the first time demands had been made. A few minutes later, back in the kitchen there was no avoiding the untidy crumpled mass of envelopes and papers lying near the edge of the table. It was a heap which had grown steadily over the past few weeks and which Stone had purposely tried to ignore.

He fumbled for the account of the Raven Garage and without looking at it squeezed it tightly into a ball and threw it into the waste bin. For a moment he felt satisfied but his ill temper would soon return. He looked up as Jo entered the kitchen. She had a bright smile, which was not unusual for her at any time of day, but Stone's face was tense with a deep scowl. Jo read instantly what it said.

'You won't mind me asking about that pile of unopened envelopes you're pushing around the kitchen table, HS?' Jo asked in a voice that she knew could not be ignored.

'I'll deal with them all tomorrow,' Stone replied irritably. 'It's on my agenda so please don't hassle about it.'

'You ought to know there is a letter from the agents who deal with Marine House reminding that you're not up to date with the rent. They rang me yesterday to find out why you were letting it get behind and I told them that the demand had just been misplaced. So where do you want me to put all these letters now so they don't get lost or forgotten any longer?'

Harry Stone ignored her, a reaction to a difficult question that Jo had seen before. But Stone had not told Jo he was letting the demands for rent on Marine House drift as he was going to move on. He was going to leave this place, it was too big, and he would find another more secluded house, hidden away in the countryside from prying eyes. Just as Arrow Hall had been.

Stone was a wealthy man, Jo had been told that when he was negotiating the lease for Marine House, but that was not how it was now looking to her. Jo always referred to Stone as 'HS', his initials as far as she knew them, and it was almost a term of endearment and totally reserved for her. It was closer than Mr Stone but more formal than just Harry, which did not seem right. Jo did the housekeeping, she followed on each day as it came but she was always there to tidy up where Stone had left his mark, usually dirty glasses and plates, or food nibbled and discarded clothes. She tidied other rooms, kept the fridge replenished as she thought necessary and looked out for anything else that would keep this grand house reflecting the elegant Regency period when it was first built in 1820.

Jo had kept house for the family of the owner for five years before Stone arrived. She had come with the lease when Stone took over, she was perceptive and had many times in the past year wondered why a sixty-year-old bachelor would want to live alone in such a large fine Regency mansion. She had seen that he had no routine to any day and that his swings of mood were extreme. And HS was becoming more untidy in his habits with the whisky bottle being drunk more quickly. But at this time, Jo knew none of the history of Harry Stone, or Claire and Arrow Hall.

'Refreshing HS's study' is what Jo called it, but it was a daily ritual of printing off his emails and responding as he decided, though to get a response at all from HS meant that you were talking about something he thought was very important. Most times, to communicate, Stone used the phone, he liked the spoken voice, he liked to shout often and he had never achieved that with an email and rarely with a letter. Jo always softened the tone of a reply that HS had dictated to an email.

'I'll go around the upstairs this morning, but I notice you again slept comfortably on the sofa last night and that's the second time in a few days,' Jo said, looking at HS now slumped uncomfortably on the kitchen chair.

'I don't remember going to sleep as I came in late. I've had an accident with my shoulder, it's painful still and I need to get to the doctor sometime to see what the damage is,' Stone said, and looked away with a distracted frown.

'We'll need to buy some more of your favourite Glenfiddich, HS,' Jo said.

'Do it, put it on the account. We still have some credit with the wine merchant don't we?'

'Yes but one of their bills is on the table that you've just shuffled away.'

Stone ignored Jo's comment, he did not want to hear about people asking for money to settle accounts, and Jo left HS sitting alone in the kitchen staring at the ceiling, his thoughts obviously very far away.

But Jo was wary and she was beginning to have concerns about the security of this large house. She went quickly to the study to send an email as the front doorbell rang. Stone breathed out heavily, placed his large mug of tea on the table, eyed the pile of bills and threatening letters, and walked slowly to the video intercom in the hall. Any diversion from his dreary mood in the kitchen was welcome and Stone pressed the button and waited just a second.

'It's Dave,' a croaky voice came back.

'What the hell are you doing here? Why aren't you on site?' Stone shouted.

'Forget the site. We gotta talk, boss. Like fast. And I do mean fast.'

'We've done all the talking. You clear out and leave me to deal with this load of thugs my way,' Stone replied. He switched on the one-way video link and saw Dave staring at him.

'Please listen, boss, let me in and hear what I got to say. It might just get you off the hook that Xavier's got you dangling on for a hundred and fifty grand. And you might even get your precious motor back. You know, that big red shiny lump of metal.'

'That crook snatched my car. They smashed my shoulder with a lump of iron. I've got nothing else to say to 'em until I decide how

I'm going to kick them out. So scoot, get out of here and back to the mud and bricks on the site where you belong.' Stone drew in his breath and looked at Dave's ruddy face in the video camera. He did not know who to trust and he hesitated.

'I really need to talk to you, sir, and urgently please.'

'You've got nothing to say that I want to hear.' Stone was becoming annoyed and it showed in his voice.

'Listen, boss, I left Sudbury to plough through the snarl-up on the motorway to get here. If you give me a bit of time I can help to sort your problem. I'm trying to protect you and it's now gone past the hour when I need a coffee, so you owe me ten minutes of your time, Mr Stone.'

Without thinking Stone released the remote catch on the door and shouted dismissively into the phone. 'Follow the hallway along. I'm at the end.'

Thirty seconds later Dave appeared, cleanly dressed with no stained or dirty jeans. Even his brown shoes were shiny with recent polish.

'You live in this castle alone?' Dave asked, breathing heavily.

'Leave it, Dave. I don't want any of your smart lip in here.'

'Worth a bit, ain't it?' Dave said, looking at the wide carpeted and elegant hallway.

'I said leave it, didn't I? I don't need you coming here and lisping that at me,' Stone said, glaring at Dave.

But Dave was interested in where he was. This place was big and grand. He spoke slowly. 'Money's nothing to me. Don't understand it, except a few hundred quid in the back pocket to keep going. Don't add up in my book how you can live in this palace but not have the readies to clear off Xavier and all the trouble he'll bring you. Simple. That's all.'

'I'll deal with Xavier when I'm ready and it's not your business how I live,' Stone said sharply.

'You're right, boss. I've got no idea. It's all a bit posh for me. As I said a few hundred quid…'

'Dave, didn't I tell you to shut it? My shoulder's aching like mad and I just don't want to hear your thoughts on how I live and how you exist. So why're you here?'

'I got a deal for you. Something to clear off your debt on Sudbury. Xavier called me to his squat yesterday. So hear what I got to say, please.'

'Get on with it and then get out. I've got other things to deal with today.'

'Where's your kitchen in this place, Mr Stone? I want a coffee, then we talk. Okay?'

Dave was in the wide hallway and Stone walked quickly into the modern white clinical kitchen that even though it had high ceilings was cluttered enough to be homely. Stone often spent time brooding in his study, but the kitchen was a place where, when he was alone in the big house, he could shout down the phone and hear his voice echo off the walls.

'Instant coffee with a dash of milk,' Dave said before Stone had chance to move towards the Italian coffee machine that dominated a corner table. 'A mug'll do nicely.'

Stone stared at Dave but put the kettle on to boil. Two minutes of silence ensued before they both sat at the kitchen table. Dave put three teaspoons of sugar in his coffee and Stone glared at him again.

'You ever dealt with large bundles of notes to hide them in somebody else's business for a few weeks?' Dave suddenly asked, stirring his coffee vigorously and noisily.

Stone again stared unbelieving at Dave and shouted. 'No, I haven't, and I don't want to, not now or ever. No notes for me. So don't be dumb repeating it all over again. I told you a couple of days ago I'm not into that and I'm not listening now. So if that's all you've got to say, get out!'

'This is different, Mr Stone. You'll know of some business that flows in cash. I mean the ones who take cash for sales every day. Shops, restaurants, cash and carries, used car lots, slot machines on the pier. Do you know what I mean?'

'Don't be naïve. I don't know what you mean and I don't want to know. So what have you come here to say?' Stone shouted again.

'You ain't got no choice, you've got to help Xavier tidy up a lump of cash, Mr Stone. Like quick. He's come into a lot of notes and he says you'll know how that sort of thing works.'

'What do you mean, know how it works?'

'You know, sorted and washed through somebody's pukka bank account so when it's paid back nobody knows where it had started from or when it was paid in. You gotta turn the cash into something that looks legal and nicely clean.'

'Is this a joke, Dave? Have you come here all the way from Sudbury just to tell me that? You're wasting my time and yours, so get out.'

'Okay, boss, you still just don't understand. Look, I'm deadly serious. You owe Xavier a lot of money, the boys are no longer working at Sudbury and maybe never will. Xavier now controls all that happens there, he'll stop your building being finished, so be careful,' Dave persisted.

'How does that thug suddenly come into a lump of dirty notes?' Stone asked.

'If you want to stay safe, don't ever ask where it comes from.' There was a pause from Dave as he took a sip from his coffee.

'You've come to talk about crooked money. You want me to handle stuff from druggies, someone running a scam, even thieving, heists, where a lot of people get hurt? How many people have been hit with metal bars around their head or had knives stuck in 'em to get this cash? Do you know where this kind of stuff leads? You get banged up for a long time if you get tangled in this mess,' Stone shouted.

'These deals happen every day. So some advice, sir, please, no questions. You do what Xavier asks and he lets you off the hundred and fifty grand debt he says you owe the boys. That's why you do it, Mr Stone. You don't have no choice.' Dave shouted back across the kitchen table.

'Of course I have a choice, you fool, and I'm not going to do it.'

'Don't push it, sir. You're in deeper muck than you know. Feel safe. Go with it.'

Stone stood and wandered around the kitchen, distracted, with his tea mug in his hand. 'I don't need you to tell me to feel safe. I can look after myself, so shut it, Dave.'

'Remember how easily they nicked your car. Dark country lane, nobody there to help you, and you could have been left lying in the wet ditch and not even awake to cry for help. These boys have only lightly tapped you on the shoulder so far, and they don't hang around, so think hard before you tell me to shut it.'

'If that thug is trying to frighten me, it won't work. This place is safe and I can watch everyone who comes and goes here,' Stone insisted.

'If that's what it takes, Mr Stone. You should be very frightened, 'cos I know what Xavier does when he don't get his own way.'

'How much of this crooked cash are they trying to push on me? Few hundred? Few thousand?'

'Let's say a quarter million. That'll get you going, it'll send these boys away for a few weeks at least so you can get the site finished and get out.'

Stone swore to himself and for a moment felt sweat on his forehead. 'This stops now. I just don't do money laundering, I know nobody who would run the cash through their business because it's just like openly handling stolen loot. That's madness and I'm not going there, so you go right back to that thug Xavier and tell him direct from me the answer is no. And always will be no. Got it?' Stone snapped.

Stone sat down heavily and placed his cup on the table with a noise that was an attempt to show his contempt for Dave's visit. But Dave, with a straight face, leaned back in his kitchen chair. For a moment he just stared at Stone.

'You're caught in Xavier's trap so you'll be easy meat if you try to run away from it.'

'Give me the address of this gangster, I want my car back,' Stone said.

Dave gulped his coffee noisily as he scribbled on a slip of paper and placed it heavily on the kitchen table. He then gazed at the floor. There was nothing more he could say that would stop Stone becoming belligerent and too arrogant to believe that Xavier was no threat.

Their silence was broken within a few seconds by Jo as she walked casually into the kitchen. She had overheard some of the talk which had been loud across the table and she looked at Dave as if for some reason she disapproved of HS's guest. She did not like shouting at any time but this sounded as if HS was being pushed around and that was something she knew he would not stand for.

'Parking attendant at the front door,' she said. 'Blue Range Rover on the yellow line. If you move it now, he says, okay, otherwise a parking ticket. Eighty quid. HS, here's the post.'

Jo placed some letters and junk mail on the table. She hovered for a few seconds as if she wanted to be part of the argument that was taking place but Stone looked at her and nodded. She read his thoughts and she left as quickly as she had entered. Dave stood and fumbled in his pocket for his car key. He finished the rest of his coffee and then walked to the kitchen door and into the hall without looking at Stone.

Stone heard the front door slam within a few seconds. For a moment there was silence, which increased Stone's annoyance at the demands that were suddenly building against him. Xavier was a madman, from the smell on his clothes probably high on cannabis and pot, trying to hold him to ransom with release only if he took on money laundering, that's where this now was. Stone ran his hand through his hair in nervous irritation. His frustration was increasing as he shouted for Jo.

'Are you in trouble?' Jo asked innocently as she walked into the kitchen. She now looked at HS with a sternness that only she could give to the person who now lived all alone in this magnificent Regency house.

'You wouldn't believe me if I said it was just a visitor getting a parking fine,' Stone replied and laughed.

'Is that all?'

'Jo, how many keys do we have to this house?'

'There's two back doors, one front door in case you can't remember the keypad code. I have keys to both back doors and you have the rest. But there's a copy key to the front door in the drawer of the table you're sitting at, just in case you lose the others. Why do you want to know?' Jo asked.

'Just checking.'

Again Stone tried to laugh but although it was still only just after midday he felt suddenly tired, on edge. Dave's visit could not be ignored. And Jo turned away. Her arched eyebrows said she smelt growing trouble around this place and for her own safety she would be wary of any other visitors coming to see HS.

Stone opened the letters that Jo had placed on the kitchen table. There was an official brown envelope from the Revenue and Customs, he slit it open but he knew what he was going to find. It was a letter following a meeting in London just a few days ago. Stone scanned the demand for £45,000 back tax and penalties; he could not run from this any more. He had continued to ignore it for the past three months but it threatened bankruptcy proceedings if payment was not made within three weeks from the date of the letter. Stone had not yet been caught in bankruptcy but he had seen it up close once before.

His credit cards would be stopped, his bank accounts frozen, all his assets worldwide taken beyond his control or he would go to prison. The thought of disclosing his Panama accounts made him feel very prickly and he let out a long breath as he threw the tax letter across the kitchen table until it fell off the far edge. For Harry Stone, finding cash was getting urgent.

He had not yet settled the insurance claim for the burnt-out pile of Arrow Hall but agreeing with officialdom was something that Stone was not good at. The insurers knew the building had been torched. The fire department had made their own report and of course Stone knew exactly who had started the fire. It was a crazed gang of druggies high on skunk who he would not pay protection money to and that extortion was not something he wanted investigated.

Stone shuffled the pile of bills. Impetuously he tugged out a formal letter and account from the agents dealing with the lease for Marine House. He crumpled the papers into a small ball and, as he had done with the Raven garage account, threw it with some force into the black bin bag that Jo had placed inside a deep drawer to take kitchen waste. Momentarily he forgot the taxman demanding £45,000 to be paid promptly or face the consequences.

Stone was lounging on a large sofa in his sitting room when his mobile buzzed on a low table.

'Is that Harry Stone?' a voice asked.

'Yes.' He had a faint memory that he had heard that grating noise before.

'Good to hear you're answering on another mobile, 'cos I got the number from the one you lent me. Just like you lent me your flashy red car. Remember it all, Harry?'

'What do you want?' Stone snapped.

'Dave been to see you?'

'None of your business.'

'Did he put a deal to you?'

'You think I'm following you down that road with dirty illegal cash that you've lifted from I don't know where, then you're on another planet. So forget it and get your idlers out of my site.'

'Okay, Harry. We won't talk over the line, don't know who's listening in do we? So just a "yes" or "no". But remember I've got your car and a number that leads me to Roger, one of your mates.'

'Leave it, you thug!' Stone shouted back.

'Okay, matey, why don't I give you a choice. A way out that'll get the site at Sudbury finished off so you can sell those nice glitzy apartments. But, first, you gotta clean some notes for me, wash 'em clean to make 'em look legal, and then I leave you alone. And, Harry, one day, maybe we'll even have a drink together and I'll hand your motor back. It's worth a few quid from what I hear. So what do you say to that, eh?'

'That's no deal. It's blackmail that you lot of gangsters try on every day. And I don't deal in that sort of money-launder peddling, never have done, never will,' Stone snapped.

'Okay, matey, we'll wait for another day. And blackmail, eh, Harry? That's not a nice word where I come from.'

'Don't come near me again with your cracked intimidation stuff because I've got other ways of dealing with that,' Stone said angrily.

'I'm not listening to that, Harry. So what about three o'clock next Friday? Look at yer map and find Birling Gap. A car park near Beachy Head. You know, right on top of the cliffs. But come alone, Harry, and I'll give you the cash to clean up for me and maybe we can then talk about a deal. Or if you want, don't come to talk and we get heavy because you owe us a lot of money and this deal ain't going away, matey. Ah, yes, I was forgetting. Before I go, sorry for one of my boys giving you a tap on the shoulder the other day and I've told him we're maybe going to do a deal and he's promised not to be so nasty next time.'

There was the same dry taunting laugh that Stone had heard in the country lane. It made him feel very tense. He flicked his phone off and his hand went to touch the throbbing ache in his shoulder.

Later that day Stone shut the front door of Marine House with a slam and walked down the steps to a waiting cab that would take him to Chelsea Football Club. He'd had an invitation from his bank, very unlikely he thought, but he would go with access to an executive box, drinks, then seats to watch a European Cup draw. Then, with minor bets on the side for each goal scored and who got it, the evening would satisfy Stone as a good way to get beyond menacing threats. The game would be fast, the crowd noisy, and Harry Stone was easily at home with other guests in this sometimes raucous environment. In the bar after the game they would talk noisily, they would often swap business cards and Stone had a talent of summing up anyone who, sometime later, might be a familiar face who could help him.

As Stone got into the cab the light sea breeze refreshed his face like a soothing, cool flannel. Whatever he did, Harry Stone, now at his most belligerent, thought he could make sure the solace of the fresh sea air would last.

6

The football match had been fast and with a winning goal two minutes into stoppage time. Stone had lost himself in the excitement and noise of the moment. There was then more reason for him to stay at the bar to talk, to have another double Scotch, although not of the fineness of the malt he drank at Marine House. Inevitably it left him the next morning with a headache. He felt confrontational, he wanted to get on with the day and he shouted at the top of his voice for Vlad. He appeared within a minute still buttoning his shirt.

'I've got a job for you,' Stone said.

'Of course, Mr Stone.'

'Get up to London fast. East End. Get to this address, go and check it out and look for the Ferrari. Look in all the side streets around the place until you find it. Take the spare keys and while you're there if you meet the slob who has taken the Ferrari, big fat bald head, give him a bloody nose. Got it?'

Stone gave Vlad a slip of paper with a scrawl where Dave had written Xavier's address and Vlad stared at it for a moment vacantly.

'Mr Stone, sir, I'll go straight away,' Vlad replied.

It was still only just light and Stone's headache lingered. For a while he sat in his study half dressed and fiddled with a card he had been given at the game last evening. He remembered the face and the man who was tall, casually dressed just in jeans and a black sweater even though the night was cold. He had a strong Yorkshire accent and he shouted and swore as if he was the only person in hearing distance. Stone held the card up and read it again. *Martyn Blake. Director and owner of Blake Markets.*

It was not difficult to remember Martyn. He was a big man who during the game drank several pints of Yorkshire bitter and was someone Harry Stone had found easy to talk to. He said it as it was, with a few expletives shouted loudly. But Martyn Blake owned a supermarket business and that had alerted Stone to quickly find out more about this man and what he did. He was not going to give in to Xavier's intimidating demands but this was maybe a way out if he was pushed into a corner by that drug peddler.

Stone knew Martyn's supermarkets were in the West Country. Coming to London to watch a top football game, he told Stone, was always an excuse he snatched to get away from being bound to a desk. And among the other enjoyments Martyn found in London was a small members' club south of the Thames where they served jellied eels and cockles and members played snooker for fun. And Martyn said he was going to be there in a couple of days' time and he easily gave an open invitation to Stone to join him.

His arm and shoulder were now aching with a throb that was hurting his neck but Stone toyed with Martyn's card in his fingers. He stood on a balcony off the large sitting room of Marine House and stared past the road to the width of the sea. He tried to raise his arm but it gave him a searing pain right down to his hand. He had left the impact from the iron bar for a couple of days hoping the raw hurt in his shoulder would calm down. Even with a few hours' sleep and a glass of whisky the pain was still intense and it was time for him to call on the doctor.

Stone called Jo and, with Vlad away searching for the Ferrari, an hour later she drove the Porsche to the surgery. It was just a couple of miles into town but the Porsche felt heavy and Jo felt uncomfortable driving it. She held the steering wheel tightly and she could sense from the corner of her eye HS's frustration. This morning she took the car as close to the surgery as she could get and left Stone with just a short walk. Jo then drove to a multi-storey car park two streets away to wait for him. But driving this big car into a very tight space, which was dark and dingy with low ceilings, left Jo feeling enclosed.

It was ten o'clock in the morning prompt that Stone arrived at the surgery and that was exactly the same time that Jo was parking the car with difficulty into a very tight bay on the fifth floor of the car park. A large green van had followed her into the concrete building and was now reversing right next to her leaving very little space for her even to open the car door to get out and stretch herself. Jo was suddenly very tense.

In the doctor's surgery Stone was tense too as he removed his shirt. He was even now feeling reluctant to let the doctor examine his shoulder because he did not want to talk about what had caused it. But the GP knew Harry Stone well and he knew too this patient never called unless he had a real problem.

'That's some nasty smash to your shoulder, Harry,' Sean said as he studied the large black bruise around his patient's collarbone. 'What hit you?'

'I didn't see it, a lump of iron I guess, but it came down hard,' Stone replied.

'Was it an accident?'

'I dunno.'

The doctor pressed on a bone and moved Stone's arm, which made him wince but he tried to hide his reaction, as if that would help the examination.

'That hurts doesn't it?' the doctor said as Stone replaced his shirt.

'Yes, it's a shooting pain when I move my arm, doc. Is there much damage?'

'You'll need an X-ray to find that out, so I'll make an appointment for you this evening. It's possible you've got a fracture in your collarbone and if that's so you'll need to have your arm strapped up,' the doctor said.

'I walked into this one. I should have known it was coming but I looked away.'

'Do you want to tell me what really happened, Harry?' the doctor coaxed.

'Nothing much, just a petty business deal that's gone astray. A difference of opinion. But I'm sure you don't want me to go into the sordid bits, doc,' Stone said.

'Shouldn't you be talking to the police if someone has brought down something heavy on your shoulder and a bit close to your neck, Harry?'

Stone looked away, it was not the question he had wanted. 'Can't do that, and anyway it was just a little scuffle, a little disagreement between friends.' Stone laughed but the doctor kept a straight face.

'Well it's up to you but you shouldn't let it happen again. A man of your age and with a hit a bit nearer your neck, you could be in real trouble.'

'Forget it, Sean, it's just my collarbone you need to know about,' Stone said.

'I can only warn you. I'll give you some strong painkillers, but don't mix them with the whisky.'

'I wouldn't dare,' Stone replied and managed a short laugh.

'I'll call you with the X-ray result. But some advice in the meantime, Harry – slow it and put the whisky bottle away for a week or two. And next time you're hit so hard you go to the police because you'll need proper protection. You've got serious damage to your shoulder and it's clearly not been hit by one of your friends in a playful gesture,' the doctor said. It was an order, but knowing his patient was unlikely to take any notice of it the doctor went to make up his notes on Stone's visit.

Stone left the surgery, his shoulder still nagging with a dull ache. He walked the short distance to a pharmacy to get the prescription for painkillers. On the pavement outside he called Jo to collect him. But by now, alone in a dark car park, Jo was very frightened. Almost before she had released her seat belt the man from the green van walked round the Porsche and opened the passenger door.

'Do you mind if I join you?' he asked with mock politeness as he looked at Jo and eased himself onto the seat.

Jo recoiled. She tried to open her door but the green van was too close and she gripped the steering wheel tightly and sank lower into her seat.

'Who are you? What do you want?'

'Was that Harry Stone driving with you?' the intruder asked.

Jo fumbled for her phone and as she started to call HS, it rang. It was HS calling to be picked up. She said "Hello" but Jo's voice was croaky and the intruder just laughed as he looked at her frightened face.

'Jo, come and collect me quickly, same place where you dropped me, okay?'

'I've got a man sitting in the passenger seat of the car and I'm stuck on the fifth floor of the car park and if I can get rid of him…'

'Jo, you all right?'

'I don't know what's happening here but he's just asked if it was you in the car when we came into town,' Jo replied.

The intruder, a thick-built black man, leant across and snatched the phone from Jo's ear. The sudden movement surprised her and she let out a scream but there was nobody to hear it except Stone at the other end of the phone.

'I'm not going to hurt this nice lady, Harry, but I bring you a message from Xavier,' the intruder said into the phone. 'You can't get away now, you gotta do what the boss man Xavier says. We know where you are, Harry, we watch your large place by the sea, so think hard before you say no to meeting Mr Xavier at Birling Gap. That's it, mate, I'll leave your nice lady alone now but I hope you've got it. No second chances, okay?'

He passed the phone quickly back to Jo and within a few seconds he was gone and was reversing the green van ready to drive at speed down the ramp and out from the car park. It left Jo shivering and she heard HS's voice in her ear.

'Jo, what's going on?'

'He's gone whoever he was but I'm frightened.'

'Come and get me and we'll drive straight back to Marine House.'

Jo threw the phone onto the seat and drove even more timidly to the corner where she had left Harry Stone just half an hour ago. She was shaken at what had just happened so quickly and this was not how her life had ever been while caring for Marine House. Ten minutes later Stone got into the car, looked at Jo's white face, but he said nothing, and they drove in complete silence back to Marine House. Jo ran from the car into the house through the back door leaving Stone to follow. As he went into the kitchen Jo was sitting at the table so frigid in the chair that she looked like a statue of white marble. Stone proceeded to swallow two painkillers from the pharmacy and then sat at the opposite end of the table to Jo.

'I'm sorry, Jo, for what happened. They're some petty crooks and they were just trying to get to me,' he said.

'I'm not sure I can stay here anymore. I can't belong to Marine House if it's going to be attacked by some very nasty people. I don't need it, HS, and I'm sure you don't need it either.'

'Please listen, Jo, I'm going to clear them off tomorrow. And when he's back Vlad'll get some more security for this house, that's what's going to happen.'

Stone stood. He wanted Jo to stay, he was guarded, he was not sure about his feeling but he knew he needed the mood of quietness and control that Jo brought to this large house. As he watched Jo leave, Stone did not know how to tell her the way to deal with some very malicious people. They were out there, they were close by and Jo would go if this happened again. And that would leave a striking silence which Stone definitely did not want.

***

Claire left the restaurant in Grosvenor Square, where she had lunched for two and a half hours with Jennie. They had only talked about their visit to Arrow Hall for a few minutes but Claire still had a nagging feeling that, whatever she did, Harry Stone would somehow still haunt her. The Panama passcodes were valuable to Stone, Claire was sure he would soon be calling, and it made her uneasy. The visit to Arrow Hall opened up again memories of all the business papers she had kept tidy for Stone and the cash he had secreted around the house. Seeing the ruins of the old building now left abandoned made her angry. Claire would keep the Panama codes and she had a fleeting thought to hide them in some secret corner, right away, until Stone agreed to rebuild the property.

As they parted the frown lines on Claire's forehead told Jennie of the uncertainty that was surrounding Claire at that time. Usually unflappable and phlegmatic, Claire told Jennie over lunch that for some reason she was not sure of, she had a nasty, claustrophobic feeling that she was being followed. She had had a stalker a couple of years ago and even though she had not seen anyone behind her this time she knew that this is what Stone would do. He would track her just to let her know he was around. And he would be looking to get access to his money.

Jennie saw Claire into a cab to take her the short distance to Rick's office in Mayfair. It was a place Claire had only been to a handful of times and that was when she first met Rick two years ago. Today, leaving the cab and walking through the glass front doors to Rick's office building made her stop. It opened up the raw memory of why Stone had sent her there two years ago. It was made worse for Claire because this was a memory which Rick knew nothing about.

Today Rick had asked Claire to meet Martyn Blake, owner of Blake Markets, a supermarket business he was putting money into. As Claire walked past Rick's PA and into his office there was a broad grin on Rick's face. He gave her a kiss on her lips and held her hand, which was cold. He looked at her hand and fleetingly at her face and saw her unusual nervousness.

'Where have you been to get your hand so cold?' Rick asked as he squeezed it tightly.

'Just lunch with Jennie. But it was cold in the cab from the restaurant.'

'This should be an interesting meeting and I'd really like you to stay,' Rick said.

'I'm finding London colder than Barcelona but it's never cold in the West Country.'

'That's good, Claire. Take a look at Blake Markets for me please. Something odd's happening down there. They should never be running out of cash.'

'I was going to call in a couple of days. Will that be early enough?' Claire asked.

'We'll find out in a few minutes. Martyn Blake's the man. He owned all of Blake Markets until I bought a share from him six months ago.'

'And what about the chateau, the vineyard and making wine, how's that all going?' Claire asked.

'It's good, you'll love it, I'll tell you all about what I've seen in Bordeaux when it's signed up and I'll take you down there. But, Claire, first there's something else, something special, something new and quite different you might like to do after you've had a couple of days sorting Blake Markets for me.'

'Wait a moment, Rick, don't go too fast.'

He pulled a chair close to Claire and took in a deep breath.

'Take your time on the supermarkets. I think you'll have to delve deep to find out what's really going on and I know you won't be put off if they're cold to you calling.'

'I've dealt with worse and I could always walk away.' Claire laughed and looked at the widening grin on Rick's face.

'What do you think of this? I've decided we should have a house, a place out of town where we can relax and entertain some of the few people I like in this business. What do you think of that idea?'

'A house out of town, you take me by surprise again. But of course I love the idea.'

'I thought you would. And I thought there's nobody better to look at this than you. Claire, you know what I like, you know how my business works and I think you know what type of house you would like to live in too. So if I ask you to start looking, is your answer yes?'

'That's a terrific idea. Yes, I've always lived in a house with space and I do find living in London sometimes confining. Tell me what you're looking for.'

'Okay, say a sixty-mile radius of London, plenty of land and with at least four bedrooms,' Rick said.

'How much do you want to spend?'

'Claire, you know what I like so I'll leave that up to you. You find the right house and I'll pay up, how about that?' Rick said.

'You're serious about this?'

'Yes. Of course I am. You lived in a country house before you came to be with me, you liked that place didn't you, so why don't you go back there and see what the estate agents have got on their books?'

Claire was stopped short by that comment from Rick. Of course she would like to go back to the countryside she lived in two years ago to look for a house. But that was a part of her life that she had kept hidden from Rick and that was how it must stay.

'You look surprised at all this but don't be because I'm decided that is what we need. Try some research with agents and online so that we can get serious about house-hunting,' Rick said.

'The whole idea is a big project and I'd love to go and look.

What say I start with my visit to the West Country? There'll be some lovely properties I'll pass on the way down to Blake Markets.'

'Yes, why not start there.'

Rick was interrupted by his PA who led a middle-aged and well-built man into his office. It was Martyn Blake and Rick moved quickly and shook hands with him. It was a friendly welcome. He introduced Martyn to Claire, not as his partner but as someone he worked with and who he had asked to spend some time looking through the books of Blake Markets.

'You're running short of cash in the business,' Rick said after they had all sat around a low table in the corner of Rick's large office.

'It happens.' Martyn's terse reply surprised Claire and she looked at him, expecting him to say more.

'Can you tell us what's going on to make the business run dry?' Rick asked.

'I've no idea, I'm not one of the clever people who look into the bowels of a business to see what's happening each day, I just make sure the shelves are stacked full of stuff people want to buy,' Martyn said. He did not look at Rick or Claire and appeared disinterested in the whole meeting.

'Martyn, come on, you're the man who started Blake Markets, you're the man who has brought it along to where it is now, and now you sound as if you don't know about your own business. So tell me what's happening,' Rick insisted.

'You see all the figures they send you each month, so take it from there.'

'Martyn, please. Have you come all this way here just to tell me that?' Rick asked.

'I had some other business I came to London for, not to sit in your fancy office to be interrogated. Yes, I know all about Blake Markets, but I thought you were going to put some more cash up front so we could expand the place with some more supermarket stores down country alongside the others,' Martyn said.

Claire looked at Rick, who she could see had sat upright as if he was about to stand and perhaps walk away. She was only an onlooker. And she had seen confrontations like this with Harry Stone at Arrow Hall, many of which had ended with Stone telling someone to leave his house quickly.

'I'd like to put some money up, but not until I know why Blake Markets is leaking cash. Supermarkets like yours should be running in it, not looking for the next penny so you can pay the staff for what they've done in the past week.'

'Leave it, Mr Austen,' Martyn said.

'I don't understand this. I don't understand why you're being so tetchy with a simple question about a business you should know inside out. I want Claire to come down and have a look over your shoulder and then perhaps we can talk about putting some more cash in to expand what's already there.'

'Send her down, I don't care. But just give me a call when you're ready to talk about the real stuff like some more cash to see the place go forward.'

Without looking at either Rick or Claire, Martyn stood and walked from the room. He was gone within a few seconds and there was silence until Rick slumped back into his chair and looked at the ceiling.

'What do you make of that?' he asked Claire.

'Oh dear, something's biting him but only he knows, not me.'

'Do you still feel like going down there to have a delve into the place? There's obviously something going on?' Rick asked.

'Yes, of course. It sounds like a hornets' nest but that just makes it all the more interesting. Leave it to me and I'll get to the bottom of things.' Claire sounded confident, eager to go and pry, and Rick put his hand out to meet hers and for a moment they both laughed.

'I'm going back to Bordeaux tomorrow to settle the vineyard and chateau. It's really looking good and I can't wait to get it all tied up. I'll be away for another few days, so as your reward, this evening I've got tickets to see the latest film in Leicester Square. Red carpet for some A-listers coming to see the premiere of their blockbuster and I'm sure they'll let us on that carpet just for a few steps. Then dinner at The Ivy. Okay with you?' Rick asked.

'For this evening that would be just fine. I've never walked on a red carpet before or even been on a magic carpet, which I might need in the next day or two. So tonight I've not got much else on that I'd prefer to do,' Claire said and laughed again.

'Make yourself at home at the flat and I'll be with you in an hour. Then we can forget all this nonsense about what's going on at Blake Markets, whatever it is.'

Claire went to Rick and kissed him gently on his cheek. He took her hand and squeezed it tightly. At that time Claire had no way of knowing of the coincidence that Harry Stone would also soon be meeting with Martyn Blake to talk about his supermarket business.

7

Stone took a train to London and as usual he gave no notice when he called on Roger. He expected Roger to be there and he expected immediate attention, whatever time of the day or whatever he was after. But this time Roger had expected Stone to visit. He had received an odd call from a man calling himself Xavier telling him all about what Harry Stone was up to. Roger tried to remain calm, detached from the brashness that Stone would deal him, but it was never easy.

Roger's assistant, Cam, opened his door and interrupted. Roger was staring through the window across London's developing rooftop skyline towards St Paul's.

'Roger, I've got your friend Harry Stone waiting in reception. Said he'd like to see you for a few minutes...'

'I need to talk, Roger,' Stone said, not letting Cam finish as he squeezed into the wide and minimalist office.

Cam stood firm and glared at Stone as he walked purposefully to Roger's desk with a mocking grin spreading over his face. From previous visits Cam knew all about Harry Stone; she had always disliked his attitude, as normal people did not act with rudeness and arrogance. As Cam closed Roger's door firmly she wondered what this man Harry Stone was demanding this time.

'Harry, why're you crashing in here as if you owned the place?

You've upset Cam and you should apologise to her before you leave,' Roger said quickly, sensing Cam's unease.

Stone ignored the request as if Roger had not spoken and slumped easily onto a sofa against a wall. It was dominated by a large abstract line drawing of the Thames around London Bridge. He had in the past sometimes gazed at it, but now he had no time for anything but the demands he had come to make.

'I want a hundred and fifty grand, Roger, and I want it like quick.'

'What's going on, Harry? What are you up to this time?'

'Get a hundred and fifty into my London account. Can you do it today?' Stone asked.

'Where do I find that sort of money just like that? I can't pluck the stuff out of the air as if it's floating there waiting for you to call.'

'Look, I need a short-term loan, just for a few weeks,' Stone said.

'What's the security?' Roger asked.

'Come on, it's my word, that's the security and you know that. We don't have time to play around with this, so get on with it straight away can you?'

'I can't find investors who will suddenly cough up that amount just, like, today. Anyone with spare cash will want to know where it's going before they let it go. So what goes, Harry?'

'Are you telling me you can't do it?' Stone rasped, although he already knew the answer.

'Give me details and I'll check it out but it's very unlikely I'll find anything.'

'It's straightforward. It's a loan to tide over my Sudbury building for a few weeks. You know what building work is like. You spend half a million before anything comes back, and that's where it is now.'

'Why not go and see your friendly bank manger?'

'Shut it, Roger. I don't like 'em, they're too stuffy,' Stone said.

Roger Garon shuffled a file wound in a pink ribbon on his desk and looked out of the window as if he wanted to get on with something else. He drew in his breath just to control his tolerance which was shortening with this man.

'Harry, write it out, make it at least *look* real and as ever I'll put it around the block for you, but it'll take time,' Roger said.

'I haven't got the patience to go through all that, so forget it. I'll make some other arrangements. But make a note that I asked you because this might have consequences, okay?' Stone replied.

'You don't change, Harry, do you? I've told you many times not to come through my door without some detail in writing about what you're looking for. And what you're going to spend it on. That's how it works,' Roger said.

'My business is fast-moving, events run quickly, you should know that, but that's too fast for you, eh Roger?'

'You're running so fast you'll fall one day. Why don't you slow it up, take a breath before you jump? But you never take my advice do you, Harry?' Roger asked without looking at Stone.

Stone stood, his impatience showing in the deep frown over his eyes. 'Cash, that's the game. Building sites run on cash. Fivers, tenners, Roger, hard cash,' Stone said in his best low-volume voice. He then took a wallet from his inside pocket and waved a fistful of twenty-pound notes towards Roger.

But Roger just turned his head away and, to keep Stone on the back foot, used his practised ploy and said nothing for many seconds. He then looked at the file on his desk as if he was ignoring him. But Roger spoke at last, very slowly, as if he was in a courtroom and Stone was a guilty party pleading to be let off.

'Your demand for cash is not connected to a madman called Xavier, is it?'

'How do you know about him?' Stone said sharply.

'He called me on your phone, that's how.'

'What did he say?'

'Tells me you owe a large bundle of cash to him and his mates on your building site and he's got your Ferrari as collateral. Is that it?'

'I've got my man searching for the Ferrari, you watch, it'll be back in a couple of days, then I'll get it hidden away until I sell it,' Stone shouted but he suddenly felt cornered.

'I don't like the smell of that man, he sounds dangerous, thuggish, right on the edge for you to be dealing with him. And I've had my investigators, who specialise at looking at gangsters, to give me a report.'

'You can't tell me anything I don't know already!' Stone shouted again, trying to hide his surprise.

'Okay, listen to this from the Fender investigators' report. That man, your mate Xavier, was in prison just three months ago, and that's almost his second home from what the report says. He was convicted of GBH after he stuck a knife into the flesh of someone he didn't like. And then he's spent time inside for drug peddling, heroin, cannabis, cocaine, you name it, he's done it. He's into extortion and protection rackets too, just like that mob who set fire to Arrow Hall because you wouldn't pay them. You'll remember that, Harry,' Roger said.

'Leave it,' was all Stone could reply with.

'Yeh, we'll leave it, but he's probably dealing with all sorts of poisonous narcotics and the vicious debt collecting that goes with it. Watch it, Harry, this man Xavier is at the nasty end of it all, so do you want me to read more?' Roger asked as he threw the Fender report across to Stone.

It fell limply on the floor and there was silence from Stone for a moment. This was not what he wanted to hear.

'I can deal with Xavier. He's just an overgrown criminal making crass demands on the site at Sudbury but he won't get away with any of 'em and he knows it.'

'What about your phone?' Roger persisted.

'I don't care about that, he'll soon throw it away.'

'Okay, but what else goes with this man that I should know if we're talking money?'

'I've got to finish Sudbury, I've got to get my cash out of that place so I've got to deal with Xavier and all his heavies around him. No other way. If I can't find the cash quickly Sudbury'll rot away, it'll be finished, gone. But don't try to frighten me off with drug dealing, GBH and other fantasy things.'

'Tell me what's really playing with this man Xavier?'

Roger was beginning to gnaw away at Stone, and he sat still for a moment. He turned to stare at the panorama towards St Paul's and he suddenly felt hot even in this air-conditioned space.

'He's pushing me to handle some cash for him.'

'You don't mean money laundering, I hope, Harry.'

'He's getting heavy. His thugs know where I live, they're getting a bit too close. That's why I'm here, Roger. For a hundred and fifty grand I can get him off the Sudbury site.'

'Get your money out of Arrow Hall,' Roger said. 'You watched it burn down. You've let it rot for two years and what a growing mess that is.'

'I want you to sell the site just as it is, a pile of ashes,' Stone said quickly.

'Yeh, if you really mean that after all this time I'll put it on the market for you but you've still got to settle the insurance.'

'There's Claire. I need her help to get that settled. She was there when the first match was struck to set the place ablaze. She knows where all the cash was that I kept in the house and she kept the codes to access the large lump of dollars I've still got in my Panama companies. All that lot went up in the blaze and all she did was double-cross me,' Stone said quickly.

'Hold it, Harry. If you were running a normal business like the rest of us you wouldn't have cash stashed away just like that.'

'Shut up, Roger, you know how I deal and I don't want to talk about it now,' Stone said.

'Okay, but you get into money laundering and the police'll be right on your tail. They'll shut you up for a long time.'

'You quickly forget that the police stood and looked at the ashes of Arrow Hall for six months and then walked away. I've heard nothing since, so I know how they work,' Stone replied. He thought for a moment and again stared towards the view of St Paul's in the distance.

'What's Claire doing now?' Stone shouted.

'I can't tell you that, leave her alone. She'll be frightened if she knew you were here chasing her.'

'She's got to help me, I'll get to her, and then we'll see what happens,' Stone said.

'Claire's not going to help you, so get on and sort your business out yourself.'

'That woman tried a fast one on me when she went to work with that other guy and I don't ever forgive that,' Stone said.

'But Claire *loved* Arrow Hall. With her flat in the west wing it was her home too, and she was excited about having the place renovated. You remember you'd promised her that?'

'Claire just wanted to see me cough up cash so she could stick two fingers in my face. And now she's getting too crafty living in her posh Knightsbridge flat. But I'll get even. You watch.'

'Harry, *lay off.* Whatever Claire did, you pushed her into it,' Roger said, for the first time raising his voice with impatience.

There was silence again, just for a few seconds, and Roger looked at Harry Stone, daring him to speak.

'Before you go, Harry, you've got to run a million miles from Xavier and his thugs. They'll drag you right down leaving you with the police crawling all over your affairs. And, as for the taxman, he won't let you go next time,' Roger said.

'Get on, like, quick with the sale of Arrow Hall's skeleton. Don't give it away but do it fast, I want the cash,' Stone said and stood.

Stone had heard enough from Roger and as he walked to the door he passed Cam who was sitting at her desk and he gave a thin smile which she did not return. The door to Roger's suite of offices closed gently with a slight hiss and it was silent in the carpeted hallway as Stone waited for the lift. Momentarily he thought of the wide-eyed girl dangling his car keys before he paid the garage for repairs. And then a demand from the tax office for £45,000 was still lying on his kitchen table.

He needed cash, he needed it quickly and his bad humour was growing. Claire walking off with his Panama bank codes was a thought that made Stone very angry. And Roger had thrown the Fender report at him as if he was a school kid who had to be brought up short. Stone already knew Xavier and his heavies were vicious, they would stab and slash if he ever tried to hide from their demands.

The lift was a short, silent descent to the ground floor and as he got out he'd made up his mind. His need for cash was growing, he would deal with Xavier's bundles of notes from the lawless underworld. And he thought he already knew someone he could bribe with a big enough payoff to wash it through their business, to make it look like legitimate money. It was his only way out.

On the street a red double-decker bus towered, passing quickly, and even though Stone was on the pavement he felt the draught of its air full in his face as if he was being punched to expel the last gasp from his lungs. Stone's temper was being sharply tested. He held his arm out for a cab. He directed it to the other side of the Thames to a narrow back street and a converted warehouse of six storeys with a façade of solid London yellow brick. Upstairs the building was converted into flats, but Stone walked down a steep wide flight of steps to the basement. There was no lift here in this snooker club that was hidden away from the noise of the street above. This was not in a stylish part of London's City area, but an old-fashioned meeting place that catered for those who wanted to play on the green baize tables or just to hide away for an hour or two with a drink and a very basic London style of eating. Cod and chips and jellied eels were specialities.

Stone had a reason to be here, he signed in at reception and paid a year's membership fee, and he sat at a corner table that looked onto a sunless walled courtyard. He ordered a plate of cockles and a double whisky. This place was unstuffy, it suited Stone's humour, and being in a basement suddenly made him feel at home after Roger's high-rise office. He sat and watched for half an hour as this was the place that Martyn Blake would come to, just as he said he would when he was in London.

Harry Stone sat alone in this empty room, it was early for lunchers and there was near silence in the starkness of the original brick walls and upright wooden, heavily padded chairs. He drank his whisky, gorged the plate of shellfish and for a few minutes relaxed. But he was here for a purpose, he had already felt the steel bar of Xavier closely around his neck, and even the smell of that man's breath was enough. And what had Roger told him about laundering cash?

Mobile phones were strictly banned from this room, and Stone went to a small booth in a dark corridor behind the empty lounge where there was a fifties-style phone. It was hanging on a cord, he picked it up, dialled a number and waited almost a minute.

'You on the site?' Stone shouted into the phone in his frustration at being kept waiting.

'Of course I am, boss.'

'What's happening there?'

'The boys aren't working and this place isn't going to move until they know you're in business with 'em,' Dave replied.

'Get on to Xavier and tell him I'll do a deal at Birling Gap tomorrow. I'll be there at three in the afternoon sharp and I'm not hanging around. Tell him no funny stuff, okay?' Stone said.

'Yeh, you're doing the right thing, Mr Stone. But be careful, boss, that man's got lots of minders round him.'

'I know how to deal with thugs like Xavier. But let him know just from me, he's got to pay off all those scruffy layabouts on the site and I don't want to see that lot behaving like overgrown school kids again, waving their tools as if they're weapons. Understand?' Stone felt satisfied, as he always did when he was giving orders.

'I'll tell him what you say, boss. But I don't know…'

Stone cut across Dave as he was feeling hot in the dark booth.

'One more thing. This deal to move a quarter million in notes through a legit business is beyond risky. Whoever I find won't do it for nothing. Ten per cent is what they'll take. It's a long stretch inside some foul pokey if they're caught, okay?' Stone said.

'I can't tell him that. That lot don't do deals. From here, boss, leave me out of it.'

'Ten per cent is what it needs. And if Xavier gets funny I'll blow his whole lot of bent and vicious gangsters into the sea!' Stone shouted.

'Please, boss, don't ever think of grassing because you won't be left standing upright if they find you.'

'Look, Dave, I didn't call you to be told what to do so get on with it. Go.'

Stone had reached his usual quick state of irritation and he wiped from his brow a bead of sweat before it dripped into his eyes, and smoothed his hair in a gesture that said he was nervous, as he placed the phone back on its cradle.

But Dave was anxious too. Stone was playing hard and that would never work, he had seen it before. The site at Sudbury was now becoming right in the view of some very vicious racketeers, extortion thugs, and Dave was not going to stand in the middle.

It was still quiet in the bar but it was beginning to fill with a sprinkling of City traders from across the Thames. Stone pushed his way to the bar and ordered another whisky. He sat at a small corner table and stared vacantly into the room. Half an hour later he heard a voice he knew. Standing at the bar as if he owned it was a big man, over six foot, his face round with a greying head of hair, and his voice from Yorkshire, easily remembered. Stone watched as Martyn ordered a beer and then Stone stood, walked across the room and tapped him on the shoulder. Stone's face offered a thin smile as Martyn turned round.

'I thought I might find you here,' Stone said.

'The executive box at Chelsea,' Martyn replied. 'That's the place.

Chelsea dumped Manchester United out of the Cup. I liked it, it was a great experience. Glad to meet you again, Harry.'

'Yeh, it's good to see you too. There's no better way to watch football than in a private box. A bank lays out the carpet to customers to see the game and then disappears as if they never knew you when you want a bit of cash from them,' Stone said and laughed as if he meant it.

'Yeh, that lot are crazy, but so what?'

The small talk lasted for ten minutes. Stone bought Martyn another beer, and as the room became more crowded and noisy Stone wanted to stay here, he wanted to find out more about Martyn because he owned a supermarket business that dealt in lots of cash.

'Fancy a frame or two of snooker?' Stone asked.

'Great idea.'

Stone led Martyn and they walked to the billiard room as if they were two contestants at the Crucible.

'Spent a long evening and some cash in the Piccadilly casino last night. Blackjack and roulette are my favourites. So let's see how we go with the green baize,' Martyn said with excitement.

'Do you ever beat the table at the casino?'

'Not always, but sometimes I can get a run and then it does feel good,' Martyn said.

'Not a place I go to, I don't like the idea of losing most of the time.'

'I'll take you and show you the tables and we'll have some fun. What do you think, Harry?'

'Maybe. But how's business running with you? Supermarkets isn't it?' Stone asked as they reached the wide expanse of green that was the snooker table.

'A bit slow at this time of year but I've sold a quarter share of the supermarket business to a partner. Just last month. And he's putting cash in and sorting it for me. So I watch from the edge most times now.'

'You were opening up a couple more outlets in Devon and Cornwall when we met. Is that still you?'

'We're now spread right over the West Country. It's all grown faster than I can deal with, so someone from outside gives me time off. And if I play them right the investors are going to give me some cash in the pocket when I like to go to the races for a day or two.' Martyn laughed.

Stone walked round the table to line the balls into the triangle and they played snooker for the next two hours. Martyn drank more beers and in the banter around the few frames of snooker he told Martyn that he had not too long ago taken on the taxman over money he had hidden away. Martyn liked that thought, as if it was something he should do, and he probed Stone for details. But Stone did not tell Martyn that only a few days ago he had been hit with a heavy metal bar in a country lane and his prized investment in a Ferrari had been snatched.

Stone's idea of playing snooker was never for fun and he only stuck at it to move his connection with Martyn forward. And then maybe he could drag Martyn Blake into a deal of washing a lump of doubtful cash through his business. But it would be dangerous and Martyn Blake was the type of man who would surely see that.

With his whisky Stone was becoming mellow but he now had growing indigestion with too much Glenfiddich too quickly and too much vinegar on his plate of cockles. After a couple of hours as the place was thinning out he was ready to go. Martyn had a contented smile on his round face as they left the old warehouse building both satisfied with their snooker. Martyn had won a few hundred from Stone at £100 a frame and Stone was beginning to find out who this Martyn Blake really was.

'Good to play, I'll win next time, so make sure you let me know when you're around again,' Stone said as he shook Martyn's strong hand.

'I come to London to get away from all the people wanting to talk to me, become anonymous for a few hours and it's always good to meet a mate to have some time out,' Martyn replied.

Stone liked Martyn's 'time out' and 'away' words, they fitted exactly how he thought about doing a deal with him and he waved as Martyn got into a cab. And half an hour later Stone took a train home from Victoria Station; his head nodded into a fitful sleep in the empty carriage and he was jolted awake as the train reached Brighton. And the thought of finding a bigger casino to take Martyn to than the one in Piccadilly where he had played blackjack, lingered with Stone.

Marine House facing the sea was quiet when Stone arrived home and he was alone as he stared from his large lounge across the road to the sea. There would be an enticing payoff if he took cash from Xavier, but it was dangerous. Money that had come from some very dark corners of the underworld would cause more pain if the deal did not float as those thugs demanded. There would be no room for anything to go wrong.

In the quietness Stone quickly remembered that Jo was not in the house. She had been very frightened as she felt the unwelcome closeness of a large man sitting next to her in the Porsche in a dark corner on the fifth floor of a concrete car park. Had Jo now left Marine House for ever, too frightened to stay? That was something Stone definitely did not want but as he poured another Glenfiddich he did not know how to show it.

8

Stone woke from a sleepless night as Birling Gap, a place crumbling into the sea close to the white chalk cliffs of Beachy Head, pervaded his thoughts. It was not until the light was filtering through the curtains of his bedroom that Stone finally cleared any lingering drowsiness with a shower. It was five in the morning, very quiet. He dressed and looked through a front bay window towards the sea. He saw a cloudless blue sky.

He had a quick coffee, which he drank wandering around the kitchen, and the image of Xavier was never far away. Meeting with that man with a shiny shaven head today he would be as helpless as facing a herd of running cattle unless he took action to hold him back. Half an hour later he took a walk slowly along the deserted Brighton beach. With a gentle breeze blowing in from the sea he stood and stared out to the limitless horizon which stretched across the incoming water lapping gently over the pebbles. With his shoulder still throbbing Stone was now aware that meeting Xavier in a scrubby sea cliff car park was risky; even more so if money was to be handled. This time Vlad would be there to protect him.

Until now Stone had always kept clear of the gangs of twisted people and the underhand deals for rough notes that was the drug dealing world. Today would be different, it would bring a payoff that would clear a growing debt in Sudbury. Xavier's cash would thread its way through to him from the grasping hands of druggies dealing narcotics and from the ones using their needles. Stone would try to ignore that twisted world but at that time he had no idea where this money laundering deal would lead him.

The burnt-out wreck of Brighton's West Pier loomed like a dragon climbing onto the beach as Stone sat on a wooden bench for a while and stared at the horizon. A few minutes later as he was walking back, he stopped for a moment to stare at Marine House, the imposing Regency mansion. It was a striking structure, but it was not Arrow Hall, it was different. Inside it was a place where he could hide but still stare from the large windows with their balconies. Arrow Hall was now finished, for Stone it was dead and he blotted the place out from his thoughts. He would never rebuild it but he would sell the ruined site, take the insurance cash, and run from it. Fast.

In the kitchen, Stone drank more coffee and crunched toast with lashings of marmalade, his usual breakfast start to the day. Just a short while later, as he was idling with the crossword on the back page of his newspaper, Jo let herself in by the back door with her own key. He had not expected Jo to return to Marine House and her face showed she was not her normal bright self. Unusually for Stone he momentarily felt awkward and did not know what to say.

'We need to talk, HS,' Jo said.

'I've told you, I'm sorry for what happened in the car park, but you weren't hurt were you?'

'Yes that's just it. If I'm going to stay at Marine House I need to know I'm going to be safe.'

'Don't worry about that hoodlum getting in the car. He was just trying to frighten me over a deal his boss wants to clear up. He would never hurt you. Jo, I really want you to stay here. This house needs your help and we'll tighten security around the place.'

'Did you sleep on the sofa again last night?'

'No, I kept to my bed this time,' Stone said and raised a thin smile.

'Let's get things settled then. First there's a few bills to be paid,'

Jo said as she shuffled the papers on the kitchen table into a neat pile.

'Okay, but I've dealt with the Raven Garage round the corner. I paid their account right up, gave them my credit card when they returned the Porsche,' Stone said, not looking at Jo.

Stone had told her nothing of the standoff with the girl from the accounts department and that is the way it would stay.

'That's good, the Raven Garage are convenient and easy to use. Is there anything special you want me to get in?'

'Get what you like and I'll eat it but sometime we'll go down the road and we'll enjoy dinner together at the Michelin starred fish restaurant. What about that?'

'Does that come as part of my job here?' Jo managed a small grin.

'Why not?

Jo hesitated but she needed to know. 'So where did you live before you came here?' she asked.

'Arrow Hall. Old Elizabethan timbers, dried-out moat around the edge. Great history. Big and rambling. But it was all destroyed by hoodlums demanding protection money. I never pay to extortion rackets.'

'Is that what the man who sat next to me in the car was after? Extortion money?' Jo asked.

'No. I promise you, Jo, he won't come again,' Stone said and leaned back in his chair, satisfied.

'Did you live in Arrow Hall alone, HS? In a large house, all on your own?'

There was a pause and Stone got up from his chair and started to pace the wide kitchen. He ran his hand through his hair, the only gesture of being unsettled he ever made.

'I had somebody who helped me on all my deals. Her name was Claire, she had a flat in Arrow Hall but as the whole place was burning to a cinder she betrayed me. Walked off with some of my papers and went behind my back on a deal. I lost a lot of cash.'

'Why would she want to do that?'

'I never asked her. She ran from the house when the timbers were collapsing. I've not seen or spoken to her since,' Stone said as he walked to the door.

Stone did not know how to talk to Jo and tell her about a crook trailing him who had been convicted of GBH. He gave Jo a stare, but Jo felt the stare and turned away.

'I like the flowers you've put in the hallway. They add a bit of life to the place, but what do I know about things like that?' Stone said as he watched Jo walk quickly from the room. Jo was back and that was all that mattered at this moment.

As he left the kitchen Stone had unusually tense lines around his mouth and a yellow pallid colour in his cheeks. He went to his study, a dark room at the rear of the house which rarely saw the sun. He sat at his desk and took two painkillers for the increasing ache that was nagging at his shoulder and neck. He would soon have to face off the shiny bald head of Xavier in a scrubby nondescript car park at Birling Gap, a place he had never been to. It was what would follow from there that was making him very wary. This time Roger was right.

'*Take the blackmailer to the police, tell the cops to sort the grubby deal he was being held to*,' was Roger's warning. But the cops already had Xavier and his mates under surveillance so grassing on the intimidation from that lot would drag him into the cops' radar too. Grassing was not his way but Xavier was getting closer and it made him shiver.

Stone opened an escritoire desk, pulled a chair to sit against the level flap and found his leather-bound address book going back several years. They were mostly notes he had not yet transferred to his laptop and smartphone and probably never would. Two cups of coffee helped him to rummage for half an hour through the address book, looking for a contact who could deal with large sums of cash. Martyn Blake was the only name so far who fitted into this wild scheme. Stone was not sure, he had to find someone in the next few days and he fidgeted. His list of contacts was getting very slim, he was losing touch with mates who could deal on the edges for him.

Flicking through the pages ten minutes later Stone came back to Martyn Blake but he had to be sure. He had his business card from the football match, he had met him at his snooker club south of the Thames and after losing several frames and a few hundred pounds, he had been drawn to Martyn. But would Martyn deal when he understood the dangers of being found out?

After sitting alone in almost total silence and drinking another coffee from the expensive Italian machine in the kitchen, Stone impulsively dialled Martyn's number on the card. The call was answered speedily. A hard sounding grunt came that was Martyn's usual response to a number calling him he did not recognise.

'Martyn, hi.'

'Sounds like Harry Stone,' Martyn replied in his easy-going, monotone voice. 'How're you doing?'

'It was good meeting you, but I'll win next time we play snooker.'

'I'm up in London next week. What about a few frames then?'

'Yeh, that'll be good. But listen, something else first. I'm planning a few things and I've got an offer of a free flight on a Cessna private jet. Would you like to join us?' Stone lied, which was not unusual for him.

'Where's this jet going then, Harry?'

'Away to a bit of sun. A couple of days in Monaco. I know a flash hotel there and what about the casino?'

'Hang on, Harry, what's this all for?'

'A bit of time out. It was good meeting you in London but this trip'll be something quite different, you'll see. We'll go to the casino in Monte Carlo, see the blackjack tables, even sit at them if you like.'

'Blackjack, eh?' Martyn mused. 'Like the sound of that. Always good for a few quid if only to watch the other punters lose.' He laughed with a casual eagerness that easily showed.

'What about your lady, Sandy? Wouldn't she like to come along?'

'I'll ask but it's really not her thing,' Martyn replied.

'Tell her "private jet". It's the only way to travel and when you've done it you won't go back to Ryanair or easyJet. Bring Sandy, she'll love it.'

'I don't like flying, but short haul… I might come along, Harry. But I don't know. We've got two new supermarket sites coming on later this year which are tying up loads of cash and it's all tight with the bank squeezing too. So I can't take too much time out.'

'Yeh, I know all about business pressure, but come on, this is to the sun to watch how the other half play. And it's only for a couple of days.'

'Sure, I'll think about it.' Martyn's voice was suddenly dulled, as if he wasn't interested in what happened in his business or even a couple of days away at the blackjack tables.

'Right, let's make it Monday next week? Shoreham airfield. Nice little place west of Brighton, I'll let you know a time. But look forward to meeting your good lady, Sandy, if you can drag her away for a few days in the sun.'

'Okay, maybe I'll come just for the ride but I'll call you and I'll let you know about Sandy,' Martyn said.

'That's good, you'll like it,' Stone replied.

Stone heard Martyn let out his breath in a sigh and he quickly cut the call. For a moment Stone stopped. Would spending cash on a private jet for fun days in the South of France, even at the casino in Monte Carlo, be enough to draw Martyn into washing a bundle of cash through his supermarkets? Would Martyn see it as too wild a deal and not his type of gamble? There would be a lot of grubby notes to handle passed down from the drug underworld and would Martyn sit at a desk to sort all the paperwork for clearing that lot of paper money into the bank?

Closing the escritoire Stone paced the room. Looking from the balcony window to the sea he dialled the number of Jetways, a private jet charter company. He had been to Paris with Roger just a couple of weeks before. Fifteen thousand pounds was the cost of that flight, but Roger had been chasing a deal and he was paying, just taking Stone along for a day out. This time it would be different. Stone would be paying. But it would be worth it if it got Martyn on side. And at that moment Stone had nowhere else to turn if that did not happen.

'How much for a jet to Nice, please? Like the Cessna Citation I flew in last time when Mr Garon took us to Paris.'

'Shoreham airfield?' she asked.

'Good airfield. Easy place. Yes please,' Stone said.

'We'll do the same price, we like to keep Mr Garon's friends happy. And I presume you'd want the same hospitality on board again?'

'Yeh, it's a longer distance to Nice, further than Paris, and we can't go thirsty on board,' Stone said.

'How many passengers, Mr Stone?'

'Maybe just two. Maybe three, maybe four. Depends who wants to come for the ride.'

'What date?'

'Monday next week.'

Stone heard Jo putting more bottles of Glenfiddich into the cabinet in the sitting room and after fixing an expensive flight to Nice it was a normal, reassuring sound. But he picked up the demand for forty-five thousand from the Revenue. That could tip him into bankruptcy and running a jet to Nice just to enjoy the casino in Monte Carlo with Martyn, a mate he had only known for few weeks, suddenly felt like madness. Stone touched his shoulder, felt the bruise and shivered at what he was being forced into.

Birling Gap was a place Stone had never been to and when he thumbed through a large road map, even though it was remote, he saw the comforting closeness to a main road. Stone brushed his hand through his hair. He was beginning to feel tension in his neck and he went to the kitchen to find food. He was not hungry but it passed some time. An hour later he put his golf cap on which hid a lot of his face and then called Vlad to take him to meet Xavier.

***

Martyn took the phone call from Harry Stone in the study of his house. It was a large room that faced onto a wide expanse of green well-tended grass that the gardener did his best in the fight with rabbits to keep even. They left pockmarks on what was once a tennis court with a fine level surface but it was all the same to Martyn, it was green and it blended with a hedge that surrounded the garden.

Martyn's study was a room that was wide, untidy and messy. Pictures of his rugby-playing days with a couple of caps and when he was a lot thinner, well below his sturdy middle-aged frame now, looked down from two walls. Martyn put the phone down from Stone and eased himself from the large Victorian desk that was positioned to look out onto the lawn. He felt at ease here and he could shut the door and be totally secluded when he wanted to hide away from everybody. And nowadays that was becoming often.

Sandy, his partner in life, rarely came into this space. She was a lady who preferred ordered tidiness and the rest of the large Victorian house on the edge of Exmoor was her space.

Martyn muttered to himself as he walked to the window that looked onto the garden. Yeh, a runaway to Nice and the casino in Monte Carlo where he could play blackjack drew him like a magnet. But Sandy would disapprove of that, and did he need her tut-tutting at him again for not giving his share of attention to her life and what she did?

Martyn took a key from a small ring that held his car fob and unlocked a bottom drawer of his desk. He removed two cardboard folders with papers that had long since needed sorting and dumped them heavily on his desk. At the bottom of the drawer there was a clear plastic folder which he removed and rested on his knee.

Betting accounts from two bookies in the local town, his code for his online account for poker, a game that held no interest beyond excitement from the uncertainty and unknown result each time he played from his laptop, a note of what he had lost in the casino in Piccadilly and on the fixed odds terminals from three betting shops as far away as London's West End. Martyn had carefully added up what had gone in the last year, it was a big figure and it concerned him. Especially as Sandy had no idea he had been to the casino in Piccadilly three times in the past month or even at all. And then there were the mundane slips from two days away at the races in Newbury and Lincoln. He had a fascination to keep the paper showing his bets and his growing losses just dragged him along to the expected gains of the next wager. It was in that instant, sitting uncomfortably at his desk, that he knew he could never have said no to the enticement of the trip to Monte Carlo.

Martyn noisily shuffled the files and dumped them all back into the bottom drawer which with one push he slammed shut. He stood upright at the desk for a moment and then walked away to the door. He stared back at the desk drawer which he had left unlocked as if he wanted someone someday to find it all and let everybody know he was a gambler and that sometimes he lost money. He placed the keys to his desk back in his pocket and felt he no longer cared what people thought. Why should he? He was wealthy, he had built a business, he told people what to do.

Rejecting any concern about his losses, gambling always gave Martyn a positive buzz. That sensation had been growing in him in the past year and it now helped him to cope with any losses at the games he played. But Sandy was perceptive, sensing Martyn's brooding aversion just to talk with her anymore, or even think about the business of Blake Markets.

Martyn ambled slowly into the garden and found Sandy weeding a small patch of vegetables, a part of the large garden that she claimed as her own and from which she produced a supply of fresh vegetables for the table. As Martyn went to the races and the betting shop, so Sandy found relaxation in the simple pleasure of digging the earth and growing things.

She had been surprised when Martyn had agreed to sell a slice of Blake Markets to an investor from London. Martyn had only once told her of a man called Rick who was buying some of his shares in the supermarket business and that alone told her he was losing interest in the future of the place. But Sandy had spoken privately to Gina, the lady who looked after much of what happened at Blake Markets. Gina, too, was very perceptive and she could see plainly that Martyn had signed off from caring about things that went on each day. He was rarely at his desk and his absence was making it more difficult for Gina to control the place. It was as if Martyn was guarding himself against his betting accounts, but he would never admit that was the reason he was now keeping his distance from everyone.

Sandy did not remove her trowel from the earth as Martyn approached, but slightly rose from her arched position as if to relieve her back.

'Do you remember me telling you about Harry Stone?' Martyn asked.

'Is he to do with business, or someone you've met at the races?'

'Business, Sandy. I told you I met him at a football match when the bank took us to Chelsea and then, when I was in London talking to Rick Austen, our new investor, I had a light lunch with him.'

'Yes, he sounded a bit of a wide boy from what you said. So what about him?'

'I've just had a call from him, he was asking if we'd like to join him for a few days out to the sun,' Martyn said.

'A bit more play, is that it?' Sandy asked, avoiding Martyn's eyes.

'Private jet to Nice. Down in the sunshine, some good food and see how the other half live.'

'Never been to Nice,' Sandy said as she stood up, holding a pair of secateurs in her hand as if she were about to cut something.

Her attention was on her vegetables, not on Martyn's attempt at conversation, and her tone was immediate disinterest at what he was saying.

'Want to come? Get the sun on your face?' Martyn coaxed, but only half-heartedly.

'You know I can't spend the time away at the moment. I'm arranging the village fete. As the rich people here we're supposed to take a lead and you need to keep your eye on Blake Markets,' Sandy replied, turning her back on him.

'I look after the business as much as I need to and that means sometimes I'm allowed to go away.'

'Do you remember Gina? She's the lady who sits in the office and organises all the people who work there and probably a lot of other things that you've forgotten about,' Sandy said with sarcasm. 'No, you've forgotten her and everybody else who makes their living with us.'

'What are you saying, Sandy? Come on let's have it,' Martyn said.

'Gina rang me the other day to find out where you were. She needed to talk about the new stores opening, she needed to talk about the money you've got to find to pay for it all, yes she just needed to know you were still around.'

'I've got a phone if she needs me that badly,' Martyn replied with rising irritation.

'Well listen, she tells me your desk in the office is piling high and it's noticed by other people that you haven't been around much lately. People talk, you know.'

'Let 'em talk then, it doesn't change anything.'

'The new investor will talk too if you're not around the place more often and where will that lead?' Sandy said.

'I've been tied to this place for fifteen years and that's long enough for me. Nice and Monte Carlo will only be a few days away and if you wanted to you could get somebody else to get on with the village fete. And so what if we're seen to be the rich people? Let's just give cash to rebuild the church steeple, that's all they really want,' Martyn said.

'You've lost interest in this place and the business, haven't you? Even before we sold a few shares, Gina kept on telling you the business was running low on cash. And she tells me, not *you* Martyn, the investors are sending someone down to take a close look. She says they want to know how much cash the business will need when you open the new outlets. It's nothing to do with me, but plenty of other people will be looking around soon.'

Martyn started to move away, his attention was wandering and this is not what he wanted to hear.

'Okay, I'll go in tomorrow to sort the papers but after that I'm off to Nice with my mate Harry,' Martyn said, taunting Sandy.

'Yes, you go, and play. But while you're away remember that there's a lot of people out there who rely on what Blake Markets does to keep their own lives in order.'

'Don't push it, Sandy. I know all that.'

'Have you bothered to find out what that man Harry Stone is up to? You meet at a football ground having some blokey fun shouting at each other, but a private jet to Nice as well? I don't get it.'

'Harry Stone's just a regular guy, got too much money and too much time too to see it blow away in the wind. Underneath his smooth veneer he's a playboy or maybe even a wide boy, that's his life, that's all,' Martyn replied.

'You going there to bet in the casino?' Sandy asked bluntly.

'Come on, Sandy,' Martyn coaxed. 'I've got a few quid to burn and so have you.'

'You just watch it before casinos grow on you. You're getting too keen on a flutter and Monte Carlo could be dangerous. So don't spend my cash as well as your own, that's all I'll say.' Sandy stood upright and felt her back ache and her face was hot in the sun.

'You're not coming are you?'

'No,' Sandy said firmly. 'You can run off with your friend

without me. But make sure you look after the new building in Truro and then help Gina look after the pennies.'

There was sarcasm in Sandy's voice and she turned her back on him again and walked quickly to the house. She had heard enough and she did not want her day disrupted any more.

Martyn marched away too. He had heard Sandy and he knew she was right as he slammed the door of his car and made for his office five miles away. As he drove along the country road with its high hedges, he thought again about the betting accounts in the bottom drawer of his study desk. He did not know how to stop them coming and he did not know how to deal with the demands that flowed from those hidden papers. And he no longer cared.

The space that was his office was tucked into an upstairs corner of a large warehouse and was unpretentious and as untidy as his study at home. It was next to the place where the computers ran, recording what happened in the business of Blake Markets, but it was all becoming a foreign place to Martyn. His little room was often hot, noisy and, if he was there, always very busy. Martyn now hated it. And, just as Sandy had said, there was a pile of papers on his desk and of course he had long known they were gathering dust. More important to Martyn, they were papers he was going to ignore, they could gather more dust until one day he hoped they would just go away.

Once in the building Martyn managed to avoid Gina. He knew she would want to talk but that would never clear away the pile of papers that confronted him. He rang Harry Stone.

'Sandy won't come to Nice, she's got other things happening. But I'm still on, never been to the casino in Monte Carlo so I'll bring some dollars and see if we can beat the house on their own blackjack tables.'

'Great. Fun is what Nice is all about. You can also see a few celebs who're always parading, showing off. Pity about Sandy. Empty aeroplane. But bring your dollars, euros, sterling, whatever you've got, and we'll play the tables and see who wins.' Stone sounded as excited as Martyn.

Martyn laughed. He would not even think about the possibility of losing more cash and anyway he would lock his record of it all away, in roughly folded papers inside the bottom drawer of his study desk. That is what he had done before and that is what he would do again. But how long could he keep his betting life from Sandy?

9

Just after midday Vlad arrived, as demanded by Stone, to drive him to Birling Gap. Vlad had returned from London early that morning without the Ferrari. He had searched all the streets surrounding Xavier's doss in London's East End but as he was alone he had not dared to knock on Xavier's door. He did look at the concrete steps that led to the front door of the address he had been given by his boss. He decided against climbing them as they would make it difficult to give the man a fist in his face without being cornered himself. But Vlad had to tell Stone of his failure to bring back the Ferrari, and he was met with a deep glare from Stone as he stood in the kitchen of Marine House. It signalled his distrust of Vlad's waste of time.

And as they left Marine House they drove in silence; the day was warming in the midday sun and the roof of the Porsche was down. Stone had worked out the route and he gave directions to Vlad as they left Brighton and drove west towards Beachy Head, a place Stone had never been to. Just under an hour later, they entered the scrubby car park of Birling Gap. It was on the chalk cliff edge with steps down to the shingle beach and it was deserted. Stone searched the outline of the few stationary vehicles, but he saw no green vans, and he ordered Vlad to park at the back by a high grass bank that gave him sight of the whole space.

'Take a walk, give it half an hour and then… well let's see,' Stone said.

'Sir,' Vlad said as he left the car and started to walk to the steps that led down to the beach.

Stone slid across to the driver's seat. He would maybe want a quick getaway even if Vlad had not come back. He called after Vlad.

'Have you got a knife?'

'What do you mean, sir?'

'I don't like to repeat myself. I said have you got a knife?'

'Sir, I always carry one,' Vlad said and slipped a large penknife from his pocket to show Stone.

'Just have it ready, I don't know how this is going to go. Okay?'

Vlad did as he was told, which is what he always did when driving Stone, and he slid the knife back into his pocket. Within two minutes he had disappeared towards the cliff edge and the sea without looking back. The sun was high and it was becoming hot. Stone put the hood of the car up – he wanted to be less visible – and he held the steering wheel tightly with the skin stretched over his knuckles, showing white. His golf cap kept the sun from shining directly into his eyes but Stone screwed his face into a deep frown.

On the edge of a steep chalky cliff facing the Channel, where on a clear day France would sometimes appear, the car park was bare with loose, rough gravel and untidy with litter easily blowing in the breeze. But it was well secluded, and perhaps that was what Xavier wanted, Stone thought as he blinked again into the very bright sun. His Porsche was black, not ostentatious like the bright red Ferrari that Xavier had taken, and he sat waiting. But he did not trust Xavier and his thugs, and he looked for an escape path if he needed to get out of here quickly.

Stone put his heavy dark glasses on to shield his eyes and set the air con running at maximum just to get a blast of cold air in his face. He stared expectantly through the windscreen, his heart rate increasing as he became impatient and irritated at being kept waiting. It was, though, still only two minutes past three. He had been lured here by Xavier, he did not know what to expect, and by now, with anybody else not on time, he would have driven off. But having come to this deserted place on the edge of the cliff, Stone knew he had no option but to see this through.

Another fifteen minutes passed but it felt like thirty. With growing anger Stone sat and stared at the blank landscape but he had now waited long enough. He could deal with Sudbury, brickies waving weapons at him he could ignore, and on a warm summer's day this scruffy car park was not where Xavier was going to frighten him again. Without Vlad, Stone drove slowly to the entrance and with a few deep breaths kept his growing aggression under control. He was going back to Marine House.

A green van entered at speed from the road. Stone's eyes met those of the driver in a concentrated stare. A bald head and round face grinned with a teasing smirk. Even in this wide-open space Stone suddenly felt cornered by the presence of this man with the menacing stare in his eyes.

'Got a message from Dave you wanted to meet so I come with a present,' Xavier said as he leant out of the window. 'Harry, you look frightened but I'm on my own, no mates with me, so relax and we deal, okay?'

Stone said nothing but he knew the voice and the face. What was he doing here, giving in to the intimidation of this hoodlum?

'Right man for this.'

Xavier threw a thin leather briefcase and Stone fumbled with it as it landed on his lap. He heard a deep belly laugh from Xavier and suddenly he felt nakedly uncomfortable in this open space. His shirt was sticking to the back of his car seat and Stone wanted away. He detested the sight of the bald head and large staring eyes, a stark memory of the heist of his Ferrari and the man's face talked of a world of ruthless and grubby deals. And whose money was really in this caseload of cash? Stone felt growing aggression in tune with his heart beat.

'I wash this cash, you get out of Sudbury with all your idlers there. I don't want 'em on the site any more. That's the deal. Got it?' Stone shouted.

'I'll decide that later, Harry. You just take this hard earned money and do as you're told. That's the deal.'

'I want ten per cent. In cash. That's ten per cent of what's in this case if you want the lot washed through one of my mates' business accounts. And when that's done this deal is over, you don't come back for more, anytime,' Stone shouted.

'Well it's like this, mate. I got your other wheels safely tucked away. That red Ferrari's a nice car to push a bit on the motorway, and remember Sudbury's my call so you leave it all to me and maybe we talk later about sweeteners. That's if you keep the cash tight, away from anyone who might want to poke their fingers in it, okay?'

'I want the Ferrari back. *Now*,' Stone said.

'Not possible, it's mine to have a few more test drives like they do in any good garage. And like I said when you lent it to me, just a bit of security in case you don't do as we ask.'

'You're just a pumped-up narco trafficker who's trying his gangster luck and it won't work with me,' Stone said.

'Well put it this way, if that's how you think, I tell you, mate, you look like a good bet to practise our gangster ways on. You got a big house, you got nice motors, I don't see many other flashy Porsches sitting around here and that's yours too, ain't it?'

Xavier, with a mocking cockney accent, blew a whiff of alcohol into Stone's face. He held a small camera the size of a credit card close to Stone and, with the briefcase in Stone's lap, pressed the camera shutter three times in three seconds. Stone blinked. This was not what he had expected. He had no chance to hide his face and he wiped his forehead on his shirt sleeve. Xavier laughed loudly, his bald head with a vein on the left temple shining in the sun and there was a menacing sharpness in his mocking eyes as he crunched the green van into gear, ready to leave.

'Just taken my receipt for a quarter million in nice used paper money. Not many deals like that around, eh, Harry? But my boys send it with a message. You've got the contacts, matey. So use 'em to turn that pile of dough into clean money that nobody asks any question about. You know what I mean?' Xavier said.

'You get real. I've got your cash now, so I'll play this game my way,' Stone said.

'If you lose a penny I wouldn't like to step in your shoes, Harry. But that ain't gonna happen, you're too good at this type of deal, I can see that.'

'Don't start your idle threats,' Stone said. He felt his hand shake as he wiped his forehead.

'Okay, but don't forget, matey, you owe a lump of cash to people like Boozy who worked for you at Sudbury and they aren't too happy. And me and me boys can be right mean if we get cross. So you've got three weeks starting from today, not a day more, to wash it through into clean cash. To get my money back my mates'll send invoices adding up to a quarter of a million and in three weeks' time you pay it back down the wire. That'll show it's clean money. Got it, Harry?

'You're crazy if you think I can deal with this tainted cash in three weeks. But you get violent and I burn the lot,' Stone said, but with increasing hoarseness in his dry voice. It betrayed his tenseness, even creeping desperation.

Stone placed the briefcase on the passenger seat and blinked as he looked at the menacing face in the green van who waved his credit-card sized camera at him again.

'I'm not listening to you, Harry. Don't run away and remember you're in it now right up to here. You're in my nutcracker, Harry. Can't you feel it yet?' Xavier laughed. He made a gesture with the side of his opened hand on his neck and then withdrew his head into his van.

'Get out of the way,' Stone shouted as he saw Vlad come back from the cliff path.

'Yeh, I'm going, but let me give you a final bit of advice, matey. This ain't my readies, Harry. It's like this, I got a mate in the island of St Vincent in the Caribbean who asked me to find a home for a few weeks for his hard-earned cash and I thought no better man than you for that job. But he says he'd like to talk, see if we can do any more work together. So you've got to get out to see him, he wants to see you've got an honest face,' Xavier said and laughed in a raucous cackle.

'Shut it, I'm not going to trashy places like that.'

'Okay, mate. Let's wait and see. You're far too clever to let our nice little deal go wrong but we'll be watching, we'll be following, we gotta make sure all those notes're safe. And my mate in the sunshine of the Caribbean… well I don't like talking about something nasty happening to boys like you if it goes wrong. Do you know what I mean?'

'Don't you listen? I just told you I'm not running to the Caribbean. And I don't want to know about money from your dirty cannabis and extortion set-ups. I do this deal my way, got it?' Stone shouted.

'Okay, if that's the way you want it. But my sunshine friend might get a bit bothered that his cash isn't safe in your greasy hands. Put it like this, he don't know you, and I mean, a quarter of a million in notes he's just lending to you on my high recommendation… well…'

'Get out of my way.' Stone shouted and he rammed the Porsche into gear.

'Okay, Harry, don't get excited. I'm not very good at writing but I've left you a note about St Vincent in there, an address for you to look up,' Xavier said pointing to the briefcase.

He then waved his large fist close to Stone as the van suddenly moved forward and noisily spun loose gravel and dust. A grey-haired lady walking her small dog stared disapprovingly and Stone stared back at her as he placed his sunglasses on his nose. Sure, he agreed with her stare, this was not a place to practise wheel spins.

Stone moved back to the passenger seat as Vlad came closer and he waved to him to come to his window.

'See that green van? Go and slash a tyre, I want it stopped so it's not going anywhere,' Stone said as he watched for the woman and her dog but they had now disappeared along the cliff path.

Vlad was not sure and he put his head further into the Porsche window.

'You heard what I said, get on, do it before it slips away.'

Vlad ran towards the green van, which had now stopped to let a car pass. He lunged at the near offside wheel. A hiss of air burst quickly from the tyre and a bald head leant out to see what had happened. Vlad saw his chance and landed a heavy fist in the middle of the wide shiny face.

Stone sat still in the Porsche with the case on his lap but his pulse raced as he watched Vlad. Just a few seconds later Vlad ran back as he saw the bald head emerge from the green van, blood streaming from the nose. Stone's heart was still racing as Vlad jumped into the Porsche and he expertly drove as they left the car park before the green van moved. Xavier was going nowhere for a while.

The bright sunlight shone directly onto Stone's face and for a moment he closed his eyes as Vlad opened up the engine of the vintage Porsche and drove towards the main road and then to Brighton. With the leather briefcase on his lap, and as Vlad expertly worked through the gears, he was sure that Xavier was not following him. Momentarily, Stone began to feel less irritated by the threatening demands just made on him.

Driving on the open road Stone closed his eyes. Rough stuff he did not know how to handle. If it became really ugly Stone would be first to run, but at this time he had dealt Xavier notice that he was going to give back if there was a fight. Vlad drove at speed and Stone slipped lower into the seat, his shoulders hunched into his neck. Holding the case tightly Stone suddenly thought that he should have counted the quarter million cash. What if it was short by a hundred grand or even more? Of course that was the sort of stunt that Xavier would use to squeeze him more tightly.

Would a jet flight into the Monte Carlo sun, as a lure to entice

Martyn into a deal, really work with this load of cash? Getting it all paid into Martyn's bank, note by note, and then out again in three weeks with nobody asking questions at Blake Markets, how was that going to work? Stone could only give instructions to get it done, then disappear until… what?

On the open road Stone breathed more freely as he looked in the rear-view mirror. His refuge, his haven, his imposing Regency mansion, Marine House, with the invisible security cameras and burglar alarms and a remote system that locked and unlocked doors; Stone knew it would be out of reach of this madman. His intimidating lunacy would be halted on the bottom step. But a deep frown still creased Stone's forehead; this man had people everywhere.

His head nodded, his eyes were closed and he clutched the briefcase as Vlad drove skilfully until they arrived at the front entrance of Stone's residence an hour after leaving Birling Gap. As Stone eased himself from the passenger seat he did not even look at Vlad, and with a tenuous feeling of bravado carrying the case, Stone boldly walked to his front door. He stood for a minute staring across the busy road to the beach and the sea.

Away from just the sight of Xavier, Stone had a growing sense of security and he went to the sitting room and threw the briefcase onto a low table. It was only five o'clock, he poured a neat Scotch and slumped into one of the heavily cushioned sofas that faced the deep semi-circular windows fronting a small balcony. Sipping his drink he stared at the ceiling and knew he had seen a vicious reality flicker in the deep eyes of Xavier. The wide face with its glistening shaven head and alcohol-stained breath said that this man came from a place of violence and intimidation, and even in the security of Marine House, Stone shuddered.

With his whisky glass in his hand he went to the small escritoire and again looked at the card of Martyn Blake. He stared at the closed briefcase with its hidden, trafficked cash, resting openly on the table. Just a jet flight to Monte Carlo and gambling in the casino was all he now had to get this deal running. He took a large sip from his whisky glass.

Jo was tidying the laundry in the kitchen, and Stone closed the sitting room door so that she could not interrupt him. Sitting on the deep sofa with his back to the window he opened the thin briefcase. On top was a sheet of paper with the address of Xavier's supplier on the island of St Vincent in the Caribbean. Stone took it out and stuffed it into his jacket pocket. He then handled the used notes, bundles of twenty pounders, fifty pounders, that had been roughly bundled with their corners creased and folded and tied with red rubber bands. Where had they come from? Who had counted them together into bundles? Who had paid heavily for them as drug mules, or racketeering and extortion and who knew what else?

Stone was now seeing the sharp end of this deal, and he began to feel very hot sitting completely alone in almost total silence. The malt whisky began to soften the frown lines over Stone's eyes but he became gloomy and tired. He was on his own, and not even Roger would know or even care if he was one of the victims of Xavier's GBH attacks.

Stone heard Jo moving about as he went to refill his whisky glass from the decanter. She had a smile and her eyes looked bright again, and perhaps the encounter in the car with a man who hid his face in a hood had passed. But he had got their cash in rough bundles on a table in his sitting room and it could happen again. Stone knew he could never be sure that Jo would be safe from the racketeers who would come around to Marine House.

Jo had finished sorting the laundry to be collected tomorrow and she peered round the door to the sitting room. It interrupted Stone who was adjusting the bundles of notes to fit back into the thin briefcase. Hurriedly he closed the lid and looked steadily at Jo as he placed the briefcase on the floor. But Jo retreated. There would be another time to talk about replacing the carpet in this room, a carpet that had red wine stains from a careless visitor just a month ago. Jo had caught a rapid glimpse of the bundles of notes and she watched Stone closely as he ran his hand through his hair.

Stone went onto the small balcony and he felt the very fresh evening air as he stared out to sea. It was calm and a warm breeze held him for a moment hypnotised as if in a daydream. Before he gave this cash to Martyn he would take his cut – twenty-five grand – and he suddenly felt confident that from this case of crumpled notes he could clear the bills Jo had shuffled into a neat pile on the kitchen table. Restaurants, hotels, suppliers of food and wine, electricians and plumbers who came to work in the house could all now be paid. But it would not be enough to pay off the demands from the taxman.

He picked up the phone and rang Roger.

'How you getting on with the sale of Arrow Hall?' Stone demanded.

'What's pushing it so suddenly? It'll take time, be patient.'

'The bill from the taxman for forty five grand and less than a couple of weeks to pay up. Or bankruptcy. I told you the clock is ticking on that, Roger.'

'Arrow Hall is an unusual place, listed with all sorts of caveats on it and with the cost of rebuilding absolutely unknown. And a lot of people run away from that.'

'Okay, but keep the pressure on. There's something else. Next Monday I'm going to Monaco with a mate to talk some business and I want you to come. Shoreham airfield, private jet, and all on me.'

'Hang on, Harry, my diary's a bit full at the moment…'

'I expect to see you at Shoreham, ten o'clock Monday morning, okay?' Stone said sharply and turned his phone off.

Stone sat heavily in a chair at the kitchen table and idly fiddled with the growing pile of junk mail and real envelopes when he saw six identical brown envelopes that Jo had neatly placed together. He slit them open and found each one had a parking ticket inside. He soon found they were from all around London, from Kensington in the west to Plaistow in the east. They were all addressed to him as the owner of a Ferrari and his own personal number plate was shown on each ticket.

A quick tally showed him that he now owed almost £1,500 in fines from places he had never even visited and did not want to know about. The tickets shouted at him in red ink that if the fines were not paid within seven days they would incur penalties that would double the cost. Stone tossed them aside and tore up the envelopes, showing the whites of his knuckles from his growing anger. He roughly shuffled them back into the growing pile of bills and correspondence on the kitchen table.

Stone poured himself another whisky and sitting at his desk he called for Vlad who was cleaning the Porsche. As soon as he appeared Stone handed him the batch of six parking tickets.

'You gotta get back up to London. That fat face you hit a couple of hours ago is driving the Ferrari around in the East and up West. They're charging all over the place leaving unpaid tickets from every parking space there is. Wouldn't be surprised if the car's been clamped by now. But go and find the address of each of these tickets, have a good look around each place, knock on doors to see if anyone knows where the car is. You know your way around London so get out and search every corner. And while you're at it go back to the address of that fat face you went to a couple of days ago, get around all the streets again and search for it. Next Monday I'm away so get off and search then, take your time to look properly but I want the Ferrari found, and I want you to bring the car back this time. Give me a call as soon as you find it,' Stone said, his voice getting louder as he spoke.

'Sir, are you sure I should go back to the East End place I looked at before? If that man lives there I won't be safe after what I did to him and his motor this afternoon,' Vlad said.

'You know how to look after yourself, you heard what I said so get on and do it.'

Stone took five twenty-pound notes from his pocket, which he pushed into Vlad's hand. And Vlad stood still and looked at the parking tickets, bewildered. But Stone waved him away before he could say any more. Stone did not want to talk about his missing car or be goaded any more by what he saw as a deliberate taunt with parking tickets from Xavier. The emptiness of the large house closed in on him as alone in the sitting room he looked at the case holding a quarter of a million in used notes, still not sure if that was a real total. There was silence for a few moments, broken as Jo came into the room again.

'Are you all right, HS? You look very tired and you were shouting at Vlad.'

Stone saw her gaze at the briefcase lying on the seat.

'I've had a difficult afternoon. Vlad gave a thug a bloody nose and slashed his tyres to stop him trailing me. And I've just opened half a dozen parking tickets from around London that somebody's running up using the Ferrari,' Stone said and looked away.

But it did not deflect Jo's glance at his half-empty whisky glass and she sat on an upright chair facing him.

'I've dealt with the laundry for a week but I think the hot water system needs servicing. Has it been hot enough in your shower?'

'Yeh, it's been a bit tepid early in the morning but I really don't take much notice,' Stone replied.

'So I'll get on and get it done but it will cost a few hundred, HS,' she said.

'Of course,' Stone said quickly to dismiss Jo's trivial bit of household demands. He stared at the briefcase.

'We should get security checked. I went to empty the mailbox and there was this black face, with a hood, smoking just staring at the door. It took him ten minutes before he moved off. He didn't come up the stairs to knock, he just stood there and then sat on the bottom step with his back to the door. I watched him from the sitting room window and he sauntered away as if he had nowhere to go.'

'He'll just be a layabout with nothing better to do in the middle of the day. Plenty of them around this part of the town,' Stone said.

Jo looked quizzically at HS. She read in his face that something was happening that he was not sure about, he almost looked frightened, with puckered lines forming around his mouth.

'Is there anything else you want me to do tonight before I go, HS?'

'Why don't you stay and have a drink?' Stone asked.

'Yes, thank you, I'd like that.'

'So what is it to be? You know what's in the drinks cabinet more than me.'

'A glass of your best white wine, please.'

It took Stone five minutes to go the wine cooler in the kitchen and uncork a bottle of very expensive Chablis that had been there since he moved into this house. He poured a full glass for Jo and took it back into the sitting room.

'It's the bottle of Chablis I've been wanting to open for some time, so enjoy it, Jo, drink up and we'll get a cab to take you home later.'

Stone sat opposite Jo and watched her intently. 'I've got something I want you to do for me,' he said.

'Just ask, HS. If it's something to do with running this house I'm here to help.'

'I want you to write a letter for me. It's to a lady called Claire Watts. She worked for me until Arrow Hall burnt down. If I write a letter in my words it'll be strong and tough, so you put it how you would write to a friend. Be business-like but it's got to say what I want.'

'I'll outline something but don't you know her well enough to put it as it is?' Jo asked.

'You find the words I need, Jo, and I'll sign it so Claire won't know the difference. That's all.'

'So what do you want in this letter?'

'Claire has access to some documents called Panama codes, and I need her to tell me where these documents are. Maybe they were burnt in the fire at Arrow Hall but she knows all the detail anyway, so she's just got to write it down so I can get hold of my Panama cash. Tell her it's getting very urgent and I don't want any delays.'

Stone paused and looked at Jo as the next part needed to have real spite and nastiness that Stone would dish out to Claire if she ignored him.

'Okay, listen to this last bit. Tell her that if she keeps playing the game of hiding the Panama codes from me then I'm going to call around to see her boss, a man she's now living with. She'll know who I'm talking about and I'm going to tell him how she's double-crossing me and now running away with secrets from my business deals. Tell her this letter is her final reminder.'

'It's your letter, HS. I'm only going to put it on the laptop but that sounds a bit like blackmail to me. Are you sure you want me to write that?'

'Yeh, why not, she's hiding my money and I want it back. You write it and she'll know what I mean,' Stone said.

'Okay, I'll draw up something. But let me tell you, HS, you need to keep it very soft to get the right response from Claire. And let me also tell you next time you should not be so careless when you ask someone to keep something valuable for you.'

Not many people spoke to HS so bluntly but he ignored Jo's comments and picked up the briefcase. It was thin and it looked like expensive leather.

'There's some cash in here. I need to have it counted. Down to the last pound. What about doing that for me too?' Stone asked.

Jo looked at Stone with arched eyebrows. 'How much cash? Where did it come from?'

'Slow it, leave the questions, Jo. I don't know the answers. You just count it and tell me how much. Not today, but why not when I'm away in Monte Carlo to do some business. Okay?' Stone said.

'Can I just look at it now?' Jo asked.

‘No, but I’m going to leave it out of sight under the sofa here.’

Jo enjoyed a second glass of Chablis and Stone refilled his Glenfiddich. An hour later Stone saw her into a cab to take her home and he thought he had done enough to say thank you to Jo for staying around. But he was still troubled by bundles of notes in a briefcase in his sitting room. He had been told a quarter of a million but was that right? Stone was going to find out and whatever was there he’d start square with Xavier and his hoods.

10

Jo was concerned at what was happening in the household of Marine House. She had seen HS becoming restless about security, and even about his own safety. She could see he was now drinking very large snifters of whisky and taking them very often, even early in the day. And now he had asked her to count a large sum of cash in a briefcase he was hiding under the sofa.

Jo arrived an hour earlier than normal the next day so that she could get the cash counted and then get on with making a list for the cleaners of the parts of the house she wanted dealt with. Sitting at the kitchen table she opened the case and was startled at what she saw. She jerkily recoiled from the bundles of rough, crumpled notes that had not been unfolded at the edges or even made into tidy denomination batches. There were many wads bound with red elastic bands, she stared at them and even thought she could smell a mustiness that would tell its own story. Suddenly Jo felt the intrusion just as she had in the concrete car park and she saw the notes as more than just piles of printed paper. Each one carried an unpleasant hidden history which HS had tried to keep away from her.

With the notes spread across the kitchen table it took her over an hour to get them sorted into separate denomination piles, edges folded back and ready to be counted. On each bundle Jo methodically placed a yellow Post-it note with the total that bundle held and then she totalled it all up using Stone's calculator from his study. She was sure she had the right figure, but handling the notes made her hands dirty and she felt contaminated as she replaced the crumpled paper into neat piles back into the case. She snapped it shut and left it where she had found it, deep under the sofa in the sitting room, out of sight. She passed her hand over the top of the case as if she was dusting the thing. This was unreal having such a large sum of cash, not knowing what it was for and all in this chintzy room. She sighed. On a clean sheet of paper she wrote a note to HS giving the total she had found and left it, so HS could not miss it, on top of the pile of unpaid bills on the kitchen table. HS would see that when he came back.

Jo had never written a letter before which she thought was blackmail. She had read the words three times and intimidation, however softly written, was what it was. She could stand away from it but it left her wanting to know what sort of woman Claire was that pushed HS to write such a letter. Jo carefully placed what she had written also by the side of the unpaid bills,

Instructions to the cleaners did not take Jo long to complete. Jo saw that Vlad was in the sitting room checking a fitted bolt on the balcony doors and, satisfied at her morning's work, about midday took some fresh air. She walked along the seafront for twenty minutes. The sea air was a tonic that she gulped in with deep breaths, a good antidote to the oppressive, almost sealed, atmosphere of Marine House with its dirty bundles of money.

Feeling refreshed, Jo let herself in by the back door and put her jacket on a chair in the kitchen. There was a small alerting noise behind her and she spun around. Her heart raced as she looked straight into the bloodshot eyes of a black face staring at her from beneath a deep hood.

'It's okay, darling, I'm not here to hurt you, like rape or something, no – you just tell me what I want and it's all much easier for both of us. Got it?'

Jo felt the pace of her heart increase and she put her hand to her mouth as if to stifle a cry. She had seen this face before – sitting on the front doorstep and next to her in a dark carpark.

'Get out of here!' she screamed. 'Leave us alone.'

'Yeh, darling when you tell me what I need to know.'

'How did you get in?' Jo shouted, expecting that Vlad would hear even though he was out on the balcony to the sitting room.

'Wasn't difficult, sweetie, when you leave the back door open, I just walked in. Very grand in here, ain't it?'

Jo felt the back door key in her hand. Had she left it open?

'I'll call the police,' she said, and stretched out to the mobile that was lying on the kitchen table.

But the hooded intruder caught her arm and pinched it tightly as he pulled her away.

'My boss needs to remind Harry he's gotta make a trip to the Caribbean, that's to a little island of St Vincent. And my boss needs to know where his mate Harry's put his briefcase of nicely folded notes. My boss needs to know it's all safe. So, darling, just a short visit for you to tell me what I need to know.'

'I don't know anything. I don't know what you're talking about so get out of here,' she shouted again as she moved to the other side of the table.

The kitchen door opened and Jo even smiled as Vlad came into the room in his greasy jeans and he looked ready for a fight.

'What's going on, Jo? Do you need my help?'

'We don't want this person in here, he's trying to rob this house, so call the police,' Jo said as she looked at the hooded face.

But he saw Vlad advance towards him and he moved back. Vlad's reaction was swift and he caught the hoodie in a rugby tackle that sent him through the open back door to the small steps. The hoodie was flat on his back lying on the concrete path that led down to the garage as Vlad piled on top of him, and smashed three quick punches into his face. Vlad yanked the hood back and stared into the dark face and glaring eyes and then stood with his foot on the inert body of the intruder. It was a kick to the side that made the hoodie groan with growing pain and he rolled over as if to protect his face from further punches.

Vlad moved to the back door and he saw Jo reach for the phone.

'Jo, leave it,' Vlad said, out of breath.

Within seconds the back door slammed with a heavy thud. Jo went quickly to the kitchen window and watched intently as the intruder slowly raised himself onto his knees like a staggering drunk. But Jo was shaken and she sat down at the kitchen table.

'What's all this then?' Vlad asked.

'I don't know how he got in, and he held my arm as if he wanted to hurt me. I can't go on like this,' Jo said.

'Are you all right?' Vlad asked as Jo took a handkerchief to wipe her eyes.

'Let me calm down for a minute or two. Then I'll be okay.'

Vlad went to the window and saw the intruder walk shakily to the small lane.

'He's gone and he won't want to come back too quickly now,' Vlad said.

'HS will be angry that someone like that got into the house. And it's the same man who sat next to me in the car when HS was at the doctor. And then I saw him sitting on the doorstep a few days ago when he was just staring at the front door.'

'Was he thieving? What's he after?'

'I don't want to know,' Jo said. She was shaking as she wiped another tear from her face.

Vlad went to the back window again and took a long stare around the garden edge.

'Leave it,' Jo said. 'I'll tell HS what's happened but you get the alarm system and all the locks double-checked. And we'll keep the doors closed.'

Jo felt the close-up intimidation from the staring eyes of the hooded intruder. It was an unsettling couple of minutes. Jo left Vlad in the kitchen and went back to the sitting room. She needed to make sure the cash was still there in its case. She pulled it out from underneath the sofa, looked at it for thirty seconds and then pushed it sharply back as if it would infect her.

***

Martyn's face was flushed. He felt a boy-like excitement at being in Monte Carlo as he walked with Harry Stone and Roger Garon onto the wide sunlit terrace of the Cheval D'Or. It was a two-star Michelin restaurant and bar which looked over the wide expanse of the harbour. It was somewhere that Martyn had never been before. As always around this place there was a fleet of motor yachts from large to not-so-big, that rested easily in the calm water in neat rows. For a moment Martyn stared at them and wondered if they ever left these marina walls. The yachts and pontoons were busy with people even in the heat of the afternoon sun and Martyn blinked and turned away. He would have liked to have been out there, not partying, but just to see who these people were.

In pressed white slacks and a blue jacket, Roger was dressed for this place but Stone kept his shirt tightly buttoned as if it was going to get cold. A Panama hat hid his eyes and it made Stone look sinister, maybe even wanting to slink away. Martyn had a sweat-stained shirt with the sleeves rolled up clumsily and deep marks under each arm from perspiring in the heat of the sun. He carried a jacket over his shoulder and his cheap plastic white sunglasses highlighted his lined face and ruffled hair.

The maître d' eyed Martyn with a long stare that registered distaste and approached with an outstretched arm that was about to bar entry. That is until Stone stuffed a fifty-euro note into his hand and stared at him with his piercing blue eyes as if daring him to stop them. Or even fumble to give him some change. Stone's stance was assured, he moved forward and put on a false smile with his head held high, and the maître d' led them to a small table on the edge of this elegant and busy terrace. But he was less than sure that these clients should take a privileged position on his sun deck.

Monte Carlo was exactly where Harry Stone wanted to be with Martyn. The flight down in the private jet had been quick and had impressed Martyn with the trappings of luxury which his new-found mate Harry Stone could indulge in. Harry had let Roger and Martyn spend time in the casino where Martyn had played blackjack and Roger had several runs at the roulette wheel, but the little white ball was not kind to him. It was obvious this was a place that Martyn could slip into easily. His confidence at the table showed through his easy concentration, helped by the many times he had played blackjack at the Piccadilly casino in London. Stone had watched Martyn handle his cards and he was sure he had brought him to the right place to talk.

Today gave Stone belief that Martyn could be tempted to handle bundles of dog-eared used notes. Martyn would see it as another fun gamble, like La Salle Des Amériques where he had twice cleared the table. And Stone watched as Martyn's eyes moved away from the yachts and he pulled his sunglasses off and squinted at the maître d'. Martyn tugged clumsily at his shirt sleeves to wind them higher up his arm just to show that he had no feeling for being part of this playground. It was only for those who wanted to dress up to look flashy. And the maître d' could put his stuffiness back into his pocket with the large euro note.

But winning 1,500 euros on the quick game of blackjack half an hour ago left a warm glow with Martyn. He had been asked to roll his shirtsleeves down and put his jacket on before he was allowed to sit at the blackjack table and he had inevitably conformed. Chasing the odds until they fell his way was what he was here for. Having a flutter now was an easy game for Martyn. It was just how he had seen all of his business life, a gamble, and he often reflected on how he had started Blake Markets with Sandy. The business had only a few pounds and a lot of trust when it was launched fifteen years before. But gradually over that time, for Martyn, the excitement had gone and his earlier nervous energy running the place had deserted him. Even online poker, a game which dragged him to his laptop when Sandy was not watching, now gave him more excitement than Blake Markets.

In the casino Martyn knew he was not playing against the others sitting round him but he had stared with animated interest at the middle-aged lady at the end of the semi-circular table with white hair and a wrist weighed with jangling gold bracelets. The cards were not running her way and she rose from the table, grabbed a large red handbag and stalked away, her wrinkled, sun-shrivelled face twisted under large dark sunglasses. You did not get that buzz watching the first past the post from Newmarket on the television, even if you had taken a sizeable online bet.

Being live in this place for Martyn was more than that. The speed of knowing the winnings and seeing the uplifted and downbeat faces of other players of the slick, quick game of blackjack was something that always showed him there was real gambling beyond his dimly lit bookie's corner shop. Fixed odds machines had no emotions, they flashed at you garishly, they sometimes took your cash and that is what Martyn savoured in this glitzy casino where he could make a quid or two, walk away and never be seen again. Even if he had lost, Martyn was sure he would have the same buzz that would drag him here again sometime.

A waiter carried an ice bucket with champagne to their table and Martyn quickly cleared the check with a tip as if to tell Harry Stone that he could afford to pay too. The sea was a sparkling blue, the air humidly warm and Martyn slouched low into his chair under the parasol as if to hide the sweat that was discolouring his shirt. He was on a high, he had won rather than lost a valuable bunch of euros. He had watched with interest as Stone slipped notes to the gatekeeper to enter this classy and very pricey place and even though with Sandy he had wealth he knew he would never be in the habit of passing it around like that just to have champagne served under a parasol.

Martyn was not sure what to make of Roger. He was stylish, he sounded more clever than Harry, he had not said much and Martyn was not sure why Roger was here. Harry had introduced him as 'coming just for the ride' but Martyn felt more than once that they were both watching, assessing him maybe. But for what? A blunt northerner brought up in a teeming high-rise Sheffield apartment block, where everybody knew you and what you were doing, exclusivity had never been part of Martyn's upbringing. But in this place snootiness was all around him and squinting under the parasol he stared at Harry and he wondered what drove this man. It was surely not just being seen in a flashy place properly dressed. Maybe it was just the fun of the visit, private jets included. Martyn leaned back heavily in his chair and laughed inwardly at the flimsy façade that he thought he saw in Harry Stone.

'You did well in there, Martyn,' Harry said, clinking his glass of champagne against Martyn's and Roger's.

'Easy. You buy the chips, pile 'em high and then get the right cards. And then don't push your luck or stare at the other players too much.'

'You looked confident, you've done it before by the way you were playing,' Stone said.

'Just once or twice,' Martyn hedged. 'But a horse here and a few quid on the number of goals scored in some football game there. That's me.'

'Sure. But you're a natural, I'd just flounder around at that table so it was great to see you play. You've got some nerve watching your cards even as that jewelled woman got a bit flustered. Don't know how much she lost but from her chips taken away, it looked a pile.'

'I guess I was born to play it hard. I've not always been lucky, but you have to follow your luck and make the most it.' Martyn laughed.

'We'll come back here sometime and I'll follow what you do at that table,' Harry said, and looked at Roger as if asking for support.

'Come on Harry, this sort of place was never your scene, you'd lose a ton at that table,' Roger said.

Stone stared at the marina. 'Anywhere's my scene but I'll never give the casino the chance to fleece me,' Stone replied.

'Never take the casino too seriously, the house always wins when it's all added up. They have to mint plenty of cash to make that place so plush,' Martyn said.

It was at that fleeting moment, sipping his champagne and hiding from the sun under the wide parasol, that Martyn thought of the bottom drawer in his study desk. There he hid a growing problem that he would keep to himself for as long as it was possible. The debts were nagging at him, though, they would just not go away.

'Tell me about yourself, Harry. We come away to play in a nice private jet and I mean, that must cost a lot of cash, so what do you get up to?' Martyn asked.

'I do a bit here and a bit there, usually Roger helps me if only with some prim and proper advice and to spin a bit of paperwork,' Stone answered with an evasiveness that was part of his life.

'I like your confidence. You got us onto this sun deck as if you owned it,' Martyn said.

'Listen, Martyn, if money'll buy it, then Harry Stone's your man,' Roger said and laughed.

'I think we should share the cost for the flight. That little jet was very smooth, no waiting to be corralled into a corridor before boarding, and I've won a few notes in the casino, so how much do I owe?' Martyn said.

'No, no, it's definitely on me,' Harry said raising his palm in the air.

The conversation lulled. It was too hot to talk or even think, and Stone sipped his champagne as he looked at Martyn's wide face which was already tingeing red in the sun. The away days were running as he had planned.

'You still building that big warehouse near Truro?' Stone asked.

'Yeh. It's a big build but I leave it all to the contractor. They run it and tell me what they're doing when I ask. Building work and mucky sites are not for me,' Martyn replied.

The thought of mucky building sites hit Stone and he gazed at the tethered yachts. The mud and mess of Sudbury was still there and he never wanted to see it again.

'What goes, Harry? You look a bit ruffled when we talk business in this sunny spot,' Martyn said.

'More champagne?' Stone steadied his hand with the bottle as he poured.

'Why not? If we don't finish it somebody else will.'

There was a pause from Stone as he looked at Roger to continue and he felt constrained as he held his champagne glass to his lips. Roger too sensed that Harry was struggling.

'Martyn, why don't you tell us about your business?' Roger asked.

'Supermarkets, we buy cheap and sell cheap. No frills in our places but West Country stuff. Keep the loos and the aisles looking clean and bright and it works. But I've just sold a lump, about a quarter of the business. We have a partner, call themselves Trifoni Enterprises, some investing guys, and I don't see much of 'em, but that might change. Couple of days ago I walked out of their flashy big office in the West End. Their boss man, Rick, had promised some cash so we could build two new stores but then they changed their mind and they want to send someone down to look over the figures and disrupt the place. I'm losing a bit of control and I'm losing my patience but so what?' Martyn laughed enigmatically and moved his chair more into the shade.

Roger looked suddenly alert. He knew Trifoni Enterprises, he knew of their boss man, Rick, and had not long ago checked out what Trifoni did and who they were. He looked at Stone's thin face and there was blankness there, not even a slight smile of recognition of the name Trifoni.

'Would you like another flutter, Martyn, you know, something out of the ordinary?' Stone suddenly asked.

'You know me, always like to play. What goes?'

The waiter hovered as if he wanted to refill the ice bucket and Stone passed him another twenty-euro note almost from under the table and then waved him away. Stone did not want interruptions.

'I might have something running that's not your usual deal. It's just a bit on the edge. But there's a big fee if you join me,' Stone said, and looked at Roger's disapproving face.

'Lay off, Harry. I support you when you need it,' Roger said.

'You don't advise Harry's deal then, Roger?' Martyn asked.

'What do I know?' Roger replied and left his seat to walk to the edge of the terrace overlooking the sea. He knew what Stone was going to put on the table and he wanted to hear nothing of it.

'Okay, Harry, let's have it, tell me what you've got.'

'This has to be confidential, just you and me working it,' Stone said.

'If you're offering half a horse so we can watch it run and have a wager for fun at Newmarket or Lincoln then I'm with you, Harry. So which part of the horse is it?' Martyn said and laughed.

'Could you pass a few extra notes through your supermarket tills?'

'You giving away some cash, mate? Doesn't sound like you.'

'Well, listen to this. I've got a contact who's got some extra cash, don't ask where it's come from but he needs to hide it away from prying eyes. Do you think you could mingle it into the takings from the till, like just for a few weeks and then pay it back when he's ready?'

'Has your mate got divorce problems, you know, hide it away from the missus until it's counted up and settled?' Martyn laughed again.

Stone laughed too. He had been there, Sofie had tickled him up for a sum he saw as outrageous but he had settled and walked away. If only this deal was that simple.

'What would you think of moving a quarter million in notes through your system? A supermarket looks a pretty good place for doing just that,' Stone said.

'Did you say a quarter million? In notes?' Martyn asked in a lowered voice as he again moved more into the shade of the parasol.

'You'll get a cut if it works. Five per cent? But it's a cool quarter million to hide and just for say three weeks.'

'Hold on a minute, Harry. Where does all this cash come from? Who's running around with a whole quarter million in their back pocket? You're not getting out of your depth here are you?'

'Well, listen, it's a mate of mine who's helping with my building in Sudbury and this is returning his favour. Have it as a loan, and a few days mix it with the real takings from your customers. Let it rest for a few weeks until you get a pretend invoice from my mate for let's say some new building work. You send him a cheque to pay it back to his own legit building business. All done and dusted. And you get your cut. Five percent, £12,500 all in cash.'

'Harry, come on, that all sounds a bit shady. Flaky. I doubt very much that Gina, our lady who looks after the numbers, would go along with it. My people are straight, I tell you, Harry, Gina's right down the middle. Won't even let me claim out of the little tin she keeps for a haircut.'

Stone knew he was not being taken seriously, and he felt the sharp edge of resistance. This Gina lady would touch the nasty side of this deal as she would have to handle all those bundles of crumpled notes. For the first time that day Stone began to feel uncomfortably hot in the sun.

'If we made your cut ten per cent of the deal right up front in cash, with no questions asked, would that make a difference? Twenty-five grand just like that. When did you ever have a flutter that gave those odds?' Stone asked in a whisper.

Martyn stared out at the harbour where a large blue yacht slipped its moorings, very gently churning white water as it moved ahead. Martyn knew that was not for him with full-blown power in your face from a motor yacht as long as a bus. And Harry's deal to move cash from who knows where did not sit easily with him either. The honesty of his roots from a hard northern upbringing where you did not cheat whatever the odds had never left him. And as he looked straight into Harry's face he was very wary of this shifty offer.

'Harry, my friend, this just isn't you. I mean, you're being pushed into this, right? It doesn't sound on the level and it's some criminal cash from God knows where being laundered. You sure it's not a scam over the telephone that hits all those easily conned out of their hard-earned savings? Do you know where this pile of cash comes from?'

'No idea,' Stone said, his voice low.

Martyn persisted. 'Dodgy money would bring all sorts of wrong 'uns around my place. With the cash we handle we've got enough problems with security anyway. And Gina and the girls…'

'Look, Martyn,' Stone broke in, 'this deal would all be anonymous. I give you the cash, you let it run through your fingers like sand and nobody knows you've even got it. And because it'll all look normal, nobody will ever ask. Your bank won't know, your people who work in the back office won't know, so what could be easier than that?' Stone asked quickly.

'You in a spot of bother, Harry? Have you got someone breathing right down your neck to do something nasty? I notice your friend Roger isn't listening to it all,' Martyn said.

'Leave Roger, he knows what I'm doing.'

'Okay, but tell me where you are on all this and I'll see if there's anything else I can do to help.'

'I've told you. It's simple, it's a quarter million in notes in, then a cheque back,' Stone replied.

'Okay, Harry, but tell me about your mate who's pushing this cash around.'

'No, I can't do that. But I promise my mate will never know you, nor Blake Markets. I'm the man in the middle, you stay totally private, you stay secure, well away from the sharp end. But you take ten per cent. Do I need to say more?' Stone persisted.

Martyn took a long sip from his champagne and stared unbelieving at a couple just being shown to a table at the other end of the deck. The girl was in a dress that covered less of her body above her waist than if she was sitting on a nudist beach and her escort led a small dog that was yapping and running at her ankles. Martyn turned away; this swanky place was not for him. Blake Markets was his home even with the problem lurking in the bottom drawer of the desk in his study. His betting debts were multiplying, Sandy was getting to know what he was doing, and Martyn now only hesitated slightly.

'I'll have talk to Gina when we get back, she'll have to handle it all. It's not my scene working with all that paper in the office. I wouldn't know how to key it into the computer to get it into the bank,' Martyn said, his attention still wavering on the couple who had just taken their seats.

'I don't have much time. I've already got the cash and I'm being pushed to have it dealt with, like quick. Today's Monday, would Wednesday be too fast to start the deal at your end? And if I came down elevenish in the morning…'

'Harry, I don't believe it. Are you telling me this pile of money is sitting in your own front room unguarded and for anyone to snatch?' Martyn asked, arching his eyebrows in surprise.

'I've got it all secure right in the middle of my house. It won't get nicked because nobody knows it's there.' Stone laughed.

'Okay, Harry, I'll go along with it, but whatever happens I can't hustle my people into something they don't understand. This lump of cash from nowhere is not what they're used to.'

'I told you it's a loan, simple as that. But this is in hard cash. Do we have a deal to start in a couple of days, eh?'

'Yeh, I like your offer of a cut in notes, mate, that'll mean I can get to the casino again quicker,' Martyn said laughing, but only he knew the seriousness of what he was saying.

They left the terrace over the harbour half an hour later and took a cab to Nice airport. Roger was aloof, quiet, and the cab was hot and stuffy. Stone thought he had coaxed Martyn into the deal but would it still stick tomorrow in the sober light of day?

The private jet was on its approach to Shoreham Airport just two hours later. There was silence on the flight and the aircraft hit bumpy turbulence over the Channel as it descended through dense cloud and made its approach. A few minutes later there was a thud as the aircraft hit the tarmac and then its engines blared loudly as it braked. It taxied easily to the terminal with a short call from the pilot.

'We were a bit long on the runway. Just had to brake hard. Sorry guys,' he said.

They were quiet as they walked to the terminal. Martyn had a stunned look clouding his face with his shirt still stained heavily from sweating.

'Don't like flying at the best of times. That landing was not for me. But thanks for the outing, it was great and definitely my turn next time,' Martyn said.

'I liked your company. You looked really settled at the blackjack table winning all those euros. Yeh, we'll come again some time,' Stone said.

'I'd like that, Harry.'

'And can we come to your office with my briefcase of cash? Tomorrow too early?' Stone asked.

'No, not the office, it's far too open. There's a pub, Ferry Cove Smugglers, right on the coast, five miles away in a village called Ferry Cove. I'll text you the postcode for your satnav and we'll meet there,' Martyn said as he shook Stone's hand.

'Take your payoff upfront and remember my contact who's lending the cash will never know you, I'll be in the middle of it,' Stone said still trying to coax the deal.

'Yeh, keep Blake Markets' name right away from the mobsters feeding you this cash. I like the twenty-five grand and… well I'll see what we can do,' Martyn said.

Roger was standing back and he had no smile as he waved limply to Martyn. They parted, and Martyn's face suddenly looked tired and strained. He was not as relaxed as Stone had hoped after time in the sun dabbling at the tables in the casino. But then Stone did not know Martyn had a bottom drawer in his study desk which was causing him concern. As Martyn slumped onto the back seat of his waiting cab he soon drifted into a light sleep and a twenty-five grand prize after winning a fistful of euros on the blackjack table wafted by in his dreams.

Stone took a deep breath. His shoulder was aching. But there would be more rough stuff coming if he did not move this cash away from his sitting room. Roger took Stone by the arm as they walked to their cab.

'I like your style but you'd better wait and see if Martyn's onside. He sees this for what it is, plain money laundering,' Roger said.

'Martyn can be bribed with a twenty-five grand payoff. That guy needs cash to go and have some fun. That's obvious to anyone who cares to look.'

'Be very careful, Harry. What you're walking into is very dangerous. It's not like playing the taxman along with fancy stories as you've done many times before. No. This is different.'

'Don't be negative. I know what I'm doing,' Stone said sharply.

'But did you hear what Martyn said about Blake Markets when we were in Monte Carlo?'

There was silence as Stone glared out of the window as the cab moved quickly onto a clear road. Roger waited in vain for a response.

'Listen, then. Martyn's sold a quarter share in the supermarkets. I've done some research into Martyn and Blake Markets and you might want to listen to this,' Roger said.

'If you're going to be discouraging, I won't listen.'

'Do you remember Martyn talking about the Trifoni Group and a man called Rick?'

'Hold it, Roger. I'm not so crazy I don't know all about them, even the connection to Claire, but it won't derail this deal with Martyn.' Stone was silent for a moment as if he had suddenly been hit again with a metal bar now on his other shoulder.

'Claire will be going to Blake Markets to comb through their books for Rick Austen and his Trifoni Group. So what'll you do when Claire gets to know it's your cash being washed through the place? She'll run to the police, that's what Claire'll do. So I'm just putting you on alert. Be very careful how you deal with this,' Roger said. 'It's all going to get very uncomfortable for you.'

'I've done a deal. I'll move the cash through Blake Markets, and I don't care what Claire and Rick Austen are up to.' Stone ran his hand through his thinning grey hair.

'Right, but you be careful. This is becoming a nasty coincidence. You'll find Claire at the back end of this deal. And it's sounding like the can of worms you usually walk into.'

'Shut it, Roger. I know what I'm doing.'

'You've got this gangster who's not short on mugging and knifing anyone in his way, and with your precious Ferrari motor car that he's nicked from you just lurking in the background. He's holding you out to dry. So that's where you stand, Harry. I warn you, but the choice is yours. And just for the record, you'd better know I'm running a mile away from this deal. I know nothing about it and I want nothing to do with it.'

'Keep on running, Roger. Martyn'll deal this cash and you won't even know when it happens,' Stone said.

'Final warning then. Money laundering is a crime high on the list with the police. They've got a whole bureau of investigators just itching to look at any cash that has even a merest whiff of laundering. It's paper money they're chasing.'

'I've got to do it, I've got the cash, Xavier's not going to walk and Martyn's on board.'

'Harry, you're not listening. Washing cash is a favourite route for terrorists, arms dealers, druggies, you name them, all trying to make their cash look mainstream. When you're banged up there's a long stretch inside. They seize anything you own like hidden Panama bank accounts. Harry, you've got to know the odds of winning in this game are stacked against you.'

Stone held his hand up as if he could stop Roger saying anything further, but it did not work.

'You're being caught in a net, Harry. Once you've cleaned one lot of cash from gangsters they'll come for more. They always do.'

'Why should I care? Money's money isn't it? Paper money, cheques, what's the difference?'

'It'll be a quarter of a million probably in a dirty bag shoved across a table in a dirty pub. Is that what you're going for?'

'Shut it, Roger,'

'Okay, last call then. Xavier's been done for GBH, drug peddling, protection racketeering, extortion. I'll say no more, Harry, but I'll visit you either in hospital or Pentonville,' Roger said.

They were silent for a slow drive along the short journey to Marine House. The cab left Stone at his front door and he did not even wave his hand at Roger as it drew away on its route to Newbury. Inside, in his sitting room, Stone looked at the briefcase from Xavier with a quarter million in used notes. In his tiredness his memory was muddled. Had he asked Jo to count them?

He sat for an hour with a Glenfiddich. But it made him more tense and he went to bed that night with a thick head and a brain that would not let him calm down into easy sleep.

11

The Fender report told Stone all he needed to know about Xavier and his network but he did not like Roger spouting it. Stone had never had a knife stuck in him, he had never had his head kicked in or a glass smashed into his face but he was wary that this was what thugs and hoodies surrounding him would do at a click of Xavier's fat fingers. The dangerous path of money laundering was where he was being driven. From there it was only a small step to drug racketeering, protection, and blackmail. And under all that there would be other scams these senseless thugs would be dealing in.

Stone went to the bathroom and looked at his face in the mirror. He saw lines forming around his mouth and a deepening puffiness under his eyes. He quickly turned away and put on a bathrobe, went into the sitting room and pulled the briefcase with the cash from under the sofa. As the reality of a new day hit him he opened the case and stared at the bundles Jo had tidied. He now saw the visit to Monaco as a charade and even the huge cost of hiring a private jet would not lure Martyn into his net. He suddenly felt very hot as his doubts mounted.

He saw Jo's neat yellow pieces of paper under the elastic band of each bundle. He pulled out a wad of twenty-pound notes, saw she had marked £5,000 on the top and slid it, satisfied, back into the case. He would soon get confirmation from Jo that the case held a quarter million and he shut it and slid it under the sofa, a gesture that satisfied him. It was out of sight and at this moment it could do no more harm.

In the kitchen Stone idly sat at the table and he fingered another letter that had come just that morning from the tax office. It read in formal printed wording that bankruptcy proceedings were now being started for full payment of £45,000 plus bankruptcy costs of a further £2,000. The deadline for payment was getting close and next to it there was a reminder from Jo that he had not yet dealt with the outstanding rent for Marine House. Stone placed both bits of paper roughly back on the pile of unpaid accounts. He had growing doubts about Marine House, it was too big, too on show and Xavier knew where he was. Somewhere smaller, less obtrusive and with a lower rent, would do but he wanted to see Jo and she was part of Marine House. From the pile of letters he pulled out Jo's crisp white sheet of paper with her neat, round handwriting. It was her note to him:

> *HS, the briefcase holds £235,000. I don't know how much you thought was in there and I have not counted twice but I'm sure that is the right figure. I've got to talk to you so I'll be in later, Jo.*

He stared at the note for only a second, he then stood as if he was going to walk away from this place but he was held back. The money was wrong as 235,000 was not a quarter million. It was 15,000 short. The house was very still, creepy in its sealed quietness and Stone clenched his fists and felt his anger rise at being short changed. Stone tossed the note away and picked up the other sheet of paper from Jo. He snatched it from the pile of unpaid bills, read it twice, signed it with a squiggle, folded it roughly in half and pushed it into its envelope. It was the letter to Claire. The words were much too rosy, but it gave her the choice of Panama codes or he would go straight to see Rick. He stuck a stamp on the envelope and put it into his coat pocket to post.

Stone still did not see the coincidence of dealing with Claire again, in a business owned by Rick Austen. He suddenly wanted to get away from the strange feeling of quiet in the house and he drove a few miles to The Lanes car park. There was a small shop window down a very narrow path, and he went in and sat for fifteen minutes to wait his turn to be given a haircut by Sol. Sol was a man who said little but whose handling of a sore head was deeply soothing. Sol always demanded payment for his services in cash, no credit cards, no cheques and he was a man Harry Stone always felt comfortable with.

From the simple thing of a haircut, Stone felt refreshed. He put Claire's letter in a post box with a satisfying thin sound and slowly walked to a small cafe on the seafront. He sat outside, idling his time with a coffee, with the sun shining on his face and staring vacantly across to the sea. He thought he saw a hooded black face lingering ten paces away, just walking slowly backwards and forwards past his table. But he saw no stare from underneath the hood and Stone dismissed it as part of his growing paranoia of being watched.

Jo's note with the total of the money in the briefcase was beginning to niggle at Stone. She had got it wrong. No, that made no sense, it was just what he wanted to believe. He would throw the lot back at Xavier, then he could be finished with this rat infested cash. It was a tempting thought but he knew he could never do that. He would soon become a target for more beatings with metal bars. And then there was Jo who would leave next time she was frightened by a black face in a hood.

It was becoming busy on the promenade and Stone left his table and started to walk along the paved path which bordered the side of the beach. He stopped and he called the number on his phone for Martyn. He needed to talk, he needed to get the cash moving out of Marine House. But the ring purred for just half a minute before voicemail clicked in. Stone spoke quickly.

'Martyn, hope you enjoyed the run to Monaco and the casino. Thanks for joining the party. Private jet's the only way to fly and we'll do it again sometime. But you know I've got the cash we talked about so I'll be down tomorrow. Elevenish, okay? That nice pub on the coast, Ferry Cove Smugglers you said, wasn't it? Sounds a good place to talk. Give us a call back on this number. Eh?'

As he drove his Porsche with the hood down along the seafront, Stone was uneasy. He could feel the tention in his shoulder and neck and getting no reply from Martyn did not help his mood. What if elevenish tomorrow was maybe a date Martyn now did not want to meet?

He then kept glancing in his rear-view mirror for a green van but he saw nothing, not even hooded loiterers, and he swore to himself. It made him hunch lower into his seat as he drove carefully through a knot of traffic. Then the road ahead was clear and he put his foot on the pedal, as suddenly he knew where he was going and what he was going to do. He was soon following the route on the motorway to Sudbury. The place was dying; his architect's vision of an old Victorian hospital transformed into classy upmarket flats, for which there would be ten buyers fighting to close on each apartment, was now fantasy. Stone wanted to see it all once again.

With his stooped shoulders severely aching, an hour and a half later, Stone drove into the still deserted site. It made him irritable as he walked into the Portakabin and found Dave speaking loudly into his phone with his legs and wide dirty boots sprawled across the desk. Dave punched his phone off and stood almost in one quick movement as if he needed to hide a guilty secret. And Stone faced Dave, staring at him blankly for almost ten seconds.

'I'm not being idle, boss, but there's nothing for me to do here except guard the place,' Dave said.

'I've got a job for you, something to get on with now,' Stone snarled.

'I'm here to help, boss, so tell me what you want.'

'I've got the bundles of notes from Xavier and I want you to go and deliver the lot to my mate Martyn Blake. He's going to clear them through his supermarkets. You come tomorrow morning, early, my place, Marine House in Brighton. I'll give you the cash. I'll give you details where to take it. Understand?'

'I don't want to be dragged into this, Mr Stone, all I want to do is get this place finished for you, so we can both get on with something else. You know this money washing deal is very dangerous, long time in pokey if caught and I don't want to get mixed up in it.'

'You're redundant and I want you out of this place. And what I gotta do is urgent. We've gotta get on with it so we're not chased by Xavier.'

'I don't know your mate, never met him.'

'You will, at Ferry Cove Smugglers, it's a small pub right on the coast and out of sight down in the West Country. I'll give you the postcode for your satnav and you've got to get there to handover the cash mid-morning tomorrow. Martyn's the right man to clear this all for me, he's straight up, no nonsense.'

Dave let out a heavy sigh. He'd tried to stay out of the way, he knew all about the gangster ring he would be dragged into if only as a runner… and if it went wrong… Dave turned and looked through the grimy window of the Portakabin and for a moment closed his eyes.

'What do you know about the Caribbean? Xavier's got a mate in St Vincent and says this lot of cash is his.'

'There's always talk around the site about St Vincent. But be careful, boss, I've heard of some of his mules coming back from that place being caught by customs at the airports. Sniffer dogs find it. The customs people, they know what's going on there so don't ever think of bringing back a bag of white stuff. You know what I mean?' Dave asked and laughed.

'I'm not carrying anything for anyone so forget it. That man'll get another fist in his face the way he's talking.'

'They grow marijuana in the Caribbean. And Xavier and his friends operate their own tight ring of dealers selling cannabis onto the streets of East London and plenty of other places. Xavier lives with his mad dogs in a squat in the East End and anyone who steps out of line like not paying their debts on time, well they get hurt,' Dave said.

'You're listening to his racketeering talk too much. I don't do drugs, nor should you!' Stone shouted.

'I'm clean, but some of those boys on site here like Boozy and his mates'll be smoking pot even while they're working. So watch out, boss, money and drugs don't go.'

'Come to Marine House early tomorrow morning,' Stone said.

Dave had been standing hesitating by his sparse and dirty desk and he slumped back into his chair. He then stared again through the smudged window to the half-finished and deathly quiet site and knew then he should have already walked away, forget all that was now going on here. He looked at Harry Stone's white face, he saw his narrow eyes and he saw in this man ruthlessness too. There would be a nasty rupture when this man and Xavier really met in a fight. Xavier, coming from a doss with mad fiery-eyed dogs slobbering all over the place, and Harry Stone, from a large elegant house on Brighton seafront would become a ferocious contest.

Before he left the site Stone sat still in his car. He tried another call to Martyn. He wanted to tell him to expect Dave, he wanted to tell Martyn that this deal was now very urgent. And he wanted to tell Martyn to get Gina ready, the lady who would deal with the grubby notes to clear them into the bank.

Martyn was brash, uncultured and said it as it was. Would a quick payoff still entice him enough? Would he see beyond what would surely come from a ruthless gang of underworld criminals if it all went wrong? Stone expected Martyn to tell him straight up that this deal was not for him. But where was Martyn? Stone looked at his silent building site and grasped the steering wheel of the Porsche to show the whites of his knuckles.

Stone drove quickly back to Marine House, by now feeling tired. His eyes were drooping even though it was only midday. He raised the hood and parked his Porsche carefully in the garage at the rear of the house and let himself in by the back door.

Jo heard the door open and walked quickly into the hall to meet him.

'You sure you got that counting right?' Stone asked sharply. 'It should be a quarter of a million.'

'HS, please, before we talk about that dirty soiled money I've first got to tell you we've had visitors,' Jo replied.

'Oh?' Stone said, disinterested in even looking at Jo.

'A hooded black guy came into the kitchen and he wanted to know about this cash.'

'What did you say?'

'I told him I didn't know about any cash. But it frightened me, I knew what we had hidden under the sofa and he pinched my arm very tightly.'

'Where's the money now?'

'Right under the sofa. And even if you don't know it, I'm going to tell you it's not safe having so much lying around in the house,' Jo said sharply.

'Did you leave the back door open for this thug to come in? I've already told you to be careful around this place!' Stone shouted.

'He got in, that's all. And listen, HS. I don't want to know your business, but this intruder wanted me to tell you to go to St Vincent. Yes, that's in the Caribbean. And yes, I've counted the cash and the figure I gave you in the kitchen is right. However many times you count it you'll find it's not a quarter of a million.'

'No, you got it wrong, you must have,' Stone said and looked away.

That was now too much for Jo. Not the first time she had been confronted and assaulted, and now the shouting from HS who was too loud and too short with her. It made her shiver. Jo grabbed her coat from the kitchen and shouted back at Stone, who was still in the hallway.

'Calm down and don't shout at me again like that.'

Stone looked at Jo unsure how to reply but she cut in quickly.

'I'm leaving. You find someone else to look after this house, someone who doesn't mind hearing your loud voice all the time and who'll take more care of a large bundle of what looks like money from some hooded gangsters stuffed under the sofa.'

It brought Stone up sharp. It was not what he wanted.

'Jo, come back!' Stone hollered.

Jo was a part of this large house, it was too empty without her. He had shouted at her, he had ignored her again and it was now too late, he knew it, as he heard the door slam. It sounded very final. He was not sure why but he needed Jo.

Stone felt very tense, any trace of a smile had gone from his face. He walked quickly into the sitting room and pulled the briefcase out. His hand quivered slightly as he flicked it open and saw everything intact but he knew he was fighting on his own with this deal. And it was already fifteen grand short.

***

Gina was studying figures on the computer screen when her desk phone rang. It was Martyn.

'How's the bank balance today?' he asked briskly.

'No better, we're still running short with a lot of bills to pay. And there's a nasty demanding letter from the bank getting very shirty and wanting to know what's going on. I can't answer it, I don't know. But I'll leave it on your desk,' Gina said.

'I want two hundred pounds and all in notes. You can leave them on the top of my desk too. I'll be in later to collect,' Martyn said. He ignored Gina's comments about the bank because he just did not want to know about it.

'If I leave cash will you please sign for it, Martyn?' Gina persisted. She had quizzed Martyn before when he was too easy taking cash just as he pleased, and it was not her way of dealing with things.

'Yeh, whatever you want,' Martyn replied.

'I've also got a betting account on my desk from Davy, the blacksmith in the village. It's for a few hundred so what do you want to me to do with that?' Gina asked.

'Gina, you sound uptight with all this, but please calm down and just leave things like that for me to deal with personally. You know where my desk is so just pile it all there, okay?'

Gina sighed heavily. She was beginning to feel flustered.

There was a pause before Martyn spoke again. 'I've arranged a loan for the business. Just to tide us over for a few weeks,' he said.

'Good, at last. How much?'

'Quarter of a million for three weeks. A mate of mine, Harry, is coughing it up so it's very casual between friends, no paperwork and we needn't tell the bank.'

'Is your mate sending a cheque or bank transfer so I can watch out for it? And when do we get it?' Gina asked.

There was another pause. Martyn was not sure how to deal with this. He had agreed to collect the bundle of money tomorrow and he knew Gina would argue about it. But Martyn no longer cared what Gina might think about it all, even his absence from his desk.

'My mate will be down tomorrow morning to meet at the Ferry Cove Smugglers pub. Elevenish. I want you to go and collect a briefcase of notes he'll bring down. Do it discreetly, don't flaunt it when you get back to the office but pay the money into the bank. Spread it over the next four to five days and run it into the three bank accounts, including the special private account where all my personal stuff goes. Split it up because I don't want the bank to notice it coming in.'

'Martyn, do you mean that? You want me to go to collect from a stranger in a pub, a lump of cash that big? Isn't that a bit dangerous?'

'No, just go and do it and pay it into the bank as I've told you,' Martyn said, his voice beginning to sound hoarse.

'Do we repay this all in cash too when the time comes? I mean how would I find a lump of notes like that?'

'No, my mate'll send an invoice to clear it back to his business. We'll do it over the internet in a couple of weeks' time.'

'This all sounds dodgy to me, money laundering isn't it?' Gina said.

'No, it's a loan from a mate, happens all the time.'

'Martyn, I find this very odd. Are you sure you want me to do this? I mean shouldn't we talk to the bank first?' Gina asked, feeling insecure about Martyn's untidy and doubtful loan.

'Get on with it, Gina, please. Just do what I ask. Okay?'

'So you're going to ignore the bank?' Gina asked.

'I'll deal with them in my own time. But they come in the queue like anyone else we owe cash to,' Martyn said. There was a pause before he continued with his voice now becoming very rough. 'But, listen to this before I go, I went to see our new investor, Trifoni in London. They're sending a lady down to have a look at the figures. Her name is Claire and she'll call you. And make sure you keep this bundle of notes that you're collecting right away from this Claire woman. Show her everything else that goes on but that bit of cash is private. Very private.'

Martyn clicked his phone off to end the call leaving Gina stunned. She looked at the cluttered space that was her office, a space which she oddly felt at home in. Built almost in the roof of a warehouse that stored food before being sent out to the supermarkets' it was confined, not glossy at all, but it served its basic purpose of a space to direct the money needs of the business of Blake Markets. She did not like the sound of this fantasy scheme. In the short call it sounded very dubious, right on the edge of what Blake Markets would ever need to do. In frustration Gina shouted the simple word 'Martyn' but it bounced off the walls of the small space that enclosed her. No one heard her.

With a quick movement she pushed the papers on her desk aside and leaned back. Of course Martyn liked a gamble, a bit here, a bit there, she had always known that but some bookies' accounts addressed to the business had landed on her desk. They needed immediate payment and they were big.

Tilting back in her chair, Gina looked at the ceiling and then closed her eyes. Gambling and money laundering, what was Martyn doing? He was getting into a dangerous game. You dealt with thugs who gave you the cash, then you had to keep it all quiet, keep the law away and keep the cash safe. And, who knows, Blake Markets had enough problems around security with the large amounts of cash the business handled every day. Why add another dubious lump to it?

Gina had not seen Martyn for almost a week but Martyn had his own routine. He liked to be seen on the shop floor early when they opened and late when they closed. He liked being close to the customers, seeing it happen, and it was his way of knowing exactly how the place looked with the shelves fully stacked in the right order. And then there were the queues that always gathered at the checkouts and a mound of unsold and out-of-date vegetables at the end of the day. Shuffling paper in an office, coping with detail and sitting still for long stretches was not something Martyn could ever suffer. He never had done and he was not going to start now. But in the last few weeks Martyn had been moody, fractious, showing his temper at small things he did not like. Twice he had locked himself in his room in the office space as if he wanted to isolate himself from the rest of the world. He did not even open his office door for a cup of tea or coffee, which was his normal ritual around midday. Gina knew that something was changing.

On a side table Gina flicked her computer screen on and stared at a page of figures for ten seconds. But she could not concentrate, she knew what they said and she finished her sandwich and sipped a cup of cold tea. She was beginning to uncover some awkward things Martyn was doing with Blake Markets' money and she had been searching the numbers in the last few weeks to find what was going wrong. And tomorrow, if she did as Martyn had asked, it would lead her to an anonymous deal to get a large amount of cash in a pub. It was a 'no paperwork' loan. At that moment Gina was tempted to walk out and leave it.

Ferry Cove Smugglers Inn was well known to Gina, she had often enjoyed a drink there with friends, usually at Sunday lunchtime when it was heaving with local people. But there was hesitation as she thought about driving there tomorrow to pick up a bag of suspect notes from someone she did not know. With growing annoyance she called Martyn again but it rang and was not answered, his phone was switched off. She left messages for Martyn to call her, saying it was urgent, but knowing this was how Martyn disappeared sometimes Gina was doubtful he would respond.

Gina scanned again the letter from the bank that Martyn did not want to see and felt hot and anxious. Why couldn't Martyn go himself to collect this bundle of money? What was he running from?

***

'Do you want to know about the visit to Monte Carlo and the casino?' Roger asked.

'A joyride for three grown men acting like boys I guess. No, I don't particularly want to hear about it,' Jennie replied.

'Well what if I say that something is going to happen that affects Claire, something that might drag her into another of Harry Stone's dodgy deals?'

Jennie sat more upright in her chair, put her half-finished cup of Earl Grey tea on a small table and then closed her eyes for a moment. 'I'll have a gin and tonic, please, before I hear any more,' she said.

Roger came back five minutes later with Jennie's glass and put it on the low table. He wanted to talk.

'You're the only person who can help Claire at this time. I don't know who else she would listen to.'

'She's listening to Rick Austen all day. They're close. They dine in all the best places and Rick seems to get reservations where we would have to wait six months for a table. And this year they've done the London Season. That's seeing everywhere and being seen in the right places. That's how close she is to Rick. But why can't we do the London Season as they have done?' Jennie asked not expecting Roger to reply.

'Look, Jennie, we've never met Rick Austen but Claire always unwinds when she talks about him. Thankfully he doesn't know of Claire's history with Harry Stone, but the whole lot could be coming back to haunt her and she could be walking into deep trouble.'

'Claire's still fragile from the last dodgy deal that your mate Harry Stone got up to a couple of years ago. I seem to remember he was chasing pubs in Brighton at a price he should have known was fake,' Jennie said. She knew Claire's history and she did not want to talk about it today.

'I agree Claire's shaky after what she went through. But she's already told you where she's going to do some more work for Rick Austen.'

'Down in the West Country. Blake Markets, a supermarket business,' Jennie replied.

'Well, listen to this. Harry Stone has got himself into a money laundering scheme. And the point of going to Monte Carlo was to entice one of Harry's mates, a man called Martyn Blake, to pass the cash through his business. And that's the same business that Rick has asked Claire to look at. It's a very nasty coincidence.'

'Claire will go and do what she needs and then come back, that sounds simple to me,' Jennie said.

'Claire's going to be walking into something bad down there if she's not careful. Claire will have no idea that Harry Stone is going to pass a lump of stolen cash into the same business Rick's invested in, that's what. If this money laundering scam of Stone's is ever found out, everybody dealing with it or even close to it could be in trouble. That includes someone like Claire, innocently handling the stuff on the edge.'

'I'll talk to Claire to let her know before it's too late,' Jennie said.

'Be careful, Claire can't walk away now. She can't go to Rick and tell him she knows Harry Stone who's about to launder a lot of cash through a business Rick has bought into.'

Jennie sipped her gin and tonic slowly. She saw the coincidence that had led to Harry Stone and Rick Austen both dabbling in the same business. It heightened Jennie's concern as to where that would leave Claire.

12

It was half past six in the morning. Stone swore as he put down a mug of coffee heavily and spilt some over the table top. He smudged the dirty marks as he wiped them quickly with his hand and looked at Dave. Dave was one of the few people that Stone would trust and today he was smart, out of his building-site clothes and he looked ready to complete the simple job that Stone was now giving him.

How much was in the brown briefcase stuffed with used notes Stone could no longer be sure of and as he gave it to Dave he said nothing. The notes, bound in red elastic bands, would be added up again and all paid into Blake Markets' bank. If it was fifteen thousand short Martyn would soon find out. But at that time Stone could not find Martyn to tell him or to make sure that Dave's journey to Ferry Cove Smugglers Inn would not be wasted.

'This isn't my job, boss, I don't want to be dragged into Xavier's nasty web, and I want your promise you'll keep me clean if it blows up,' Dave protested as he took the case.

'You'd got your feet up on the table at the site yesterday and you looked as dead as the place you're supposed to be building for me. Until you get Sudbury moving again, this little trip'll keep you busy. So don't whinge before you've started the day,' Stone said.

'You'd better know Xavier's been rooting around the site looking for anything valuable to cart away. But I cleared him off, I stopped him taking a whole load of power tools and a couple of pneumatic drills, all valuable stuff, but he'll be back. You see.'

'Get today right first and then we'll start Sudbury running again. I want to see this lot gone from my doorstep,' Stone said.

'Xavier'll want to know exactly where this cash is being dealt, so he'll be calling, boss,' Dave said.

'My mate Martyn's expecting you after eleven this morning,' Stone said. He passed Martyn's mobile number to Dave with the postcode of the Ferry Cove Smugglers Inn for his satnav that Martyn had texted.

Stone's fuse was getting short again, he had heard enough. He pushed Dave out from the Regency mansion by the back door. It was still early in the morning and the small lane behind the house was empty, but Dave drove slowly onto the main road. He had seen up front the methods of extortion that Xavier and his wasters of druggies, layabouts and real-time criminals applied. He was now running their cash and, if it went wrong, it could drag him right into the middle of something nasty. It was then that he shuddered at the thought of his visit to Xavier's dingy East End squat with mad barking dogs.

Dave had not driven a long distance in his battered and rusting Range Rover for a while. His vehicle was noisy, heavy on his shoulders and driving fast on the motorway he had a growing headache from tension. It was making his eyes water. He glanced at the briefcase many times and he squinted in his rear-view mirror for anyone following. But he saw nobody, and three hours later he relaxed more easily and his hunched shoulders dropped as he drove down the narrow lane that led into the car park of the Ferry Cove Smugglers Inn just before eleven.

It was secluded, standing on its own and it overlooked the breakers noisily moving in from the Atlantic. Dave switched off the car radio to let in the moodiness of the place for a moment as he stretched and yawned. He had never visited this part of the rugged and green north coast that led from Bristol to the westerly tip of Cornwall and as he watched the sea beyond it was momentarily more enticing to him than the scrubbiness of the site at Sudbury. He wiped his eyes with his handkerchief and wondered why he had agreed to come here.

He threw his peaked cap and sunglasses onto the seat, breathed in heavily, brushed his hair back with his hand, and quickly set the car alarm. With the briefcase hidden out of sight under the passenger seat Dave slammed and then locked the car door. There were just two other cars but no people around and Dave stood still for a few seconds to be sure he was really on his own. It was right on time as he ambled towards the secluded pub.

The dimness of the low-ceilinged bar contrasted with the light outside and as he entered he felt uncomfortable. He was going to hand over a quarter of a million pounds to someone he had never met and he blinked. This place was different to the pubs he knew, there was no etched glass on the windows, and he lowered his sweating forehead to miss a beam as he walked in.

A lady in her late forties but looking some years older, with streaked, elegantly coiffured blonde hair and a round, high-cheeked face, was sitting alone in a corner, a small glass of orange juice on the table in front of her. She was the only person in the bar and she looked at Dave closely. He went to the bar to buy himself a pint and then he sat, looked at his phone for any messages, and sipped his beer noisily. But the lady was unsure, he was not carrying a briefcase full of cash so this was not Harry, Martyn's mate.

And Dave looked at his watch. Where was Martyn? he wondered. Dave stood to take some fresh air outside with his pint but the lady called to him across the empty bar.

'Are you Harry, Martyn Blake's mate?' she asked sounding foolish at the flimsy question.

'Who are you?' Dave called back.

'I'm Gina. Martyn couldn't get here and he asked me to meet you. You've brought something for him.'

'I'm not Harry but where's Martyn?' Dave snapped as he sat heavily on the high backed settle beside her.

'If you're not Harry who are you?'

'It doesn't matter who I am. Where's Martyn?'

'Martyn's at home. Not feeling too good, he tells me he has a cold,' Gina said easily.

'What? A cold in the summer?'

'I don't know, that's all he told me. Does it matter?' Gina replied.

'I'm not giving you anything. Martyn's got to be here. I'll call him.'

'Okay,' Gina said. 'That's all right by me, but if he doesn't answer we'll both go and get on with something else.'

Gina moved to the edge of her seat and stared at Dave. He flicked on his phone and called Martyn's number. It rang for a minute with no voicemail and, staring back at Gina, in frustration Dave flicked it off.

'Take me to his house. I need to find him.'

'No. He won't be there. You leave it to me. I can deal with it, I'm the one who handles all this stuff at Blake Markets, nobody else,' Gina said sharply.

'Okay, so what did Martyn tell you about meeting today? What instructions did he give you?'

'You've got to give me a packet that's got some cash in it. Martyn said it's a loan he's arranged from Harry, a mate of his, to tide the supermarkets over for a few weeks. But who are you? Are you another of Martyn's mates?' Gina persisted.

'I've never met Martyn so stop quizzing me,' Dave replied but trying to be evasive.

'How much cash have you brought?'

'A quarter of a million. Okay? Is that right?'

'If that's what Martyn told you, yes okay. Where did you get all this cash? Is it yours?'

'No it's not mine, my fingers aren't on it. Martyn's asked for it and I'm bringing the lot down here for him. I don't know any more,' Dave said quickly.

'So are you now satisfied I'm not here to thieve the lot of lousy cash and run away?'

Dave was becoming irritated at what he had found after a long drive. But he had heard enough, he did not feel that this lady was right and he walked quickly to the low door. Once in the car park he made a call to Harry Stone. But he only spoke with his boss for less than a minute and the instructions were simple. If Martyn had sent someone to collect the cash then that was how it was. Get rid of the stuff in the place Martyn had agreed and ask questions later.

'Want another drink?' Dave asked when he came back into the bar.

'No, thank you.'

Gina's face was blank with no smile as Dave took two minutes to get himself a half of beer and with an audible sigh sat with Gina on the high-backed settle.

'You sound a bit uptight, lady. What goes?' Dave asked.

'Meeting a man I don't know in a pub and collecting a quarter of a million in notes is not something I do every day, that's what. And I'm very busy and don't have time to spare for all this shady stuff that seems to be what you're at.' Gina's mouth sagged and her usual easy smile was absent from her round face.

The bar was still empty, too early for lunchers or drinkers and Dave fidgeted on the wooden seat, unsure how he should now deal with Gina. This meeting was not right, he knew money was more important to Xavier than the white narcotic powder he controlled with his ring of dealers, and if cash went missing they did not ask questions. They got physical, they inflicted stab wounds with knives or even machetes and they would demand to know of the hidden pub by the sea where he had handed the case over.

'Has Martyn told you what the deal is with this money?' Dave asked.

'The more I hear about it the more I don't like it. It's dodgy, I don't get involved in anything that's not right down the line so it's

Martyn's deal, not mine. Just don't tell me anything more about it because I'm not listening.'

'Okay so, yeh, we'll leave it at that. It's your problem now but be careful how safe you keep this cash when it's swilling around. Okay, lady?' Dave asked.

The pub was filling with a noisy group of walkers in for a rest and a pint. Dave was getting jittery, this was no place to linger, he stared at Gina and he saw her cheeks were flushing pink with nervousness.

'Come outside and I'll give you the case,' Dave said.

Gina picked up her handbag from the low table and, without looking around at the walkers, followed Dave from the pub. She had heard enough, wherever Martyn was hiding he would have to come out and get on with this charade himself. She was walking out of it and once in the car park she turned to face Dave.

'Is this how you earn a living, handing out dodgy cash?' she asked.

'Shut it,' Dave replied.

Dave looked away. He did not like to have his honesty probed and he now had a throbbing in his head. It was time to get away from this place, back to the mud of the building site at Sudbury, and he pushed past a group of walkers mingling in the yard. Some hikers were milling around and admiring a gleaming BMW with its hood down that had parked close to his rusting 4x4 and Dave stood back. He gently held Gina's arm.

'There's no going back now,' he said in a low voice. 'Get it paid in, like, quick. Simple as that, because I don't want you to get into trouble. So look after yourself.'

'Yes, I'll do that but you tell Harry whoever he is that you've handed the parcel over and I'm giving it straight to Martyn when I find him. And tell him I've not counted the cash so it's on trust that you've given me a quarter million in notes,' Gina said.

'Get Martyn to call me when you find him. Agreed?'

Dave wrote his mobile number on a crumpled scrap of paper

from his pocket and gave it to Gina. The gang of walkers had moved away from staring at the standout BMW but Dave was still wary of being watched. He flicked the passenger door of his rusting Range Rover open and grabbed the brown briefcase from under the seat. He walked the few paces to Gina's car, waited for her to catch up and without meeting her eye placed the briefcase with a hard thud on the bonnet.

'It's yours now, lady. Get Martyn hauled out of bed or wherever he is, because his mate Harry'll want to know how it's going.'

There were no goodbyes. The wind blew Dave in a gust as he walked back to his car and he did not see the tears in Gina's eyes. In his car he sat still for a moment and as he put his golf cap firmly on his head and his sunglasses on his nose he decided this was a number one stupid place to come to with a quarter of a million in used notes. Martyn's summer cold did not sound right, and why was this lady shielding Martyn from the meeting at the pub? Dave knew how these things worked, where lies always showed up. So who was Gina? She looked too fragile to deal with a quarter million in nasty paper money, owned by ruthless crooks like Xavier and his racketeers. Dave suddenly felt that this morning he was doing something wrong. Yes, Dave felt truly sorry for Gina.

The car park was filling and Dave did not look back to see Gina fumbling with the case as she unlocked her car. His ageing Range Rover gave out a cloud of black smoke as Dave left. He drove fast along the narrow winding lane with high hedges that led away from this isolated pub to the motorway.

The day was now hot and humid, his old car becoming very heavy to drive. The air conditioning had long since ceased to work and hunched over the wheel in slowing traffic Dave was becoming more uneasy. This deal was all wrong. The traffic was slowing to a stop-start crawl and Dave called Martyn on his hands-free. It was just something to do, it would pass an irritating few minutes tailing at snail's pace the red lights of the car in front on the gridlocked motorway. Martyn's phone purred for at least a minute with no response, not even going to voicemail. Dave tried to sit upright in his car seat but it made his back sweat freely as he held the steering wheel.

With growing frustration at the crawling traffic, as he passed Heathrow Airport, Dave pulled into a service station. He parked at the top end of the wide expanse of places, rested his head on the backrest and closed his eyes just for a few moments to relieve the ache building in his back and neck. A minute later he left the car, removed his cap and blinked in the sun as he walked to the services shops.

With no warning a flashy blue coupe with its hood down drove very close to him and almost in one movement the car was parked and its engine turned off. A few people stopped and turned to register their disapproval at what they thought was the excessive speed of this vehicle in a motorway car park. And Dave too turned to stare at the driver. Within a few seconds the unmistakeable large body of Boozy emerged showing his weight, suddenly looking even bigger than he ever did on the Sudbury site. Boozy walked towards Dave with a mocking smile.

'Hello, Dave, are you doing something for our friend Harry?'

Dave's surprise at seeing Boozy quickly turned to anger.

'What're you doing here?' he shouted.

'Same question to you, Dave!' Boozy shouted into the air, not even looking at Dave.

'What I do is none of your business,' Dave said.

Boozy was oblivious to a family who had just parked close by and who were all now staring hard at him with contempt. This man was showing off and nobody liked that.

'No, Dave, that ain't how it works no more. Me and my mate Xavier, we need to know what you're up to, where you go and what you do for Harry. A quarter million on loan's gotta be safe,' Boozy said with a jeering laugh.

'You haven't been following me all day?' Dave suddenly exploded. Did he recognise Boozy's car as the one in the car park at the Ferry Cove Smugglers Inn that attracted attention from the hikers?

'None of your business where I've been.'

'Why aren't you on the site?'

'Nothing doing there, mate, and 'sides, I got other things to do till your mister comes round with the cash.'

'You watch it. Harry'll get you before this is finished!' Dave shouted. More heads turned to see what was going on and at that moment Dave was not sure why he was defending Harry Stone. That man had picked this fight himself.

'You sound a bit screwed up, matey, so calm it and listen to me. Your man Harry's got a large pad at the end of the motorway, we all know where he hangs out so he can't run off and hide.' Boozy was in full flow and he even sounded eloquent but, as Dave turned away to leave, Boozy put his hand heavily on his shoulder and spun him round.

'You stay right there. We're gonna talk. We've got a tail on you, we know you had to come back this way sometime. Mr Xavier wants to know where you're floating all his cash, we gotta know it's safe and not being spent unwisely. After all, a quarter million's a big pot to have for a scheming bloke like your mister. And I hear he spends loads on private jets going off to fancy places in the sun.'

'Whatever you're up to, Boozy, just get out of my way,' Dave shouted.

Boozy towered closer and Dave, for the first time since he had known this man, smelt his stale tobacco breath. He went to remove the grip on his shoulder but Boozy's hand suddenly squeezed close to his neck as if it was a garrotte. Dave for a moment was helpless, he was the one who gave people like Boozy instructions but today it was different. It could get ugly with people watching and Dave could see Boozy was under the influence of something nasty. Dave wanted away and his hit was barely a tap against the stained sweatshirt covering Boozy's wide belly. But it was enough to make Boozy react fast, he released his grip on Dave's shoulder, spun him round and gave a heavy slap to Dave's face. Dave felt it sting and his eyes watered. He let out a noise but it was muffled by Boozy's arm across his mouth. For a moment Dave was stunned. Its suddenness, with the gathering crowd gawping, left Dave with a feeling of nakedness in that wide-open concrete space.

'We're watching so don't play funny. Okay, mate? Oh, and one thing I nearly forgot. Remind Harry that he's got to get a jet to the Caribbean just as Mr Xavier told him. Let him know it's urgent.'

Boozy started his car engine with as much noise as he could make from pushing the pedal. He waved a large fist from the window as he left the car park at speed. The mingling crowd of onlookers gradually walked away from a road-rage tiff coming from the drivers of an eye-catching soft top and a battered old 4x4. It was just a heated argument that had only lasted a few minutes. But more would have stopped to stare had they known a quarter of a million pounds in laundered cash stood between them.

Dave walked quickly to the services entrance, rubbing his cheek, which now tingled. In the restroom Dave splashed water from the tap over his face and looked at himself briefly in the mirror. This deal was madness and he felt angry at what Harry Stone had asked him to do today.

Just over an hour later Dave drove into Stone's garage, his temper boiling. He walked to the back door, the dingy back entrance to Stone's imposing mansion. He wiped his watery eyes, and without knocking he walked into the kitchen. He was met by Harry Stone, a glass of whisky in his hand. Stone gave no greeting as he looked at Dave who pulled out a chair to sit at the kitchen table. Dave thumped his wide fist onto the table top and swung back in his seat.

'I want out from this money dealing, Mr Stone. The cash's gone, gave it to a lady called Gina. Don't know where she is now, she could be cruising in the Caribbean for all I know. And I called your mate Martyn three times and it was no go with him. He's gone, it's all very loose, untidy, all left in the air, and if that madman Xavier gets on to it again, well I don't want to be here,' Dave said.

'Martyn sent this woman, you've handed it over, so leave it, that's all.'

'Yeh, but on the way back I got slapped in the face by that man Boozy from the Sudbury site. Waving his trowel probably high on skunk. Remember him?' Dave replied testily.

Stone looked away and started pacing around the large kitchen. Jo had smelled one of the thugs as he sat next to her in a dark concrete car park, a hooded man had been asking Jo about the cash right inside this kitchen and it told Stone this squeeze was getting tighter.

'Leave it, Dave, the cash is now Martyn's problem, not mine.'

'No, sir, it don't work like that. It stays your problem until every penny's back in the hands of Xavier and his mob. And that's a quarter of a million pounds.

Stone ran his hand through his hair. Without saying anything to Dave, Stone walked to the study. Dave followed just in time to see Stone grab the whisky bottle and pour himself a large measure. He then slumped into a chair at his desk and stared at Dave.

'You're not finished yet. There's something else you've gotta do for me,' Stone said.

'What're you talking about?'

'That case of cash you took to Ferry Cove Smugglers was fifteen grand short of a quarter million. Xavier's trying to short change me and he's got to know, like quick. I want the fifteen grand repaid to me, like now,' Stone said and closed his eyes.

13

Gina was unsure about Dave. Who was he? His roughness was no more than a thin veneer and underneath there would be a calculating ruthlessness that he would have shown had she not taken the cash. He was driving a rust heap of a car, not the man she had been told by Martyn to meet. As she watched him leave the isolated car park she had a feeling of despair. What was happening?

Gina was confused, she did not know how to deal with a meeting like this and, on the bonnet of her car where Dave had left it, she snapped open the briefcase. The wind gusted, she felt the case move and she hurriedly closed it without looking at the bundles of money. Was this cash just a loan as Martyn had told her, a loan to keep the bank away for a few weeks or did it already smell of something very nasty, secretive, something that Martyn did not want to handle. Gina was tense; she felt very alone.

She walked to the edge of the car park and watched the large breakers on the sea with white foam thunder onto the rocky coastline. For a few moments she looked mesmerised out to the far horizon heavily covered in cloud. She wanted away from this lunacy that Martyn had led her to. The walkers had left the car park for the pub and, alone, Gina felt a strong urge to toss the caseload of cash over the cliff. That would be the end of it. The bundles of dishonest cash consumed by the waves with the bad money never to be found again. That simple act would distance her from being part of Martyn's senseless scheme even before it started.

It was an enticing thought, but it was a wild thought. It was beyond Gina's character to chuck any money away just like that. Inevitably, reality now drove an impulse to hang onto the case. But if it did not land in the foaming sea, the cash would have to be dealt with, and with Martyn hiding, that would be her job. Gina did not want that and where was Martyn? What was keeping him away from dealing with his mates? Gina was becoming overwhelmed by this thought.

Gina returned to her car, threw the case onto the back seat as if it was a shopping bag, and she drove through the narrow but familiar back lanes for the ten miles to Martyn's house. The world of Blake Markets now had the smell of being lawless with all that that would bring. The only way for Gina was to step back; it was Martyn's contract with a mate and it was now his alone to clear into the bank.

But Gina was perplexed. Handling dodgy money was never Martyn's way of doing business. The most he would do was to come to ask for more twenty-pound notes. He liked to put them in his wallet for a visit to the pub, a haircut or paying the village blacksmith who ran a book on the horses at Newmarket. But he kept the funny stuff away. He was basic, down to earth, known as 'the Guv' to those who worked around him. With his broad Yorkshire accent, he would always poke fun at anything not quite straight up. Martyn gave fools the sharp edge of his tongue. But did he know who was really behind this load of cash? Did he know who this man called Harry was? Or did he just not care anymore?

As she drove slowly along the back roads Gina regained her poise and her frustration turned to anger at what Martyn had asked her to do this morning. Sure, Martyn would know where this lot had come from, sure, he would know they were hot, tainted, lethal bundles of cash. But did he know how many innocent people had been badly dealt with on their way to her desk? No, Martyn had closed his eyes to it and Martyn did not care anymore. He had disappeared as if he wanted to shut the door on Blake Markets. And Gina was now going to confront Martyn with that after she had thrown this load of cash at him.

Everything Gina did was methodical, expecting all in her world, just like herself, to be neat, tidy and, above all, certain. She took the supermarket business as it came, she never got ruffled by the daily pressure of organising other people to do the work of keeping everything in order as she wanted it. Gina felt hot as she drove past her own cottage in a village close to Blake Markets and turned off into a long driveway that led to Martyn's house.

It was a late-Victorian red-brick building with large rambling gardens surrounding the place. As Gina swung her car across the loose gravel that bordered one side of the garden of Martyn's house, she waved to Ken, the Scottish handyman who kept the lawns mowed and the borders clear of weeds. This place was trim, well kept, but it was still ordinary and Gina stopped for a moment; why should this offensive case of cash interrupt this tranquil place?

Briefcase in hand, Gina knocked on the back door ready to throw it all back at Martyn. The door was ajar, she pushed it open and walked in. The house was quiet, peaceful and cool from the summer sun. Gina went to the kitchen, threw the briefcase onto the edge of a cluttered table. She called for Sandy, Martyn's wife, a lady she knew well, but there was no reply. She sighed heavily with despair and at that fleeting moment again wanted to return to the pub by the sea and toss Harry's case with the poisoned cash over the cliff edge.

'Martyn!' Gina suddenly bellowed at the top of her voice. Her scream loosened her jaw and released growing tension. But her voice echoed against the high ceiling. She waited a short moment and there was no reply. Somehow she did not expect one. But where was Martyn? He had left yesterday morning to 'visit', his word for calling in on a site unannounced, and for the third time in the last few hours Gina picked up her mobile and called his number.

Voicemail clicked in ten seconds later. She flicked it off and stuffed the phone back into her bag with a deep sigh.

Gina grabbed the briefcase from the table and although she never broke into a run these days her walk to the back door was as close to a trot as she ever went.

'I know Sandy's at a village meeting but do you know where Martyn is?' she asked.

'No, Gina, I haven't seen the Guv since yesterday morning nor his car in the yard. But that's not unusual for me,' Ken said.

'Please keep watch and let me know if Martyn comes. And get him to call me please,' Gina said, more as something to say than expecting it to happen.

She slammed the side door of the house with a satisfying thud and in an unusual rush, propelled by a strong feeling of helplessness, she left for her office. At that moment Gina was not sure what she was going to do. She did not want the briefcase from Dave anywhere near her for much longer. She would now leave it where it belonged, hidden in her office waiting for Martyn to collect it.

Half an hour later, her cheeks flushed pink from rushing and growing tension, Gina walked quickly into her office and she slowly closed her door to her own small working space. After this morning she wanted it to be private and quiet. There was only a small window high in the wall to give natural light and a computer screen blinked blindly but quietly in a corner. This box-sized space was just a few yards away from a room full of people. They were people who dealt with all the numbers for Blake Markets. Sitting alone Gina now knew for sure that keeping Martyn's rotten deal secret was not going to be easy. There were just too many bits of paper to hide from too many people.

Isolated and flustered, but driven by her curiosity, Gina opened the case. What would a quarter million in used black economy notes look like? She placed the briefcase on her desk and, with her hands trembling, clicked it open. She took a bunch of dirty and creased twenty-pound notes from the top of a pile. The Post-it notes that Jo had put on each wad were still there but Gina removed the red elastic band. The folded edges of the paper notes, told her that many times they had been very quickly and roughly handled. Her curiosity was quickly settled; whatever dark, corrupt money was in the case it looked no different to real everyday cash. Gina slowly replaced the bundle into the case.

She stared at the shabby, dog-eared mess that now confronted her, that once again made her want to scream out to Martyn. He'd got to clear this trash into the bank himself or send it back to Harry, his mate. She put her head in her hands in despair. Martyn was never going to count these random bundles of cash, he would never even get to touch them, he had just left it all to her. The money was to help Blake Markets' bank account from running dry. That was what Martyn had said, but seeing the paper money in front of her Gina now knew that was a big lie.

It was quiet in the small space of her room and she started to count one of the bundles of notes. It did not take her long to see that it agreed with the number that had been written on the Post-it note stuck to the top. Gina looked at all the numbers written on the yellow slips of paper on each bundle and handling them deftly she quickly added them up on her calculator. Her total came to £235,000 and that was definitely not a quarter of a million. She started again but it still came to the same figure. It was short by exactly £15,000. Gina was incensed; she felt betrayed, taken as a fool and her impulse was now to get the lot out of her sight. She did not care anymore. She was very alone.

These bundles of cash had a venomous feel and she decided her only way out was to pay the money, whatever it came to, into the accounts of Blake Markets. She would now do that as quickly as she could. Then she would go, close her office door, wash her hands and feel clean again before it dragged her down.

With a few deft key movements, Gina completed a form for the bank input. She was going to split the cash over three accounts just as Martyn had said and the first one was to be the special private business account. She knew her decision to start paying the money into Blake Markets' bank was a line from which, once crossed, there could be no going back. But Gina controlled the thought, she knew exactly what she was doing and she swore to herself that this was the end, this would get rid of it.

But for a moment Gina hesitated. In a quick movement she called Martyn by pressing a button on a direct-dial phone. Gina wanted him here, sitting right next to her. She wanted him to feel this bootleg deal close up and to handle some of this tainted money as she had that morning. Gina wanted him here to tell him he had been short-changed by £15,000, and… Gina just wanted Martyn here to let him see this charade was all real. She sobbed quietly as she listened to the ring tone as it filled the quietness of her room. It rang for a minute before Gina flicked it to stop.

The special private business account was controlled by only Gina and Martyn. It was secreted away from all her assistants sitting outside her room. It was a good place to start as Martyn paid school fees and holidays and lots of other personal things from this special account. It was settled up at the end of the year, Martyn always grumbled that he had to pay too much, but it could not be hidden from the hard-noses at the bank.

Gina completed the form to list the value she was paying into the bank and added her pin code. With an adeptness that showed she had done this many times, Gina shuffled the first pile of twenties and tens, which came to £85,000. She pushed them to the side of her desk and felt better that she had started to clear the poisonous lot away. Gina completed the same task for the next batches of notes, which totalled £70,000. Somebody had counted these all before, it made her job very easy, she did not know who it was, but she now worked deftly and accurately. She placed the two bundles totalling £155,000 in a sealed bag to be taken to the bank by the regular security firm that called each day. In the outer office Gina placed the bag in the chute that took the cash down to a safe holding box. It would be collected an hour later. Gina's relief at getting some of this paper money away from her soon drained away. Now there was no going back.

The bunch of notes still to be dealt with were sprawled across her desk. She quickly counted the Post-it notes on them and they came to £80,000, as she expected. With what she had already paid in, that squared the total cash that had been in the briefcase to £235,000. That was not a quarter of a million. Satisfied with what she had cleared away from her desk, Gina decided that she would deal with the rest of the notes in the morning. At that time Martyn would be with her. But Gina was becoming very annoyed from the meeting with Dave at the Ferry Cove Smugglers pub. The case short by £15,000. The figures were not right, and it infuriated her long-held feeling of fairness. She called Dave.

'You did know, didn't you, that the money was fifteen thousand short?' Gina shouted into the phone.

'What are you saying?'

'I don't know how low you lot can stoop to do something as nasty as that. It's sly, deceitful and later I'll get Martyn to call his mate Harry to tell him what he thinks about you gang of thieves,' Gina shouted at the top of her voice.

'Hold on a minute, that's nothing to do with me,' Dave shouted back, surprised at the call.

Gina was feeling insulted at this deceitful way of planting a load of cash on her and she cut the call to Dave. Her breath was coming faster and her right hand trembled slightly as she hurriedly started to throw the remaining bundles of cash into the briefcase. She was startled as her door opened. A young woman she had never seen before, somebody who looked business-like, entered without hesitating.

'Can I come in?'

Flustered and feeling exposed, Gina nodded.

'Are you Claire? I thought you were coming tomorrow.'

'Yes. I had to be in the area today so I decided I would just call in to say hello and then come back to look at things in more detail with you tomorrow. Is it all right if I come in for a few minutes?'

'Yes, please do,' Gina said. She could see Claire staring at the bundles of notes on the desk.

'It sounded as if you were having an angry exchange on the phone so I hope I'm not interrupting anything,' Claire said.

Gina did not know how to reply, her shouting at Dave was private, as was this cash.

'You know how things are sometimes when somebody wants to argue with you,' Gina said and looked away. She had never met Claire before, what had happened today was still hurting, and Claire's unexpected presence was suddenly overwhelming. Gina was not sure how to deal with this visitor and, as Claire focused her smile across the desk towards Gina, Claire could see that her interruption was not welcome.

'This is Martyn's cash, money he's got from selling one of his precious cars and I'm just counting it up for him. But I do need to clear it quickly so it's not a security risk,' Gina found herself saying but she felt very guilty.

'That looks some pile,' Claire said, eyeing the open briefcase.

'I don't know why Martyn has to deal in notes like this, but it's what he gave me,' Gina replied.

'Isn't there some law that says dealing in cash over a certain amount by car dealers, estate agents, lawyers and a few other odd people has to be declared somewhere?' Claire asked.

'You might be right but you tell that to Martyn and see what answer you get,' Gina replied.

Gina was sure Claire's inquisitiveness about what happened at Blake Markets wouldn't work with Martyn; in his straightforward way he would tell Claire to run away and maybe that is what she should do now. But Claire continued to look at the bundles of notes with growing surprise which showed on her arched eyebrows.

'I hope you have no security problems here then,' Claire said.

'You've caught me at a bad time. I've got to be away in a minute to catch up with Martyn.'

Martyn selling a car was a myth, Gina knew that, but it sounded true as she put the last bundle of notes back in the briefcase. What else could she say after she had just met a man at a pub hidden on the coast and been asked to take this cash to wash it clean?

'Forgive me for barging in like this but you know why Rick has asked me to come. He'd like me to talk with you about Blake Markets' cash problem. I assume this money you've got there is nothing to do with the business.'

Claire remembered Martyn stalking away from Rick's office just a few days ago when he asked about cash and Claire moved as if she wanted to touch the briefcase on Gina's table. There was silence from Gina and she sat back in her chair, stared at the ceiling and then placed her hands heavily on her desk.

'Okay. It's like this. Martyn's done a deal with a mate of his who is lending Blake Markets a quarter million to tide us over a tight spot. It was all in paper money and I'm now paying it into the bank,' Gina said.

Claire saw Gina's unease in her deep frown and she sat down next to Gina's desk. The bundles of dirty notes looked unreal.

'Do you really mean he arranged a loan all in notes?' Claire asked.

Gina's forehead was perspiring and her hands were cold as she sat upright in her chair. She closed the lid on the remaining cash, and slid the case onto the floor. Gina was tense, and her head was throbbing.

'I'm only doing what Martyn has asked for. I don't like it, it's very dirty handling crumpled bits of paper like this. But I want to get rid of it all, I've already paid some of it into the bank and the sooner I get the rest away from here the better,' Gina said.

'Someone's brought you a quarter of a million in notes to your office here?' Claire asked.

'No. Martyn asked me to pick it up at one of the most out-of-the-way pubs you'll find in this place. I was given it just a few hours ago in the pub car park from a man I'd never met before. Martyn knows him but I've no idea where he comes from.'

Claire looked at the case of notes and then at Gina. Rick was astute, open in all his deals and he would not stand for floating, under-the-counter, cash. Claire wanted to know more.

'I ought to say hello to Martyn. Is he here?' Claire asked.

'No, I'm not sure where he is at the moment.'

'Do you know when Martyn arranged this? I'm not sure if he's told Rick.'

'All he told me was a mate of his called Harry offered him a lump of cash as a short-term loan. Short term means three weeks. The deal was we had to pay the cash in, then we'd receive an invoice for some building work to pay it out again. Sometime soon, in somebody else's hands, it ends up looking like good money, not just bits of dirty paper. That's the story anyway, that's what Martyn told me,' Gina said unsure if Claire would understand.

'Gina, please, this is real money laundering. I don't know about Martyn's mate but it's usually cash from crooks trying to use someone else's regular business to wash their cash in. Please be very careful. This could taint the business of Blake Markets, even get it closed down. I've seen it before and it'll also bring lots of shady people around,' Claire said.

'I didn't want to leave the cash lying around, I didn't like touching it, so I've dealt with most of it,' Gina said. Her voice was becoming hoarse, scared by all that had happened so quickly that day.

'How much have you paid in?'

'A hundred and fifty-five thousand. It's gone, it'll soon be in the security van on its way to the bank. This is such a mess. When I counted up all the grimy notes from the briefcase I was given, the money was fifteen thousand short of a quarter of a million so now I've only got eighty thousand left to clear,' Gina said.'

'Are you saying somebody's short-changed you in this supposed loan?'

'I've counted it all twice but that's what it looks like.'

'Martyn's putting you in the most dreadfully compromising position. You're not going to pay the rest of the cash into the bank until you've spoken to him, are you?'

'Martyn's out visiting the venues and I can't get him on his usual number,' Gina said and she bent down to pick up the closed briefcase. 'I don't want ever to see it again and I'll let Martyn know what I think about it all as soon as I see him.'

'I don't like this, Gina, and I don't think you do either,' Claire said.

'I'm going to shut the case away in our strong room, I can't deal with it anymore.' Gina's eyes were becoming watery. She had a feeling of guilt at what she had done and that was only paying some folded and creased paper banknotes into the bank. Her conscience troubled, she placed the case heavily on her desk.

'Should we take what's left to the police straight away?' Claire asked.

'No, that's Martyn's job. I'm not going to do it for him and he can tell them exactly what this is all about. He can tell them who his mates are, where the cash came from and what the deal was. But why have I been so stupid to let myself stoop so low as to go and collect this grubby cash from a pub car park?' Gina asked.

Claire did not respond but she looked at Gina's tired watery eyes. Feeling hot and flustered, Gina stood as if she was about to leave. It was enough to finish the conversation and, two minutes later, Claire left Gina's small office. Claire's short visit upset Gina, it made her feel guilty about Martyn's squalid plan that she had been dragged into it. She wanted to get away for a few hours to blot out all she had done from eleven this morning. And that meant blotting out handling tainted cash in the Ferry Cove Smugglers Inn car park. She drove to her cottage in the country as quickly as the winding lanes would let her.

In the small conservatory at the back of her house, Gina surveyed the green countryside and decided that if Martyn continued to hide from this deal she was going to walk out from Blake Markets with her hands clean. Going to the police, that definitely was Martyn's job and she was not going to do it for him.

But it made her stop as in the past couple of weeks she had unearthed what Martyn had really been doing. Now was the time he should be confronted with it. Gina had slowly come to understand why he had kept away out of sight from her. Martyn had used fake invoices to take cash from the business. The amount he had siphoned off came to a very large figure, he had been clever to hide what he was doing, and he must have known that a three-week loan would only be lost if it was ever paid into Blake Markets' bank. But what was Martyn really hiding that he had to commit a fraud on his own business for money? Gina sat in a chair and stared into the garden for a few minutes. Uncertainty was surrounding her.

***

As Claire reached her car she too sat still for a moment. Claire had only called in to Gina as she had time to spare after starting her house search for Rick in the area around Bath. She had only met Martyn once when he had stalked out from Rick's office after only staying for a few minutes. Then she had not been sure what to make of him. *But what was really happening here?* she asked herself. If this cash had been planted in Blake Markets to be laundered, it would leave a tainted trail that would be hard to cover. And at that time, if Claire had known it was Harry Stone, Martyn's mate, trying to launder a large lump of grubby notes through the business of Blake Markets, she would have been very wary. She would have alerted Gina to be on guard for her own safety and she would have called the police straight away.

Claire thumbed through some property details she had left on the back seat of her car. She had kept her house search for Rick along the route west of London and so far she had been very disappointed at what she had seen where nothing matched her expectations of what a country house should offer. Perhaps she had underestimated what Rick would pay but with her disappointment growing she drove to the next property where she had an appointment to meet the agent and view the house.

As she expected, her house-viewing that afternoon left her in despair at the clutter in houses that vendors were presenting to be viewed and she easily compared it to the orderly tidiness she kept inside Arrow Hall. From the details of country houses she had so far had from agents, the choice was small, nothing that would excite her to give to Rick, and she made no more appointments to visit in that area.

After the viewing, she took the long drive back to London and she felt tired as she opened the door to her apartment. In her letter box there was an envelope which she opened and read the letter quickly. She stuffed it in her pocket and, at that moment, with Rick away, she felt low and upset. In her small sitting room she reread the letter and it hurt that a man she had helped with his business matters, keeping them clean and tidy for many years, could write with such stark threatening demands.

Panama bank accounts had always been Harry Stone's dark secret. Rereading Stone's letter she felt a sudden temptation to rip the Panama papers into tiny shreds and put them in the waste bin, never to be seen again. Her file, taken from the stable block, was lying with other papers waiting to be tidied up, but she quickly flicked their pages and then threw them onto the floor. She put Stone's letter in its envelope and placed it with the Panama bank codes. Claire would deal with Harry Stone later in her own way.

In the small bedroom of her Knightsbridge flat Claire started to pack a few clothes and personal items, all ready for the move into Rick's penthouse apartment. She had photos of her mum and dad, which she had positioned on a window ledge of her kitchen and bedroom. Both were now deceased but she missed them as close friends and advisors who had always been willing to listen when she was undecided about something. She had often spoken to them about Harry Stone but they had wisely kept their distance from him.

As she placed the photos in a large box, Claire again felt misgivings about leaving this place. She had found it to be a haven of quiet when she needed time to herself and Harry Stone's letter added to her nagging thoughts that Rick would one day soon find out about that man and Arrow Hall. And if he did find out about her past and what she had done for him just two years ago what would Rick do? She did not know. In the early evening Claire took a call from Jennie and she was eager for a time to stop her packing.

'Thanks for lunch last week, are you calling to make a date for next week?' Claire asked quickly.

'You're the busy one so it's your call,' Jennie said.

'I'm packing a few things before moving into Rick's apartment. I've been down to the West Country today for Rick and I think something funny is going on just as Rick had thought,' Claire said.

'Well, listen, Claire, I've got something from Roger to tell you about your visit. It's Blake Markets you're looking at isn't it?'

'Yes. But how does Roger know about Blake Markets?'

'Be careful. Roger has been away with Harry Stone and, would you believe it, also with the man who owns Blake Markets. Couple of days ago they went on a boys' jolly, private jet and all, down to Monte Carlo. But that's not all. Roger has learnt that Harry Stone's like a blunderbuss trying to get his mate to work cash through the supermarkets.'

There was silence for a moment as Jennie finished and just the name of Harry Stone made Claire shudder.

'Am I hearing right, Jennie? What I'm doing for Rick will get caught up in Harry Stone's web?'

'Coincidence, call it what you like but that's what it adds up to.

And Roger says to be very careful when you're there. Just don't get caught in Stone's scheme,' Jennie said.

'This is money laundering, That's what they're doing.'

'Run away from it, is Roger's advice.'

'I can't do that. I'd have to tell Rick about Harry Stone. Jennie, that man is haunting me, wherever I go, whatever I do, he's there,' Claire said.

'Can't you tell Rick this is a job you just don't want to do? He'd surely understand that,' Jennie said.

'No, I've already called down there and in a few days, I'm going back,' Claire said.

'This time it sounds like something ominous is going on down there.'

'Harry Stone's sent me a letter,' Claire said.

'Do you want to tell me?' Jennie coaxed.

'It's very threatening. Blackmail at its worst. Unless I give him access to his long-lost cash, his pile in Panama, he's going to run to Rick. And he's going to tell him a made-up story about Arrow Hall and how I found my way into Rick's office two years ago.'

'He's just trying to frighten you. You've got what he needs and you hang onto it and let Stone squirm,' Jennie said.

'Of course I'm not giving in to him, I would never do that.'

There was a pause. For a moment Claire's uncertainty that she should leave this small apartment hit her again. Her future could unravel.

'When shall we have that lunch next week?' Claire asked.

It took Claire and Jennie five minutes to work their diaries for next week but when she put the phone down Claire sat on the sofa and she thought of Gina. There was something sinister going on and Gina was now being put into the middle of a nasty deal from Harry Stone. She would visit again tomorrow and she would be careful.

Rick's call from France an hour later left her feeling doubtful that she was making the right move to leave her flat. Their conversation was short; it was mainly about the chateau and vineyard he was viewing in Bordeaux and he did not ask one question about what Claire was doing. After the call Claire read again the letter from Stone. It made her certain Stone would carry out his threat to get to Rick. But alone in her empty flat Claire could not forget the case of creased paper money she had seen in Gina's office.

14

Vlad left Brighton with a spring in his step but also with parking tickets from addresses all over London. They were places where his boss's Ferrari had been left with no worry about how big the parking fine would be when it overran its time. Stone had shown Vlad the detail on the tickets and Vlad had looked vacantly as if he did not understand. But this was a job Vlad would enjoy, he could see London, a place he liked and he could be on his own away from Harry Stone for a few days.

But it was raining, Vlad was wet and cold and he soon saw what a big job this would be. After two calls on side roads outside Harrods in Kensington, Vlad saw nothing that could lead to the Ferrari so he took the underground, to a parking lot at St Katherine's Dock. It was just a five-minute walk to the iconic Tower of London. Having seen the bald, shaven face of Xavier and slashed his van tyre, Vlad's instinct was that the most likely place would be in the maze of streets that make up the East End. Around the Tower of London it was busy, it was summertime and tourists swarmed everywhere. Vlad looked at the ticket and it had been issued exactly a week ago at ten in the morning. Vlad cast his eye around, he walked around the dock area but saw nothing, just ordinary, inconspicuous traffic, boats and people.

He walked back to the Underground station by the Tower of

London and took a train to Bromley-by-Bow where he looked hard at the next ticket. This was a less sophisticated part of town, less developed, but he found the spot where the ticket had been issued. It was off-street parking and he wandered down a side road that led into a cul-de-sac. Cars and vans were parked close together and at the end there was a small covered garage with no sign but with three cars lining the road all in a different state of being taken apart. These cars had not moved for some time but under cover in the decrepit run-down garage building he suddenly saw a bright red car covered in a thick layer of dust. The size and sleek lines of this car stood starkly against the oil-strewn floor littered with paper and plastic cups. The place was empty of anyone working there. Vlad walked in slowly and he stared at the number plate. It was the Ferrari. The car stood to the back of the garage and Vlad fingered in his pocket the duplicate key he had brought with him.

Vlad strolled on to the end of the short road, bordered by once-elegant Victorian town houses, it was very quiet with no moving traffic or people walking. He sauntered back to the garage; it was sparse, it was empty and Vlad saw his chance. He looked carefully around and walked quietly into the repair shop. The Ferrari was facing inwards and parked up close to the wall of the building and he was going to have to back it out if he was to get away with it.

Making only a small sound as he opened the driver's door he sat still in the seat for ten seconds listening. He placed the key in the ignition and wiped a smear of dust across his vision on the windscreen, aware that his next step would awaken the whole street when he started the booming engine. He closed the driver's door by tugging the handle until it shut with just a click and without the normal satisfying slam. He fingered a knife in his pocket he had brought with him remembering the scrubby car park at Birling Gap, and he started the engine. The place was still empty; he cautiously pulled the gear lever into reverse and slowly backed the car from this enclosed space.

There was the sudden noise of a landline phone ringing in a

glassed-off space further down the building and he moved the car more quickly. He heard footsteps coming from behind and in one move he put his foot down and swung the steering wheel until with the roar from the power of the engine he reversed to the road. He did not hear the voice shouting at full pitch but he briefly saw a face as the rear of the car hit a black man who spun away and collapsed against a wall of the building. Vlad did not know if he had caused serious injury with a thump that felt hard and he was not going to stay to find out.

On the road, Vlad was ready to leave the narrow cul-de-sac when for a moment an approaching green van blocked the exit. But Vlad saw a space, very tight for a wide car but he had to keep moving. At a reckless speed for such a narrow enclosed road, Vlad squeezed the Ferrari past the green van which had now stopped and he heard the noise of a searing scrape on the back wing of a parked car, long abandoned for its spare parts. Without thinking, Vlad drove at speed up a side road until he came to the High Street and then pointed the car to take an eastern route which was signed to a motorway. Frequent stares in his rear-view mirror made him think he had got away, he would soon find the motorway back to Brighton and no car was going to beat him for speed on that journey.

There was a clear ping from the instrument cluster with a small icon of a petrol pump. It showed that he was now very low on fuel and he would soon have to stop to fill the thing up. Vlad swore to himself, he was not far enough away to be safe from the green van and he had left somebody injured on the ground. On his offside he could see the lights of a garage a hundred yards down the road and with thin traffic coming towards him he drew across and went to the farthest pump from the road. He was not hidden but he was not openly on view. Within two minutes he yanked the hose from the car, it registered twelve pounds and thirty pence, he locked the cap and ran quickly to the kiosk. There was a woman in front but Vlad brushed her aside, slapped a twenty-pound note on the counter and shouted, 'Pump number eight, keep the change.' He was gone within a few seconds with a shout from the startled cashier. There was an agonising minute's wait before he could join the High Street traffic but Vlad settled on his eastward run until he came to a motorway. The route from there would be straightforward.

He called Stone on the hands-free.

'I've got the Ferrari, boss, I'm on the way to Brighton, I've done a bit of damage to someone who got in the way and they'll hunt me down. So when I get back can we hide your motor, sir?'

Stone was surprised at Vlad's quick success, he was in his study still having morose thoughts about where he had sent a quarter of a million in used notes. Where to put the Ferrari out of sight was not something he had yet given any time to. But he was alert quickly as if the car was an insect coming to bite him. The garage at Marine House would be the first place Xavier and his thugs would search and his mafia would soon be sniffing around again.

Stone quickly called Raven Garage. He had been made to pay their account right up and the memory of the girl standing next to the bonnet of his Porsche had not left him. But Stone pushed that aside, they had a storage shed on the northern edge of town where they would keep his valuable car secure and hidden. It momentarily lifted Stone from his anxiety about running a quarter of a million in notes through Martyn Blake's supermarkets.

In just ten minutes he had paid up front on his gold credit card for a month's rent for storage. He called Vlad back, gave the address of the garage's storage shed and at that moment Stone saw this snatch of his Ferrari as a major punch on the nose for Xavier.

***

The pile of envelopes and bills that Jo had were now sprawled over a corner of a low table in the sitting room, Stone could no longer avoid them. She had sorted them into junk mail and other envelopes and on top with a short note she had placed the parking tickets returned by Vlad. As he walked through the door he saw them and clumsily he tore each one in half and placed the paper into the open fireplace that was otherwise spotless from the cleaners who Jo had arranged just yesterday. That was the end of that irritant, Stone thought, and he cleared his plate, finished the rest of his Glenfiddich and suddenly gathered the remaining pile of envelopes. Without opening any of them, he wrapped the bundle in a padded envelope with a terse note requesting quick payment and addressed the whole lot to his accountant. And for Harry Stone that would leave him free of petty demands.

From a drawer in the kitchen he found a couple of stamps which he stuck on the parcel and he put on a light raincoat to walk the quarter mile along the seafront to a post box. There was an uncomfortable, damp, misty drizzle, but Stone felt better breathing the sea air, if only for half an hour. The parcel went easily into the red cast-iron post box that had adorned the side of the road since Victorian times.

After being splashed from a passing car that hit a roadside puddle, Stone crossed over to the sea where he could walk for a few hundred yards back to Marine House under the cover of kiosk awnings. Stone slowed his step to keep under a canopy as the drizzly rain increased in a sudden gust. In an instant there was a heavy hand holding him roughly by the thin lapels of his coat and it spun Stone round. In one move another heavy hand was threaded through his arm just as if he was being led out for a stroll. There were two hooded men, both taller than Stone, and they stood either side as they held him rigidly.

'Leave me alone, you trash!' he shouted, but his voice was feeble.

'We're taking you, mate, so shut up or you don't get to come back to your nice big warm house. Okay?'

Stone's hand was now behind his back and he was marched quickly along the pavement away from the direction of his house. He tripped but he was held upright and lifted from the ground like a marionette on strings. Rain was falling more heavily now, which had cleared most of the beachside of people. Stone was frightened, he felt the pain of his arm twisted high up his back, and he instantly thought of the malodorous Xavier who had forced him from his valuable car in a country lane. This time, though, he was being manhandled right on his own doorstep and there was no way he could move or shout for help. They passed a few strolling walkers who looked curiously but moved away quickly as this was not their problem. Three minutes later the two hoodlums dragging Stone between them reached the entrance to the pier.

It was lighter here and their feet thudded on the wooden boards as they moved quickly, past the entrance, past the funfair lit with hundreds of bulbs but at this time with few visitors, past the fish and chip restaurant that wafted a tasty aroma, until they reached the pier end. Stone knew where he was, he had been on this jetty many times but always in daylight when he wanted the taste of fresh sea air. This place was close to his big house on the seafront but the garish and flashy visitor offerings were a blunt contrast to the elegance of his home. Stone had often stood on the balcony of his Regency sitting room staring at the lights, feeling the attraction in their stark gaudiness. But his view now was blurred as his arm was twisted higher up his back.

There was a struggle as Stone tried to free himself and he flayed out with one free arm and leg, but they stopped at the railings that bordered the pier end and he stared out to the dark sea beyond him. He was heaved by his shoulders and legs as if he was a lump of wood that was about to be dumped into the sea but Stone's shout for help came out as no more than a squeal. His back rested on the iron railings, which ground into the bones of his shoulder. Below, he heard the water slurp and splash against the iron girders of the pier but it was all inky black, he could not see anything and he was frightened. These thugs were about to toss him away from their grip and down the thirty feet into the coldness below. There he would splash helplessly until he swallowed more water than he could…

A nightmare of nearly drowning had awoken Stone many

times and the waking had always happened before he was in the water. But in the darkness of this place it was now reality, it was different, he was already awake and a hooded face was speaking to him as his arms and legs were held with a pinching grasp against his struggle.

'How'd you like to go in and have a swim, Harry, mate?' a voice asked beneath a hood.

'Get me off here, you rats!'

Stone's shout drifted away unheard and in a mocking move he was pushed further away from the holding arms making it his turn to grab at the two men.

'Shall we toss him in, Cooky?' a hooded face asked.

'Yeah, that's where he's going. And this is from Mr Xavier. He don't like you thieving back that big shiny red motor car and he wants to know where it's hidden. And don't tell us it's in your garage, we've already poked our noses round there. So where is it, Harry?'

Stone struggled desperately but the grip on his arms and legs was even tighter now and he said nothing as if he had not heard the demand.

'I said, where's the wheels you stole? Where's it hidden? You got ten seconds or we drop you over the edge.' It echoed into Stone's ear and all he could do was to listen helpless to the hoodlums' demand. They were not playing.

'You let me down first, you scum,' Stone said.

He felt their grip loosen as he was dropped on his back to the floor of the pier like a sack of coal and for a moment he was stunned, his breath driven from him by the fall. He gasped as he lay on the damp boards for half a minute, dazed as if his nightmare dream had not yet finished. Stone started to get up but Cooky put his foot on his chest.

'You stay there, mate. It's where you belong until you tell us what we gotta know. And then we all go to our nice warm homes till the next time. Got it?'

'Raven Garage,' Stone shouted and pulled from his wallet a card which he held up to a hooded face that was staring down at him. 'Where they store cars, north of the town.'

'That's better, Harry. You're just too soft to hold off, we knew that. We'll give this little card to our boss, and he will be pleased,' Cooky mocked. 'But the boss says just frighten Harry today, teach the man a lesson so he understands how we do things. And this time we let you go home. But who'd know if you just had an accident and fell in that bit of icy water down there? Yeh, you'd float out a long way before your lifeless body was found. Dark enough, ain't it, to swallow up anyone who tries to play funny with us. You've got a nice big pad over there, mister, so when you wake tomorrow, all comfortable, don't forget where you've been tonight. Got it?'

'Get out of my way, you scum, I'll deal with you later,' Stone shouted.

'No, matey, you listen hard. Remember what you were told? Eh? This money you're handling is from the Caribbean. You'll find St Vincent is a nice place. You go there, mister, and you find we might start to leave you alone. But then again we might not.'

Stone moved to get up but fell back after a heavy kick into his shoulder. He howled as it hit the bone that had been thumped with an iron bar just a few days ago.

'That's for my mate you hit when stealing the Ferrari. He's got a few bruises too.' There was laughter from the two men and one stopped and pulled the hood down of his mate to show his face. 'He's called Vincent but he left the saint off, man.' The loud cackle from the two men continued, deadly threatening, Stone thought, and he struggled to his feet.

Vincent pulled his hood back to cover his head and shouted at Stone. 'You don't like this place do you? But we'll bring you back to the seaside again if you do any more thieving. You know like taking motors or nicking Mr Xavier's lump of cash. So you got just two weeks left, matey, or we come again?'

'Shut it. You tell that crook Xavier and his gangster friends in the Caribbean that the cash was fifteen grand short that he threw at me. So fifteen grand less is what he'll get back.'

The two men were not listening, they quickly melted away and Stone's words were lost in the air. Stone's whole body ached and the back of his head and shoulder blade were very painful. He kneeled and then stood up, feeling dizzy. No, he hadn't swallowed salty water, and unsteadily he looked at the jazzy lights of the pier. He held onto the rail as he looked over at the dark water and trembled at the thought of one dark night being dropped into that black hole. It would engulf him quickly.

With big strides that made his calf muscles burn Stone walked quickly to Marine House. His shoulder was throbbing and his arm was aching from being dropped on the wooden floor of the pier and he could feel the boot that had given a hard kick with menace to his thigh. As Stone unlocked his front door he was wet and he just hurt all over. A flood of light in the hall met him. He took off his coat and flung it onto a small chair that stood below a large mirror. He saw his dishevelled hair which he flattened with his hand as if his appearance mattered. He turned and was met by Jo.

For a short moment Stone was uncertain of where he was. Jo's face did not have its welcoming wide-open smile but he had just come from a dark hostile place at the end of the pier. It was a face he had not expected to see again. Ever. In the sitting room he impetuously flung himself into a chair and let his arms drop by his sides. He felt beaten.

'My goodness, whatever's happened, HS?'

'Thugs twisting my arms. That's all.'

'You're shaking. Your jacket's torn. Have you been mugged or something? We really must call the police,' Jo said as she moved to pick up the phone.

Stone shouted at Jo which made her jump in its harshness.

'No! Not the police, never. I'm not hurt and they were only some chancers after a bit of cash.'

Jo moved away, uncertain what HS was really up to. She had

only come back to pick up another coat which she had left hanging on the kitchen door and a bag of food shopping she would need for her own house tonight. But HS had been hurt and she was not sure he should be left on his own. Jo went to the cupboard and poured a generous measure of Glenfiddich, which she handed to Stone. He took it, raised a thin smile and said 'Thank you'.

'Do you want me to stay, HS?'

'No I'm okay. But I need to speak to Vlad. I've got to tell him to keep guard at the Raven Garage storage to make sure the Ferrari is not being taken.'

Stone had barely finished his sentence before his whisky glass fell from his hand onto the carpet and Stone slumped forward in his chair.

15

The black Range Rover had deep-tinted rear windows that for many reasons were intended to repel inquisitive inspection. Glistening dew from the still-early summer morning covered the car's roof and condensation clouded inside the windscreen. The vehicle stood silently on the uneven farm track as if it had every right to be there.

'What the hell is this doing here?' Gemma said out loud, even though she was on her own. This was not the first time Gemma had found it necessary to fight a trespassing blot, even fly-tipping, on her many acres of carefully cultivated farmland.

'Taz, come away,' she commanded as her golden retriever ran towards the vehicle, sniffing and prancing around eagerly.

Her dog crouched as if to pounce on his prize. Then he suddenly bounded round the Range Rover with an excited eagerness, barking loudly as if he had found the prey he wanted to retrieve.

'Taz, come away,' Gemma repeated sternly. The dog stopped immediately and sat staring at the car, slobber rolling from its mouth. Gemma strode to the driver's door, ready to give a piece of her mind, and, quite used to dealing with cattle, any animals come to that, Gemma always said it as it was.

The door was locked and with a gloved hand Gemma wiped a streak of dew from the window and put her nose close to the glass. Instantly she stepped back as if there was a nasty smell but she saw the hose running like an uncoiled snake from the exhaust to the rear window and onto the body of a large man slouched in the driver's seat. Lightly dressed in an unbuttoned green shirt, with the sleeves rolled up despite the chill of the early morning, the body sat skewed, a white face, puffy as clouds, its eyes open, staring vacantly ahead.

Gemma swore and tried the car door on the other side, but it was locked and she stood back, momentarily stunned. Steadying herself against the vehicle she grabbed a mobile from her pocket and punched in triple nine.

16

Dave was lounging heavily in his chair as he had often done in the past few weeks and he was staring vacantly at the grimy window of the Portakabin that hadn't been cleaned for the last year. He ran his finger along the edge of his desk just to check the amount of dust that had settled and he held it up to the light as if it could talk to him. It was grimy but he did not care as he would be out of the desolate site that was Sudbury in a few weeks.

His phone rang four or five times as the number was not on his list of close people he would want to talk to. He snatched it from the table. Any diversion from the gloom that he could see from his Portakabin window was welcome.

'Yes?' Dave said sharply.

It took only a minute for the call but as he snapped his phone off he stood as if that was the right thing he should do. He quickly regretted his harshness. He was jolted at the news from Gina and he walked outside for a moment and just looked into the sky, with his heart rate quickly increasing. The difference between life and death was not something he had ever contemplated much, but it now confronted him as an ugly fact that his boss had to face.

***

Stone's early morning routine was almost as tight as the ritual of monks in retreats. Early was the time to get up and early was the time to get on with the day. A small gym took up a dark room in the basement of Marine House and his workout was encouraged by James, his personal trainer, who called every few weeks to measure and weigh him and guide his routine.

But last night Stone had taken a sedative supplied by his doctor and he had slept heavily beyond the early time he normally rose. And he felt different this morning with a cloudy, heavy feeling to his body which ached and hurt on his shoulder and he sat for a while in his dressing gown in the kitchen with a cup of coffee. He had come round from losing consciousness last evening just as Jo was about to call for an ambulance. He had shouted to stop her and she had shouted back what she thought of his life being disrupted by thugs who even got into Marine House. Stone had said sorry and had agreed that Jo should call his doctor and as a private patient ask for immediate call-out.

The doctor had arrived half an hour later and meticulously checked his patient and declared him fit and well but again with high blood pressure that now needed treatment. And that treatment included advice, as ever, to put away the whisky bottle for a period. And as Stone was feeling alarm at what could have happened after being held by thugs over the murky water at the end of the pier, it was not long before he poured out the whole forty minutes of the frightening attack. But Sean looked away, he had already told his patient to go to the police.

And this morning Stone was alone in the kitchen; he was unsure how to deal with the ominous reach of Xavier and he finished his coffee feeling fragile and bruised from the attack last night. The call from Dave at midday made his skin tingle in the back of his neck.

'You've got a problem, a big problem, boss!' Dave shouted.

'Don't bring me problems, I don't like 'em,' Stone replied almost light-heartedly.

'Your mate Martyn's dead.'

Stone held the phone away for a moment and frowned deeply.

'Dead. Martyn dead?' he repeated, as if he had not heard the words correctly. 'What do you mean?'

'I had a call two minutes ago from that Gina lady who I gave the brown leather case to. She told me Martyn's dead.'

'What's happened?'

'Looks like he killed himself.'

'Martyn, suicide? Where? How?'

'Down a country lane. Gassed himself from the exhaust of his Range Rover.'

'Who found him?'

'A woman walking her dog.'

'Why the hell did he do that? Any note left?' Stone rasped.

'I don't know any more, boss, that's all she told me.'

'What's going on? Martyn was okay when I took him down to Monte Carlo. We had a good time, he even had a punt in the casino. Had his sleeves rolled up in the sun as if he owned the place.'

'He's not there anymore, boss,' Dave said.

'The deal with the cash was all straight with Martyn when I left him, there was nothing funny about that. And this'll bring the cops in,' Stone said sharply.

'Yeh. She said the police've been, they asked for a lot of details about Martyn and then took her to identify the body in the morgue. Not a nice job for her.'

'Martyn's got a wife. Where is she?'

'Don't know.'

'What about the money? Have the cops asked about that?' Stone whispered into the phone.

'Dunno, boss. But Gina says she's worried, terrified even, about the load of druggie cash you sent to her to handle.'

Stone felt again the tingle through his hair. A suicide was not on his list of things that could go wrong on this deal and he suddenly felt nervous, defensive, almost as if he had killed Martyn with his own hands.

'Go and get the money back and I'll look for somewhere else to place it.'

'No. Don't even ask me to. Gina told me she's already paid a large chunk into the bank,' Dave said.

'Get down there, bring back what you can and get her to transfer the rest back to my bank,' Stone shouted.

'This Gina lady's in shock and there's no way I can get anything from her like that. And you'd better know there's some lady called Claire who's looking over her shoulder at what's going on down there,' Dave said.

Stone stopped and drew in his breath. Someone called Claire looking over Martyn's books was not something he wanted to hear.

'You've cut the line dead, I hope. You haven't left it so any of this cash can be traced back here, have you?' Stone asked.

'It's not my deal, I don't know how these things work so leave me out of it, boss. It's all getting too hot for me.'

'Yeh, but you haven't told this Gina woman about me have you?'

'Unless Martyn told her, she don't know who you are. She just knows you as Martyn's mate Harry,' Dave replied.

There was another moment's pause.

'Yeh, Martyn was untidy, I could see that when I took him to Monte Carlo. We'd better get his office cleared,' Stone said, hoarseness rising in his voice. He was rattled, this was devastating news and he did not know how to handle it.

'Cleared of what?' Dave shouted back.

'Records, anything that might get questioned by the cops on the bundles of cash. Traces of bank accounts. Files. Diaries. Anything for God's sake, you know what I mean.'

'You want me to get all that, I wouldn't know what I'm looking for and that Gina lady won't be able to help. She's in shock. She couldn't face it.'

'Are you still lounging at the site?' Stone asked.

'I've told you many times, until you pay the boys here, that's the way it's going to be, sir,' Dave replied firmly.

'Get off your backside then, do as I tell you and go to see this lady, do what you have to do to get all the cash back, I want it like now, or we'll be at the end of a knife from Xavier and his thugs,' Stone said. He was now sweating on the palms of his hands and he ran his hand through his hair.

'I don't like it, boss, I've given the cash as you told me, it's now gone and you're never getting it back,' Dave said.

'For goodness' sake, man, be sensible. Cash is cash, they've got bank accounts and it's not their money it's mine that we're dealing with. So go and get some sense into Gina before it all runs away. Don't play games, don't make it worse, don't add problems,' Stone said sharply.

'This is your problem not mine, Mr Stone, and don't you think we'd better wait to see what's happened to Martyn first?'

'He's dead, isn't he? Wake up, Dave. The police'll go through the place like ferrets and investigate Martyn's death as very suspicious. They'll search for a motive and they'll take anything away that looks odd, and that includes lumps of untraced cash.'

'I've told you, leave me out of it, sir,' Dave said firmly. He had heard enough and he closed his phone.

Stone swore and then threw the phone across the room where it made a noisy clang as it hit the floor. He stared vacantly around his study for a moment and a fleeting image of the large shiny bald head of Xavier flashed in front of his eyes. Laundering somebody else's money from crack cocaine and heroin dealing would always be dangerous as he had seen only a few hours earlier right down the end of the pier.

For an irritable ten minutes he walked distractedly around his study. He had a strong impulse to lash out and punch whoever was in his path. But Stone was in his usual state of loneliness. He took a deep breath and felt overwhelming pressure to get down to Blake Markets himself, get his hands on some cash and rummage through Martyn's desk. He had to stop any papers or notes that would lead back to him from getting into the hands of the police. And he was sure he knew who this Claire woman was, but where would that leave him once she knew where the cash had come from?

Dave's call made Stone's head spin and in a small closet off the hallway he filled a glass with water and drank it in a few gulps to help his parched throat. He walked slowly to the front door and stood motionless on the top of the steps that led down to the pavement. He just stared blankly towards the sun before a cloud quickly enveloped it and made the place gloomy. The road was empty of hooded faces staring back at him and he slammed his front door shut.

Compulsively, he went to his study and took his passport from the top drawer of his desk and upstairs in his dressing room placed it carefully in a ready-packed bag of clothes. Leaving the country, running to a safe place, even to the Caribbean, was suddenly a persuading thought. He'd leave Dave to tell Xavier that washing their cash now had run out of space. That looked like the only way out.

Stone stared at the neat pile of clothes he had placed in his bag and finally reality hit him. He punched his fist into his palm in frustration. Of course he could never hide right away from physical violence, even torture that he would get from the mob trailing him. And if Claire blew the whole scheme wide open, leaving him with stretches from the law in some dungeon-like prison, he would be surrounded inside by cronies of Xavier. They would taunt him day and night and that would be beyond what he could take.

Stone walked around his study for a couple of minutes until he felt calmer, until he no longer felt the sweat on the palms of his hands. He walked distractedly into the hall and suddenly noticed the large array of flowers that previously that morning he had ignored. Their strong aroma drew him to them and he leant towards them for a moment as if they could bring relief from the gloomy air that he had been breathing in his study. Stone grabbed the newspaper resting on the hall table and took it to the sitting room where he slumped into an armchair that easily enfolded him.

But what had pushed Martyn, this outgoing man, into a dark corner? And what was going on that Martyn had kept secret, a secret that would now be peeled wide open for all to see? Stone needed to know. Urgently.

***

The call from Gina came just at midday.

'Martyn's dead.'

'Gina, did I hear that right?' Claire replied.

'I'm afraid you did. Suicide. Killed himself sitting in his car.'

'That is absolutely awful. But why?'

'I can only guess. He had been gambling heavily and I'm finding that he had been taking cash from the business to pay for it. I had to go with his wife Sandy to identify his body and it has left me in a state of disbelief. The police are buzzing around starting to ask questions and I'm sure we'll know more as it unfolds in the next few days,' Gina said.

'Do you want me to come down today? Just to sit with you if you like?' Claire asked.

'No let's leave it for a day or two. But I thought you ought to know straight away and the money that Martyn brought in, the loan deal or whatever it was, will now come right out into the daylight.'

'Have you still got the cash in the briefcase? Eighty thousand pounds wasn't it?' Claire asked.

'Yes, I'll keep that cash and then we must decide when to go to the police.' There was a pause from Gina and Claire thought she heard a sob. 'I now understand why Martyn wouldn't answer my calls in the past couple of days. He was hiding.'

'Yes, I'm sure the police will hunt around for reasons for this tragedy but are you sure there's nothing for me to do if I came down today?' Claire asked.

'No, please leave it for now. I'll have to go to see Martyn's wife Sandy again sometime. She was absolutely stunned by what's happened,' Gina said. 'I can't tell her about the loan cash Martyn brought in but she'll need a lot of help if Blake Markets is going to get through this.'

The call ended and Claire felt mental numbness at the news. She had only met Martyn once but the suddenness of the death hit her leaving her mouth feeling dry and her thoughts wandering quickly to what she could see would follow from this tragic news. The laundered money with £80,000 still in a briefcase could now never be repaid. And Claire would have to talk to Rick about Martyn and the tainted cash. And how could she hold back on the name of Harry Stone as the lender of the cash?

When Gina's call came Claire was viewing a country house that was a potential property for Rick to buy. But the place suddenly felt cold, uninviting, and with sparse furniture and high-vaulted ceilings, she had seen enough. She left quickly and she sat in her car outside this house, concerned at what her next visit to Blake Markets would uncover.

17

There was a slip of paper in his letter box which he read quickly.

> *Just a nice reminder Harry you got 11 days to send my money back sorry about my boys taking you for a walk down the pier*

It was signed simply with an *X*, and the crumpled piece of paper enraged Stone. He screwed it up and threw it away. But he could feel the menace that was coming from that simple bit of paper and he did not know how to stop it. The note had been delivered early that morning and it made Stone's anger surface in Roger's office when he called in later that day. Stone needed cash, he now needed it very urgently and he would hustle Roger.

'Arrow Hall's got to go, like quick. How many agents have you got on the job?' Stone demanded.

'One at a time, that way they take a real interest in getting it going. But you can't exactly do a glossy brochure of the place to get someone excited when it's just a heap of rubble with even the garden running away with long grass and weeds. You surely know that, Harry.'

'It's a valuable site, close to London, rebuild it as it was and you'll have all the high spenders out to have a look. Can't you get a list of the people who've been to see it so we can follow them up?' Stone asked.

'Forget it, Harry, no, they won't do that. Anyway, most buyers of a speculative plot like Arrow Hall want to remain anonymous until the deal has gone through and they've started rebuilding.'

'What if I increase your fee if you get it sold in the next two weeks?'

'Harry, please, you don't understand. I've got the top agents on the job, it's circulated to all their known people interested in developing buildings, so increasing my fee will make no difference at all. I'm right on top of it and I talk to the agents each week,' Roger said.

'I'm being driven to the edge by the Revenue people and I don't want the bankruptcy leeches getting their hands on Arrow Hall. They'll sell it at a knock-down price, they won't care what it's really worth.'

Stone looked away. Of course Roger was right. Arrow Hall could not be sold quickly but he urgently needed the cash to repay Xavier and to clear off a large tax bill to the Revenue. Stone did not like Roger's office and half an hour was a long time for him to spend there. He got up to leave.

'I hear you've written to Claire,' Roger said just as Stone reached the door.

'So what?' Stone said without looking back.

'Claire gives you the Panama codes or you go to call on Rick Austen to feed him some trash. Is that the deal you put to Claire?'

'Yeh, and that's the way it's going to happen.'

'What I hear is that Claire doesn't like blackmail so she's going to tear your precious Panama codes into tiny small pieces and then burn them. She'll then explain to Rick after your visit what really happened two years ago and wait to see who Rick believes is telling the truth. So be careful, Harry, this isn't going to work just as you want. Lay off your heavy-handed bullying, is my advice.'

'I'll get her, she'll come begging me not to go to Rick. It's not only Panama codes, I also need to clear the insurance parasites on Arrow

Hall. And Claire knows all the bits I had hidden and how much cash was burnt into the ashes of the Hall. There were a lot of notes tucked under the stairs, Claire looked after it, and she owes me. She's got just a few more days to come to me with the Panama codes otherwise... well her life then gets interrupted and she won't like it.'

'If you did your business like anyone else then you wouldn't be in this trouble,' Roger said.

'Martyn's killed himself,' Stone said and took a step back into Roger's room.

There was a pause. 'Martyn's killed himself? You're not trying to be funny are you, Harry?'

'Found dead in his car. The guy's opted out, and now left me in a black hole.'

'Harry, that is very sad news. I liked what I saw of Martyn in Monaco, no sides and graces with him. But if Martyn's dead then you have got problems, mate.'

Stone did not turn to look at Roger, he already knew he'd got problems and he left with his usual abruptness. Time was running out, he could not face what was surely coming and he did not know where he could turn to next. He was on his own on a fast train back to Brighton when his phone pinged. It was Dave.

'Remember Gina down at Blake Markets, boss? She says we've got to meet urgently. She says there's a whole lot of things you'll want to know.'

'Is that woman going to give me the cash back? That's all I want to know.'

'Look, boss, I don't know. But she's just called and I'm passing the message on. She wants to meet and I've got to give her a time and place to fix it.'

'Are the police onto something? They're not getting closer are they?'

'Hold off, Mr Stone. I've told you I don't know and she wouldn't tell me anything more over the phone.'

'Well, you get yourself down there, like quick, to find out, okay?'

'I'm not going boss,' Dave said with a firmness that stopped Stone from his usual aggression.

'What do you mean you're not going?

'I've done all I'm going to do and I'm finished with this dangerous game.'

'Do you want to keep working for me?' Stone shouted.

'I don't care, boss. I'm finished with all this funny stuff. Remember this whole lot of nasty cash is yours not mine.'

Stone was stunned. This was not how people he employed talked to him. But with Dave it was somehow different, he was as blunt as Stone himself. It was a dangerous mess.

'Tomorrow. Midday in London at Victoria station. Tell her there's a big clock and I'll be waiting there. Don't tell her any more. So no funny things, eh, Dave?' Stone said quickly.

He heard a grunt from Dave and took it as his answer. In the empty carriage as it drew into Brighton station, Stone was again unsettled. He searched for more hooded eyes as he paid off the cab outside his house and climbed the steps to the front door. He saw nobody but they knew where he was. At that time he could only think of one way to respond.

Since visiting the scrubby car park at Birling Gap, Stone had been carrying in his pocket the scrap of paper with an address in the Caribbean. It would be very hot there and he did not want to meet more druggies in the chain that led right down to Xavier. But he was now hesitating. Martyn's suicide was changing everything, and sometime soon he was going to have to talk to the man who owned this money. He needed more time.

Stone took the scrap of paper from his back pocket and for the first time read it carefully. He knew nothing about the island of St Vincent, except what Dave had told him, but he knew all about the island of St Lucia just a few miles across the sea. Two years ago he had built a seafront hotel in that lush tropical paradise but it had ended in being razed to the sand. And it left a drug-fuelled cartel chasing him right back to London.

In St Vincent they grew marijuana. It came down the line to people like Xavier and he had a bunch of narco traffickers who dealt the powders, sometimes contaminated, to innocents on the streets. At the top of the heap Xavier took the cash but he had to launder it to make it look legit.

The deal with Harry Stone had now gone hideously wrong, the notes had gone into a deep hole dug by Martyn's gambling and his death. Stone did not know how big that hole was and at the start he had been short-changed by fifteen grand. But when the thugs hauled him over the water at the end of the pier, they just laughed at him. They didn't want to know. Stone tore up the note from Xavier reminding him there were eleven days left; that date could not now be met and he felt a nervous energy to get something done.

With a glass of Glenfidddich in his hand, Stone weighed up the only chance of getting out of this trap that was enclosing him. He stared towards the sea and knew he had to follow the scrap of paper that had been in the case of a quarter of a million of paper money. The Caribbean was a place he never wanted to visit again after St Lucia but that was now changing. He checked his account with the travel agency and it was running dry, so he booked his flight to the Caribbean direct through an airline website. It was not something he did often, it took him half an hour to get what he wanted including a hotel and he was sweating when he finished. Staring at a screen tested his short level of patience but he booked a first-class flight to St Vincent via Antigua and checked the dates twice before making payment on his credit card. He was now committed.

The sun beat these islands into a torpor that stopped any bustle in daily life and Stone thought of the underworld that spread its tentacles from this small rock in the Caribbean. As he pressed the computer button it confirmed that he had paid £8,500 to visit this place. Driven by the reality of not repaying Xavier's cash, Stone was going in a couple of days' time. This visit would be his sign-off from Xavier and all his violent intimidation.

He sipped his whisky, he was alone with not even Jo to talk

to. He went to the kitchen and he raided the fridge, found some smoked salmon and with a few slices of bread sat at the kitchen table for half an hour and brooded. Bankruptcy was looming and the television flickered in the background as if he needed its unobtrusive comfort.

***

In France, Rick was enjoying himself researching the commercial side of winemaking. As ever Rick was thorough and he was now sure that he could invest in vintage claret with some idea that he knew what he was doing. He was making his third visit to the wine areas of the Loire and Bordeaux and he had been learning about ripening fruit before harvesting, fermenting into alcohol and importantly letting the process work itself for some time. Bottling for the chateau was done by a neighbouring plant and he had met the owners but talking to them he had needed an interpreter. It was all fun for Rick, this was something new he was excited to get involved in but it was unlike Claire's house-hunting west of London.

Rick's call to Claire came at nine o'clock that evening.

'Okay, so what say I tell you about vineyards and chateaux where I've been today?' Rick teased.

'Rick, please. I've got some terrible news to give you.

'Whatever's happened?

'Martyn Blake's dead,' Claire said.

'Oh, goodness.' There was a pause and Claire's eyes felt watery. 'Claire, I'm so sorry. I shouldn't have blurted in like that. You sound very tense. Do you want to tell me more?'

'He committed suicide in his car down a country lane. The police are buzzing all over the place and Gina, poor girl, is in total shock.'

'Is there anything we need to do?'

'There's not much we can do. But there's something very odd going on down there. There's a lot of other issues I need to tell you about at Blake Markets. Their cash isn't quite as easy to trace as I thought. So we'll talk more when you're back,' Claire said.

'Do we know why Martyn took his life?' Rick asked.

'I haven't heard anything other than from Gina. She tells me that Martyn had been gambling heavily and she thought he had made big losses.'

'I had growing doubts about Martyn as he stalked from my room and to me it sounded that he did not like to talk about money. Now perhaps we know why. I had felt something was going on down there and this now puts it all into perspective. But it could never be enough for him to take his own life. What an ugly mess,' Rick said.

'There's a lot more to tell you.'

'Go on then.'

'It looks as if Martyn had started a deal to take a loan for the business. It's all very vague but it was all in paper money and it's sloshing around in Gina's office,' Claire said.

'Paper money, lots of twenty pound notes? That can't be right.'

'I think she's had nearly a quarter million on her desk in the last few days.'

'That's dealing right on the edge. I don't like the sound of it. Hard cash like that is way out from normal for a loan.'

'I'll talk more with Gina but I'll need to dig around to get a full picture of what's really happening.'

'Did Martyn tell Gina who this loan was from?'

'Gina says she met a man called Dave in a pub and he gave her the cash in a briefcase, and she doesn't seem to know more than that.'

'Claire, you're right, this is not something to talk about over the phone. It sounds like money laundering which is very serious these days. The police will track this even if nobody else does.'

'I'm not going back for a few days as there's just nothing I can do there at the moment. With Martyn's suicide, everyone is in shock so I'll let it settle a bit before I return. I've got a few appointments to view properties down that way first. But the house hunting's been disappointing, I've not seen anything that makes it interesting enough to second-view,' Claire said.

Rick did not reply and the call finished quickly. Rick was in a hurry to get surveys completed on the buildings he was about to buy and even though it was getting late in the evening he was not yet winding down from his excitement at the chateau and wine making he was investigating. For the past two days Claire would have liked to join Rick in France. That would have given her space, a few days to get away from Blake Markets and the awful tragedy of Martyn's so sudden death. But Rick had not asked her to travel with him.

As she put the phone down it left Claire with uncertainty and it made her suddenly feel on her own, isolated. She always felt better after Rick's calls but this time she shivered and tomorrow her only diversion from the dreadful news about Martyn would be house-viewing

18

Stone picked up another scrap of white card in Marine House's post box that morning. It told him there were just ten days left and it finished with the words 'or another walk to the end of the pier', with a flourish of the letter X. Stone had seen enough of these crude reminders from Xavier which he tore up as soon as they arrived but the invisible pressure that came from a bald-headed thug was building.

It did not delay Stone's early morning appointment at the surgery. The doctor quickly saw the tired look on Stone's face with rings under his eyes and a tense frown on his forehead. Stone's shoulder was nagging with pain. He was shortly going to call on a small island in the Caribbean, he was going to be on his own and after fainting in his chair he wanted the friendly face of his doctor to tell him he was okay.

'No fracture, you'll be pleased to hear, Harry,' the doctor said, looking straight at his patient. 'But how's it feeling now?'

'It's painful, Sean, and those painkillers you gave me don't help too much. They just make me a bit drowsy. They made me crash out the other evening.'

'A bit nearer your neck and you could be in the mortuary by now.'

'It won't happen again, I've taken precautions.'

'Okay, that's up to you, but let's check your blood pressure. Last evening it was running high.' Without commenting further the doctor wrapped the blood pressure band around his patient's arm.

As well as a doctor, Sean was a friend of Harry Stone's, he had known him for many years and he knew the type of man he was. He knew too of Harry Stone's fast, corner-cutting lifestyle and of course it all added up as he peered through his glasses at the anxious lines on his patient's forehead.

'Still too high, Harry,' Sean said a minute later. 'And you look a bit heavy in the face so I'll say it again, lay off the whisky for a while. You've blacked out once so take that as a warning.'

'I have nothing before midday, Sean.' Stone tried to laugh but it was hollow.

'Leave business alone too. Just for a short time. It's obviously causing you problems so take a break from it.'

'Just had a friend who's committed suicide. Gassed himself in his car.' Stone was folding his sleeve down and the bald statement of Martyn's death suddenly sounded cold and final. And his doctor managed to ignore it.

'Take my advice, Harry, slow it up. If you don't, you'll find bigger problems down the line.'

Sean looked at his patient as they shook hands and he could easily see that he was not being told the truth about Harry Stone's problems. And Stone felt unusually heavy and lethargic as he left the surgery, uncertain how to deal with Martyn's suicide, uncertain how this lady, Gina, would cope with the bundles of cash he had sent down. But he had to go to see Gina in London, he had to hear that the cash was all there for him to collect. He was hopeful, he had a date to see her and he called Vlad.

'Have you tightened security round this house?'

'Sir, I've checked every window, they all have window locks so I think you're safe.'

'What about doors and the garage. Is it all secure from loiterers there?'

'Yes, sir, but I don't know about Jo, she's only been in quickly and then gone but she always checks the doors when she leaves,' Vlad said.

'If she's not back tomorrow you go and find her and find out what she's doing. Tell her I need her here, okay?'

'I think she was upset when she left, Mr Stone. She slammed the doors.'

Stone ran his hand through his hair and there was silence for a moment. Vlad was waiting for his orders, unsure whether to stay or go.

'You're keeping a tight watch on the Ferrari at Raven Garage I hope. They'll try to thieve it back.'

'Sir, I was there early morning and last evening and it's quiet, nothing's moving.'

'Bring the Porsche round to the front steps, we're going to London, Victoria Station,' Stone said.

He watched Vlad leave and he stood on the back doorstep for a moment just to be certain that the CCTV camera was scanning a wide area. He walked through the house, grabbed a coat and then peered out of the front door spyhole to see there were no snoopers. Satisfied, he quickly ran down the steps and slumped low down in the front seat of the Porsche next to Vlad.

Stone had not yet faced reality about Martyn's death. He thought that his own aggression would get the money back as that is the way it usually worked. But then what would he do with it? On the drive to London his head dropped and he closed his eyes.

With thickening traffic and Vlad driving slowly it made Stone frustrated. He was silent, he thought again of his increasing blood pressure that Sean had told him of just a few hours ago, he had been scared after blacking out, and now he had to face a lady who would tell him… he had no idea but he would not let her go without finding the quarter of a million Dave had taken down. They arrived well in time and Stone left Vlad at the rank of queuing taxis that always waited at this station.

'Stay close by and keep your mobile alive,' Stone barked as he slammed the door shut. 'I don't know how long this'll take but I'll call you when I'm ready,' he added.

Inside the station concourse it was as Stone hoped. It was milling with people, and he walked to the familiar clock and stood with his back to a small piece of blank wall. His timing was perfect, it was nearing midday and Stone smoothed his ruffled hair. He could feel his pulse race as he stood still just people-watching, and he suddenly saw a middle-aged lady with a round face and blonde hair. She was staring directly at him as she approached.

'You look like Harry, Dave's mate,' she said.

'Yeh, okay. But you're Gina, okay? And are you alone? I mean nobody else knows you're here?' Stone asked with a thin smile on his face.

'If you're Dave's mate, yes I'm alone, but I'm not staying long. So you'd better listen for five minutes then I'm off,' Gina replied.

'Do you want a coffee?' Stone asked and started to walk towards a coffee bar just a few metres away on the concourse.

'No I don't have time for that,' Gina replied.

'Okay. No nor do I but I want to know you're going to repay in ten days' time all the cash that my mate brought down.'

'Don't you get sharp with me,' Gina retorted.

'Where's all the money?' Stone rasped back.

'In the bank, but eighty thousand pounds I've still got in my purse.'

'I want it, where is it?'

'I might give it to the police, I haven't decided yet, 'Gina replied.

'Don't you dare let the police near it. I don't want them interfering. This loan's on a tight time limit for repayment! Martyn told you that,' Stone shouted.

'You did know that it was fifteen thousand short of a quarter million didn't you?'

He looked at the ground and half turned away. 'That's between me and Martyn so leave it, okay?'

'Look here, whoever you are, Martyn's dead and that changes everything. All the cash I paid into the bank for Martyn's mad scheme is now lost. Listen carefully because you're going to get nothing back.'

'Sounds as if you're not taking this seriously, lady. I did a deal with Martyn and I expect it to be carried out, okay?' Stone said.

'Martyn's not here anymore. So you'd better understand your crooked game is dead, finished,' Gina said.

'No, that's not the way it works. So you'd better understand, lady, what'll happen if this money goes missing.'

'Okay, if you're really Dave's mate, it's now your turn to listen to me before I go. Martyn was a gambler!' Gina shouted but it was almost lost in the tannoy blare of a train announcement.

'What do you mean, Martyn was a gambler?'

'Just what I said, he was a gambler. Big time.'

Stone looked stunned by Gina's announcement and he continued in a low voice. 'So Martyn bought lottery tickets, so he had a punt in the casino at Monte Carlo. Is that what you mean?'

'Martyn's gambling has cleared the whole lot out. There's no money left. Not yours or our business at Blake Markets.'

'But my man Dave has just brought you a quarter of a million so what're you up to?' Stone asked.

'Don't you understand? Your dodgy money is just going to cover a little bit of Martyn's gambling debts and it'll stop your gang of crooks not even getting a penny of their money back.'

'That's rubbish, I don't believe it, you're just trying to squeeze the cash away from me. I've seen it done like this before so don't try that one, it won't work,' Stone said.

'Martyn saw you coming, Harry. He's been gambling big time. Horses at Ladbrokes, poker online, the casino in Piccadilly, all over the place, he's been throwing the cash around and it's all money he's taken from the business.'

'Who else knows of this?' Stone asked.

'Me, you, the bookies. And I shall be telling Sandy, his wife, what Martyn had been doing although I expect she knows already. That enough?'

'Keep it away from the police. Okay?'

'You sound very frightened, Harry.'

'I've got a lot to lose and so have you if this deal gets fouled up,' Stone replied.

'This is going to come out into the open whether you like it or not. It's not only the police buzzing around the place now, there's accountants doing their yearly check on the figures, and Blake Markets has another investor alongside Martyn. And they've sent a very bright lady called Claire to look over my shoulder.' Gina's lips were pursed as she spoke, giving her voice unusual tenseness.

'The cash was a loan, it's nothing to do with Martyn's gambling and I'll come down and get it if that's the way it's got to be,' Stone said.

'Come on, Dave's mate, don't you understand how business works?' Gina taunted. 'Your money's lost. There's nothing left in the bank at Blake Markets so don't you go away thinking you'll get anything back. Martyn's gambling has seen to that.'

'That's not possible,' Stone said, and then covered his mouth with his hand as a close passer-by looked at him as if startled.

'This is final. Martyn's dead and the cash has gone with him. Finished. Gone. And I don't want any of your mates hanging around my office searching for any crumbs. Did you hear that?'

Gina started to move away. She wanted to finish this meeting in this noisy place. She had nothing more to say to this odd man at Victoria Station. But she was anxious. Had he brought anyone with him who was watching her and who would get venomous later now she had told him the cash had gone? Gina was unsure, but she wanted distance from the shady underworld that had seeped into Blake Markets.

Stone stood close to Gina and tried to take her arm as if he did not want her to go. For him, this meeting was not finished until

Gina told him she could give him his money back. To Harry Stone it was as simple as that.

'Take your hand off me,' Gina said angrily.

'Have you checked Martyn's desk? Cleared it of any papers, notes, scribbles, anything he might have left about this cash?'

'That's none of your business. His room is locked until the police take a look. You seem to be very naïve about how the police do things when a strange death happens, so get out of my way and go back to where you came from.'

Gina pushed Stone and he steadied himself from tripping backwards onto the hard floor. She let a white envelope slip to the ground and pointed to it as Stone glared at her. 'It's addressed to you but the postman delivered it to my office. Looks like Martyn's writing,' Gina said.

Stone stooped to pick up the envelope and then watched Gina walk quickly to the taxis that were queuing outside the station. Yes, this meeting was over. A large whisky was what Stone craved at that moment, he wanted to feel the elusive calmness it might bring. But he walked to the tables and chairs standing outside a cafe where he could drink a coffee from a cardboard cup.

Five minutes later Stone called Vlad to collect him from the spot where he had left him not long ago. Sweat penetrated Stone's shirt as he fixed his seat belt and shouted at Vlad to get back to Brighton. Fast. As they crawled through the knotted London traffic Stone tore the white envelope open that Gina had taunted him with. He read it twice before he believed what it said. It was in a scrawl, but the message was quite clear.

Harry

I've got something to tell you. You'll be the first person to know that in the last year I've taken one million, one hundred and fifty pounds from the Blake Markets' business. Exactly that figure, I've kept a record of it all, it covered gambling losses

I couldn't get away from. But, Harry, that was all it was, my own money I lost.

You came with a quarter of a million, money from drugs trading and you'll know what other nasty places too. I paid your shady cash into the bank as I wanted it to be sunk deep down into the same big plughole that had taken my money.

Harry, here's a lesson. I've done a great job to remove dirty money from the hands of crooks and thieves who tried to wash it through an innocent business.

I hope you survive this, mate.
Martyn

Martyn's signature was just a black scrawl. Stone closed his eyes. He had been wrong to trust Martyn and the police trail would quickly turn to Martyn's gambling and a quarter of a million pounds in rough paper money that Stone had brought to Blake Markets as a loan. Stone shuddered. He quickly tore up the note from Martyn into very small pieces and let them scatter from the car window as Vlad drove at speed on the motorway.

It was mid afternoon when Harry Stone let himself in by the front door. In the sitting room he flung his coat over the back of a chair and poured a large Glenfiddich from the glass decanter which Jo had refilled. The western sun was still streaming in through the deep French doors and he slumped into a sofa and threw his arms across the cushions. He sat still for a few seconds and savoured his drink. Unexpectedly, Jo appeared.

'Do you like what I've done, HS?' Jo asked.

'If you mean the flowers they look good but I didn't think you wanted to be here anymore,' Stone said and tried to laugh.

'You were sharp and you were rude and you don't need to be, HS, so please do not do it again.'

Jo looked at Stone's face which, not for the first time, had tiredness showing under his reddened eyes. She was not going to ask what had caused him to look so exhausted and she knew he had not really even noticed the flowers or their scent. But Stone, with a large glass of whisky in his hand, accepted Jo's bluntness which he took only from her.

'Haven't you finished your day working in this place? It's gone past your usual time,' Stone said.

'I just wanted to hang around until you came back. I want to let you know that the carpet in the lounge needs changing, you've had quite a few people around in the last year, and not all your guests are that careful. Lots of spills making marks, particularly that red wine. The carpet man has been and left his samples in the kitchen. There's no hurry and they're just for when you're ready to look at them,' Jo said.

'Give me time and I'll look at it. But help yourself to a drink. There's enough gin in the cabinet I hope,' Stone said.

'Thanks, I'd like that,' Jo replied as she walked to the cocktail cabinet in the corner.

'I've been up to London. Catching up on what's happening after my mate Martyn committed suicide.' Stone finished his whisky and looked at the ceiling for a few seconds.

'Suicide is terrible for those who know the person, but he was only a casual acquaintance, wasn't he?'

'Yeh, but the cash you counted Martyn had been handling for me and it's left a few problems,' Stone said.

'It's not my role in your household, HS, for me to comment on your private deals. But they do sound as if they're causing a lot of trouble. And I do need to know that Marine House is a safe place if I am going to stay on here,' Jo said.

'Sorry if I shouted at you, Jo but it's just how it was. And, yeh, Vlad is looking at everything round this place and he's had all the windows and doors checked.'

'The hooded man who came into the kitchen and sat right on the front doorstep, he was back there again today and he gives me the creeps.'

'I've told Vlad to clear him away. I've told him to get tough with him.' There was a pause from Stone and he refilled his whisky glass. As he sat down he looked at Jo who was staring from the balcony across the road to the sea.

Jo was uncertain about Harry Stone. He did not know how to say sorry after shouting, he had been roughed up by people he met when doing business and he was getting in arrears for the rent on Marine House. The hoodie who still sat on the doorstep all day just to watch Harry Stone made Jo very uncertain about feeling secure in this large Regency house.

'Jo, please, I like you to be around this place and why don't we have a drink more often?' Stone said and held his whisky glass up as if he was inspecting what was inside.

Jo refilled her glass but an hour later, with half of it left, she had to leave. She had an appointment at the hairdresser but Stone said sorry to her again for shouting as he led her to the front door. He watched as she got into a cab, he did not know why but he wanted Jo's presence around the empty rooms of the large building that was Marine House. With his whisky glass in his hand Stone closed the front door, hopeful that he had done enough to keep her. But his thoughts did not linger on Jo and he went to his study and called Dave.

'The money's all gone, wasted away with Martyn's gambling. I saw the lady in London and Martyn's been siphoning off cash leaving his supermarkets bare,' Stone said quickly.

'I hope that's not true, Mr Stone.'

'Don't argue. You get off straight away to Xavier's place. Tell him of Martyn's death and tell him it'll delay things for a bit. Tell him it'll take a few more days to get the cash back to him.'

'Please, boss, that man'll go wild if he hears that,' Dave said.

'I don't care what he does. Tell him to lay off and I'm going to St Vincent, his Caribbean island, tomorrow. I'm gonna talk to his real boss.'

'You've still got some days left to get the cash back, can't you borrow some money to clear Xavier off, you know, just to keep that man and his mad dogs away?' Dave asked.

'Shut it, Dave, that's not going to happen. You remind that thug he short-changed me fifteen grand. Then I'll deal with him.'

He had given his instruction and he closed the call to Dave. He sat back more heavily into the cushioned sofa but his anger was rising. The cash was not there, it probably never would be. Then there was the steamy island of St Vincent in the Caribbean; they will need to get used to knowing that the cash has been gambled away. It was in a charged and angry moment that Stone had that thought, but doubt lingered that he could clear these brutal gangsters out of his way.

***

'You better come and see me mate,' Xavier said. 'Sounds like we got a lot of things to talk about.'

Dave called Xavier within ten minutes of hearing from his boss, Harry Stone. He had a strong compulsion that made him drive into the East End of London on this bright summer day. He felt nervous though as he walked up the outside concrete steps that led to Xavier's doss above a charity shop. There were now sinister shadows enfolding Harry Stone, and you did not even blink in deals with Xavier if your side of the pact was not going to be delivered.

Dave had sometimes seen the consequences of the 'tidying up', a vicious system of beatings, stabbings and broken bodies, that was carried out by this fluid gang of thugs who could appear from almost anywhere. Dave reminded himself he was only here as a messenger and after he had seen Xavier's shiny face today and given Stone's message, he would get out. Quickly.

'My mate, come in. I'm pleased you've called on me to have a cup of tea,' Xavier said as he put the mug he was drinking from onto a table.

'Where are the dogs?' Dave asked looking through to the hallway.

'Out on a job.'

'Those animals are threatening, nasty. Makes me scared just coming to see you.'

'One of my boys has taken 'em down to a site where there's been a bit of mischief, you know what I mean, some thieving, taking without the okay some of the tools and other stuff. Nasty that, ain't it?' Xavier said without even a tight grin on his wide face.

Dave saw the irony but he was just pleased that this time he did not have to run the gauntlet that was Xavier's narrow passageway that led from his front door.

'It's Harry Stone,' Dave said.

'He won't like me dogs either but they're pets really. And with our friend Harry, sometimes we gotta make a bit of noise to let him know where we are. Nice and close. Just in case he runs out on us. You know what I mean?' Xavier said.

'Look, Harry ain't my friend. I just run the Sudbury pitch for him,' Dave said.

'Yeh, that's good. So what've you come about, mate?'

'You'll want to hear what's going on.'

They had by now walked into the dingy room that overlooked the street and Dave stood in a corner near the door. Even without the menace of snarling dogs this was not a nice place to stay in too long and he held his car keys tightly in his hand.

'Do you want to sit down?' Xavier asked and wiped his hand across a stained sofa as if to remove dog hairs.

'Harry's got some trouble with the cash,' Dave blurted.

'Do I hear you right, mate?'

'I don't have to be here, but I just want to tell you what Harry's doing.'

'Yeh, I'd like to know that because to me sometimes he looks as if he's becoming a bit slippery.'

'Harry's placed the cash right down in the country, with a mate of his who runs Blake Markets, that's supermarkets with plenty of the liquid stuff running through their tills.'

'You got their address, mate?'

Dave reeled off the postcode for Ferry Cove Smugglers Inn. ‘That’s all I know, I took the cash down and met a lady there from Blake Markets with offices a few miles away.’

‘Yeh, that’s good, my boys’ll find ’em, they’re good at searching out wrong ’uns. I’ll send ’em down to have a look.’

‘You got to listen some more. It’s not as simple as that and you need to know his mate down there who owns the place has jumped out of the deal, committed suicide. Just a couple of days ago.’

‘Yeh, lot of that around at the moment,’ Xavier said as if he had not heard the words correctly.

‘The money’s been washed into the business but it’ll take a bit longer to get it out again,’ Dave said.

‘Why isn’t that man, Harry Stone, standing here right in front of me telling me all this?’ Xavier said without raising his voice.

‘He’s going to meet your man in St Vincent. He’s going tomorrow and he wants to know your boys won’t try to feel him again once he’s been there,’ Dave said.

‘We had a deal and Harry’s running from it, that’s what I’m hearing, so we gotta do what we gotta do to remind him that he’s not walking away from our agreement. And if that means roughing him up… well that’s what we gotta do.’

‘That’s not all I gotta tell you. Harry tells me the cash was fifteen grand short when he counted it and it was fifteen grand short when the supermarket counted it up, and Harry don’t like it,’ Dave said.

‘Sorry, that one of my boys ran his fist at you in a car park on the motorway. He shouldn’t have done that and I told him off, okay?’

Dave ignored this outright lie and he knew Xavier would not ever talk about the cash being short and he would just blame Harry for being careless. That was how Xavier played this game.

‘The cash has been lost in some big stint of gambling and it’s never coming back. Not any time. His mate’s wasted it having his own fun and it’s left a lady right down there in the country very upset with Harry who’s demanding the cash back. I thought you ought to know all that. But it's nothing to do with me,' Dave said and put his hand on the door handle.

'Not so fast, my friend. Where is our mate Harry? Is he afraid to come here?'

'Last time I saw him he was in his large place down in Brighton,' Dave said.

'Is he hiding or running?'

'No, mate, I dunno what he's up to.'

'You go and tell him, Dave, the island of St Vincent is going to be very upset at this news.'

Xavier had by now lit a cigarette and he was blowing smoke rings in the air. The momentary silence made Dave feel more insecure in this ugly place and he looked at the door.

'This is not sounding good for Harry,' Xavier said with a mocking grin. 'I'm very pleased you asked about my pet dogs…'

'Don't you let 'em loose in Sudbury, 'cos I don't want to be there if you do,' Dave said.

Xavier laughed and his smoker's deep crackle bounced from the stark walls of this unlovely place.

'Like I said, I'm off. But Harry says to tell you he's maybe got some other cash coming and he'll clear it to you when he can,' Dave said.

'This is all sounding very foggy, a bit unlike our man Harry Stone. He's gonna walk out on a deal. And that's not nice is it, mate? It could make me a bit cross,' Xavier said.

'Missing cash is nothing to do with me. All I want to do is finish Sudbury,' Dave said again quickly and opened the door and walked onto the top concrete stair.

'You won't stay for a cup of tea will you, mate?'

'I haven't got time,' Dave replied.

'Okay, so you go and tell Harry he's not playing fair. We'll need to get him sorted if he's mislaid a quarter million due back like in just nine days' time. Don't know if Harry understands nasty but he'll find out when the boys get going,' Xavier said.

‘He don’t like the parking tickets coming at him,’ Dave said as if he had just remembered it.

‘Our friend Harry has been very naughty. He’s snatched back that lovely red Ferrari and that little man who works for him hurt one of my boys badly. He’s gotta know he can’t do that’

‘I’ll be at Sudbury, mate. Call me if you need me,’ Dave said.

Dave was now halfway down the stairs and the shout from Xavier he only caught in one ear as he reached the bottom step.

‘Tell Harry he’s in my sight, we’re watching him and we’ll be calling on him very soon.’

Xavier’s shout was packed with menace. He would become volatile, anything could happen and Dave did not want to watch it. Within a few minutes Dave was away and straight into the large pub at the end of the High Road. It was empty in the bar for those who were prepared to pay a little more for their beer and Dave sat at a table, taking a big sip from his glass. The bizarre place Xavier lived in was unreal and with his dogs ‘out on a job’ they could be licking up the water in the puddles at Sudbury for all he knew. And Harry Stone could be part of the meat on the table for their next meal.

Dave was hot and, unusually for him, flustered. Living in a big house, a big ego, no, Stone would not last long, he told himself, sitting uncomfortably on the well-worn upholstered seat of the pub. But Dave’s pint of beer was refreshing as he shuddered at the thought of a cup of tea with Xavier.

19

The taxi was waiting and, as he stood at the bottom of the steps, Stone glanced back at his front door as if he was looking for reassurance. He did not find it and as he climbed into the cab to take him to the airport he was in a foul mood. It was not helped by being searched with his shoes, belt and watch all taken off to get through security at Gatwick airport. Even an hour later as he rested anonymously out of sight from his fellow passengers in first class, Stone knew he was jumping to the tune Xavier was playing. But he knew too he would stop it as soon as he got back.

On the flight to Antigua, Stone read, napped for a while, watched two films and drank whisky as he nibbled at a small lunch. His foul mood deepened when he had to transfer to a little six-seater aircraft which took him to St Vincent. From there it went very smoothly, even Stone's small travel bag was handled for him, but he was beginning to feel tired and tetchy when he arrived at the little airport on the island. And he was only coming to tell them to keep away, that's if they wanted their cash back sometime.

It was very hot, humid, dusty and disorganised, and his shirt was sticking to his back as he found a cab to take him to the Old Fort Hotel. To keep his visit to this small island anonymous, Stone had tried to make a reservation to stay in another name but he had to give his credit card details and that made him jittery. Five stars was always Stone's choice of hotel since it usually bought him privacy, even a restful type of secrecy, but he had no idea what he would find in this strange place.

Refreshed, but in the humidity of a new day, he took a leisurely breakfast in the shade of the terrace of his suite. An hour later, eager to get this visit finished, Stone took a cab to Kingstown, the island's capital. He gave the driver enough dollars to tempt him to stay around in case he might need him again urgently. But where he could run to, he was not sure.

Ten o'clock was early in the morning for a Caribbean island. The street was not busy, it was already drowsy from the overpowering heat. Stone sat at the roadside table of a bar for half an hour drinking two freshly squeezed orange juices. He had been given an address when Xavier had thrown the case of cash at him in a scrubby car park and he would now take his time to stroll to this place if only to see if it looked more than a run-down shack. Stone was feeling lethargic, maybe he should take a ride around this town first, but he stood on the roadside for a moment. It was peaceful and his cab driver pulled alongside as if he was tailing him. But not for the first time in his life Stone felt totally alone, isolated far from anyone who could help him.

Stone opened the door of the cab, he would come back to this town but first he would take a ride around the island. He wanted to find where they grew the illegal marijuana and all that went with it, he wanted to see it for himself. Abruptly he felt a heavy tap on his shoulder and he spun round. It was just like the sudden touch of the hoodie on Brighton seafront.

'You're Harry Stone,' a dark-faced Caribbean man said to him.

'How do you know that?' Stone shouted back.

'We know everything that goes on in this island, mister. Every man who comes, every man who goes, we know 'em all,' he said.

The heat of the day penetrated to Stone's face even though he had a Panama hat that shielded part of his head. He hesitated as he looked at the round Caribbean face with gleaming eyes. But this voice was suddenly sinister with its coldness.

'I've got a cab waiting so if you want me I'll be at the Old Fort Hotel. If you know all about this place you'll know where that is too,' Stone said as he moved to sit inside the cab.

'Don't be funny, mister. It don't help. You and me we gotta talk, like now. So you ain't going nowhere until I say so and that driver is one of my boys so he'll only take you where I say.'

A second black man sidled up and stared fiercely at Stone. But Stone had heard this talk before, telling him what he could do and where he could go and in his fractious way he had always ignored it. This time he was alone and his protest would be lost in the humid air. His anger was quickly rising, he hesitated, the cab door was slammed shut against him and Stone was dragged away by his shirtsleeve along the dusty, lifeless street.

The sun was bright in his eyes and on his face, he did not struggle, he was tense and silent. He tried to release his arm from the tight grip of the Caribbean man but it was a futile gesture. For a few minutes he was pulled along two dusty roads and then pushed into the shade of a dark cafe on the edge of the road and shoved into a white plastic chair. It was out of the gleaming heat of the sun and a large fan whirled overhead as a waiter in a shirt with bright Caribbean colours brought two fruit drinks with straws. The Caribbean man nodded in the direction of the bar and a clean-shaven, white-faced man with a head of grey hair came forward. He joined them at the table.

'My people tell me you're Harry Stone. Is that right?' he asked in a strong grating Glaswegian accent.

'What do you want?' Stone shouted.

'Well, Harry, first let me welcome you to St Vincent. As you can see it's a calm place away from all the noise and smell of traffic you get in Brighton. I've been to that place too but this island is warm all the year; we get a hurricane sometimes but none of the nasty winter rain from the sea. My friend Mr Xavier tells me that you have a large house right on the seafront. You must be a man of money.'

'Shut it. You're wasting my time,' Stone said.

'Okay, straight up, Harry. You've got a problem and it sounds like a big 'un. You owe exactly a quarter million in crisp notes that my man Xavier gave you to look after. Let me tell you that is *my* money and let me remind you it is due back in exactly seven days' time. My friend Xavier also tells me you may have some problems paying it all back as we agreed. Is that where we're at together?'

'Who are you?' Stone blurted.

'That's not how this works. You don't ask the questions, you just do as I say and you'll be okay. If you don't, well, let's not go there today, eh, Harry?'

'I've not come here to hear all that crap. Xavier will get his infected cash back when I'm ready and only if you keep your thugs away from me. That's all there is to it. So unless you tell me what you're after and you leave me alone until I get your dirty money back, I'm leaving now,' Stone said.

'Okay, Harry. But I hear too that you also owe a large debt to all the boys on the mud-filled site you have in a place called Sudbury. It sounds to me you're in some deep trouble.'

'That cash you threw at me was fifteen thousand short, it was crooked drugs money. Drugs is what happens here, isn't it? Fields of marijuana hidden up the hillsides, you grow it, you sell it. But don't drag me into it because I don't deal in dirty narcotics that kill.'

Stone was irritable, he was very hot and he wanted out quickly from this place. But he looked at the calm Glaswegian and he became anxious. The Glaswegian lit a cigarette, leaned back in his chair and stared at Stone. He had got this man just where he wanted him.

'You finished your little speech about my nice peaceful island here, Harry?' he asked.

Stone waved his hand and looked away.

'First, my friend Xavier tells me he took a picture of you taking the case of cash from him. So if somebody has pulled out a bit of commission for handling it don't you now try to tell me it was short. That don't work today, okay.'

Stone took his phone from his pocket and tried to stand but he was firmly pushed back into the chair. He felt the pain in his shoulder as his phone was snatched before he could see to stop it.

'Okay, you sit still and do exactly what we say. We'll keep your phone safe for you but first we talk about the building site in Sudbury. It's in the ground, it's going nowhere, and I can tell you it'll never get finished. My friend Xavier'll make sure of that. So, it's worthless to you and that's the way it stands unless…'

'What're you really after?' Stone asked sharply.

'Before you leave this place the whole Sudbury site'll be mine. All you have to do is sign the papers I'm now going to show you.'

Stone watched as the Glaswegian drew heavily on his cigarette, just as he had seen Xavier do.

'Okay, you steal the site, so what do I get? How much are you paying me for it?'

'No, Harry, it don't work quite like that. I get Sudbury and you don't pay the interest on the quarter million of my money you got floating around that you can't pay back on time.' The Glaswegian blew cigarette smoke into the air and Stone stood, getting ready to leave.

'Where're you going?' he asked, looking at Stone intently and daring him to move.

Stone had seen stares like that before, he knew the intent behind them was real and he knew what would follow.

'I'm getting out of here. Do you think I do deals like that, heads you win, tails I lose?' Stone asked. 'No, don't try that one.'

'I'd calm yourself and sit down again if I was you, Harry. You're not going anywhere until I say and that's not until you've signed my papers. That little aeroplane that flew you into my island doesn't leave here until I tell the pilot he can fly and I'm not ready for that yet.'

Stone hovered for only a few seconds and then pulled his plastic chair away from the table and sat staring into the bright sun, ignoring his captor. He drew on his drink until the straw made a strangling sound on the bottom of the empty glass.

'What do you think you're up to? I've already poured a lot of cash into my building at Sudbury and I'd need my lawyer to get papers ready and all that stuff if I'm going to sell the place. So that's where we are. Okay?' Stone asked.

The Glaswegian snapped his fingers and a girl with a pigtail in a colourful dress to match the waiter's shirt came to the table almost from nowhere. She had a large white envelope which she placed into his open hand. He pulled from it a document which he placed in front of Stone.

'You sign this and you go home. You don't sign this, you don't go anywhere. Even the Old Fort Hotel won't have a bed for you, but in St Vincent you'll find it warm enough to sleep on the beach, but not something you're used to I guess, Harry. Is that right?'

There was mocking in the narrowed eyes of the Glaswegian but Stone turned away. He did not attempt to pick up the document in front of him as if it was tainted and might infect him. The Caribbean minder stared at Stone with strong white eyes as he stood over him and pushed the papers closer to his side of the table.

'You'd better read these, man, and just do as my friend says.'

Stone snatched the document and flicked through the pages in silence with both men watching his movements closely. After a minute he threw the document onto the table.

'This looks as if it transfers Sudbury into a company called Elon Ltd. Who is that?' Stone asked.

'I've said, you don't ask questions, sonny. But it's me. Elon was my dad's name, biblical from the book of Judges. But I own it, all of it, and all my quarter of a million you're washing for me will soon come back into there. It'll soon finish the journey you set it on through that supermarket business bank accounts.'

'Well I don't sign then,' Stone said, and got up from his chair.

'Sit down, you don't listen do you, Harry? I'll tell you when you can go.'

Stone hesitated and then sat and stared at the Glaswegian who blew another ring of cigarette smoke into the still air.

'You're trying to thieve the lot, you think I've got no way of stopping you fiddling me like this. And I don't deal with crooks,' Stone said.

'You read the document again, Harry. It doesn't say anything about a transfer, it gifts your building site at Sudbury to my company, that means you don't get a penny. No payment. Nothing. That's the wording and someone as educated as you, who knows all the twists and turns in business deals, will know what that means. You give it to me. Plain isn't it?' the Glaswegian shouted in frustration.

'Forget it. I don't care who you think I'm giving it to because this isn't going to happen. Plenty of people know where I am and if I don't show up back home in a few days well…'

'Don't force me to get heavy, Harry. I could have you taken anywhere from here, leave you in the middle of some jungle high up in a mountain on another island, surrounded by trees and snakes a metre long and that would be some place you really wouldn't like,' the Glaswegian said slowly.

'Who wrote this document? How do I know it's real?' Stone asked.

'I have lawyers all over the place, in Glasgow, in London, and even in St Vincent if I want 'em and they've checked all of your ownership details and made out this nice deed. Sit here and read for as long as you like but you don't move until you do sign,' the Glaswegian said as he put a pen in front of Stone. He lit another cigarette and looked satisfied that he had got his man.

Feeling increasingly hot and uncomfortable, not only from the humidity in the air but also from the intimidating Glaswegian and his sidekick, Stone sat for another fifteen minutes. It was in absolute silence he read the final pages. He was not a lawyer, he didn't even have the critical eye that Roger gave to documents, but he knew it said the property he owned in Sudbury. And this paper was saying it was now gifted to this crook in St Vincent, into an untraceable shell company registered in the tax haven of the British Virgin Islands.

But sitting in the torrid heat Stone was beginning not to care what happened to the Sudbury site. Most of it had been built so far with borrowed money, not his, so what did he have to lose? The place had not worked for him, he couldn't finish it and he never wanted to go there again. Throwing Boozy and his mates at the Glaswegian suddenly felt as if the deal was becoming as simple as that. But he hesitated.

'You listen to me, you narco pusher. It'll take a few days longer and you'll get back the polluted money your handler gave me. But I'm not signing this fake bit of paper, you take Sudbury away and you get no cash back, ever. Got it?'

'That's good you let me know, Harry. Some of Mr Xavier's boys have already been talking to you and till I get all my money back they'll be watching. Closely. And I might leave you alone, but then again I might not,' the Glaswegian said. He was mocking Stone with his firm voice delivered with a smile.

Stone looked away from the cigarette smoke that in the still air was floating heavily around. He was trapped, stranded until he did what the Glaswegian demanded. This small cafe was empty, he had already been dragged openly down the street and nobody had even looked across the road to see what was happening. But what if he now ran down the street and shouted for help? There had been no sign of police anywhere since he came to this small island but surely somebody out there would see him if he called loud enough? It just made his anger rise and as Stone was leaning on the table ready to leave, the Glaswegian was expecting his move. He spoke in his taunting tone.

'You want me to call some cops to see if they'll let you go? That what you want, Harry?'

It was just the stare from this man with jeering narrowed eyes that Stone now wanted to get away from. He could feel the sweat running down his forehead and he took a handkerchief from his pocket to wipe it. His hands were very clammy too, and reality hit him. His only reason for calling here was to buy time on the pot of cash that had been lost by Martyn's gambling but it was not working like that. He could see what would come if he struggled against this lot. Or get into the cab and drive away for a while.

It was with an agitated gesture with his arm gently trembling, that Stone took the pen and with a squiggle signed the document on its back page. He did not even think to ask for a copy he could take home to see if it really was all legal but the deed was signed and the Caribbean sidekick snatched the paper and added his own squiggle as a witness to Stone's signature. He then slowly folded it and presented it to the Glaswegian who stubbed his cigarette on a saucer and, for the first time in their meeting looked as if he approved of his visitor.

'Thank you, Mr Stone,' he said. But his voice always had a sneer and even the thin smile on his face showed that he was in charge. 'Can I offer you a drink to celebrate your first step in unwinding your contract with Mr Xavier? You have done well.'

'I'm on the next flight out of here,' Stone said. He stood and began to walk to the road. He had not yet understood the suffocating sham he had found in this little cafe.

'Not so fast, we have more business to discuss. So come on, Harry, sit down again, we have lots of time to talk,' the Glaswegian said with firmness.

'I said I'm going. I'm finished and I want the flight out tonight. People will be looking for me, expecting calls, and when my phone's not answered it'll blow your little games wide open,' Stone said.

'Why don't you take a seat, Harry? Stay, relax a bit and we'll talk. I want you to do me a favour, after all, you do still owe me a large amount of cash which you've got on trust and just in case we don't see it when it's due…'

'I've told you when you'll get it back, but for every hour you keep me here it'll take days longer,' Stone interrupted.

'Yes, I'm sure we'll get it back, Harry, because I can tell you now you won't want to be around if it isn't returned. We had a deal when you took the notes in the first place. And I can't always stop my boys in London as they can be very nasty if their pay packet don't turn up at the end of the week.'

The thin lips of the Glaswegian turned to a half smile as they had done several times that morning and he again clicked his fingers. His Caribbean minder instantly dodged behind a screen that led to the kitchen of this shabby place. In only a few seconds he reappeared holding a leather travelling bag, just the size of the one that Stone had brought with him. He lumped it on the table and stood back.

'There we are, Harry, that's what you've got. Something to travel home with just as a smart gent like you would carry. But inside you won't find your crumpled clothes but just fifty thousand in US dollars. All nice fresh paper money. How about that?'

Stone looked startled, he turned away and said nothing.

'So, Harry, when one day you leave this island in the sun you carry this with you and when you get back to London you'll be met by one of my boys who'll take it and then he'll let you go on your way. A free man. How about that?'

'You don't think I'm going to do that and get caught in some airport scanning machine or a dog sniffing at me for running cash from drugs, do you?

'I've got people everywhere who'll smooth your passage but some places are still open. You've got a risk. Take it as hand luggage and as you clear London's airport a smart man like you should have no problem looking confident as you walk through the green channel. What do you say now, Harry?'

'You might just as well have loaded that bag with the cannabis stuff you grow in this place, all those green leaves and the white powder, for your drug louts to deal in London,' Stone shouted. 'Dogs sniff money as if it's their dinner so shut it, I'm not doing it.'

He was feeling hotter as the sun was becoming higher, he was feeling thirsty for a Glenfiddich and he was missing Dave and Roger who should have come with him to this steaming place. It had been beyond stupid to be here on his own, cornered with a smirking crook laughing at him. He turned to the Glaswegian and restrained himself from landing a solid punch on his face right where it would hurt most. But the Glaswegian spoke, seeing Stone's fist twitch across the table.

'Well, put it like this, Harry. I've told you many times today you're going nowhere until you do as I ask. So you just stay around, enjoy the hospitality we offer here and then in a few days we maybe talk again,' the Glaswegian said as he left his chair. He shouted to the Caribbean man who was now standing right behind Stone.

'Take our friend, Mr Stone, back to the Old Fort Hotel, tell the girls there he is to have everything he wants as my guest while he rests and thinks it over.' The Glaswegian lit another cigarette as he looked unsmilingly at Stone.

Stone stood, put his Panama hat on, placed his clenched fist in his pocket and walked past the Glaswegian to the roadside. There was another click of fingers and the Caribbean man took Stone by the arm and led him to a waiting cab.

'The boss says he'll be around to hear from you, man, but enjoy our island until you're ready to talk.'

'I'm getting out of this stifling place before you try any more of your thieving tricks,' Stone shouted. 'I'll get that property thing torn up when I get back, and I'll make sure the cash isn't there anymore.'

The Glaswegian again narrowed his eyes and smiled as the Caribbean man looked away. He had seen his ruthless and cunning boss work before. And Stone's temper was rising but he held it in check long enough to climb into the cab and drive back to the Old Fort Hotel.

He showered, put on a clean shirt and then walked around his air-conditioned suite in a state of deepening despair. He ordered an American whiskey as he sat on the suite balcony and watched the clear blue water of the Caribbean. But he wanted out, back to London, before this farce ended in a fist fight.

Stone looked at the bulging leather holdall filled with large bundles of US dollars and he flinched at the thought of carrying that lot back from this island. This place grew cannabis, and who knows what else, and carrying that bag would be a journey lethal to his own freedom. He sipped his bourbon and as he mellowed he had a forlorn hope that if he sat it out long enough he would be missed at home. Surely somebody would try to find him, Dave would know where he had gone, or even Jo's perception would now be taking hold. But it would take another few days for him to be missed and Stone knew it.

It was only mid-afternoon. Stone went to sleep in the torrid Caribbean sun, lying in a hammock strung along the veranda of his suite at the Old Fort Hotel. He was not sure what he would wake to.

***

Marine House was empty and Jo was quite alone. She was busy but wary, intimidated by the quietness. It was only in the middle of the morning and she was tidying the contents of the fridge and the wine cooler to complete a list that she could email to the supermarket to be delivered. Why Harry Stone kept bottles in the wine cooler she was unsure as he never drank from it and the bottles, although of a certain vintage, would not last forever.

Jo was startled when the front doorbell rang. She looked at the video camera and saw two large men in dark uniforms. She was not expecting anyone and all tradesmen called at the dingy back door, which was always in the shade from the sun and was less than inviting. Hooded hoodlums were the last people to sit on the front step. What had HS been up to this time? Jo quickly moved to open the door.

'Is this the home of Harry Stone?' a man in uniform asked.

'Why?'

'We are High Court Enforcement Officers. Is Mr Stone at home?'

'No, he's away on business,' Jo said.

One of the towering men, who dwarfed Jo in the small space of the door, showed Jo his ID card and started to push past her into the hallway. 'Can we come in please?' he said.

'Please don't push,' Jo said, and tried to stand in the way of the two men. 'Just tell me what you want, I will talk to Mr Stone and I'm sure he will deal with it when he's back at the end of the week.'

'Are you Mrs Stone?' The question was unexpected.

'No, I'm the housekeeper,' Jo replied and was not flattered by the question.

'Harry Stone owes three thousand eight hundred and thirty-seven pounds including costs for an unpaid account of a law firm, Gard &Co. We have a warrant to seize anything of value to cover that amount if Mr Stone cannot pay us while we are here. But we will not stay more than the next thirty minutes before we start to do an inventory of property that could be removed and sold. I hope that is clear.' The officer looked at Jo with little sympathy as he surveyed the wide imposing hallway of Harry Stone's house. People who could pay but did not, brought out a different attitude in him.

Jo was still standing close to the door feeling vulnerable, unsure who these men really were. They did not look like the hooded man who had held her in the kitchen and sat on the front steps a few days ago but HS had been badly mugged not far from his house.

'How can I be sure who you are?' Jo asked, standing squarely before one of the men.

'This is the High Court writ, these are our ID cards, so please be sure we are genuine officers from the High Court. Do you know if Mr Stone can pay to clear this debt?'

'Of course he can,' Jo said, becoming irritated.

'Well, please understand we can't leave here without payment or goods from this house to go to auction to cover the amount.'

'I've got a debit card. It's mine not Mr Stone's. Can I pay the account for him?' Jo asked.

‘Of course, but may we now come in from the front doorstep to settle it?’

Jo led the two large men to the kitchen. She was taking them on trust but what else could she do? She had seen the account on the pile of unpaid bills in the kitchen, it was to do with his building at Sudbury but Jo now felt intimidated. It took ten minutes to clear the amount owing with Jo’s debit card and she looked hard at the official receipt as if she still did not believe it.

The bailiffs were only on the top step when Jo closed the front door and she shivered as a tear crept into her eye. She went to the sitting room, sat in its quietness and eyed the cocktail cabinet. But, no, she would just tell HS when he returned that she could not carry on like this. Reluctantly, she was going, as she could never feel safe again alone in this big house.

***

The office door that led onto the car park was always closed and securely locked by Dougie, an older man who, in snow and sunshine, in the dark and when the evenings were light, had a strict timetable in keeping this door secure. It was a part of his life that allowed him to go to bed knowing he had kept a certain order in an otherwise uncivilised world. Dougie lived in a cottage down the short lane that led to the Blake Markets warehouse building and he never even bothered with a torch as he walked on the track. Even when it was dark he knew every pebble that might be loose in the road and all of the many stars that lit the sky on cloudless evenings.

Martyn had taken Dougie on when the business was growing just as the new warehouse was being built, often paying him cash out of his own pocket. He was only short, an elderly man well into his seventies, but Dougie took his job of locking up seriously and with unrelenting reliability.

He had often wondered why this door at the end of this

usually quiet, small lane that led nowhere needed to be secured. But Dougie was a man who was loyal, who liked his routine and who liked his place in the outside air. Tonight he would secure the office door again as he had done for the last fifteen years. But tonight, as Dougie was carrying out his usual ritual of closing the door and turning the key in the mortise lock, he heard footsteps on the stairs that led up to the offices. He immediately thought that Gina was working late and perhaps she was now leaving. He stood inside the door to greet her with a smile already on his face. But Gina would have secured the door herself if she was the last to leave that evening and Dougie was confronted by a heavy hooded figure. There was a thumping noise as he almost jumped down the last few steps.

'You got the keys to the safe?' the intruder asked angrily, standing over him.

Dougie was startled and did not reply. The hooded face, with eyes full of madness that were screwed half shut as if in pain, stood almost face to face to Dougie and then towered over him.

'Didn't you understand what I say, old man? Come on, keys to the safe, or else.'

'I don't have no keys,' Dougie replied. 'I just shut the…'

'Don't lie or I'll put my fist in your face. Last time, I want the safe opened.' The hooded man again stood close to Dougie, now with an intimidating smile on his face.

'How many times you gotta know, I don't have safe keys so get out of here. I don't listen to scum like you,' Dougie said, facing up to the hooded man towering over him.

'Listen, old man, I want the quarter million you got in there and owed to my boss, the big man up in London. You know where that is?'

'Don't call me old man, and get out of my way,' Dougie blurted. 'You can do what you like to me, I've got no keys, I've got no money and all I do at this place is the front door. That's nothing to do with you, so get…'

Dougie was not allowed to finish and the hooded man held him upright as if he was propping up a drunk.

'Do you want my boss to come here to get his bundles of notes himself, do you want him to do this place over? You wouldn't like that, so give me the keys to the safe where they're all hidden.'

Dougie turned and shouted into the air, 'Get out or I'll…'

A hard fist smashed into Dougie's face. He fell to the ground and felt a tooth at the back of his mouth in his throat. A hand roughly tore at Dougie's coat, searching, and Dougie was too stunned to resist as his right hand went to his face as if to shield from another blow.

Dougie felt a hand over his chest and through his trouser pockets and the search ended after only a few seconds. The hooded man found Dougie's front door key, threw it onto the ground and spat at it.

'I'll be back so don't be so stupid next time if you want to get up and walk away, old man,' he snapped.

The suddenness and force of the attack dazed Dougie and he felt for his ring of keys, one to the front door here and one to the front door of his small cottage down the lane. He scrambled to find them and picked them from the floor a few seconds later. He pulled a handkerchief from his pocket and held it to his bleeding nose.

Dougie never carried a mobile phone, he had never needed one and even the cajoling from Martyn that he should put one in his pocket for his own safety had never taken root. But there was a button he remembered just at the level of the bottom tread of the stairs and which Martyn had pointed out to him several times in the past fifteen years, a button that would call for help if he ever needed it.

His hand reached out, he pressed the button and it released a siren noise that blew into the air. Dougie saw the hooded man run from the outer door of the warehouse offices and then he heard the spinning sound as wheels tore into the tarmac of the car park.

He looked up and saw a green van move into the lane that led to his cottage. Then it was quiet and Dougie tried to sit upright as he stared at his hand that was filling with blood streaming from his nose. A few seconds later he fell unconscious onto the uncarpeted floor at the bottom of the stairs.

20

As the Glaswegian had promised, the security and border control checks for leaving the Caribbean did not detain Stone. He was anxious as he threaded through security at the small island airport and even the bag with plenty of dollar bills did not raise an eyebrow in his direction. But the departure areas were hot and humid and Stone wanted out of this place where he had been mocked by a cigarette-smoking Glaswegian. Even though security had not detained him in the Caribbean he was uncertain about carrying a bag of dollar bills through London. He would have no answer if he was caught, they would be forfeited and his life would then soon be behind prison bars. But Stone was going to carry them. These dollars, bundles of paper, would be very useful to him.

In the first-class cabin, after a large malt whisky, Stone slept on the overnight flight from Antigua. But he did not feel refreshed as he landed early in the morning at London Gatwick. He put his passport in his pocket and left the plane with an acknowledgment from the male flight attendant who stood at the door to the aircraft. The coldness suddenly hit him after the humid heat of a few hours ago but he had put on a jacket that gave him a professional, upright appearance as he confidently walked with the two travelling holdalls to the inevitable queues before he could leave this airport.

Border control was busy but Stone checked through the face scanner queue quickly and he walked more slowly straight past the luggage carousels. Approaching the green customs' channel Stone slowed to the pace of the moving crowd. He wanted to run but he just stared at the back of the woman in front of him. The crowd momentarily stopped as the customs' officers pulled over three young men in their sweatshirts and shorts that they had probably worn for the past week in some hot place. Stone wanted to slip through this narrow walkway but for a moment he hesitated. He walked on slowly, staring straight ahead, unconsciously gripping both bags tightly.

He reached the sanctuary of the arrivals hall and he breathed out deeply and put the bag with the dollar notes on the ground just for a moment. He could not be sure whether he had been videoed but, if stopped, he knew he could not have exposed the Glaswegian and his drug running empire. There would be consequences too from these vicious people, they had given him a quarter of a million pounds in dirty notes and now a bag of dollars almost certainly from drug running. Stone was now deep in this murky world, a place he had always carefully avoided.

But Stone suddenly felt relief and he walked slowly with his head high as he exited the noisy terminal. His prearranged cab to take him to Brighton was waiting. He now felt the cold air in the dawn coolness and he breathed in deeply. The charade of visiting St Vincent lingered and it did nothing to lessen his temper. He now had a bag full of dollars he had carried through the customs' channel, it had risked his freedom, but this bag stuffed with dollar notes would now be his to deal with as he decided. He would take his time but he would get even with the Glaswegian's smooth blackmail in St Vincent.

He walked quickly to his driver who was holding the cab door open and ready for a fast drive to Marine House. But for a moment Stone felt vulnerable and after being held captive in a Caribbean island he was wary. He looked around expecting somebody to be following him with instructions from the Glaswegian to get the cash.

Just a few metres away he thought he saw one of the hooded men who had dangled him over the pier. He quickly threw his two bags onto the back seat of the car just as the hoodie got near. Stone tried to slam the cab door shut but the wide body of the big man was now lunging across Stone inside the car to grab the holdall. The driver had already started the engine, he saw what was happening and the cab started moving.

'Get me out of here and fast,' Stone shouted to the driver.

The driver heard Stone's call and the cab moved away. It hit a speed bump in the road which jolted the large body of the attacker from the vehicle. After the howl of pain which came from the road it took only a couple of seconds for Stone to shut and secure the door. He turned to see the man stumble and roll to the pavement. Stone suddenly felt his own smugness. He had done the first thing and kept the bag of dollar bills away from the Glaswegian's runner.

Stone wiped his forehead, adjusted his jacket and sat back with a heavy sigh. The drive to Brighton was quick and as Stone walked the few steps up to his front door, and punched on the keypad to let himself in, for a fleeting moment it was as if he had not been away. Someday soon he might even clear the outstanding rent on Marine House once he had cleared these chancers out of the way. Stone walked down the wide hallway, he threw his coat over a chair, and as he looked in the mirror he smoothed his hair. His mood was upbeat.

It was still early morning. Stone had slept heavily on the flight to Gatwick and walked into the kitchen ready to make a quick breakfast. But at that moment he was not prepared for Jo, nor she for him.

Jo was looking at the garden from the kitchen window with a deep scowl on her face.

'You're back early,' she said.

'Overnight flight, they tip you out crack of dawn at Gatwick.'

'I want to talk to you, HS, this is urgent' Jo said.

'What about?'

'You sure you don't know what's going on here?'

'Come on, no I don't,' Stone snapped.

But he walked away, his head was starting to thump with a headache stretching across his forehead. He reached for the paracetamol off a top shelf. He was filling a glass with water as Jo followed him, determined to get Stone's attention. She placed a large empty flowerpot she had been cleaning heavily on the kitchen table.

Stone looked at her, uncertain. 'What goes then?'

'You'll want to sit down before I tell you.'

'Come on, don't play with it, what's happened?'

'We've had visitors. Two big men who said they were bailiffs. Demanding money to pay for outstanding solicitors' fees. Gard & Co, do you remember?'

'I'm not paying their account they didn't do what I asked them. That's it,' Stone said.

'I had to face these two big men who wanted to see you. They showed me their ID cards and said they wanted three thousand eight hundred and thirty-seven pounds. So what could I do against two big men just like that?'

'You didn't let them in did you?' Stone asked, turning away from Jo and walking into the sitting room.

'What do you think I did? Me against two big guys with smart uniforms and a warrant to enter the house to collect money?' Jo asked, raising her voice.

'You should have called me, I'd have sorted 'em,' Stone replied. 'The last thing I'm gonna take is some trigger-happy debt collectors coming round.'

'Your mobile was switched off, not even on voicemail. They were threatening to come in and find something to sell, anything from this house to cover the outstanding money. And I don't think you'd want them foraging around this place searching to see what they could take away. So I've cleared it. I paid it all on my own debit card and you owe me,' Jo said and started to walk away.

Stone turned to watch as Jo left the room. He had heard her walk straight to the front door before and the place suddenly felt cold and lonely. He wanted to go and tell Jo to come back, he knew he had been sharp, but he could not even call out to her. He swore to himself as he slumped into an armchair in the sitting room, his head still thumping.

Yesterday Jo had tidied the pile of bills from the kitchen table and she had put them on the low table where HS often sat in this large room. On the top was the demand from the taxman and even Jo suspected that was becoming serious. Stone rested for a full two minutes before he picked up the official letter and put it down again quickly. He stood and walked to the long window that opened onto a small balcony. He peered through the heavy drapes that hung to the French windows of the large empty sitting room. Seeing no one, not a hoodie staring back at him and not even Jo walking along the road with her back to him, he breathed out heavily.

It was still early morning but a few minutes later he fixed a long measure of Glenfiddich. He was now going to fight his way from the corner that Xavier and the Glaswegian had been pushing him into. He had been carrying greenback dollars in a bag and they were valuable and were now his.

***

Just last evening Dougie's wife had called Gina. Dougie had received a senseless beating from a hooded intruder and it was what Gina feared, the same hoodlums who had lent Martyn a quarter of a million in notes. Gina knew they would come. They were now knocking on the door to have it back. The usual security company and a locksmith had been since last evening repairing the door with a new lock and they had rung Gina to give her the new code. Early next morning Gina had pressed the five digits on the pad that opened the door and she examined the place at the bottom of the stairs where Dougie had fallen. Suddenly she felt very vulnerable in this quietness.

Gina always started early when nobody else was around but this morning, before Claire called, she was now very cautious. Martyn's money laundering deal had kept her awake last night. There had to be more to find, how had Martyn plundered cash from Blake Markets, and with her mouth dry, her eyes heavy through lack of sleep, Gina did not want visitors. She went to the cooler in the empty office, filled a small glass with water and sat at her desk.

But as she entered her office Gina saw papers which had been scattered around the floor in an untidy mess. See looked for the large sum of paper money in a briefcase, £80,000 she had left last evening under her desk. It had not been touched. Feeling nervous she took it out, flicked the lid open and poked at the untidy bundles of notes. They were all just as she had left them. In the stark quietness of the early morning Gina was fearful of how this was going to end.

Martyn's death had been very sudden and Gina's feelings were still very raw. Gina had wanted to look for Martyn again, she could not yet believe he had gone, and it left her with an uncomfortable feeling about how Blake Markets would now survive.

It was mid-morning that Claire arrived. She knocked on Gina's door and saw she was just staring at the ceiling.

'Are you all right?' Claire asked seeing the white pallor of Gina's usually fresh tinted face.

'I'm worried. Martyn's left Blake Markets with a huge problem,' Gina said.

'Do you want to talk? And what are the police saying?'

Gina was silent and her hand was trembling. A strange air of quiet had settled around the place, even though it was a working office space that just a few days ago was full of business and personal chatter.

'Suicide. It's terrifying, it's all so sudden.'

'Perhaps you should go home, take some time out. Would you like me to drive you?' Claire asked.

'No. I've got to find more about Martyn's deal. Laundering money just isn't right, is it?' Gina asked.

'Gina, don't even think about that at this time. This must be a terrible shock for you.'

'Why didn't Martyn tell me more of what he was doing?'

Claire sat on the edge of the only other chair in the room. This tragedy was something new to her. She had only met Martyn once and from what she had seen of the man who walked out of the meeting with Rick… no, suicide was not like Martyn, Claire thought.

Gina paused, her hand still shaking as she looked at Claire.

'I'll need to do something with the cash still in the briefcase. And it's eighty thousand pounds,' Gina said.

'Keep it safe, don't bank it and we'll deal with it once we've been to the police. It's all going to come out into the daylight and even about the man who brought it to you,' Claire said.

'I don't think we should go to the police yet. A man I just knew as Dave gave the cash to me. I'd never met him before but he looked a bit rough and he was very abrupt.'

'But Gina we do have to go to the police as soon as we can. Do you want a lawyer with you?'

'No,' Gina replied quickly and firmly

'Did Martyn tell you who was really behind this very unusual loan he had arranged? Did Martyn not give you any more names or where it had come from?' Claire asked.

'No, it was just a simple loan from a mate of his to tide Blake Markets over a tight patch. I've paid it into the bank accounts exactly as Martyn told me and he said we'd get an invoice to repay it over the internet and he thought that would be in about a couple of weeks. I don't know what'll happen when we get to the repayment time and the cupboard is bare.' Gina took a sip of water from a glass on her desk and she stared straight ahead as if she was expecting somebody else to enter her room.

'You do understand I'm going to have to tell Rick all about this?'

'It's all going to tumble out soon, so what?' Gina said and she looked at Claire as if she was uncertain.

'I'm here to listen, Gina, if there's something else on your mind.'

'Blake Markets is short of cash so in the past few weeks I've being going through checking all the big payments we make to our suppliers. I found some very strange invoices which were all cleared for payment by Martyn. And when I delved further, these invoices I found, they were all forged. They were from people Martyn had made up and who we had never dealt with before. When I asked around none of the managers who run the venues knew of them either. Martyn never, ever got involved with the detail of signing off invoices for payment. He didn't like detail but this time I've traced the payments. They were made into Martyn's personal bank account in London. I'm still counting it but he's taken out over a million pounds in the past year from Blake Markets. I don't know how he got all these invoices printed and looking like the real thing but they were all bogus, made up for Martyn to get the cash he needed. I was going to confront him tomorrow with it but…' Gina put her head in her hands and gently sobbed.

A large policeman came into Gina's small space without knocking and looked at Claire as if she was somebody he should be interviewing. Claire looked away and moved towards the door.

'Leave the deceased's office closed. Nobody's to go in there until we say so and that might be a day or two yet. Sudden death like this, even though it looks like suicide, we do have to be sure and we need to find a motive for Martyn Blake taking his own life.'

The officer did not wait for a response to his very short clinical analysis and left Gina's office as quickly as he had come in. Gina looked at Claire disbelieving of this sudden upheaval in her usually well-organised space.

‘That does sound like chaos with the cash running through the business,’ Claire said.

‘Martyn has too easily plundered Blake Markets for his reckless gambling. Why on earth did he do it? It leaves our bank accounts running dry.’

Gina kicked the briefcase under her desk as if she was kicking Dave who had brought it to her. There were some very nasty people out there. They would beat up anyone in their way and after Dougie who was next? But Gina was sure Martyn knew exactly what he was doing. He would have known the loan from his mate Harry could never be repaid.

‘What if this cash *is* money laundering? Will I be in trouble for paying it into the bank, drawn into the ring of crooks who are trying to wash this money? I would never want to handle cash from underworld drug dealing.’

‘Gina, don’t even think of it like that. You go home, take some time out until we know more about what has driven Martyn into this awful corner.’

‘This business might not survive. I don’t know where all this is going to end,’ Gina said, becoming red in the face and looking very flustered.

‘We’ll look at that when you feel able, and after the shock of Martyn’s death has lessened for you. But be cautious, Gina. The man who brought the cash to you will be getting anxious too when he hears of Martyn’s death. They’ll come knocking on your door to get it back.’

‘I’ve already thought of that. I can only guess what Dave and his mates will be like when the cash is not repaid. Yes, I’ll be careful,’ she said.

Gina showed Claire the summary of what she had found about Martyn’s cheating. The fake invoices had been going on for nearly a year. Together they looked at the briefcase holding the remains of the cash, £80,000, as if it was an exhibit Claire should see. Gina hated the smooth leather of the case and what it held inside. And

Claire was not sure what to do with it. Claire stopped for a moment and looked at Gina's tired face and she saw the strain in her eyes. She sat in the chair facing Gina's desk.

'Let's take this step by step, there's something I need to tell you before we go to the police,' Claire said.

It halted Gina's vacant stare and she sat more upright in her chair.

'Do you know something that I don't about what's going on here?'

'Yes, I do. I know the man who might have pushed the cash onto Martyn. And he's blackmailing me about some papers I've got that he wants. And I'm not sure what I should tell the police about him,' Claire said.

She looked at Gina whose face straightened as she stared back.

'Blackmail? Are you being threatened?'

'Yes. I am. Rick doesn't know, I can't tell him but I can't keep it hidden for much longer,' Claire said.

'This is dreadful. Someone dealing in dirty cash threatening you. Are you sure you're safe?'

'Stay alert, and we'll go to the police together. I've got to continue house-hunting today but can you make tomorrow? Early?' Claire asked.

'I'm going home to look over some papers. I need to get the total of all the cash that Martyn creamed off from Blake Markets. And I'm taking the case with eighty thousand in it just to be sure it's safe after last night's break-in. Yes, come down early, but will you tell the police of your blackmailer?' Gina asked.

'I don't know. That is going to be difficult for me,' Claire said.

House-hunting for Claire had so far not gone well. All she had found was two or three properties that looked ideal and places Claire knew she would be happy to live in too. But all that she was finding at Blake Markets, and all that could come out of it when Rick was told, dented Claire's enthusiasm to search for more properties. Uncertain about the future, Claire waved to Gina as she left the car park half an hour later but she would be back tomorrow.

And tomorrow, Gina decided, she could be rid of all the tainted cash as she would hand it all over to the police. But she wanted to know who was blackmailing Claire. Was Claire safe? Gina was concerned for what was happening to Claire and as she left the warehouse offices with the remaining cash she held the steering wheel and stared straight through the windscreen. Gina put her small car into gear to get away for a few hours. She glanced at the briefcase she was taking home, she needed to see that it was still there, and she did not notice the green van that followed her.

***

Gina lived in a terraced cottage in the middle of a village with a dog as a pet but otherwise alone. The house was immaculate, as was the small garden. She parked her car in her usual place at the end of a lane where she rented a garage and with some papers and her laptop, she carried the briefcase to her cottage. Just this short distance from the reality of laundered money calmed her. But she still remembered starkly Dougie's beating and what Claire had told her about blackmail. Extra security at Blake Markets was being arranged and mugging in this place just would not happen again. And now Gina wanted to be alone to untangle a web that she could feel was drawing her into something she would not know how to handle.

The green van that had been near the office had followed at a distance, far enough to be out of sight, but as she walked to her cottage, she was being watched by two men, almost invisible, sitting in the front.

With some important papers she had printed off Gina was going to comb through the files on her laptop. She sat in the large conservatory at the rear of her cottage and she placed the briefcase on the floor. The sun was shining and she closed her eyes. Her head nodded and for an half an hour Gina found silence as she fell asleep.

A demanding, heavy knock on the front door, a knock which felt as if it was right inside her head, woke her with a jolt. Gina did not want visitors. She did not want to talk to anyone. But the knock was too loud to ignore as if it knew she was at home. She swore to herself as she walked slowly to open the door. A large policeman and a petite policewoman were standing there looking directly at her. They blotted out any light that would have come into this house. Gina's heart started pounding.

'Are you Mrs Cole?' the policewoman asked.

'Yes,' Gina replied.

This was the end; she had been caught laundering a lot of dirty notes, she knew the penalties were severe, fines, prison. Gina held her tears back.

'Can we come in, please?' the policewoman asked.

'Yes, of course,' Gina replied.

She stepped back and led the way into the conservatory. Her mind was whirling almost uncontrollably as she hurriedly closed her laptop and moved the few papers into an untidy heap and placed them on a low table.

'Sorry about the mess. I've a lot of extra things to think about with all that's been happening in the last few days. And there's always so much to do at times like this,' Gina said, feeling very flustered.

Her unease at two uniformed police officers knocking on her front door was not possible to hide; after all, how often had she ever had two members of the local constabulary in her house?

'We know how you must feel after the tragic death of Martyn Blake and we know that must have had a big impact at Blake Markets, so we're sorry for bothering you at this time. But just a quick word we thought might be helpful,' the woman PC said.

'There's a lot of things in the air that are unsettled and it'll take me time to get everything straight. Goodness knows what's going to happen to the business,' Gina replied.

'We'd like to talk to you about the attack on Dougie Wells. Your man who opens and closes the offices each day. Early morning, late evening, is that right?'

'Yes, that was horrible, and those thugs, whoever they are, need to be shut away. Would you like a cup of tea?' was all Gina could think to say at that moment. She wanted these two people to go, and quickly.

'No thank you,' the policewoman replied. 'We don't want to disturb you and we won't keep you long.'

'After Martyn's death, Dougie getting beaten was just awful,' Gina said with a deep sigh.

'We need to find out more about this attack, it's not something we see often in this quiet corner of the world.'

'I really can't help you with that but like you I'd like to see them, whoever they are, caught,' Gina said.

'Dougie tells us that his attacker shouted at him before he landed a punch on his face. The attacker was after a quarter of a million in notes that he said were owed to his boss in London. That's all very strange, so do you have any idea what that might mean?'

'I've absolutely no idea at all. I keep on thinking maybe it was something Martyn had arranged that he hadn't told me of.'

'We're still investigating Martyn Blake's suicide but Sandy, his wife, has told us that there's a lot of cash missing from the business.'

'We handle bundles of cash here every day and at the stores as you probably know we've had a few attempts from gangs at breaking in in the past. That's why we spend a lot of money on security. We use security companies to move all our cash around. Armoured vans, CCTV and all that. But we never keep much cash in the offices, why would we?'

Vagueness was not Gina's normal way of dealing with things. She had given easy detail, she was not being convincing, and she was just clutching at straws. Of course she knew exactly what it was all about. There was a shiny leather briefcase with £80,000 in paper money on the floor close to her. She began to feel hot.

'Yes, Dougie tells us his attacker was hooded which hid most of his face and we're still scanning your CCTV tapes. But our main concern is that this wasn't a random attack especially after Dougie told us what this hooded man shouted at him. It was about cash in your safe. We're looking at DNA and finger printing, but we think if this gang really are after such a large sum of cash they'll call again. And our concern is they'll be much nastier next time,' the policewoman said.

'Who on earth was this hooded thug? He could have been anyone, couldn't he? Those hoodlums could have come to the wrong place searching for their quarter million couldn't they?' Gina asked with true contempt at this nastiness in her voice.

'We doubt that very much. We have Martyn Blake's death under investigation but could he have been involved with something that was on the edge of your business, something to do with his gambling?'

'Everything here is Martyn's, he built Blake Markets from nothing and a lot of the time he kept things close to himself. But his death was sudden, unexpected and shocked all who knew him.'

'We understand he was into gambling in a big way and we believe he's lost a lot of money,' the policewoman said. There was a pause as she let the statement sink in and she looked at Gina's face for a response. All she saw were the tense lines that were marked around her mouth.

'I've already spent time going through Blake Markets' books trying to get to the bottom of Martyn's gambling and I don't know all of it yet. But yes, it's left some large debts to clear and it's left a hole in the business. So maybe you're right, perhaps there's something more to find,' Gina said.

'Dougie is recovering well and he wasn't too seriously hurt so we won't prolong this interview, but please give us a call if you do uncover anything else. And then our security advisory team could call if you think they could be of any help to review security around your business. Attacks like Dougie's are not nice,' the policewoman said.

'No, they're awful. Dougie was a defenceless old man just doing his everyday work,' Gina said.

Gina also had a lot more to say but it would wait until she could go with Claire to the police station tomorrow. Then she would have to tell them how she had met a man called Harry at Victoria station in London. It was just to tell him all his laundered cash was gone. And to leave him with an odd envelope from Martyn. And where would that lead?

Gina was very unsettled by this visit and she stared into the garden but she did not notice the colourful array of flowers and shrubs which she cultivated. She felt guilty doing just what Martyn had told her to do, and also after she had found Martyn's way of stealing from his own business until it was bled dry. She wanted this nightmare to finish.

After the police officers left it took another two hours looking through her laptop files and bank accounts for Gina to be satisfied. It was a mountain of cash that Martyn had taken. The sum was daunting, it was just over a million pounds. For a moment Gina stared at the pile of papers on the table. The supermarket business was sliding to the edge of collapse and would Harry, Martyn's mate, ever care about it? Gina knew the answer was never.

Gina looked at her watch. She needed to talk to Sandy, Martyn's wife, but it would not be an easy discussion. Sandy was deeply shaken and she would not want to hear about the fake invoices that Martyn had used to siphon cash from the business of Blake Markets.

In the late afternoon, Gina was very nervous as she left her cottage. Nervous at carrying the briefcase to put back into the strong-room beside her office, and nervous too that she had let herself be part of Martyn's money grubbing scheme. Martyn had opted out, it was no longer his deal and she walked quickly to her car. But her decision had been made. She would join Claire, she would tell the police everything and all she knew of the money laundering scheme. And she would give the police the case of cash that was left over. But as she thought about it she didn't know much about the people she had met, they were only Martyn's contacts, and all she knew of them were the names Harry and Dave. Was that all she could tell the police?

It was not until she was getting into her car that Gina heard the soft pad of a footstep behind her. She turned and saw two men in hoodies very close and with a reflex action she threw the papers and the briefcase onto the seat of the car, started the engine and put her foot on the pedal to get away. But the car door was open and the taller hoodie lunged past Gina to snatch the papers and the case.

'What you done with our money?' he shouted, and then landed a very heavy, wide fist full into Gina's face. Gina's head dropped sideways, she was still clutching the steering wheel and with the car door still open the hoodies ran away towards the green van, one of them with the briefcase under his arm.

But Gina's foot was wedged on the pedal and she was heavily slumped over the wheel, unconscious. The car started to move at a growing unguided pace. It raced towards two very large oak trees that had stood on this little bit of road for at least the last 150 years.

21

Stone wandered aimlessly into the sitting room and took a desultory look at the carpet samples Jo had left there. The one she favoured was arranged on the floor and covering the red wine stain. Stone knew that her choice was exactly right for this elegant Regency room and he turned away. He was unsettled, feeling hot and uncomfortable. He walked onto the small balcony that overlooked a road to the sea beyond with its wide openness and the sun was still moving higher in the sky. Jo had left and Marine House would be colder still without her but he had a bag of US dollars and that is all that mattered to him at that moment.

Stone took another small glass of whisky around midday and summoned enough resistance against taking a second. Twice he flicked on his phone to call Roger and twice he turned it off. He needed cash, he fingered the tax bill for £45,000 and decided he would clear that today. Stone stared from the balcony window. As usual he was feeling belligerent but with a growing anxiety that the truth about what had happened to a quarter million would soon lead Xavier and the Glaswegian to strike him.

He reread the creased slip of paper that had been pushed into his letter box early that morning. It told him he had four days left to clear the cash back, all washed white and clean with no smell of the dark corners of drug dealing and extortion it had come from.

The scrap of paper like the others had a large scrawled X. Without thinking he screwed it up and threw it in the bin as he walked through the kitchen. Four days was longer than the taxman was now giving to clear the sum owing of £45,000. And it left him with only one route to raise that cash.

Stone shut and securely locked the back door, and walked down to his garage. He was very wary that somebody from the island of St Vincent was even now following him and ready to snatch back the bag with $50,000 US hidden in it. His mood was darkening as he sat in the Porsche and set the satnav to Camberwell in south London. It was not a journey he wanted to make, it was to what he saw as a dingy part of London. But today this was something he could not put off. Bankruptcy, and all that would mean with starting again and grubbing around for help, was getting too close. Before he left his garage he called Dave on his hands-free. His voice was insistent; he was about to give an order.

'I want you to come straight away to pick me up from Camberwell.' Stone reeled off the satnav details before Dave could answer. 'I'm back from St Vincent and we've got to talk, like quick. Camberwell. You've got two hours, get there and don't be late,' Stone shouted.

It was a terse instruction and Stone knew his aggression to Dave would make him respond. Stone drove cautiously and it was well over an hour before he swung the Porsche into a small space just off the Peckham Road, SE15. It was a car lot and even before he had switched off the engine he was met by an obese man with a clean white T-shirt and jeans tightly belted under his wide belly.

'So these are the wheels, Harry. Looks a nice job. Haven't seen one quite like this before,' he said.

'You're offering way under what it's worth but you know what it's like, sometimes you need a few readies urgently.'

'I'll get one of my boys in the workshop just to look underneath and then we have a deal.'

‘Fifty five thousand, bank transfer today. That’s, the deal. Take it or leave it, Billy,’ Stone replied.

They shook hands easily. Billy the salesman looked pleased with the deal and Stone suspected he already had a buyer for this unusual car at a price that would leave him a large profit. But standing on the narrow pavement alongside the wide and gleaming bonnets of used cars for sale, Stone was satisfied. He was going to have fifty five grand in his bank by the end of the day and he would clear the taxman. That would push bankruptcy away. He still had the Ferrari and then there was Sudbury. But that was a sham piece of paper. He was not going to allow that.

‘What about your other motor, the big red Ferrari, Harry? Are you in the market to move that one too?’

‘I’ve got someone trying it at the moment. Yeh, I’m going to sell, but I’ve got to get a big price, too high for you, Billy. I may put it in an auction with a two hundred and fifty grand reserve. But I’ll let you know when that comes up.’

Five minutes later Billy left to talk to another customer and Stone, brooding alone, sat in the Porsche waiting for Dave to arrive. Dave arrived ten minutes late and Stone climbed into Dave’s rusting 4x4 ready to give instructions.

‘Take me straight away to see Xavier. You know where he lives,’ Stone said.

‘Are you sure you want to see him, boss? He’s not too happy from the last time I called. You know, problems with the cash.’

‘Don’t argue, get me there quick. I’ve gotta tell him what’s going to happen. This is urgent, okay.’

‘You won’t like his doss, it’s right up in the East End. Wouldn’t you prefer to meet the man at Sudbury?’

‘Look, I’ve been to the Caribbean, I’m not going to Sudbury so get me there fast and don’t argue,’ Stone said without looking at Dave.

‘Did you get some room on the deal when you went to the Caribbean?’ Dave asked.

'You're not listening, just shut up and get me to Xavier.'

Stone left a pause and watched Dave's face as he stared straight ahead to the clog of traffic.

'That man lives in a seedy couple of rooms, you won't want to see his dirty place that stinks of dog fouling, honestly you won't like it boss,' Dave said.

'You don't understand what I gotta do.'

'Okay, whatever you're going to say, remember Sudbury's not working. There's just puddles of mud and that's the way it'll stay until you clear the debt,' Dave said.

'I don't care about Sudbury. What happened to the fifteen grand short, cash that crook tried to rob from me? What does that jailbird say about that?' Stone asked.

'Yeh, he just laughed. He said nothing until I told him you might have difficulty getting the lot back on time. He wasn't happy then, boss, so be careful, he'll want to see blood run.'

Dave lent his arm against the side window, and he began to think that this would be the last time he would talk to this man, Harry Stone. And what would he tell the police when Stone's body was found floating in the water off Brighton pier? There was silence for the next hour until Dave navigated the knot of traffic leading to the High Road in East London. Stone was becoming restless, aware that he was getting close to Xavier's squat above a charity shop.

'It's along the next road but I'm not coming in with you, Mr Stone,' Dave said as he pulled heavily on the wheel to park in a tight space.

'Yes you are. I want you close by and I don't trust that man. You know his history, he's ready to do GBH on anyone he don't like standing close to him. Then you've got to run me back to Brighton,' Stone rasped back.

Keeping safe while making a visit to Xavier was not something Stone had thought about before, but he had work to do and Xavier wouldn't chance anything in a built up place like this. It was an hour after leaving Camberwell that Dave led Stone up the bare concrete steps to the door of Xavier's squat. Harry Stone was silent and brooding. He knew the East End but this was different, not how he remembered growing up in a Victorian terrace house when there were few cars and when all shops either sold food or other basic necessities for living.

Dave had told Stone what to expect, how this man lived, but something was driving Stone. His irritability from sitting in Dave's car for an hour through dense London traffic would soon be replaced with trepidation as to where this visit might lead. It was quiet on the top step with only the noise of traffic on the road below as Dave thumped on the wooden door and waited.

A ferocious noise erupted of dogs barking, Stone jolted back in utter horror and stood behind Dave. Xavier opened the door holding by their collars two pit bull terriers, one white, one black, both growling and snarling and showing their fangs through slobber that matted their fur. He was probably wearing the same sweatshirt that he had worn when carjacking Stone in a country lane, it had once been white and it now made Xavier's body look gross and intimidating. Stone shuddered but he was not going to retreat.

'Come in my friend. And you've brought Harry with you this time, Dave, that's good,' Xavier shouted at them.

The dogs were bundled into a side room as if they were small pets and Xavier closed the door quickly. It barely subdued the noise and Xavier gave Stone a cynical grin as he waved them to follow him into the dingy sitting room. Stone was silent but seeing the big shiny face of Xavier in this squalid place gave him gritty determination to deal with this menace. With a slam, Xavier shut the door to the hallway as if to keep out the din of the dogs yapping. It brought out Stone's phobia of closed spaces and suddenly gave him a feeling he was being locked in. It reminded him of St Vincent and he was going to get this over quickly.

'You listen to this,' Stone shouted staring at Xavier.

'I'm listening, mate, but you'd better bring me good news

because last time Dave called he told me you'd got a problem. Me and me mates don't do problems,' Xavier said.

'I've just seen your conman in the Caribbean and I carried home a bag full of dollars right past all the staring and invisible eyes at Customs and Border Control. Being a runner from that island is dangerous stuff, I only got through because I don't look shifty like you and your ring of thugs. So I keep the dollars. Got it? And then maybe I return them when you tear up the bit of paper he made me sign. Or maybe I don't. But don't you try your fancy heist to snatch Sudbury from me. That ain't gonna work. So that's it, take it or leave it but that's what's going to happen.' Stone was out of breath, he had spoken quickly and loudly.

'Harry, quieten yourself. We know all about what happened at the airport when you came in. You hit one of my boys when you were thieving and getting away with our dollars and that's not good so we're coming for you. A couple of my boys'll be around soon to your place but why don't you make it easy for yourself and give back the greenbacks now? What do you really want, Harry?' Xavier yelled.

'I've told you what's happening,' Stone yelled back.

'Is Harry being straight with us?' Xavier turned to ask Dave.

'I just come with the boss to show him where you live so I don't know any more, okay?' Dave said.

'You're just a con and you'll soon be back inside when I've been to the cops.' Stone moved towards Xavier as if he was squaring up to him but he stopped short. He did not want to get any closer to this malodorous man.

Dave looked at Stone and saw the red rise in his cheeks.

'Harry, mate, don't get excited. And before you talk about doing porridge let me tell you what'll happen if you run this to the cops. Okay, so you've got a lot of stuff you can tell 'em, but we'll know who's grassed and then inside the cosy prison walls, well you won't feel safe, mate.'

'You tried your trickster games with fifteen grand missing from that case of cash you threw at me. I've seen worse scum than you cower away. I know how to deal with you.'

'Don't talk tough, Harry. And what's it all about that Dave told me? The money you were going to clean up for me is now wasted, gone by someone having fun gambling and burning our cash away? That story don't sound good, you're lying to me and if you think you're going to pinch some more of our hard-earned notes, well that don't work out, mate, does it? So get back and find the cash I lent you in Birling Gap. You remember that place by the seaside?'

'It's time you listened to me. Sudbury's mine. Clear your layabouts off the site, let 'em go smoke pot somewhere else, and Dave'll get the place working again. So don't you ever let your Caribbean embezzlers think I'm giving the site away like their fancy try-on,' Stone said.

'Shall we wait and see, Harry? Sudbury's gonna make cash. One day. But don't you hang around because I don't think you're going to see it. Sound good?'

Dave was silent. He had been here before, he never wanted to come again and he was sure Xavier was a bit high and would do some serious damage to his boss.

Stone moved toward the door and shouted at Dave. 'We're going, we'll leave this lot to fester in their own putrid make-believe games.'

But Xavier had not finished and he looked at Dave who had started to move with Stone to the door.

'Harry's getting too shifty, not a man we can rely on, he's not keeping his part of the deal, is he, Dave? My friend in the Caribbean trusted him with some dollars and where are they now? And, Harry, just four days for my cash to be back all nicely washed and clean to use so it looks like legit money,' Xavier said.

'It's not there, you're not getting it until I'm ready, so shut it,' Stone shouted back.

'And before you run away we gotta settle another big debt. It's outstanding on your shiny red motor car. One of my boys got run over by your friend when he stole it so he ain't too pleased in his hospital bed.'

The noise of the dogs intruded but Stone was already at the door of the dingy and cheerless room. This place had its own menace, a chamber of squalid humanity. It was now made worse as Xavier lit his cigarette. It did not smell as if it was just tobacco, and dogs scratched scarily at the small piece of wood that was the only barrier that kept them away.

Dave joined Stone at the top of the stairs. Stone's face was white, Dave followed him at a quick trot and at a gap of two steps to his rusty car parked a hundred yards away in a side street. This man in his unlovely cell with a side room as a kennel for his mad dogs would expect blood to run now he had heard what Stone was up to.

22

In the wide hallway of Marine House, Stone looked into the lounge which was empty and quiet. He went to the kitchen which was just as empty and quiet and sat at the bare table and took painkillers for his headache. He ambled aimlessly through to the sitting room and peered past the heavy curtains towards the sea. It was a view that had often mesmerised him and quietened his random thoughts. But today was different.

Stone was agitated. He picked up the carry-on holdall which had been lying on the sofa in his lounge and as he felt its weight his determination increased. Stone was a man who automatically disliked authority and clearing the Revenue's demands for £45,000, even with costs of £2,000, he saw as a small price to pay for his freedom from bankruptcy. But he owed the rent for the last quarter on the lease for Marine House and he had received another letter just that morning. It was threatening recovery and eviction if not cleared. Stone was becoming more unsure about continuing to live in this imposing mansion. Marine House was very big, many rooms ghostlike and if he was to stay it had to be with Jo's friendly face around this large house. But he still owed her for settling with the Bailiffs who came knocking, he had shouted at her again and she had seen close up some of the thugs shadowing around this place. She would never want to come back.

Stone weighed the holdall heavily in his hands; its value to him was now more than the notes inside. All of Xavier's cash had gone, lost in the crumbling bank accounts plundered by Martyn's gambling, but he could now play the crooks, who had tried to hustle him out of everything, at their own game. Stone felt a high as he called Vlad; he appeared from the kitchen within ten seconds of the shout.

'I've got a job for you to do.'

'Yes, boss, I'm listening, just tell me.'

'This bag has got a load of cash in it, you're not to open it and I want you to hide it for me, okay?'

Vlad nodded and stood from one foot to the other.

'The Porsche has gone, I've sold it. Get a hire van from round the corner, get one that's absolutely plain, no markings on the side that says where it's come from, and here's the postcode you've gotta go to, so listen hard.'

Stone thought for a moment and then took five twenty-pound notes from his wallet in his trouser pocket and gave them to Vlad.

'Take the bag and you'll need this key when you get there. It's a derelict site with a building that's been burnt down and with just a stable block standing behind it. There's a room upstairs in the block and, if it hasn't been lifted away by some yobs after the fire, against the back wall you'll find a safe. There's a lot of broken bits of everything in that place but this key opens that safe. Stuff this bag in, lock the safe, and then replace the broken furniture and other junk to make sure it looks undisturbed. You know how to do that, so get it done like quick,' Stone said.

Vlad looked at the postcode, looked at his watch and nodded.

'Yes, sir, I'll do that straight away for you.'

'And make sure you're not followed when you leave here. And when you've done that get back to Raven Garage, I want you to keep your eyes wide open up there, I don't want the Ferrari taken again. Do you understand all that?'

Vlad nodded and with the holdall he moved towards the door.

Stone looked closely at him. He was not sure how much he trusted Vlad to do exactly what he had told him with such a large sum of money. But Stone's bargaining chips were in that bag, Vlad did not know what he was carrying and the zip was held with a small lock at each end. At that moment it was enough for Stone to be sure he could now keep Xavier and the Glaswegian singing for their cash.

Idling his time and now with not even Sudbury to visit, Stone drank his Glenfiddich with at least one refill as, alone, he wandered aimlessly around his large house. An hour after Vlad had left his phone rang and it startled him as he was staring from the small balcony in his sitting room across to the sea. It was Dave.

'What do you want?' Stone snapped.

'There's some new iron gates been delivered to go up at the entrance at Sudbury. Did you order them, boss?'

'No, what would I want those for?'

'I think they're from Xavier. He's going to put them up and lock you out.'

'I employ you to look after that place so get a truck and take 'em away,' Stone shouted.

'I've told you, this fight's nothing to do with me, Mr Stone. So unless you're going to come here and stand in front of them, those gates'll go up in a couple of days. That's what's going to happen here, and there's nothing I can do to stop it,' Dave said.

Stone felt the cold contempt that was in Dave's tone. But Dave's call ended after only a minute and Stone walked to the cabinet to refill his whisky glass. It just added to his uncertainty. As he placed the bottle back in the cabinet his phone rang again. He was feeling very aggressive and without looking at the caller's number he shouted into the phone, 'What do you want?'

'Sir, it's Vlad. I'm at the place you told me, I've put the bag in the safe but I think somebody else has been here. Some of the broken furniture has been moved away and the handle to the safe has been wiped clean and there's no dust on it. The safe was open with a key still in the lock. It's empty and I think somebody else has been looking at this place so do you still want me to leave the bag here?'

'What do you mean, somebody has been there, have you seen 'em?' Stone shouted again.

'No, sir, but the place looks disturbed, there's some broken bricks lying around,' was all Vlad could respond.

'Can you see anyone else there? Is the place empty?'

'Sir I'm alone, there's no noise here at all.'

'Leave the bag where I told you and get back to Brighton to look after the Ferrari quickly, okay?' Stone boomed and he flicked the phone off.

Claire had been there. She was the only other person who knew where the safe was hidden, she was the only other person who had a key. He did not know what she'd want from the safe but she had not replied to his letter demanding the Panama codes. That was enough and as he paced the large sitting room he decided it was time to carry out his threat to visit Rick Austen. He would leave it no longer. He would deal with Claire and let her know where she stood.

Marine House was quiet again, and he needed to call Jo. Jo spoke to HS as she saw it, and he took that as part of how he thought about her. He did not know how to say sorry but at least he could ask her outright to come back and deal with him as she had always done over the past two years. But her phone was not answering and on her voicemail he left a halting message asking her to come back to Marine House. At that time he did not expect her to reply.

23

Claire had spent two days moving into Rick's apartment, a sixteenth-storey penthouse that overlooked the Thames in Westminster, London SW1. But there was still the nagging doubt about Harry Stone. The blackmailing letter he had sent her with its threat to call Rick would not go away. It told her this move was not settled until she had dealt with him. Rick was in France, excited about the vineyard and chateau he had found, and Claire again felt alone.

Yesterday she had spent searching for houses around the south of Hampshire and she had driven past many properties some well hidden behind acres of garden. She was searching for places that were elegant, not new, but with plenty of space around, and she had found two that matched what she thought Rick would like. At last she had been excited in a house hunt which she had found a great anti-climax. Just the thought of living in the country again and in a place where she could plan gardens and even the interior with furniture and decor was enticing.

Today, as always, Claire dressed carefully in muted colours to feel comfortable in the country, a place she was about to visit. She looked at herself in the mirror as she left Rick's flat. She was insecure about what she was going into but she had a growing determination to find out what was really happening at Blake Markets. She had to see if the mess that Martyn's suicide had left could be sorted. And, with Gina, it was now urgent they both went to the police.

The concierge waved to Claire as she left Rick's apartment and a minute later she was leaving the underground car park on her hour and a half drive to Blake Markets. What if Martyn's odd loan deal all in cash was for money laundering? That thought worried her.

That morning, first, Claire went to view a house not far from Blake Markets. But she knew immediately it did not feel right. It was just too big and what on earth would Rick do with all the land that surrounded it? For Claire this property was just in the wrong place, somewhere that was not familiar to her. She would show Rick the agent's brochure with all the others she had collected and she would look at more houses before she became excited.

Claire felt tense as near midday she arrived in the Blake Markets car park. It was unusually quiet and there was a lack of bustle which made her wary. It felt wrong. Claire was not sure what she would find but she was going to look with Gina into Martyn's cash machine. It had become a lifeboat for him, with big money taken out. And Blake Markets was damaged.

There was one police car and it was parked again on the cross-hatch by the front door to the office space upstairs. Claire was alert as she climbed the stairs and found a policewoman sitting in Gina's chair. She was on her phone and ignored Claire. But Gina was not there and Claire hovered. Claire looked at the cluttered space and waited until the policewoman finished her call.

'Is Gina here?' Claire asked.

'Who are you?' the policewoman replied.

'Claire Watts, I represent one of the shareholders of this business and I've got a meeting with Gina.'

'Do you have ID? I'm sure you will understand with what has been going on here in the past few days and in Gina's absence, we need to check everything and everybody.'

'I'm looking at the business for a shareholder of Blake Markets.

And today I'm here to help Gina finalise some figures. Is Gina around?'

Claire passed her driving licence across to the officer.

'Gina's had an accident in her car. We don't know full details yet but she's in intensive care and we're waiting for the hospital's latest report.'

Claire's face was pale and a frown deepened over her eyes. She looked at the policewoman and just her air of alarm asked what was going on here. The policewoman noticed Claire's sudden pallor and stood to face her.

'Are you all right?' she asked.

'Yes, what you've said is a shock though,' Claire said.

'Can I get you some water?'

'No, I'm fine. Let me sit for a moment.'

But Claire then hesitated. Gina in hospital in intensive care was something added to what was already a dangerous place. For a moment Claire returned the stare of the policewoman but after a pause she decided now was the time to talk. She had much to say about an odd amount of cash flowing through Blake Markets and the people supplying this cash. Claire was angered by what Stone had put in writing to her just a few days ago and this was a time when she would show Harry Stone how she would respond to his blackmail. Rick was very important to her but this money laundering ring she had uncovered would not go away. And Martyn Blake's suicide, still unfolding, had made the search for answers crucial.

'I think I should talk to you about what I think is going on here,' Claire said to the officer.

'What do you mean by that?'

'I don't know anything about Martyn's death but I do know that some cash that has been flowing through this place.' Claire hesitated for a moment. 'It may be money laundering.'

'I'm here to listen but I will call one of my colleagues to join me if you will wait a moment.'

Claire sat solidly still and there was silence after the policewoman called on her phone. A bulky officer arrived two minutes later and just his large, uniformed presence made the room hot, even intimidating. The policewoman opened her notebook and sat forward staring at Claire.

'You said money laundering. Take your time and let's hear what you've got to say.'

'I think someone is trying to pass a large sum of paper money, dirty notes, through this business.'

In the next ten minutes Claire told the two officers all she knew about the cash. She had seen Gina handle some of it, all in crumpled bundles of notes that Martyn had asked her to pay into Blake Markets' bank accounts. Claire thought the cash totalled a quarter of a million but she then hesitated. She was sure she knew where the cash had come from. She knew of Harry Stone and what he had done at Blake Markets but she still hesitated. Claire was feeling the pressure, as soon she would have to write it all down in a statement and sign it.

The policewoman was scribbling furiously and suddenly put her pad on the desk. She had heard enough.

'There's a lot to follow up from what you've already told us and we shall need to find if this has any connection to Martyn Blake's sudden death. But for now we will ask you to come in for questioning at the station by the special crimes officer. The Money Laundering Investigation Unit section of the police deal with this type of scene and I think you should come down to make a full statement. You could of course have your lawyer with you. Would that be okay?' she asked.

'When do you want me to come?'

'Now would be a good time.'

***

Claire left the police station two hours later feeling hungry and thirsty. She had not called a lawyer, she had been quite clear what she was going to say and she had signed a statement. But she was apprehensive. With the claustrophobia of the police station and Gina's shock accident, Claire just wondered what she might have left out or what she had said in the pressure of the moment. But she decided she had dealt with enough today. She felt very insecure about what could now follow from all that she had told the police.

Money laundering by racketeers, who would do anything to keep their ill-gotten cash secure, was a nasty business. Was Gina in intensive care part of this cruel web? Claire did not know but at this time visitors were not allowed to see her. It sounded as if Gina was really badly hurt and Claire was sure driving down a lane into a tree could not have been an accident. It made Claire shiver as she had now seen enough to be concerned for her own safety. She drove cautiously on the motorway, she needed to talk but with Rick still in France a telephone call was not good enough. She needed to see him face to face. She needed to unload all that was in her thoughts and she called Jennie on her car phone. Jennie was shopping, the conversation was brief, but dinner at Newbury together with Roger was easily arranged for that evening.

'You look tired,' were Jennie's first words when Claire came through the front door of the Newbury house a few hours later.

'I feel it, goodness what a day. I've been house-hunting for Rick, and I've been to the police to make a statement. There's been a nasty car accident, there's cash sloshing around down there and it's scary. I mean there's huge bundles of notes that Harry Stone has been trying to wash through the business. And Rick will be horrified when I tell him what's going on,' Claire said.

In this large house with Jennie, Claire, for a while, was able to feel distant from the dirt and the mean part of money laundering she had seen. But she would still soon have to tell Rick all that had happened.

'What have you told the police?' Roger asked as he passed a gin and tonic to Claire.

'All that I know, but there are gaps. Gina knows a lot more.

She will need to describe the man she met in a secluded pub on the coast, what Martyn told her to do, and how she paid it in to the bank of Blake Markets. But that's not going to happen quickly. Gina is suddenly in intensive care from a car accident. I was not allowed in to see her but I can't believe what I was told.

'Harry Stone took me on a spree with Martyn Blake down to Monte Carlo. We had a couple of days where Martyn looked to be in good form. He seemed a regular guy, got on well with Harry and not someone who'd walk away from a problem. But he did like the casino and he played blackjack like a professional. But there was nothing he said that made me think there was this turmoil that was obviously hidden right inside him,' Roger said.

'That's not quite what I saw when I met him. It was in Rick's office. He got up and stalked out without a word because Rick was questioning what was going on at Blake Markets. Martyn knew very well that cash was running tight and Gina was getting to the bottom of what he'd done with bogus invoices. He was syphoning off cash from his own business just to hide his gambling losses. And he didn't like Rick's probing. Even then perhaps he was running away from what he knew was a big hole. And he's now left a lot of pieces to be picked up,' Claire said.

'Martyn using forged invoices is a fraud. Even though he owns most of the business the police would still start proceedings against him. Perhaps he knew that,' Roger said. 'And where does the police statement you gave leave you with Harry Stone and his blackmail threats?' Roger asked.

'I had to bring it all out into the open, and I've only told them what I know.'

'Harry rang this morning asking to meet you at the Arrow Hall site with the insurance assessor. And a last chance, he says, to give him what he needs with the Panama bank account codes. If not he'll call on Rick. How do you feel about that?' Roger asked.

'I'll come to Arrow Hall with you if you want to go,' Jennie said quickly.

Claire thought for a moment before she replied. She had just signed a witness statement on money laundering and she had received a letter from Harry Stone which she saw as deliberate blackmail. Her answer to Jennie was easy.

'No. I'm going to tear up all the codes to his Panama bank accounts and I've already torn up the letter he wrote to me with his demands. Whatever I do he'll never promise he won't go to visit Rick. It's obvious he's getting desperate for cash again and that'll make him aggressive. I don't care about his insurance. It would quickly open up all the old wounds and I'm never visiting Arrow Hall again,' Claire said.

Claire stood to look into the garden. She knew this was going to be a difficult time and she was not sure how to face it.

'Still be careful, Claire, Harry Stone doesn't like losing, and when he gets mad you don't know where it'll take him,' Roger said.

'Tomorrow I'm going to see Gina. I rang the police half an hour ago and all they could tell me was that she was in a critical condition. There was no other car involved, it was down a small country lane, she was driving fast and she went full throttle into a large tree. So what do you make of that?' Claire asked.

'You're being dragged into the middle of some spiteful dealing I can see that. These people, yes that's Harry Stone as well, will do whatever it takes to make a few quid,' Jennie said.

With Harry Stone again intruding into her life, Claire could see the good times from being close to Rick draining away. And what about the country house she had been searching for and why had she already packed to move into Rick's penthouse apartment? Claire sighed heavily. Even after some cocktails, the closeness of the disaster that Harry Stone had started and Martyn Blake had left, just added to her thoughts of the ruins of Arrow Hall. Claire shuddered at what tomorrow might bring. She passed her glass to Roger for another gin and tonic.

Roger stood and turned towards the dining room of his elegant house. The housekeeper had prepared an evening supper of Italian food and she was beckoning them towards the dining room. Claire relaxed into the place and let it enfold her. One day she would maybe invite Jennie and Roger to join her in the company of Rick at their new country house. It was a thought that quickly came, but just as quickly Claire pushed it aside. It probably would never happen now.

Halfway through dinner Roger was called to his house phone by the housekeeper.

'A Mr Harry Stone wants you urgently,' she said.

'Claire's now going to get what's been coming to her for a while. Her past deception, and now she's looted my safe at Arrow Hall. It's open and she's the only one I ever trusted with a key. Panama codes to bank accounts, that's what she's taken,' Stone said without stopping.

'Harry, hold on, calm down,'

'Tell her I'm going to see her man Rick Austen tomorrow. Tell him about her thieving and betrayal.'

The phone went dead after only thirty seconds. Roger slowly returned to the dining table and sat down heavily.

'He's going to see Rick Austen. He's thinks you've stolen his Panama codes and he's going to spill out everything to Rick. Your past deception. And, Claire, those are his words not mine,' Roger said.

Claire froze. She knew sometime Rick would know what had happened two years ago, and now it was too close.

24

Vlad had left his small room at the top of Marine House early that morning to walk the two miles to check the safe storage at Raven Garage of the Ferrari. Just before six in the morning it was light and Vlad peered through a window of the disused farmer's barn where it had been laid up with several other cars. It was still just as he had left it only a couple of days ago.

Vlad hauled himself on to a lump of wood below the window to get a better look and he thought he saw someone moving between the stored cars. But a heavy hand on his shoulder pulled him backwards and he fell heavily to the concrete path. He felt it push the wind from his lungs and he let out a loud groan. Lying flat out with his head on the ground Vlad opened his eyes. A huge hooded figure looked down at him with a terrorising glare and Vlad froze. Yes, he knew that face.

'You come to get mister's car back?'

Vlad rolled over and tried to get up but he was pushed back with a firm foot on his shoulder.

'You been looking after mister's big house by the seaside? You been keeping that pretty lady safe when I called? And you thought you'd seen the last of me but here I am.'

Vlad was pinned to the ground with a heavy foot on his chest and the hooded face spat at him.

'Yeh, it's my turn now. You broke some of my bones in the backyard of mister's big house. You remember when you tried to chase me away. And I can tell you, you won't get up from the dirt where you belong very quickly, when I've finished with you. But something for you to watch. Look at your mister's nice shiny big red car over there first.'

The hooded face pointed to the storage garage and it suddenly glowed red inside with smoke coming from a vent in the roof. With no warning there was a muffled exploding noise and a large finger of flame burst through the window where Vlad had looked earlier. Vlad tried to remove the foot of the hoodie standing over him but he was kicked to the ground and felt the pain in his ribs. He was supposed to keep his eye on the valuable car inside this garage belonging to his boss; but what now?

The flames were taking hold of the storage garage and, with petrol that had been sprayed around the floor of the place, there would not be much left when it was all finished. Vlad was in pain from the hard kick and again he tried to get up but the hoodie saw his movement and started to kick Vlad's body and his head with a vicious rage of hatred, until Vlad was senseless like a rag doll. He was only stopped from injuring Vlad's lifeless body further by the noise of a fire tender, a little distance away yet but getting closer.

His mate ran to him from the garage, gave a wanton kick to Vlad's torso and they both ran off laughing and into a field where their getaway would not be noticed.

***

Stone had not heard Vlad leave Marine House. He was not yet dressed as the hard ringing tone of the entry button on his front door startled him. It was six-thirty in the morning and he grabbed his dressing gown and quickly threw his arms into the sleeves as he walked down the stairs. He saw on the video camera several men standing outside on the steps to his front door, two with 'Police' blazoned over their uniform. Stone stood back at this unexpected early morning call. He did not like the police. They had never helped him and he classed them as authority people who meddled into your privacy.

'What do you want?' Stone asked into the video speaker with a shout.

'Is this the house of Harry Stone?'

'I said, what do you want?'

'We have a police warrant to enter and search the premises of Mr Harry Stone. So tell me before we force entry, are you Harry Stone?'

The house was empty and cold. He had been working right on the edge of the law and is this what happened if you were caught? Stone shivered at this early morning call. He guessed they had come to comb through Marine House but they would find nothing here. There was nothing in writing concerning Martyn's deal and even his Panama accounts, Claire still held everything that would lead to them. But how had they found him so quickly after Martyn opted out?

'What're you looking for?' Stone shouted.

'If you don't let us in within the next minute, we shall take measures to force entry. So stand back from the door until we are inside,' the officer said.

Stone stood back and pressed the release button to open the door. Within seconds there were two police officers in the hallway with the first one flashing a warrant card at Stone and followed by three other casually dressed men.

'I'll ask again, are you Harry Stone?'

'Yeh, but what's going on?' Stone mumbled looking away.

'You're not to make any phone calls except to your solicitor and you're not to remove anything. One of my officers will be with you as we search the whole of these premises so if you want to get dressed he will accompany you to the bedroom. We will also require keys to open doors and we may remove any computers and copies of any papers we find in this search. It will save a lot of your time if you cooperate and leave us to search this house and I can assure you we will not disturb the place more than necessary.'

By now all the men had pushed past Stone, running up the stairs and into the sitting room with a noisy stampede of boots on the floor.

'I said what's going on?' Stone repeated, now beginning to feel angry.

'We have information that these premises may be used for laundering money from narcotics dealing and we will search for evidence. We have been investigating a large narcotics' ring and we have made arrests late last evening of people we believe are involved with laundering cash from drugs and circulating it on building sites around London. Our investigations have led us to a building site in Sudbury. We understand you own and control that place, Mr Stone. And depending on what we find here and how you cooperate we will release you on police bail at the end of this search.'

'Why so heavy?' Stone said to the officer standing next to him.

The officer ignored the question and Stone walked away to the stairs and to his bedroom. He was followed by a large officer who said nothing but who then stood at the door as if to ensure Stone did not escape. Stone had much to hide, but there was nothing in this house that could arouse interest. He was being pushed into money laundering with a case of cash that had gone to Blake Markets, but he could deny knowing anything of that. Stone was not a man who wrote much down, and all he could think of was the copy of a letter to Claire demanding his Panama codes still on his computer. He had only one laptop, and piles of papers on other deals that had gathered dust in his study. And there were several demands from the taxman for a large sum of money which he had now settled.

Followed by the large officer as closely as a shadow, he went to the kitchen. Making a cup of tea for himself and in total silence except for the heavy boots of the police in the hallway, Stone's anger was rising. There was constant noise around the house as if they were expecting resistance to their search. The next hour for Stone, who knew this process was now unstoppable, was a time to decide what he would do once the law had left.

With his mug of tea he sat at the kitchen table and switched on the television for the early morning news just to divert himself from listening to this intrusion. He looked at his watch, fidgeted with his wallet as he counted the cash he had, and fumbled in a drawer for a card that he found to check an address. It was a place he would visit as soon as the police had cleared out.

The visitors methodically searched the large rooms of Marine House, bedrooms and bathrooms, elegant sitting rooms, but found nothing to interest them. They even moved on quickly from Stone's dusty study. Stone had never dealt in narcotics, this house was clean of packets of white powder, injection needles, everything. And Stone felt very smug that he had beaten them by sending Vlad with a holdall of US dollars, drugs money from St Vincent, to hide in Arrow Hall.

They would find nothing in Marine House but what would Claire have told them? She did not know about Sudbury, she would not know much about the money flowing through Blake Markets. And Martyn was no longer there to be questioned. As he stared at the flickering image on the television screen while not seeing anything, an enticing thought came to Stone. He stood, neatened the pile of bills that were growing again on the kitchen table and then walked into the large sitting room with balconies that looked across the road to the sea beyond. He knew he should have thought of this long ago.

Late last evening they had probably arrested Boozy and his mates from the site but Xavier was higher up the pyramid. He would be able to keep two steps away, hidden behind his ring of druggies who dealt for him. And now even with hearing the trampling of boots, Stone's anger cooled. Of course this heavy-handed visit was nothing to do with him.

It took two hours for the search to finish and the officers had meticulously scoured every corner of the house. Stone escorted the intrusive team to the front door and they were all now grinning and laughing as if their very early morning visit was a real triumph.

'So what're you taking?' Stone asked.

'One laptop you should sign for please, sir,' the lead officer said. 'But we won't know how we shall progress these enquiries until we've put it all together. We still have information that has been passed to us that may lead us to question you further.'

'I'll have my lawyer deal with that,' Stone snapped as he closed the front door.

***

After the police raid Stone had a shower and dressed slowly. He had not heard from Jo for the past three days and walking around the kitchen he called her. He wanted her back but just as it had been in the previous times when he called her, Jo's phone rang and was not answered. Marine House was not the same without her, it felt very empty and at midday in a dark mood he took a cab to the train station. After the police raid earlier that day he had a pulsing headache around his temples caused by his blood pressure rising and his overfill of whisky the day before. But Stone was now driven in a way he could not stop, he had one outstanding place to visit and he was going to deal with it right now.

At Victoria station in London, with falling rain in the capital causing a shortage of cabs, Stone queued for half an hour at the rank. In the slow-moving line of impatient people, Stone rocked from one foot to the other, peering anxiously around in case another traveller took a cab in front of him. He was now feeling very belligerent with a growing state of nervous energy driving him forward to get this visit finished.

He paid off the cab in Mayfair outside a glass-fronted entrance to offices. This place was not his scene at all but he knew how to dress for it and appearing smart with a well-cut grey suit, a tie and polished shoes, he looked a likely visitor to do business here. In the reception area in front of the usual security desk a group of people were noisily talking and he walked over to stand close to them. He scanned on the wall the list of businesses in the building. A lift door opened almost in front of him and then, alone, he darted into its dimly lit interior and pressed the button for the fifth floor. He had dodged security.

The lift doors opened quietly onto the fifth floor and Stone looked around, unsure which direction to take. He walked slowly down a carpeted corridor until he saw the name that had been on the wall in the entrance hall. A sign, 'Trifoni Investments' was against a half-open door and boldly he walked into the reception room. Harry Stone had come here with a smirking arrogance that would push everything aside until he got what he wanted. Even though his headache had increased he was now in the right place. He buttoned his jacket, pushed the door open and quickly marched into the room.

'Is this Rick Austen's office?' Stone asked. He shouted to make his voice sound like a command.

A startled secretary looked up at the visitor and put the paper she was handling onto the desk. 'Do I know you?' she asked as she stood to face Stone.

No, he should not be here but Stone ignored her as he could see a man, sitting at a desk on the phone, through a glass panel. If it was Rick Austen, this was his chance.

'Whoever you are you can't see Mr Austen this afternoon and you will have to make an appointment,' the secretary said.

'This is urgent and Rick Austen will want to hear what I've got to say,' Stone shouted.

He ignored the secretary who was now trying to hold his arm but he roughly pushed her aside. Without knocking he yanked the door handle almost without stopping his forward movement. The secretary backed away as she saw Rick turn towards Stone. There was no physical danger showing from this unwanted intruder, he was well dressed and Rick, a big six-foot man, had learned to look after himself. Rick Austen was finishing a call, he put his phone down and he turned to face Stone.

'I'm sorry, Rick, this man has somehow dodged security and managed to get straight up here, I don't know what he wants, and

I don't know who he is,' the PA said and looked flustered as if she had not managed Rick's diary correctly. For her, the presence of this intruder was her failure.

'I'm Harry Stone, remember my name and you'd better stop and listen to what I've got to say. Claire Watts worked for me until she pushed herself into your business. She lied, she was deceitful and she was the one who lured you to the Cotswolds where you had a nasty beating. You remember, two years ago? That woman's not to be trusted, she's a fraud, she got to you by double-dealing, she's stolen the codes to some of my bank accounts which have valuable money in them and whatever she says…'

'Stop it whoever you are!' Rick shouted at the top of his voice.

'Remember me, remember what I've said because you'll want to know it all when I've finished,' Stone said.

'What the hell are you up to?' Rick shouted at Stone who was now approaching him to come face to face. But Rick was not frightened. He stood his ground and he looked at Stone with a penetrating stare and Stone did not see Rick press a button under the top of his desk. Stone just saw his stare, cold with glaring blue eyes as if he would wring his neck if his secretary was not watching closely.

'Claire Watts will undermine this swish place just as she did my business until I found her out.'

'Mr Stone, if that's who you are, get out of here, I've got nothing to say to you. And I don't like your manners barging in here and shouting your head off.'

'Don't hide her because I'm going to get to her. She worked for me at the same time she pretended to work for you. She has a nasty cunning way with her which I don't like,' Stone said.

'What on earth are you talking about?'

There was silence for less than twenty seconds before a large, neatly dressed man in a security uniform entered Rick's office and looked at him for instructions.

'Sir, you rang,' he said.

Stone could see what was coming and he moved further towards Rick.

'I've got more to tell you about Claire Watts. You've sent her down to Blake Markets but don't believe what she tries to tell you, she'll lie, she'll let out everything that you think is private, all your business secrets, and she doesn't care what damage that will do.' Stone stopped as the security guard moved towards him.

Rick stood back a few paces from Stone and spoke quickly to the security guard.

'This gentleman would like to be taken to the street door at the back of the building and then asked to leave. I'm sure you can deal with this quietly,' he said, pointing to Stone and then looking at his secretary who was frozen at her desk.

But Stone folded his arms. 'I'm not leaving, I've got a lot more to say,' he shouted in defiance. 'Say goodbye to your business because, with Claire Watts in it, it won't be safe. She'll try to thieve the lot from you.'

The security officer moved towards Stone and towered over him. 'Please come with me, sir,' he said. 'It will be best for you if you don't make a fuss about this.'

'Leave me alone!' Stone shouted. 'I'm not going anywhere until I've told this man what he needs to hear. So don't you dare touch me.'

The guard looked at Rick who nodded towards the door as he moved closer to his desk knowing that this would only end with some form of nastiness. The guard firmly took Stone's arm but with a swift movement of his other arm Stone hit the guard with his fist, hard in the face, causing blood to spurt freely from his nose.

'Shall I call the police?' the secretary shouted.

'No, I'll deal with it. Just tell them downstairs I've got a difficult situation so they know when we reach the outside door,' the guard said as he grabbed hold of Stone.

They moved to Rick's door in a noisy tumble and with Stone's arms now flailing in the air, hitting anything that was in the way. The

PA peered round the door trying to see the extraordinary sight of the physical removal of this grey-haired, well-dressed man. Rick watched as security dealt efficiently with this shouting, uninvited visitor. Rick kept calm. He did not react to the tirade spouted by Stone and he turned away. Whatever this fracas was all about he had other urgent business to deal with; the papers for the purchase of a chateau in France had to be returned to his French attorneys that afternoon.

The PA watched as Stone was lifted easily by the security guard who let him tumble to the floor outside Rick's office suite. Stone lay there for a moment breathless but he scrambled to his knees, his shirt hanging out from his waistband and his usually well-tended hair dishevelled across his forehead. The speed and force of being ejected had stunned him and he looked back to the door of Rick's office. He wanted to finish what he had come to say. But any movement was barred by the large security guard who stared at Stone, daring him to get up and go back.

'Now are you going to leave quietly, sir?' the security guard asked. 'Or do we have to carry you from the building and call the police?'

Stone staggered to the door from the outer office into the corridor. He made for the lift but another guard took him firmly by the arm.

'Not that way, my friend,' he said. 'Back stairs for you today and then out from the back entrance to this building. Got it?'

Stone did not reply but quietly walked in front of the guard to the uncarpeted stairs that were the fire escape route from the fifth floor. The guard held Stone's arm firmly as for the next few minutes they continued in silence down the five floors. At the bottom he was taken to the door where the exit bar was pressed for him. Without a word he was then pushed with force into the busy London street. Stone caught his breath and swore. He stared back at the building, annoyed his meeting had been short but he was sure he had shouted enough to pin Claire's name to the exit door too.

***

Stone was uncomfortable on his train journey back to Brighton. He was dishevelled and uncertain how much he had got through to Rick in the short time he was in his office. But he was sure he must have made some mark just by the disturbance he had caused in the otherwise very quiet office space. He had shouted his name and Rick would soon find out who he was and he would then know why he had come. The more he recalled what he had said the more he was sure that he had killed off any friendship Claire had enjoyed with Rick Austen.

But Stone was left with the problem of his Panama bank accounts. Claire still had the codes, his access to thousands of dollars. He would perhaps make plans now to travel the long journey to the high rise buildings of Panama City. He knew the name of the offshore office Claire had used to set them up and there he would present himself with his passport, and any other details they needed to start the accounts running again. But as he walked up the steps to Marine House he wavered. That was a long way to go and he could just let the whole lot rest until he started on something new and forgot about them. They would not be lost and maybe sometime he would still find a way to get them from Claire.

Once in Marine House he kept to his ritual and walked into his study to find the Glenfiddich bottle. Feeling satisfied with his visit he took a sip from his glass but he stopped. There was movement in the kitchen. A few seconds later Dave poked his head around the study door.

'How did you get in and what do you think you're doing here?' Stone demanded.

'I've got things to tell you boss.' Dave sat in a chair and faced Stone across his desk.

'It'd better be good.'

'The new gates have gone up at Sudbury.'

Stone waved his hand and looked away as if he no longer cared.

'Is that all you've come to tell me?'

'Listen to this, Mr Stone. I've heard from mates who came to fix the gates. Rumour is the cops have done a big drugs and money laundering bust around London. And rumour is they're still looking for more of the big boys. And some of Xavier's ring are caught up in it.'

'Where is Xavier? Is he behind bars?'

'Don't know, but Boozy has been taken in for questioning, and some other boys from other sites around London. They won't talk, they won't say much, they daren't because the lot at the top of the chain will be looking out to see where all this leads.'

'Nobody else nosing around the site?'

'Only the gates going up. No sign of Xavier so I went to his East End doss. I wanted to find out what's up. But his place over the charity shop was all locked up and not even any sound of mad dogs scratching at the door.'

After he had taken another sip of his whisky Stone leant back in his chair and looked up to the ceiling. It had been very quiet since he had brought back fifty thousand dollars from the Caribbean but he was wary. That money would be missed and there would be danger lurking round this place soon.

'Get out, Dave. Go and keep your eye on the site and let me know what goes. But I like the thought of Xavier taken out by the cops. What could be better than that.' As an afterthought Stone stood and walked towards the door. 'The police were here, came early this morning, they searched and what did they find? Nothing. This place is clean. And so am I.'

A thin smile spread across Stone's ashen face. At that moment he believed the threat from Xavier and his thugs was receding fast.

***

Claire's mobile rang when she was alone in her Knightsbridge flat. It was seven in the evening. It was Rick. When he had not seen Claire for the day, Rick always called at this time, and although he had been back for two days from France he had been too busy in his office to meet with Claire. Much of her flat had now been moved into Rick's apartment but she was tidying the place and she was placing into boxes the clutter to be thrown away. Then she would hand the keys back and her move would be final. As she took the call her flat had a cold, empty feeling and she again felt alone. At Arrow Hall she had never been alone even though the house was deep in the countryside.

This evening she had called up some friends to meet for dinner. They were going to a small restaurant in Covent Garden and Claire was about to walk to the main road to take a cab there. This evening's call from Rick was short. Again, Rick was in a hurry.

'Sorry, Claire, this is just a quick call, I'm still at my desk but just to see how your day has been. The dreadful news of Martyn Blake is still sinking in. Do we know anymore about why he did it?' Rick asked.

'Things are slowly coming out and I think that Martyn was up to something very odd before his death but it'll wait until we meet because there's a lot to say,' Claire said.

'Sometime we'll need to decide what to do down there. But not yet as I've got something more pressing. The deadline that I've got to meet on the French chateau is tomorrow. But it'll be a fun investment when it's done.'

'I'm looking forward to seeing it and I hope it works better than Blake Markets. When I went yesterday I found Gina in intensive care after a nasty car accident. Whatever Martyn was up to, Gina is an important cog in the wheel who can tell us how Blake Markets work.'

'Claire, you sound worried. Are you all right?'

'I've dealt with an immediate problem and please, Rick, I don't want to talk over the phone,' Claire said quickly.

'Are you sure there's nothing else I need to follow up straight away?'

'No. The police are buzzing around the place, let them comb through and see what they come up with.'

'All right, you still sound worried but we'll leave it alone for a day or two as there's something else I need to talk about with you. Claire, get yourself ready, please because tomorrow I need to take you away. So don't fix anything else for the weekend,' Rick said.

'Sounds interesting, where are we going?'

'I'll pick you up at your apartment Friday afternoon fiveish and we'll take it from there. Is that all right?'

'Yes, but I'd like to know where we're going. What do I need to pack?' Claire asked.

'Well, let's just leave it we're going out of town, nothing formal, just casual. But we do need to talk,' Rick said.

'Of course, I'll hold everything until then.'

'Sorry this call's got to be short but I really am up against it, so see you tomorrow.'

It was just yesterday Claire had been in a police station making a voluntary statement on what she had found at Blake Markets and the memory of it was still raw. And Claire would need to pick her time to talk to Rick. She would have to tell him of money laundering by Harry Stone a man she thought Rick knew nothing about. But what she would tell Rick might not be quite the same details she had given to the police.

And where was Rick taking her for a few days because 'we need to talk and I've got a lot I must tell you'? It sounded too formal for how they would talk together, and usually Claire would be excited at the thought of a mystery weekend away with Rick. He always planned breaks like this to make them very special but this time Claire was anxious about going away. She was very unsure about the accident that Gina had suffered and she was having growing misgivings about closing the door of her Kensington flat for the final time. Tomorrow, should she tell the agent to keep it open for another month before she left it with bare furniture like a skeleton?

Claire was very uncertain as she put her phone down from talking to Rick. She was disappointed that he had talked quickly about buying a chateau with its vineyard but he did not even ask about her search for a country house. In the last few days Claire had spent a lot of time with estate agents, driving to isolated spots to look at properties most of which she had discarded. And now Rick's call made her wonder if he was really serious about buying a house in the country. Or had he changed his mind?

Two minutes later Claire slammed her front door shut and took a cab to be with her friends for dinner. She needed the space it would give her, she needed to keep her distance for a few hours from the thoughts around Gina and Blake Markets. But Claire was now uneasy and it left her feeling even more isolated from Rick and suddenly very apart from him.

25

Vlad was in hospital but Stone was not going to visit. He could never face the stark whiteness of a hospital ward and its lack of privacy with other people lying in their beds. The news that Xavier had got to the car, left Stone angry. He was angry with Vlad for letting it happen but he had quickly forgotten that he had given the address of the Raven Garage when he was facing the deep water at the end of the pier. Stone's only immediate reaction was to find and examine closely the insurance certificate for the precious car. It looked good, it was in date, his investment was still there and he stuffed it in an envelope to post to Roger with instructions to chase hard for the cash to cover the burned out Ferrari.

Stone had always shown condescension to Vlad. In the last two years that Vlad had worked for him Stone had shouted at him usually demanding instant action on something if only driving him around in one of his very big cars. Some of Xavier's thugs were still out there, not yet caught in the police web, which had included searching his house. His hope was that Xavier was being detained and questioned but Vlad had been treated like a punch-bag. Stone would not want that to happen, as from Vlad, it was only a short distance before they got to him.

Stone was sure he could ignore the final day for the return of the quarter million which was looming. He was still smarting from the try-on from Xavier of short changing by fifteen grand, but the bag full of US dollars was now his, his to keep until his site at Sudbury was handed back. As he had done often in the past few weeks, he stared through the long French windows to the sea and, unusually, it was even too early for a glass of Glenfiddich. The emptiness in Marine House gave it a stuffy feel. The windows and doors were closed and with no air from the outside it was sealed in its own smell of staleness. And early that morning, Jo had called and left a terse message on his answerphone. She was coming in later.

It reminded Stone he still owed her for chasing off the bailiffs and the account for lawyers' fees on work they had done in setting up Sudbury. He walked back up the steep flight of stairs to the dressing room behind his bedroom. It was a dark corner of the house with only a dim light but from a small safe, well hidden in the wall Stone counted out £4,000 in crisp new twenty-pound banknotes. His brooding mood continued as he went back to his study, placed the cash in the top drawer of his desk and poured a glass of whisky. And just for a short while he worried on the state of Vlad. He had been badly beaten and he would no longer be around to help answer his calling.

Stone heard Jo as she came in half an hour later. She was tidying the kitchen, clearing into the dishwasher the dirty plates that he had left from his breakfast. He waited several minutes as he heard her go to the sitting room and rearrange the long drapes into a tidy and neat pattern. This time he would greet her with a smile and release the tension in his face.

'This house is very quiet when you're not here,' Stone said as soon as Jo came into his study.

Jo looked at Stone, her usual smiling face now very subdued. Stone stood and moved towards her. Marine House had let her down in the past few weeks and he needed to tell her that was all changing now.

'It's been a bad time in Marine House, HS, so I want to know if you've sorted yourself out yet,' Jo said.

'What do you mean? Nothing's happened that I can't cope with,' Stone replied. He moved towards the drinks cabinet in the corner and looked at Jo for a response. She hesitated but then shook her head.

'Too early for me today, and I've got too much else to deal with.'

'I've got to repay you for getting the bailiffs off my back,' Stone said as he sat behind his large desk. He reached in a drawer and took out the four thousand in crisp new notes he had taken from the safe. He handed them to Jo who was hovering as if she was not going to stay there for long.

'It's for the bailiffs. Keep the change and I'll make sure it doesn't happen again,' Stone said.

'I felt threatened, I felt very intimidated.'

Stone looked at Jo as if he was searching for something that would tell him what she was really thinking. Jo was always optimistic, but today her hair was not meticulously combed and there was little colour around her face.

'Yeh, it's been a demanding few weeks, but I've sorted all the troublemakers. There'll be no more loiterers in the house or sitting on the front doorstep and we'll get on with replacing the carpet in the sitting room. And then life here in Marine House will all settle back into its usual routine.'

'I'm going,' Jo said, and put her head in her hands. She wanted to hide a tear from Stone's gaze.

'What do you mean, you're going?'

'I don't like you shouting at visitors and shouting down the phone and sometimes I find it very uncomfortable to be around you because you don't know how to relax away from the Glenfiddich bottle.'

'I have to shout, that's how my business works. There's some nasty people out there I have to deal with. And yes I do enjoy a glass or two but it doesn't interrupt what goes on in Marine House. So surely that's not a reason to leave.'

'HS, please, you don't have to explain to me the people you

do business with. Most of the time I can take all that. But now is different.'

'No it isn't,' Stone said quickly and immediately knew he was being too loud in talking to Jo.

'Listen, please, HS. Give me space to talk for a moment. I don't want to go but I have to,' Jo said.

'No you don't. This house is as open for you to be here as it has always been. Jo, you're part of this place and whatever you think of me there's no reason for you to leave.'

'I had a phone call. Early yesterday morning. My father's just had a stroke, he's in hospital and my mother has early-onset dementia. I've got to go to look after them, they need my help twenty-four hours a day. They live in Bury, outside Manchester, a long way from here, and I'm off in the morning.'

'Jo, that can't be right. How can you deal with somebody with dementia let alone a stroke? Go and find professional carers to take that on.'

'I won't know much until I get there, but you can take it, HS, that I won't be around Marine House again for some time.' Jo stood and started to walk towards the door.

Stone walked a few paces behind her.

'Jo, please do you really have to go that quickly? Have you no time for another day perhaps to have a drink to say goodbye?' Stone pleaded.

'I'm going in the morning because I have to. Then I'll see what can be arranged for carers but they would never survive for long apart in a nursing home.'

'Do you need money to get it sorted?' Stone asked.

'If that's what you're offering, no. They've got plenty in the bank.' Jo had picked up her coat, she was halfway down the hall to the front door of Marine House when she turned and looked at Stone. 'Would you be able to keep the job of housekeeper open for a few weeks if I am able to come back?' she asked.

There were tears in her eyes rolling easily down her cheek. She did nothing to hide them and Harry Stone looked at Jo again as she hesitated at the front door. He did not know how to deal with this type of scene and the barrier of his coldness was difficult for him to thaw. He had shouted at her, he had told her to go away when he was angry with himself and he regretted the times that he had shown his uncontrolled irritation.

He went to the front door and held it open for her. Jo had wiped tears from her cheek and she gave him a pensive look as she stood for a moment on the top step.

'Please come back, Jo. I need you here,' Stone said.

'That may not be possible but I shall miss you, HS, and Marine House. I want to say goodbye to Vlad, is he upstairs in his room?'

That question was the last one Stone could face up to that morning and he turned away.

'He's in the County Hospital. Had an accident. If you call on him make sure he has everything he needs because he's missed in Marine House just as you are.'

Jo was quickly down the few steps to the pavement and into a waiting cab. Through the window Stone saw her wave with a handkerchief held to her eyes.

Stone shut the front door quickly. It was not so long ago that he had decided he would walk out and leave the landlord to chase for the debt of the last quarter's rent on Marine House. But suddenly that had changed. Today he would pay the rent right up and hold the front door of this large house open until Jo could return. He would still be there to welcome her. And till then he would toast the thought with another glass of whisky.

***

For the first time since Claire had known Rick she felt nervous at meeting him. His call yesterday had been short. Those words *'we need to talk'* she could not clear from her thoughts. It had sounded a formal call from Rick; Claire packed a case of clothes with no idea where she were going but it did not sound like a mystery fun weekend.

There was uncertainty, and with what she had seen at Blake Markets in the past few days, Claire was tense. She had long ago decided she would not respond to Stone's blackmail threats but she knew Stone well. The money he had poured into Blake Markets was lost and by now he would be running short of cash. Soon he would do anything to get access to his offshore bank accounts and Claire was nervous where that might lead.

There was much Claire needed to tell Rick but she would be careful. She was still unsure why Rick would now want to take her away like this now, and Claire had a nagging feeling that her last two years of her closeness with Rick might soon end. And what would happen then? Rick would leave, probably immediately, but Claire hoped with at least a civilised goodbye. Then she would stop the final removal of her personal items to Rick's apartment, terminating a very important part of her life.

Rick had said fiveish to collect Claire and it was just five minutes after the hour that her doorbell rang. Minutes later as she was sitting in the car, Rick gave her a light kiss on her cheek but he had few words of greeting. He was in a hurry and she felt a remoteness holding him back from what she had believed was their growing intimacy of the past year.

'So where are you taking me?' Claire asked, unable to hold back from her need to know.

'I can't tell you that,' Rick replied, and in a dense traffic queue concentrated on the driving.

This last year had been busy and exciting with so much to do and see in the London Season. And she had completed work for Rick, troubleshooting for him, and everything she had started she had finished with the problem solved. She would write a detailed report on Blake Markets and give it to Rick who would then pay her a fee and that would end their business relationship too.

Today, Claire had already decided she would let Rick talk first and then she would say sorry for what Harry Stone would have told him about her. Of course she had been deceitful to Rick, but only from the pressure of Harry Stone, and for some time she had braced herself against what Rick might say if this came out. He had a lot of friends, she would not be missed, and he would get on with his business and social life quite easily. But being underhand, no, that was never her way, she told herself. And if that is what Rick really thought today she would just say goodbye and not try to argue with him about the past. Leaving Rick was going to be upsetting. To soften the parting, tomorrow she would go and talk to Jennie and Roger; they had never met Rick but they knew all about the deviousness of Harry Stone.

Released from the traffic onto the motorway Rick had been driving fast with little talk between them. It was an hour and half later that she noticed a familiar village of sandstone houses covered with thatched roofs.

'I've been here before,' she said to Rick as the car slowed.

'I thought you might recognise it.'

It was just ten minutes later that he drew the car under an arch and into a hotel driveway that Claire recognised. She remembered a walk through a garden from the car park that led to a mellow brick hotel. It was here exactly two years ago that Rick had brought her here and Claire remembered meeting the crooked businessman demanding money for a contract Rick was bidding for. And she needed no reminder of the savage beating Rick suffered by thugs, mistaking him for Harry Stone. Claire shuddered as she remembered the horror of that evening, the wounds of which would now all be opened up again.

There was little conversation between them as they showered and changed in a wide suite that looked out onto a colourful rose garden. In the bar it was very busy and noisy and dinner was in the high-vaulted dining room where there were hushed tones with little chance of talking easily. It left Claire questioning what this was all about. In the past two years Rick had never talked about being viciously assaulted in this place. But perhaps Stone's visit to him two days ago was now going to change that.

Over dinner, where she could not easily escape, Claire was certain Rick was going to unload all the disappointment he now felt about her. It was not until the main course and after they had both enjoyed cocktails, champagne, a glass of wine, that Rick leaned back in his chair and looked hard at the frown on Claire's face.

'Sorry I haven't said much in the car but I've had a busy week and I'm still winding down from it.'

'So why drive all the way here? Why not stay in London?' Claire asked.

Rick leaned forward in his chair and took Claire's hand across the table. Claire did not flinch but she knew her hand felt cold.

'Two years ago to the day we started a relaxing few nights away in this hotel and it didn't work out quite as I had planned.'

'You had a terrible beating on the pavement just outside this place so, I don't understand, Rick, why come back now to open up all those dreadful memories?' Claire asked.

'You know Harry Stone don't you?'

Claire froze. So coming here was just to drag her through it again and then say goodbye. She took her hand from Rick's, and with a deep frown again over her face she looked away, feeling so tense her hand was shaking with nervousness.

'Yes, of course I know him. But I don't ever want to talk about him. I'm sorry, Rick, for what I did, I know I should have owned up a long time ago but you were so badly hurt by those thugs that...'

'Claire, please,' Rick said, and leaned closer to Claire across the table.

'I've been living with it for two years, I feel I've double-crossed you and all for a deal that Harry Stone wanted to take from you,' Claire said quickly.

'Do you know Stone came to see me?'

'I guessed he would, he had been threatening, almost

blackmailing me, against our friendship.' Claire's voice croaked and she stopped.

'I didn't listen to him. I know all about Harry Stone.'

'But I've found Stone's blighted cash flowing through Martyn's supermarkets. Rick, I have a lot I need to tell you about that place and what Harry Stone is trying to do there.'

'Claire, not now, there's plenty of time for you to let me have all that another day.'

'Did Harry Stone say a lot about me?'

'I had him ejected from my office. Security took him. He was bundled out as he was shouting nonsense at me about you,' Rick said.

'I've been devious and I'm sorry.'

'You're not a devious person, I know that. You're clever and clean in all you do. Claire, let me tell you, I've known all along what happened on the pavement just outside this place two years ago. I've always known all about Harry Stone and what he's up to but I never wanted to hurt you with talking about it and I hoped it had gone away.'

'But what about the beating you had when they thought they were beating Harry Stone? And Rick, that's a beating I led you into.'

'Claire, please believe me that I know you didn't lead me into it at all. I had hoped that I would never have to talk about this with you and the attack was all finished but after Stone called on my offices… well, it just came tumbling out again.'

'I'm surprised that the police didn't probe more at the time. You were badly hurt,' Claire said.

'I never left it to the police. After the mugging I was so concerned at being beaten up for no reason and I was worried it was something to do with a business deal I had gone through although I couldn't think of anything or anybody who'd want to do that to me. All my deals are clean, so after the attack I hired my own private investigators to probe into the mugging and they found all the details about Harry Stone and what happened on that day.'

'Rick, were your investigators checking up on me? To find out if I'd been lying to you?' Claire looked away and she suddenly felt uncomfortable.

'I hope you know I would never, ever try to do that. Please trust me,' Rick said.

Claire used her handkerchief to dab her eye. The memory of the last two years flashed into her mind, with all the times they had enjoyed together when Rick could have chosen many other girls to be his partner. Of course Rick had trusted her all the time, there was now no doubt about that.

'Can we together now draw a line right under it all and move on just as we have in the last couple of years?' Rick said.

'So, this evening?' Claire asked.

'It's to complete where we left off the dinner at this table in this restaurant two years ago. It's to say thank you for all that you did in looking after me in my convalescence. I needed you and you did it without stopping or asking for anything.'

'I just wanted to make sure you were looked after, I owed you something and I couldn't run away just like that,' Claire said.

'Nothing was your fault. It was all down to that man Harry Stone. But we've now moved on and moved on together. Okay? Let's enjoy tonight as we should have done two years ago before we were interrupted.'

Claire kept her tears back and she managed to whisper to Rick, 'Okay.'

'There's something else I need to show you, something else we need to talk about but that's for tomorrow,' Rick said as they clinked their glasses together over the table.

26

Stone woke early. His head was still pounding in tune to a beat from his heart and he felt queasiness in the pit of his stomach as he left his bed and made for the bathroom. This nausea was different, he knew he had indulged in too many large measures of whisky in the past few days and the volume had been growing imperceptibly as he freely poured the whisky into his glass. Jo had noticed, Jo had told him, but Jo had now gone.

For a moment he was unsteady on his feet, but he turned the shower full on and with the water barely warm he stood under it and closed his eyes. For a few minutes he stood still and gradually the thumping in his head subsided but he was sure he could see and feel Xavier's menace, even the smell of his stale alcohol stained breath. Stone left the shower and, with his dressing gown around his shoulders, he shaved and gradually felt fresher. But looking in the mirror he dabbed at the black ring under his eye and he rubbed the ache in his shoulder.

It was now indelibly stuck in his mind that yesterday he had finally dealt with Claire. By squaring up to Rick Austen, he had said all that was needed to make Rick doubt anything Claire might try to tell him. And Stone never expected to see Claire again, the Arrow Hall site was now being sold and he would settle himself the insurance from the fire that had reduced the building to rubble. He would then pay the next quarter's rent on Marine House.

It took black coffee and even a slice of dark toast before Stone felt able to think about how he would get away from Xavier and his thugs. While they were being chased by the crime squad from the police he would go to hide in some secure London hotel. Claridges was his ideal place, security was discreet there, and he trusted it. His two gold credit cards had open card limits and when dressed he would pack and call a cab to take him to London. He would stay away for as long as it took to clear Xavier's lump of infected cash and keep the man from ever finding him again.

Sitting alone at the kitchen table with his second cup of coffee, Stone was suddenly aroused. There was a thumping and scrabbling noise he did not understand, a noise he was not expecting. Vlad was still recovering in hospital from a merciless beating, and it left the house very quiet, almost sealed from the outside. The scuffling and plodding persisted and Stone went to close an open window that looked onto the gloomy back garden. There was a snarling dog barking at full pitch in the narrow lane below. Stone swore at a neighbour for letting that happen but, of course, it did nothing and the sound came closer.

Suddenly, Stone was fully aware that something he did not understand was happening. In a moment of panic he ran up the stairs to his bedroom. He tossed the bathrobe onto the floor, and ran to his dressing room to grab a shirt from a hanger. However fast he tried to run behind him was a thumping of feet on the carpeted stairs and a deep snarling bark of a dog. It quickly came close, Stone flinched, and for a reflex reason tried to button his shirt.

He moved to the wardrobe in the corner of the room for his trousers but he stopped as a black pit bull terrier padded through the bedroom door, its slobbering mouth ready for any sudden move that Stone might make. The dog yapped at full pitch and it approached Stone with menace as he moved back and stood on his bed. But it was a useless act trying desperately to shield himself from the foaming mouth that showed two white fangs.

'Off, Blackie!' a cockney voice shouted as Stone stood cowering away from the dog.

The shiny head of Xavier suddenly appeared in the doorway and lunged to hold the collar of the dog. He missed and swore loudly. The dog jumped at Stone, catching his ankle and as it fell back to the ground it left a spurt of blood on the white duvet. Xavier's voice boomed as he swore again and almost jumped on the dog to stop its vicious snarl. Xavier was overweight, unfit, he had run up the stairs and he was breathless. He stood for a moment panting, holding the dog's collar with one hand, a cigarette in the other.

'How did you get in here?' Stone shouted at full pitch frightened at what now confronted him.

'Not difficult, mate, I got ways.'

'Get that thing out of here.'

'Stand, Blackie,' Xavier ordered, and the snarl of his voice was enough to bring the dog to heel.

'You putrid lump of humanity, I've got nothing to say to you so clear out of here before I call the police,' Stone said as he reached for the phone by the side of the bed.

But Xavier let the dog drag on its halter closer to the bed and there was a loud roar of laughter from Xavier as Stone recoiled from the phone and flinched.

'Get that animal away!' Stone shouted again.

'I might do that but first I've come to remind you my quarter million in hard-earned notes I lent you was due back yesterday. Where is it?' Xavier said in one deep breath.

'I've got no money here,' Stone said as he stood uncertainly on the bed.

'What I hear from Dave is that you can't keep your part of the deal. So, Harry, I'm beginning to think you've stolen my money. And if that is what I find out my pet Blackie here can get very excited.' Xavier let out a deep, throaty laugh.

'So this is where I find you, Harry,' a Glaswegian voice suddenly interrupted from the doorway.

Stone looked bewildered but he knew the voice. A steamy hot Caribbean island where he had been held for a couple of days quickly came into focus. Yes, as prisoner, he knew that. They forced him to sign away Sudbury and then he had been a carrier for drug-running cash.

'What do you want, you crooks?'

'Listen hard, Harry. You've got to know we always get back the cash that we lend, but this time my friend here from the Caribbean can't wait. His big bag of cash should have been handed over at that big airport you flew into but you thieved it when you thought nobody was watching. So why don't you get dressed and if you ain't got it here we'll set off to find it,' Xavier mocked.

'We're going nowhere, those dollars are mine now, they're going to pay for my Ferrari that you've burnt up in the garage,' Stone said.

'Yeh, remember that little fire, that's just to let you know how we work when you try to be clever. And your little foreign friend hit one of my boys when he stole that Ferrari in London. Big car, he should have been more careful.'

'Get out of here it, you gangsters,' Stone said tightness in his throat.

'Harry, just calm down, it won't do you no good shouting so much. And calling us gangsters are harsh words coming from you. But you remember who we are, we're people you're running away from, so now we've caught up with you, you gotta stop and do what we tell you,' Xavier said.

'I'm going nowhere with you lot of thugs, so get out of here and take that foul stinking animal with you,' Stone shouted.

'Harry, mate, please don't call Blackie names, he don't like it. And he's coming with us as we go for a ride in my comfy green van until we find the missing dollars. You got just two minutes to get dressed, or we carry you out just as you are. And let all your neighbours have a leery laugh at you. Which way do you want, matey?'

The slobbering dog was a sight Stone could not deal with. He was wary of even moving away from it as the vicious animal was ready to leap right at him wherever he moved. But Stone jumped from the other side of the bed and grabbed his trousers from the wardrobe. He stared at the dog which was sniffing through its saliva. It was still showing teeth amongst its slobber but Xavier now had the animal more firmly under control.

Stone went into his dressing room watched closely by the Glaswegian who, with his thin face and cold stare, looked just as menacing he had in St Vincent. He had been frightened into a corner, boxed in and he knew it. Stone swore to himself, he should have known this could happen, that these narcotics' dealers would come for him. He dabbed his still-bleeding foot and the dog was growling heavily. Through its messy nose and mouth it still looked hungry, ready to bite into anyone if it was let free to run.

Stone had nowhere to go. With two ruthless men standing guard in his bedroom and with a snarling animal ready to tear anything apart on command he was helpless. He dressed quickly, replacing the blood-soaked handkerchief on the wound at his ankle. He slipped into a pair of shoes and a very tight-fitting anorak he had not worn for two years. For a moment he sat on a stool in his dressing room and looked at his mobile on a ledge, but his thought was immediately interrupted. The dog, on a long leash, padded into the dressing room.

There was a sneering laugh from Xavier and Stone saw him stub his cigarette under his foot on the carpet of the bedroom. A minute later, almost in silence, Xavier pushed Stone in front of him down the stairs and out of the front door to the waiting green van parked on the double yellow lines. The dog was now held on a short tether but Stone turned away, the thing was abhorrent to him and he found its closeness base and revolting.

'Harry, my friend, you struggle now and you get hit, just as we had to do in that dark country lane. But I know you're too sensible and you won't do that, so you sit still and give me the postcode for my little gizmo and we take a drive together to find those greenbacks that have gone missing.'

'I'm not giving you any postcode. And you'd better know I've torn up that fake agreement which you tried to snatch Sudbury away from me with. Only a load of fraudsters would try that on,' Stone shouted.

'No, mate, it don't work like that. You've given my Caribbean friend a building site that ain't working and your gift pays for our deal that you're trying to undo. Remember we trusted you with a lump of cash? Me and my mate from St Vincent don't like the way you're trying to twist and wriggle from what you owe.' There was a snarl in Xavier's voice almost as shrill as that which had come from the slobbering dog.

Xavier looked at the Glaswegian, who was lighting another cigarette, and he nodded back. Stone was thrown into a seat in the back of the green van and there was silence as the vehicle was started. The dog was in a cage alongside Stone and he turned away as he saw watery foam on the front of its fur. The animal was very close but secured, its noxious smell pervading the air that Stone was breathing. Stone could not ignore it, wherever they were going.

As the van moved away Stone noticed the driver – it was one of the hoodies who had held him over the railings at the end of the pier. For a moment he thought he could hear water sloshing twenty feet below. Again he was in the hold of Xavier and his cold-blooded heavies and he would now be taken wherever Xavier wanted this green van to go to. He knew too there was no one out there today who would ask or even care where he was.

His leg was sore with the gash from the dog's teeth and even his shoulder still ached with a dull twinge. In this enclosed space at the back of the van it was hot, it smelled strongly of dog sweat, though the animal had now settled to the lull of the van's movement. Stone closed his eyes. He could not follow where the van was going, the hoodie driver had been moving fast and the van was now jerking with the stop–start of motorway traffic.

What was coming from the three thugs who now held him Stone did not know. He was their prisoner. He closed his eyes in the back of the van for a few minutes and in the lull it brought back Stone's belligerent self. He was never going to give the Glaswegian his dollars back and he would soon get out of this rumbling dirty thing. It would then be time to show them how ruthless he was too if pushed into corners like this.

It took an hour and a half before they entered the high industrial iron gates that were now the entrance to the Sudbury site. The place was quiet, too quiet, and Stone felt squeezed, very uncomfortable in the cramped space of this jerky van. He needed to stretch himself, he was ready to get out, away from the slobbering stink of wet dog fur and he wanted to dab soothing water onto his throbbing foot. But now, even in this familiar site, Stone was again on his own. Dave was not there and he was suddenly confronted close-up by these three coldblooded hoods.

'My site looks good, eh, Harry?' the Glaswegian said as Stone was led by the hoodie towards a corner of the old Victorian hospital.

Stone said nothing. He was trapped, he could not run and the dog was now making a howling noise that echoed loudly from the enclosed space of the van. Xavier held Stone's other arm firmly and took him a few yards around a large puddle to a yellow digger that had its driver still inside the cab with the engine running. The Glaswegian whistled and the cab driver withdrew the vehicle a few paces to leave a large hole it had recently dug with a tidy earth bank on the side.

'Now, are you going to lead my friend here, who has come all the way from the Caribbean, to where you've stashed his dollars?' Xavier asked. 'He wants 'em back, like now.'

'What're you doing?' Stone was bewildered and becoming jumpy.

'Well, mate, you see that hole, that's where you're going tonight when it's dark and nobody else is around, that's of course unless you give us the place where you're holding our money.'

Xavier's tone was sharp and menacing and Stone resisted a large fist pushed into his back. He was as terrified with claustrophobia as he had been when looking at the inky dark water that slurped below him at the end of Brighton pier.

'You'll never get away with this. My man Dave'll know and he's straight not bent like you lot of narcotics' pedlars.'

'We now run this place, not Dave, he's moved on. So that lot of dirt'll be piled on top and nobody'll know where you've gone. You'll just be lying at the bottom, helpless. Of course it's just a nasty accident for anyone looking for you. So what do you think, eh, Harry?'

The Glaswegian walked round and looked into the hole. 'I like this place, haven't seen it before. That was a nice gift you brought when you came to meet me at my home in the sun. Yeh, Sudbury'll do well,' he said.

Stone stared into the pit, helpless, for the first time feeling a frozen numbness about Sudbury and all it had stood for. Standing there on the edge, powerless, he had no doubt what this madman, certainly high on weed or some other narcotic, would do. He yanked his arm free from the tight grip and turned round to walk back to the green van. He said nothing as his two captors came behind him and he was pushed through the open back doors of the vehicle. It set off the dog barking ferociously, its noise bouncing off the metal walls around its cage. Xavier shouted his command of 'Shut up', and the animal slowly obeyed, but Stone could smell again the caged dog's breath with its slobber on its matted fur and he became very tense.

In a subdued, and very nervous state Stone gave the hooded driver the postcode for the derelict site that was Arrow Hall.

27

Dinner with Rick had been beyond what Claire, just a day before, ever expected. Later the next day the tenseness and the frown over her eyes had gone and at the start of a warm new day Claire felt refreshed, different and rested. This was how she had always been in Rick's company.

After a leisurely breakfast and in the warmth of the sun they walked into the small village that surrounded the hotel. After walking up and down the road twice, in an antiques shop Rick bought a Louis XV mahogany writing table. It was a fine-looking piece of furniture, Claire thought, though she knew not much of tables and desks made around 1750 and so long ago. But she saw the price and she closed her eyes. This was a typical purchase by Rick, something that looked superb quality and never mind the price, and it was just as their outings had been that year to events around London. The table would be delivered to Rick's flat in Mayfair by the end of the week.

This was a writing table for his apartment. As they walked back to the car he told Claire he was starting to run down his business hours in his Mayfair office and start to do more from his apartment. In the last two days he had not taken one call on his mobile phone and she had never seen Rick so calm and easy with himself. As they were having coffee in the hotel lounge he told her all about his chateau and vineyard purchase in France.

'It's just about to be completed with titles being verified by a French attorney. It's a vineyard with a grand chateau built about 1850 and still looking very fine with its turreted corners. And as a present from the current owners they've sent a case of claret to the apartment, wine that could become vintage. The whole vineyard's in great working order, and its wine is sold to many London restaurants. Sad really that it's for sale because of a family break-up. Best bit, too, is parts of the family will stay on to run it. They've been there for three generations and they'll live in the top part of the chateau and when we visit the first two floors will be ours to enjoy. How about that?' Rick asked.

'When do I get to see it?' Claire asked.

'As soon as it's all settled we'll take a drive down there.'

They left the hotel and Claire watched as Rick punched in the postcode details on the satnav of where he was going to take her. Claire was surprised Rick had not asked about the country houses she had visited for him in the last week, a time which had been difficult for her. But she had really found nowhere special for Rick to view, she would let it pass her by and yesterday had been important as a big step in clearing Harry Stone from her life. But Claire had no idea where she was being taken today. Rick was holding something back. He still needed to talk.

She looked away and settled into her seat. As they reached the motorway Claire told Rick all she had found at Blake Markets, with nearly a quarter of a million in black economy cash being filtered through the business. She told him of her visit to the police, what she had put in her statement including what Gina had done and all she knew about Harry Stone. Rick let Claire talk. He listened closely but said little even though he could see his money in Blake Markets was no longer safe.

'I owe you a big thank you for what you have done for me on this, Claire. I can see it's not been easy for you especially with Gina in an awful car crash but you've done the right thing in going quickly to the police. I know the police won't let it go until they've investigated and got to the bottom of the money laundering scam.'

'I'm going back to see how Gina is and I'll do some more probing if you want me to. Gina was finally adding up all that Martyn had taken from the business with fake invoices to cover for his gambling. The place is in a mess.'

'I met Martyn several times when I was putting my investment into the supermarkets and he never looked or talked like a gambler. But you'll remember he did stalk out from the office just a few days ago when we started to talk about money. It shows how you can be deceived by some people. But, please, Claire tell me about Gina.'

'The accident was very nasty and I don't think it was her normal driving that caused it. She really does control a lot that goes on at Blake Markets but she was pushed by Martyn into meeting at a secluded pub to take the cash from someone she had never met before. But when the police put together what I've told them and when they check on Martyn's gambling I expect they will uncover what has really being going on there.'

Rick drove fast, they soon reached London and the route then unfolded away from the centre and towards the eastern suburbs. They were places that Claire began to recognise and places she knew well. Soon they had left the streets and rows of houses behind and were in open country.

'Where are you taking me?' Claire asked.

'I think you know by now. This countryside must be very familiar to you, and I really hope you enjoy coming back here. There's something I want you to see, so relax for the next few miles,' Rick said with a grin on his face.

Claire knew where they were going and she could feel her heartbeat quicken. It was more from anxiety than excitement. They were going to Arrow Hall. It was a boarded-up site of ruins, it was the last place she wanted Rick to see, and it held too many bad memories for her. But she could not stop it now as they were driving down the lane with trees that arched over the road. The large iron gates to Arrow Hall as always were still wedged wide open.

'Rick, please, do we have to go any further?' Claire asked.

'Claire, trust me, sit back for a moment. I know how you must feel and I don't want you to be upset about this place. We won't stay long.'

As they passed through the tall iron gates the expanse of the site confronted them, unchanged since Claire and Jennie had been there just a short time before. But there was a green van parked close to the stable block that had withstood the fire. The van had its engine running, two men were walking towards the back doors and they had not yet noticed Claire or Rick.

There was the sound of a dog barking heavily as a man was bundled roughly from the van. He fell to the floor and was pulled upright by his arms, which he tried to yank free from his captors.

Claire put her hand to her face.

'That's Harry Stone!' she shouted. 'Rick, what's going on here? Is this what you've brought me to see?' She was frightened and startled just from the sight of Harry Stone at Arrow Hall.

'No I don't want you to see this mad scene, let me find out who these people are.' Rick left his car without closing the door or stopping the engine and walked quickly to the fight that had now started.

'Stop it, what are you up to?' he shouted.

The two large men took no notice and holding Harry Stone firmly by his arms marched him towards the stable block. It was a handling Stone could not resist and he was forced into a run by the two men. Rick was not sure how close to follow. They forced Stone up several low steps and as they went into the building it became quiet with only the continuing loud barking from the dog in the back of the green van. Rick stood back as a minute later the two men suddenly came from the building holding a brown holdall bag. They ran to the green van with the dog still howling and within a few seconds they left the empty site. Stone emerged from the stable block, blood over his face. He suddenly doubled up and collapsed on the ground.

‘I think we’ll get out of here,’ Rick said as he got into the car.

On the car phone he called the police. ‘There has been a fight and there is a man in trouble on the ground. It’s the site of Arrow Hall and he’ll probably need an ambulance.’

Without looking back they left this forlorn place, winding down the road and under the overarching trees. Claire had her hand covering her mouth and she could not hold back a tear.

‘If this is what you’ve brought me to see, I don’t like it,’ she said.

‘Claire, believe me, that’s not what I expected to see at Arrow Hall. Let’s get out of here and find a pub for a glass of wine to wipe that sight away,’ Rick said.

‘First I want a post box, I’ve got an important letter to post,’ Claire said.

She directed Rick to a small village just a mile away and she quickly fumbled in her bag for an envelope and slipped it into the post box by the village shop. She sat back quickly in the car and put her face in her hands.

‘Claire, what on earth’s the matter?’ Rick asked.

‘Harry Stone being beaten is not something I ever wanted to see. Watching you lying helpless on the ground two years ago was bad enough. And I’ve posted back to Harry Stone the codes that will give him access to his Panama bank accounts. I kept them when the fire was blazing, they’re no use to me anymore, and I don’t ever want to talk about it again.’

A couple of minutes later they were sitting in a country pub at the other end of the village. The Chess Board, a draughty inn, was just a few lanes away from the nastiness they had just seen. But Claire was distraught, her tenseness had come back with a deep frown over her eyes. A glass of cheap wine in her hand, sitting at a table in the busy garden was not what she would have chosen after an indulgent two days in the Cotswolds with Rick. Claire was sure this could never be what Rick had promised as a mystery few days away, but it was how it was ending.

Claire sipped a small amount from her glass and Rick excused himself to go to the toilet. As she looked at him he had a teasing smile on his face, a smile she had seen before.

'Give me a minute, please,' he said. 'There's something else I want to talk to you about.'

It was barely two minutes before Rick returned holding a folder under his arm. He sat close to Claire.

'This is for you,' Rick said, passing the folder over.

Claire put the folder on the low table in front of her and slowly opened it. There was a coloured line drawing of Arrow Hall, a *rebuilt* Arrow Hall with a landscaped garden full of colour. Claire forced a smile and she looked at Rick.

'Why have you done this, it's not a bad joke is it?'

'Listen, Claire, please. I keep a sharp eye on the market and as soon as Arrow Hall came up for sale I bought the derelict site. And Claire, more than that I want you to be the person who rebuilds it and makes it look grand again.'

Claire thought for a moment. She spoke slowly.

'Harry Stone once tempted me to do this and it never happened, so do we have a date I can start?' Claire asked.

'Claire, this is your house now to rebuild and then it'll become our country house. So please start as soon as you like.'

Rick kissed her gently on her lips and Claire was overcome. She felt an instant excitement at what Rick had handed to her, but she suddenly wavered. She could not entirely blank out the image of Harry Stone crawling on the floor of the ruins of Arrow Hall with a bloodstained face.